THE STRAND

THE STRAND

a novel

ELLEN VAUGHN

WORD PUBLISHING

NASHVILLE

A Thomas Nelson Company

This is a work of fiction.
Apart from obvious historical references
to public figures and events, all characters and
incidents in this novel are the products of the
author's imagination. Any similarities to people
living or dead are purely coincidental.

Library of Congress Cataloging-in-Publication Data

Vaughn, Ellen Santilli.
The strand : a novel / Ellen Vaughn.
p.   cm.
ISBN 0-8499-1328-4 (hardcover)
ISBN 0-8499-3728-0 (trade paper)
I. Title.
PS3572.A88S77   1997
813'.54—dc21
97-1769
CIP

Printed in the United States of America
0 1 2 3 4   QPV   7 6 5 4 3

To Lee
with a heart full of love and thanks

With Gratitude

UNEXPECTEDLY, when *The Strand* was about three-quarters complete, my husband and I adopted toddler twins. This was no doubt a surprise for them, and a delightful shock for us: God has very long sleeves, and you just never know what's up them. Walker and Haley, then nineteen months, joined big sister Emily, then four, in jumping up and down in the background whenever I sat at the computer keyboard, trying to write. So my first order of business is to give thanks to God, because it is one of His miracles—a minor one, but still well beyond the scope of normal physical probabilities—that I was able to finish this book.

I owe great thanks as well to so many wonderful friends: Grace McCrane, Gloria Pratt, Lisa Barnes, John Dawson, Sandy Smallman, and Gail Harwood, who read and critiqued the near-final manuscript; my best friend Patti Bryce, and Jeannie Edwards, who gave rich insights at earlier stages as we mused together by the Atlantic Ocean; Mary Ann Bell, who did the same thing as we mused over Lebanese food; Dr. Tony Kowalski, for his information about Poland; Dorothy Wilkes, for whisking me into the Vermeer exhibit when the lines of people waiting to get into the National Gallery of Art stretched for miles; attorney Matt Britton, who connected me to F. Rea Harper, retired D.C. homicide detective, whose real-life stories of crime in Washington curled my hair and whose expertise was immensely helpful. Similarly, Beth Wise, Richmond, Virginia homicide investigator, lent great technical help while polishing her horse's saddle one fine summer evening.

I also thank Jan O'Kelley, Norma Vaughn, Jan Pascoe, and Mildred Santilli for their wonderful help with childcare. I salute the New Song Fellowship in Baltimore, whose vibrant Christian community and tremendous neighborhood development provided the spark for my fictional church and learning center. I am grateful as well to Jan Johnson for her thoughtful and thorough critique of the first draft of the manuscript, and to the good people at Word Publishing for their enthusiasm, humor, solidarity, and expertise: Kip Jordon, Nelson Keener, Jana Muntsinger, Nancy Norris, Allen Arnold, Pamela McClure, Debbie Wickwire, and Jennifer Haney. I thank Emily Vaughn for her patience with and enthusiasm for this project. And, as the dedication indicates, I thank Lee Vaughn for his gracious support for this book, and for the ongoing adventure of our marriage.

Ellen Vaughn
February 2, 1997

Batter my heart, three-personed God; for You
As yet but knock, breathe, shine, and seek to mend;
That I may rise and stand, o'erthrow me, and bend
Your force to break, blow, burn, and make me new.
I, like an usurped town, to another due;
Labor to admit You, but O, to no end;
Reason, Your viceroy in me, me should defend,
But is captived, and proves weak or untrue.
Yet dearly I love You, and would be loved fain,
But am betrothed unto Your enemy.
Divorce me, untie or break that knot again;
Take me to You, imprison me, for I,
Except You enthrall me, never shall be free,
Nor ever chaste, except You ravish me.

—John Donne, 1633
Holy Sonnet #14

ONE

THE YOUNG MAN PEERED into the dim mirror. One of the bulbs in the old bathroom light fixture had burned out, so he couldn't see very well. But it was all right. He had shaved his head so many times before that he could do it by feel as well as by sight.

He dipped the blue plastic razor back in the tepid water in the cracked sink, swirled it around, and drew it in a precise arc across the tight, gleaming skin of his dark scalp. Once, twice more, and he was done.

He bent and mopped his head with the brown towel hanging from the rack and looked again at his reflection, turning to one side, then the other. The face in the mirror was that of a tall, black man, nineteen years old, with widely spaced dark eyes, a broad, flat nose, and a hairline mustache above his upper lip. He was in his prime; he had already lived longer than most of his friends. The only scar he bore from his years on the streets was a ragged left earlobe, torn in a gang fight years ago. He liked it. It made him look tougher.

He put on his jacket, patting the gun in the right front pocket, and appraised himself one final time in the mirror, nodding with satisfaction. He liked to look good when he went out to do a job.

TWO

TWO

WHICH DO YOU WANT?" Paul Lorelli asked, raising an eyebrow toward the dessert cart. Anne gazed at the silver platters as the waiter solemnly held them aloft. The torte was a consideration, its layers of chocolate, truffle, and cream rising high on a hazelnut hull, drifting slowly across a languid lagoon of rum sauce.

On the other hand, the cheesecake looked creamy and simple, the sort of comfort food that capped off a memorable meal like this. But then there were the fresh raspberries, each a plump jewel. You could have them with fresh whipped cream or Grand Marnier. Or both.

"I can't decide," she said to Paul. It was a longstanding ritual between them. "You choose for me."

Paul turned to the waiter. "My wife will have the raspberries with cream—and could you put a good chocolate sauce on that for her? I'll have the crème caramel. And two espressos, please."

As the man left, Paul glanced at his watch and drained the last swallow from his wineglass. "So don't you ever think about it?" he asked, picking up the strand of their former conversation. "Don't you ever think what having children would have been like? Don't you wonder what we'd be like now if we had two or three kids at home, terrorizing some poor baby-sitter?" He rolled his eyes.

Ten years ago on this night they had been at the Hyatt near Dulles Airport, eating leftover hors d'oeuvres the caterer had boxed and added to the piles of luggage in their limousine, laughing about Great-aunt Harriet's shoe, trampled on the dance floor, wondering why the best man had caught the bouquet, and contemplating an early flight to Saint Johns.

After the honeymoon had come several years, for Anne, of benign solitary confinement. Paul's legal work kept him away from home for long hours, but then he made partner four years into the marriage, and he and Anne both felt that the payoff was worth it.

Anne had worked on Capitol Hill for the first few years. Then her congressman had decided not to run again; she had not pursued another job. At home, she'd kept herself busy with cooking courses, Junior League volunteer work, a heavy social calendar. Adept with words, she had also toyed with writing children's stories. A slender stack of them lay neatly stapled, nestled in her desk drawer. Paul kept telling her to go ahead and submit them somewhere. But she hadn't felt ready to take the plunge.

She was the same way about children. When they had talked about kids early on, Anne had wanted to wait a few years, and Paul agreed. Better to be in a position where they could provide properly for children, have the base in place for private schools, piano lessons, and all the rest.

Eventually, however, Paul had been able to envision them, small replicas of himself and Anne: a strong, dark-haired boy whose future golf swing had been imprinted in his genes, and a lithe blond girl whose blue eyes would follow him anywhere. He could see them, smiling from a heavy gold picture frame on the credenza behind his office desk, a credit to his good taste in marrying their mother.

But, he had realized over the years, Anne didn't have that same picture in her mind. He wasn't sure what was on her mind. As time went by, she removed herself more and more from him. That had at first confused, then offended, then angered him, until the very things that had first drawn him to her now repelled him.

In the beginning of their relationship, Anne's ordered world had meant a calm contrast to the chaos of Paul's stormy family. He had loved her social graces, her reserved sense of control, her thank-you notes sent the day after any occasion, written in that rounded, sloping backhand on heavy Crane's stationery engraved with her initials. The "Ice Queen," some of his law school friends had called her, and at the time Paul had taken pride in that.

But over the years her reserve had stood stubborn against his growing compulsion for control, and the gulf between them had widened. Gradually its tides had pulled Paul to destinations other than family and home, and so now he found that he no longer cared very much about children at all. But it was a topic he liked to bring up now and then, just to see Anne squirm.

Anne sighed and looked around the small French restaurant. At the corner table by the window a man and woman were leaning close to one another, laughing and licking chocolate mousse off a heavy, silver spoon. She looked away.

It used to be that anniversaries were golden milestones. Anne had loved their new beginnings, these annual rituals to catalogue the past and plan the future. It used to be that Paul's expectations would sweep them both to the next logical step. She remembered Paul raising his eyebrows and his wineglass years ago, back when he still looked at her expectantly as he proposed a toast: "To next year, to making partner," he had said. And so it had been. Then, "to next year, to the new house," and "to next year, to Europe," and so on, each new dream realized, year by year . . . but now to Anne it just seemed that next year would bring more of the same, though she and Paul both still played the charade of new beginnings when they were out in public.

The maître d' appeared with a bottle of Perrier Jouet. Paul nodded as the man peeled the gold foil, pried off the guard wires and deftly eased out the tight cork. He poured the champagne into two tall, fluted glasses. Anne watched as the bubbles rose in the candlelight. The waiter arrived and set their desserts and espressos before them, then hovered for a moment, so Anne smiled at Paul as they clicked glasses, then tipped the cold champagne into her mouth.

I am drinking stars! she thought, as she always did when she sipped champagne, though she never could remember just whose quote that was.

She dipped her spoon into her fruit. "These raspberries are perfect," she said to Paul, even as she felt some perverse need to plow on through the stony soil of their kid conversation. "You know I used to think about children a lot. I love children. But at first we wanted to wait, and then I kept thinking there would be some signal, you know, all kinds of maternal yearnings, and that would be the sign that we should get on with it. But I never felt that way. I mean, I could never imagine us really having a baby. What do you do with it once you bring it home from the hospital?"

Paul spooned his crème caramel. "Other people seem to know what to do," he said. This was well-traveled ground. "You change its diapers. You let it spit up on you. You teach it its ABCs. You pray that it gets a full academic scholarship—"

"You make it sound so easy," said Anne. "Just one step after another. But I never felt like I could do it. Some of my friends turned from normal people into this boring person called 'Mommy.' They referred to themselves in the third person. They didn't talk about anything but Pampers prices and preschool. They couldn't lose weight. Their houses were a mess."

"You make everything so hard," Paul responded. "We don't need to get into all that again right now. Life just isn't that complicated. You make choices and go with them. When our parents were young, they got married and they had kids. They adjusted. They raised them. No big deal. You try to figure everything out too much. It has to be perfect or you're scared of it. Why can't you ever just go for it?"

Anne took a breath and looked down at the ripe red berries in their crystal goblet. No need to have that same argument again tonight. Maybe, if she could think carefully about it later, without distraction, she could abandon her fears and let go of the past. They still had time to have children if they really wanted them. Maybe children would help. *Right*, she thought. *Nothing like stress and mess to restore a marriage.*

Paul was looking at her, his chin down and his eyebrows up as if he was cross-examining a stupid witness. "After all, if Molly can have three kids and still keep up with life, you should be able to manage it, since she's the most disorganized person on the planet."

"What does Molly have to do with anything?" Anne asked. Molly and Anne had been best friends since they were thirteen years old, and Paul had known her as long as he had known Anne. But in the last year or so it seemed like Paul couldn't even talk about Molly without putting her down one way or another.

But the mention of Molly's name reminded Anne of something. Might as well change the subject. She cleared her throat.

"You know, there is something I've been thinking about doing, especially now that summer's over and school has started. Molly told me about this tutoring program that's in some inner-city neighborhood off North Capitol Street. There's a church there; they're working with Habitat for Humanity, renovating houses for poor people, and they have a job center and a health clinic and this tutoring program for little kids. They're looking for volunteers to do things like read or tell stories to the kids."

"So?" Paul said.

"Well," Anne plunged on, trying to get something out on the table that might turn the tone of this deadly dinner, "I thought it might be good for me to try something new. I've been pretty insulated for the last few years. I need a change. You just said, why can't I just go for things. I told stories at that after-school program at the McLean Community Center; I should be able to do it for five- and six-year-olds in the city."

Paul took another sip of champagne. "There's a big difference between kids in McLean and kids on welfare," he said dryly. "You do need a change. But tutoring in D.C. is just about the last thing you should do. You aren't tough enough. And besides, it doesn't help us at all. Why don't you do something where you can build some connections with people who might be helpful for us down the line? I shouldn't have to be the only one here looking out for our future—"

"What do you mean?" Anne broke in. "Our future looks fine to me. Your position is secure; we've got the money we need."

"That's just it," Paul whispered, his teeth clenched. "You always think everything's just fine. You've always had the money you need. You've never had to work and plan to get somewhere. You've always had someone to make things comfortable for you. Your dad, or me—"

"What does that have to do with tutoring in the inner city?" Anne asked. "Lately you're ready to blow up for no reason at all. Why are you so angry all the time?"

"Why are you so passive all the time?" Paul shot back. "You'll never go tutor in the city. You'll just think about it for a year. You wouldn't last one second in some ghetto program anyway. You can't even decide what you want to have for dessert unless I decide for you."

Anne's eyes filled, and she looked down at her raspberries, blinking quickly. Paul just sat and stared at her coldly, draining down more champagne. Anne looked up at him again, and then he snapped to attention. Anne could tell without looking that someone he knew had come in the front door.

Paul was on his feet, smiling, hand outstretched, and Anne half-turned to see one of his law partners and his wife moving toward their table. She quickly dabbed her eyes with her napkin.

"Charles, Elise, so good to see you," he was saying. Anne stood as well, reaching toward Elise and giving her the little half-hug and air kiss that seemed appropriate. "We're just out for a little anniversary dinner," Paul said. "Ten years tonight."

"Oh, Anne, congratulations," Elise said. "You're the perfect couple!"

"Ten years?" Charles broke in. "You should be away for the weekend, off somewhere a little more exciting than here. At least a bed-and-breakfast in Annapolis or the mountains or somewhere. Paul, you've got to treat this beautiful woman better for sticking with you for ten years."

Anne smiled gamely, hoping they would go away soon, even though that would leave her alone with Paul. She hated the inane exchanges that passed for repartee with the people from the firm.

Paul smiled too, but Anne could see that the muscle in his jaw was tight. Sometimes any kind of challenge, even a joke, seemed to get to him.

"Be careful," he said to Charles, grinning conspiratorially and placing his big, graceful hand on Charles's shoulder. "You don't want to mess up any surprises I just might have planned for the weekend."

Oh, no, Anne thought. *I hope he doesn't really have a getaway planned. I can't imagine he would. I don't want to go anywhere.*

Charles and Elise moved on toward their table, and Paul sat back down, blotting his lips with his napkin and smoothing his tie over his chest. Anne bent down and retrieved her purse from the wide wooden window sill next to their table. "I'm going to the ladies' room," she said. "I'll be right back."

Paul glanced at his watch and held a gold credit card toward the waiter without looking at him, staring out through the thick-paned windows into the narrow street. He shook his head, then looked at his watch again.

Anne and the waiter returned together. Paul slipped the credit card back into his wallet. Anne stared at it absently while he signed the receipt. "Why are you using your old wallet?" she asked. She had given Paul a supple new Gandolfo billfold for his birthday, and the worn black wallet it had replaced looked out of place resting on the snowy, starched tablecloth.

Paul looked at it without saying anything, his dark eyebrows down, then stood as the maître d' appeared to help Anne from her seat. The host ushered them toward the door as Anne gave a little half-wave toward Charles and Elise. "Thank you for coming," the host said to Anne. "Please, Madame, take this rose. Happy anniversary!"

Outside the warm glow of the café's lights, Anne crossed her arms around herself, the crisp and scentless red rose in her left hand. Its thorns had been shorn; its petals were tightly wrapped. She shivered a little, but Paul didn't offer her his jacket. They crossed the narrow street. Anne's high heels wobbled as she picked her way across the cobblestones.

"Do you want to walk down and look at the river?" Paul asked.

Anne shivered again. It would be pretty, and maybe it would help put some romance into their anniversary, but she was cold and didn't feel like walking.

"Come on," he said abruptly. He turned toward the left, his heavy arm steering her as they walked under the Whitehurst Freeway and headed toward a patch of parkland next to the waterfront.

Anne could hear the whoosh of cars above them on the elevated freeway, but here, in spite of dozens of restaurants just a few blocks away, it was deserted and silent. They picked their way along a brick sidewalk leading to a path that ran next to the river.

The Potomac was high; it had rained a lot over the past week. Anne could see the trees of Roosevelt Island ahead of them to the left, and in the distance to the right, the lighted office buildings of Rosslyn.

She was thinking how the leaves would change and fall would come soon, when two men walked from between the dark trees. At first Anne was glad that they were no longer alone on the path. But then she felt alarmed, and then felt it wasn't polite to be alarmed: these were probably just tourists, or maybe businessmen wandering around after dinner—weren't they?

And then, as they got closer, Anne saw the gun. Her stomach lurched and her chest felt tight, her heart thumping wildly against her ribs.

"Get up against that tree," one of the men said, pointing the big gun toward them, right at chest level. Anne couldn't really see him in the darkness; he was tall, but she realized he probably wasn't even twenty yet.

Paul stiffened, but spoke calmly. "It's okay," he said evenly to the teenagers—or was it to her? "Just take it easy."

He eased Anne toward the big oak tree, his hand on her arm. He took the wallet out of his pocket and extended it slowly toward the young man with the gun, his palm flat as if he were feeding a particularly dangerous dog.

The mugger kept his eyes on Paul, took the wallet without looking, and flipped it back to his partner, who stood in the background. He half-turned, as if to go, and Anne felt Paul exhale next to her. He took his arm from her side and started to say something, but then the teenagers turned again.

The one with the gun came forward. Anne saw the glint of the thick earring in his right ear; the lobe of his left ear was ragged, part of it missing, as if someone had once torn an earring from it. His bald head was smooth, shaven. He raised the gun toward Paul. "Your watch, man."

Paul jerked his head. "No," he said, his teeth clenched. "You've got the wallet. Get out of here."

Anne drew her breath in sharply, blinking quickly.

"Paul, just give him the watch!" she quavered. Paul hesitated, then unclasped his Rolex. The other man came forward and took it, his eyes now on Anne's thick, three-strand necklace of Mikimoto pearls.

"Take those off," he said.

Anne froze. The guy in the background spoke. His voice was soft, even a little high-pitched, and the unexpectedness of that made Anne look away from the gun and toward him.

"If you don't take them off, we can do it for you, you know," he said quietly. And then he smiled, his eyes empty and dead, like a shark's, and the smile terrified Anne more than anything else that had happened.

She reached up around her throat, hands shaking, her fingers bent behind her neck.

"No!" Paul hissed at her, his voice harsh. "No!"

Anne couldn't make her fingers work. The necklace was ten years old tonight, a wedding gift from her parents. Its heavy clasp had been hard to manage at the best of times, and this was the worst. She fumbled; she couldn't squeeze the catch just right, and then in her panic, to her horror, she found herself apologizing to these thugs who were robbing them that she was sorry, she couldn't get the necklace off.

The man with the gun moved forward and raised his hand, and Paul suddenly lost control. "No!" he shouted in fury, lunging toward him. "NO!"

Trapped by the tree, her heart convulsing, all at once Anne smelled the man's sour breath, felt his gloved fingers raking her throat and the pop of her pearls, then heard the explosion of the gun as Paul struggled with their attacker. Paul fell back against the tree and slid slowly to the ground.

At the same moment, Anne heard a man call out in the distance and saw the shadowy shapes of people approaching from the restaurants near the waterfront. Cursing, the muggers ran into the darkness.

Trying to scream but paralyzed, just as in her bad dreams, Anne looked down for part of a horrible second. Her pearls were scattering across the brick sidewalk, rolling into cracks, bouncing slowly toward the grass. Most of them were spattered with Paul's blood.

THREE

Molly and Clark O'Kelleys' repeat dinner guests knew to eat a late lunch. Molly was a generous cook, but her creations usually encountered unexpected delays. Tonight had been no exception, but the two couples the O'Kelleys were hosting had survived happily on conversation, white wine, and smoked salmon until 9:30, when the main course finally met the dining room table.

Molly had been in a Caribbean mood that September night. Maybe it was nostalgia for a summer that had fled too fast. At any rate, as she finally laid out the food on the table, a steel drum band chimed from the sound system, the grilled jerk chicken steamed on a platter next to a bright pottery bowl filled with red beans and rice, along with a round plate full of broiled plantains, dotted with butter and cinnamon.

In the middle of the table was the crowning touch, spotlighted by the chandelier's bright glow: a heavy Waterford bowl, filled with water, lined with smooth, sparkling stones, and newly inhabited by the six tropical guppies Molly had bought just before her guests arrived.

"Great centerpiece, Molly," Mary Bell said when they all sat down at the dining room table, shaking out her bright yellow napkin and spreading it in her lap. "I feel like I'm in the Bahamas. Almost. You always know how to give things a certain, uh, flair."

The fish, their pink fins swirling the water, had gamely contributed to the island environment, but they had a problem: the water Molly had run into their bowl was just a little too hot. During the meal, each turned belly up, gills heaving urgently, and expired.

By dessert, there was only one still alive. Clark O'Kelley, who worked as chief of staff for the legendary southern senator Red Wiggins, was telling the latest Wiggins story, in which the aged senator asked a junior aide to wash his back after a workout at the health club.

"He just held out the soap and asked Rob to scrub him down," said Clark. "Rob didn't know what to do. But he's a party man. He took the Safeguard and lathered the senator right there. He said Wiggins needed ironing, though."

"I don't know how you can work on Capitol Hill," David Bell said. "That kind of stuff would drive me crazy."

"I don't know how you can drill holes in people's decaying teeth all day," Clark responded good-naturedly, taking off his round, gold glasses and polishing them with his napkin. "'Thank you. Now swish and rinse, please. You can spit into the basin.' And don't you get tired of people lying to you about how often they floss?" He put his glasses back on. "There goes the last fish."

"Oh, no," Molly said. "I've poached them. I'm so sorry. I think there's one of those little nets in one of the kids' rooms. I've got to get these things out of here."

"Oh, I don't know, dear," Clark said. "It's kind of existentially artistic to have this live centerpiece dying right before our eyes while we eat our dinner. The band plays on. It's a great commentary on modern culture, life, death, decay, all during the course of one meal."

"There's one missing," David said. "Didn't you have six?"

They all looked. There were five small floating corpses. Clark looked around the tablecloth as David took a sip from his water glass. Mary turned to Molly. "It was a great idea . . . next time you could do little lizards with colored pebbles or something—"

"Aaauuugghh!" David slammed down his goblet, mopping his mouth with his napkin. "It's in my glass!" Molly leaned over and took his glass. There, nestled under an ice cube, was a pink-and-blue-striped fish. Deceased.

"Wow," Molly said. "I didn't know they could jump like that!"

"Aaauuugghh!" David moaned again.

"At least it happened to you," Clark said. "You're the dentist. Do fish have teeth?"

"It's all right, dear," Mary said, patting her husband absently on the arm and turning back toward Molly. "Molly, where's Anne been lately? I haven't even seen her since you had that cookout in August, when she came alone because Paul was working late."

"Anne's fine," Molly said, watching David gargle with Mary's water. "I would have had her over this evening, but she and Paul are out for their anniversary. Ten years."

"I can't believe they've been married that long," Mary said. "They don't have that well-worn look that comes at about seven years. I guess it's because they don't have kids. Did you know her back when they got married?"

"Oh, we've been friends since middle school," Molly said. "Then we were roommates in college, lived together before we were married, the whole thing. I was her maid of honor."

MOLLY HUNT O'KELLEY and Anne Madison Lorelli had been best friends since the day after Molly's family moved next door to Anne's.

Molly had climbed the big mulberry tree in her new backyard and sat on a branch reading a tattered copy of *Gone with the Wind;* Anne was practicing cheers on her parents' back deck.

At that time Molly felt far more at home in the Civil War than in suburban Washington, D.C., but she needed a friend—which Anne proved to be when she scaled the fence, flung her saddle-shoed foot over a low branch, and made her way up the tree.

"I'd like to be just like Melanie," Anne said, pointing at Molly's book. "She's so good, and everyone loves her."

Molly wrinkled her nose. "Melanie is boring. Scarlett gets married three times, she starts her own business, she knows what she thinks. I want to be Scarlett."

And so it began. Anne the good girl and Molly the rebel became inseparable. Molly's three brothers teased and danced around the tight circle of their friendship; Molly and Anne became closer than the sisters they didn't have. There was something, even in those fickle days of adolescence, that made them realize that their bond was an unusual gift.

They talked for hours, in torrents. When one faltered, groping for the precise way to describe a feeling, the other would finish the sentence with just the right metaphor. When one failed, the other would boost her up.

So they weathered the emotional hurricanes of high school and the social storms of college better than most. After graduation and a summer in Europe, they returned to Washington, ready to take the city.

Through the years, Anne's cotton button-downs and wool sweaters had changed only with the seasons, evolving each spring into Ralph Lauren shirts and khaki shorts. Dozens of velvet headbands lived in flowered boxes on her dresser; gold earrings mated spontaneously in her jewelry box to create near-identical new offspring.

Meanwhile, Molly enthusiastically embraced—and somehow survived—every fashion "don't" of the late seventies and early eighties, from polyester pantsuits with platform heels to a brief flirtation with purple hair. She had an extra hole bored in one ear to sport lone ear-rings whose mates had been lost.

She ate prodigiously, ran five miles a day, and draped her slender frame with long, loose coats with deep pockets. She lugged gigantic leather handbags full of dog biscuits, theater ticket stubs, packets of Flora-life, a corkscrew and bread knife, purple eyeliner, and a ragged address book crammed with friends. Anne favored trim Aigner hand-bags with neatly organized compartments, everything in its place.

But in spite of their differences, Anne and Molly had remained best friends over the years. Anne met and married Paul, and Molly dated her way through a salad-bar assortment of Middle-Eastern graduate students, a freelance photographer, two poets, and an entre-preneurial brownie salesman.

She met Clark when they both volunteered at the annual Thanksgiving turkey distribution at a D.C. homeless shelter. They married soon after, had three children—Scarlett, Lincoln, and Amelia—in rapid succession, and now lived in happy chaos in a stone house in Lyon Village in Arlington. It was a reasonable commute for Clark's work on Capitol Hill, which called for long hours—and fre-quent late-night phone calls.

So Molly didn't think twice when the phone rang after dessert. They were still sitting around the table, sipping a second cup of coffee. David continued to mop his fish lips now and then with his napkin. It was a few minutes before eleven. "You get it," she said to Clark. "It's probably the senator."

Clark got up and went into the kitchen. But in a moment he was back again, the portable phone in his hand and a strange look on his face. "It's Anne," he said to Molly. "She's in the emergency room at GW Hospital. She needs us."

FOUR

In the waiting room outside George Washington University Hospital's surgery suite, Anne stared at the phone. She felt numb, even as she sat erect, her back not touching the back of her chair, willing herself to go ahead and make more calls. At least Molly and Clark were on their way. A nurse had brought her here after Paul's gurney had burst through the double doors toward the operating room, tubes swaying and dangling, everything crashing, Anne running along beside the doctors, still clutching her purse.

They had told her that the bullet had gone through Paul's sternum and ricocheted off his ribs, that there was massive internal bleeding. He had flatlined twice, on the way to the hospital and again in the emergency room. They had cracked him open and brought him back. But his chances were slim, and the homicide detectives were waiting to talk with her. Anne wondered how to get her own heart started again.

The large waiting room was a cluster of seating areas, light blue padded wooden chairs facing one another in groupings of five or six, separated by six-foot partitions made of teak-colored wood. Artificial plants sat on low coffee tables. There were phones at strategic intervals around the room, and boxes of Kleenex posted regularly as well, as if some hospital interior designer had determined that crying could be anticipated every twelve feet or so.

A young hospital chaplain sat with Anne, his stranger's face creased with concern. A nice enough man—his name was Tinney—but he kept pushing her, as if his grief counseling training had been on the aggressive side. Anne could imagine him taking notes: *Keep them talking, ask lots of questions, get them to express their shock and grief, and they'll do better over the long run.* Well, he was asking her too many questions, presuming some sort of connection between them just because he happened to be on duty when she happened to be in shock and grief.

But Molly and Clark were on their way, and so were her parents. Now Anne knew she needed to call Paul's mom and dad. It was a call she dreaded on the best of days. Paul's parents lived in Philadelphia, where his dad owned a small Italian restaurant and his mother's mission in life was to terrorize the staff. The senior Lorellis were contentious, opinionated, second-generation Italian-Americans who alternately bullied and flattered Anne, never letting her forget her good fortune at marrying such a smart, handsome man.

Anne remembered the party her parents had given when she and Paul had gotten engaged. Her mother had never met Paul's parents before, and Virginia Madison's precisely plucked eyebrows had risen a few notches when Paul's mother had entered her home.

Celia Lorelli sailed into Anne's parents' foyer on a cloud of drugstore perfume. She rushed to Anne to embrace her and then held her left hand aloft as if it were a flag, waving it to make the diamond solitaire catch the light, and then clasped it to her own generous breast, her eyes glued all the while on the heavy silver hors d'oeuvres trays the caterers were passing. "You're a very lucky girl," she proclaimed, over and over. "A very lucky girl."

Sal Lorelli, his tie too short over his too-large belly, had moved right in and stationed himself near the bar, where he initiated a one-sided conversation with the man already standing there, one of Anne's parents' neighbors. Benjamin Hudson was executive vice president for the largest public relations firm in Washington.

"It's ridiculous," Anne heard Sal saying when she passed by a few minutes later. The topic of choice appeared to be welfare. Ben was nodding politely as he took off his horn-rims and began polishing them with a white handkerchief. "These people just gotta get a job, get on their feet. They're on welfare cause they wanna be. Look at me. My parents came to this country with nothing. We built a business from the ground up, worked hard, paid our dues. And here we are today. My son's a lawyer, we got a great restaurant, full every night, vacations in Florida, the whole nine yards. These people gotta get up and get to work."

Never mind how that's supposed to happen, Anne had thought as she glided by, allowing herself to raise her eyebrows ever so slightly as she nodded to Mr. Hudson. "Anne!" he called to her, desperate to escape. She waved, smiled brightly, and kept going, back toward the living room, where Paul and her mother were standing by the French doors.

For his part, Paul seemed to have built a buffer somewhere inside himself, smiling graciously whenever his parents were near, but with his teeth and eyes set. Anne had watched Sal try to engage his son, but Paul wouldn't pick up the banter. She had wondered how long ago Paul had decided to reject the Lorelli way of life. Probably around the time the college scholarship had come through. Paul's parents' angry incomprehension that Paul was not going to work in the family business had eventually been assuaged by the fact that their son had become a lawyer.

Even back then, in the beginning, Anne had wondered, too, how much Paul's love for her was woven together with his affection for her family's way of life. From the first time she had brought him to McLean to meet her parents, he had sized up the large house, the grand curving staircase in the entrance hall, the well-modulated conversations—no shouting and food falling out of people's mouths at *Anne's* parents' home—and seen it as his own. Anne had teased him that perhaps he'd like to take her name when they married; he seemed more like a Madison than a Lorelli. He hadn't laughed.

Over the years of Anne's marriage, her relationship with the Lorellis had gotten better. Or easier, at any rate. She had no idea what they really thought about her. They weren't the sort of people who evaluated the difficulty or ease of relationships. They just had them. They didn't even use words like "relationship." But Anne had worked hard on building something with the Lorellis, brightly asking her mother-in-law to teach her how to make marinara sauce, and eventually she had seen a little something in Paul's parents that she had begun to like.

Not much, but she had worked on it. *At least,* she had thought, *they're human. They feel, they express, they're not all walled up inside. Like Mother.* Virginia Madison was a woman who kept everything within, unfailingly gracious, disciplined, pruned, and controlled like the perfect roses she cultivated, their slender stems obediently climbing the white trellises of the Madisons' side garden.

Now, sitting in this hospital waiting area, Anne could not imagine how she would tell Paul's mother what had happened. Celia's emotions would be loud and messy, but her grief would be real. Anne thought of the blood on Paul's chest, his long frame shrunken on the hospital gurney, the passive droop of his arms at his sides. No mother should see her son that way.

Anne closed her eyes. She had to call them so they could get on the road.

But still she paused, her stomach churning. The chaplain was still there, no doubt searching his brain for the next round of queries. She stood up, a Kleenex crumpled in her hand.

"I need to walk for a minute," she told Chaplain Tinney. He started to stand up. "Alone," she said sharply. She had to get away from this thin, earnest man with too many questions. But then, as usual, she immediately regretted the luxury of honesty. She softened her tone. "I'm sorry, Reverend, I just need to be by myself for a moment. I'll be right back."

She picked up her purse and pushed open the waiting room door. The operating room double doors across the hall were still closed, but then, just as Anne stood staring at them, one slowly swung open. A doctor, probably in his early fifties, emerged. Anne could see bloodstains on his surgical greens, stains that matched the ugly blotches on her blue silk dress.

He drew closer, his face blank. "Mrs. Lorelli?" he asked. Anne nodded. Her voice had dried up inside of her.

Then she heard the sound of flapping clothes, a heavy purse thudding on someone's shoulder, two sets of feet running down the long corridor. Molly and Clark rounded the corner, out of breath. Molly's face was pale, her eyes searching for Anne. She got to Anne just as the surgeon did.

FIVE

Jozef, would you like some tea? The kettle's hot. I had a good nap this afternoon and I'm not tired. I'm going to watch the news before bed."

Jozef Kowalski looked up from the *Catholic Quarterly* lying open on his lap. He had been reading the same paragraph, the one about the pope's new encyclical, for the past fifteen minutes. He had been dozing again.

"Yes, please, Danuta," he said to his sister. He stood and stretched his long arms above his head, lacing his fingers together and cracking his knuckles. "Thank you."

He stared out the old apartment's big picture window. It overlooked the trees and hills of Rock Creek Park and reflected his thick white hair, bushy dark eyebrows, pale skin stretched over prominent cheekbones—an angular, rumpled priest draped in an old-fashioned black cassock. The plate glass didn't mirror the sparkling blue eyes or the crisscross of small wrinkles creasing his temples.

Danuta emerged from the apartment's small kitchen with a wooden tray in her hands, picking her way carefully across the tapestry carpet toward the coffee table. She was a comfortable-looking woman in her seventies, with laugh lines like her brother's, her gray hair twisted into a bun at the nape of her neck. She clicked the living room television set to channel 4.

A reporter was already profiling the evening's top story: "A Washington attorney was gunned down this evening after dinner at a Georgetown restaurant. After dining at Chez Grandpere, he and his wife were walking toward the river when they were confronted by two assailants who robbed them and shot the husband. The victim's name has not yet been released, but he is now fighting for his life at George Washington University Hospital."

Danuta shook her head. "Poor man," she said to Jozef, passing him a porcelain tea cup. "Poor wife." He shook his head slowly. The victim was in grave condition, the assailants still at large. Police had released the detail from the wife's description that one of the muggers had a disfigured left ear.

"It's the same every night," Jozef said to Danuta. "People can't even walk the streets, even in nice places." He scratched his left forearm, where the blue-black numbers of the old tattoo etched his flesh.

"It's one thing to know that death is coming," he said slowly. "We came to know that. Death was always with us. It's another to have it spring out at you when you least expect it."

DETECTIVE TOM HOGAN was staring at the matted grass near the tree where Paul Lorelli was shot when the bright television lights dimmed and the NBC reporter finished.

Tom looked up from his work. Two local stations were reporting from as near the crime scene as they could get, but they were a reasonable distance away, kept back by the police tape blocking off the perimeter of the park where the attack had occurred.

Tom and his partner, Otis Jefferson, had already talked to most of the people who had appeared on the scene after the shooting. The mobile crime-lab guys had already picked up most of the evidence, but now and then somebody would find another part of Anne Lorelli's necklace. They had about twenty-five pearls in evidence bags already.

"How many pearls was this lady wearing, anyway?" Otis asked. Tom shrugged. Something about the pearl thing didn't seem quite right. The wife had told police that one of the muggers had lunged toward her necklace. That's when the husband had lost his temper and when the guy had popped him.

In Tom's experience lately, most muggers just shot their victims and then took the jewelry; it didn't make much sense for the guy to break the goods. But then the wife had said they looked young. Inexperience often made for overly efficient assaults, in which anyone remotely nearby would be blown away.

Or sometimes, like when someone came unexpectedly on the scene, as had happened here, young kids committed inefficient crimes. Like leaving the wife alive to make an ID. And the husband, too, if he pulled through surgery.

Several police cars sat on K Street, under the Whitehurst Freeway, their flashing lights illuminating the night; other lights shone on the tree where the victim had been shot. There was little blood at the scene, just the spatter from the impact at the point of entry. The guy probably wasn't going to make it. Tom had been told he had taken the bullet right at the center of mass, close-range, and that meant internal bleeding. Lots of it.

Tom flipped another page on his notepad and began to sketch a diagram of the crime scene. He was a tall, lanky man in his midthirties, with a narrow face, alert green eyes, a long nose, and short, dark brown hair shaved a little closer around the sides of his head, a little longer on top.

Tom Hogan loved the cold, methodical, tedious process of assembling the pieces of a crime in order to determine its perpetrator—in spite of the stresses, the hours, and the frustration. Soon after Tom had started with the homicide unit, some years ago, D.C. had become the murder capital of the country, with almost five hundred homicides annually.

The Washington, Maryland, and Northern Virginia jurisdictions worked in close cooperation, but, as locals liked to point out, most of the D.C. cases were black-on-black crimes, young guys plugging each other in drug turf wars. Not much variety for the D.C. police, and the perpetrators of the crimes tended to get killed before the cops could arrest them.

Tom used to suppose that the crime rate in D.C. would go down just as soon as that generation killed itself off. Except that now the young kids coming up—the eleven- and twelve-year-olds—were even more violent than their predecessors and even less hindered by any hint of conscience. It scared him to think about the murder rate a few years from now.

There was more diversity in suburban crime. Carjackings, jealous husbands shooting estranged wives or girlfriends, then killing themselves. And most recently, the two sons of one of the area's wealthiest families were convicted of putting arsenic in their widowed mother's cocoa. She had complained of headaches and fatigue for weeks, then neuropathy. She had been hospitalized and would have survived, but the younger son had come to the hospital with a huge bouquet of red roses and a big McDonald's chocolate shake for his aged mother.

She drank it greedily and went into convulsions at about the same time as the results of a heavy metals serum test—which showed high levels of arsenic—were just coming back from the lab in Atlanta. She died just after her doctor arrived; the police weren't far behind. Tom himself had found the milkshake cup, with its arsenic residue, in the hospital trash can.

But this Lorelli case didn't look quite so creative. Probably just a robbery that got out of hand. Two kids, very sketchy descriptions—except for the ear detail—a stolen wallet, watch, and a broken strand of pearls. The victim was in surgery. Tom had found one 9-millimeter shell casing in the grass; he doubted that the surgeons would be able to repair the damage the slug had done to the guy's chest.

Tom flipped his notebook shut. "Okay," he said to Otis. "I'm going to the hospital." He felt in his coat pocket, pulled out two Snickers bars, only slightly linty, and offered one to Otis. Tom still hadn't had dinner when he got the call to come to the waterfront, and now it looked like he wouldn't be back home for some time. It didn't matter; he had chocolate for dinner more often than not.

One of the police radios crackled, and Otis walked over toward one of the cops standing near the yellow-tape perimeter of the crime scene. Tom watched as the officer said something. Otis shook his head, then walked back toward Tom. "Yeah, go interview the wife," Otis said. "Except now she's the widow."

SIX

In the middle of the night, Clark and Molly drove Anne back home to McLean. They all sat in the front seat of the O'Kelleys' Sable station wagon, Clark driving, Molly in the middle, with her arm stretched around Anne. No one said anything.

Anne stared out the window, watching the familiar landmarks rush by as Clark sped from the hospital. She closed her eyes as they drove over the Whitehurst Freeway. Right under this arch, down there next to the river, she kept thinking, Paul was shot. She opened her eyes and stared again as they curled around over Key Bridge and onto the George Washington Parkway, toward Route 123 and home. She still felt numb inside, as if she were standing on a high cliff watching herself and the others from a distance.

The cliff helped keep her emotions at bay. The horror of how Paul had fallen so suddenly and finally away from her, the shame of the drab anger of their final conversation, the confusion of the homicide detective's questions, the guilt of the distance within. Shouldn't she feel more pain? She shook her head, watching the trees along the parkway fly by, and rolling Paul's gold wedding ring around and around between her fingers.

Then they were home. Clark parked in the driveway, since the garage door opener was in Paul's car, still in Georgetown. He took Anne's key, and they walked up the brick steps to the front door.

Molly propelled Anne toward the kitchen. She rummaged around in the cabinets, found a mug, filled it with milk, set it in the microwave, and punched a button.

"You need to sleep," she said to Anne. "You need your strength for tomorrow, when Paul's family gets here."

Anne leaned against the counter and watched the seconds count down on the microwave as the milk in the mug began to sizzle. "You're right," she said automatically. "I'm so tired, but I'm scared to sleep—it just means I'll wake up and know that this really happened, that it wasn't a dream."

"I know," Molly said. "But you've got to sleep. These'll help." She took the mug out of the microwave and handed Anne two small pills. "Mary Bell had these in her purse. They're prescription, but I think you'll be all right if you just take them tonight, and then we'll try to get through one day at a time."

By the next morning, Molly wished somebody had given them some Valium as well. Paul's parents arrived, dragging suitcases and relatives into Anne's big brick townhouse as if they planned to stay for months. Anne's mother and father were already there; Bill Madison was in Paul's study, going through papers and files; and Virginia was in the kitchen, making arrangements with caterers to bring lunch and dinner.

Celia wrapped Anne in a smothering hug, crying loudly, her mascara running down her cheeks. Behind her were Sal, Paul's two sisters, their children, and Paul's Aunt Ellie, dressed entirely in black and cradling an ancient miniature poodle, who had once been black as well, but was now a quivery shade of gray.

By early afternoon Anne's eyes were red and swollen from crying, and Molly was worn out.

"Why is it people have to make so many decisions right after a death?" Molly said to Clark when they stepped outside for a few minutes of fresh air. They sat down on the curved brick steps leading up to the townhouse. "When someone goes suddenly, at the very time you're most in shock, you have to make dozens of choices you'll remember for the rest of your life.

"There ought to be some rule that you have to plan your own funeral when you turn eighteen and then update it every five years or something. Then your family just pulls out the file and does whatever it says. No questions. No arguing. No decisions having to be made by people who are already devastated."

"That's what people do when they get old," Clark said. "But people don't think about death when they're young. I mean, Paul had his paperwork in order, his will, his life insurance, all that. But he was like the rest of us. We all live in denial that we'll ever die. Not now, or tomorrow. Later. Much later. Meanwhile, carpe diem. Or eat, drink, and be merry—"

"Do not get going with general observations about the human dilemma," Molly interrupted, talking deliberately, without contractions, as she always did when she was angry. Clark never got angry. "We are not talking about the human condition here. We are talking about Paul. And Anne. I hate seeing her going through all this.

"It's bad enough what happened to Paul. None of us can begin to understand that. But now she has to fend off the entire Lorelli family. She's never been able to deal with them. Paul always did. And they're out of control."

"Well, then, you go fight for her," Clark said quietly, turning to kiss her on the cheek. "I'll go home to the kids and give your mom a break. We'll bring you some clothes. You stay here again tonight."

He stood up and held out his hands. Molly grasped them, and he pulled her up. She hugged him hard. "I'm sorry," she said. "You've been so wonderful through all this. Thank you."

As she reentered the chaos of the living room, Sal and Celia were holding forth about the funeral, dead set on a Mass. Paul hadn't been to Mass since high school, and Anne went to church only for occasional services, Christmas concerts, Easter. To Molly, it didn't make much sense for Paul to return to church just because he was dead.

But it wasn't worth a battle. If Paul had been there, he would have prevailed, as he did when he insisted to his parents that he and Anne be married in Anne's parents' Methodist church. Molly looked toward Anne; she was ready to fight if Anne wanted a Protestant funeral. They went into the powder room together to talk it over privately.

"It's not worth it," Anne whispered. "What does it matter? Paul's gone. It doesn't make any difference to my parents. Having the Mass would mean a lot to Sal and Celia."

"What about the cemetery?" Molly asked, folding and refolding a burgundy hand towel. "That's the next thing they want—to take Paul back to Philadelphia and bury him there. You're right. I don't think the funeral really matters. But I don't think it would be good to have Paul buried somewhere far away. You'll need to visit him sometimes. You don't have a plot reserved somewhere around here, do you?"

"Well," Anne said slowly, "I do. When Paul and I were married Mother and Daddy gave us a double plot at Columbia Gardens in Arlington. They had bought it years and years before, just before they had me, and they wanted to upgrade to a better location, so they gave the old site to us. I didn't think much about it then, except that it was a morbid present. But Daddy's so practical. I didn't know I'd need it so soon . . ."

Her face twisted, and tears spurted out of her eyes.

Molly hugged her and sat her down on the closed toilet lid, ripping off some toilet tissue and helping Anne dab her eyes, talking the way she talked to her children when they were hurt.

"Well, then, we can put Paul there, and that way we can visit him whenever you want. I don't care if Sal and Celia go into hysterics, that's what we'll do. I'll take care of it."

"Thank you," Anne said. "You heard the other thing Sal wants, right?"

"Right," Molly said grimly. "Open casket at the funeral home. I heard Aunt Ellie say that people need to see him, to say good-bye. I also think she's going to bring that poodle to the funeral, but that's beside the point."

"You've got to do something," Anne said. "I can't fight them all on this, but we absolutely cannot let them have an open casket. Paul told me years ago about some aunt who threw herself onto her husband's coffin, and she was kissing his face and flailing around and actually knocked the casket to the ground."

"Oh, no," Molly said. "No way. I'll take care of that."

They emerged from the bathroom, and Molly led Anne toward a chair. "All right, everyone," Molly said brusquely, folding her arms and addressing the assembled Lorellis. The poodle was helping itself to smoked turkey off a buffet tray. "About the casket. Closed. Right?"

Anne groaned to herself. Even in tragedy, Molly's tact was at its usual level.

Celia tottered toward her, mascara still streaking her round face. "Oh, Hon," she said. "Of course. We sure don't want people to see what they did to him."

FOUR DAYS LATER, on the morning of Paul Lorelli's funeral, Tom Hogan sat at his metal desk on the third floor of D.C. police headquarters, looking at the Lorelli file. There was little to go on, like most of the cases Tom had dealt with over the past year.

Outside murders were usually harder to solve than a killing in a victim's home. There, it was easier to establish relationships and motives by basics such as whether the entry was forced or not. In Tom's experience, most victims knew their killers and left evidence of that by opening the door for them.

And inside crime scenes were more likely to be undisturbed, with higher chances for finding fingerprints, or hair, or clothing fibers. Particularly if the killer was stupid, or high at the time of the crime, as in the Maryland double murder that Tom remembered from a few years back: two attorneys, married to one another. The killer had shot them execution style in the bedroom, then stopped in the kitchen to drink a glass of water before he fled in their car. Detectives had recovered his fingerprints on the outside of the glass, and enough of his saliva inside, to run his DNA and make a positive identification.

The street murders were more likely to be disturbed and contaminated, either by weather or curious people, and it was harder to get any context for the crime. After Paul Lorelli's shooting, the killers had fled into Georgetown's maze of narrow streets and alleys, probably into the anonymous crowds that always filled the corner of Wisconsin and M Streets on weekend nights. They had not been courteous enough to leave any fingerprints or DNA calling cards behind.

And so far, Anne Lorelli's ID had been of little help. The perps were black, young, wore baggy dark pants, probably jeans, big jackets, dark gloves . . . the only unusual detail he had was the earlobe missing on the one with the shaved head, but that hadn't yielded anything yet. Tom guessed that the ear suspect was an import or new in town. He had visited a few guys he knew on the streets, and nobody seemed to know anything about a kid with a ragged ear.

He had asked Fairfax County police to keep an eye on Anne; Witnesses in D.C. murders sometimes ended up dead, though that was more often the case in gang killings than random street crime. Tom had also made sure that the newspapers printed that Anne hadn't been able to give any clear identification—an added precaution, though Tom doubted that the perpetrators of a crime like this spent a whole lot of time perusing the *Washington Post*. And he had withheld from the media, as always, some of the key details: the caliber of gun used, the particular items stolen, the fact that fibers and hairs not belonging to the victim had been recovered from his shirt.

But even though the Lorelli shooting was likely just a mugging victim going ballistic and getting himself shot for doing so, there was something about this case that bugged Tom. Something about the wife's distance. Even though Anne Lorelli had been in shock when he interviewed her at the hospital right after her husband's death, she didn't have the raw, bleeding anguish he had seen so many times before.

It was probably nothing. She seemed like she had a reserved personality anyway. She was probably just stunned, frozen by the shock of sudden death.

But history had taught Tom to follow his instincts. He closed his file and prepared to go to Paul Lorelli's funeral. There would be a lot of people there, and he'd blend in with the mourners and see if anyone unusual showed up.

ANNE WENT THROUGH PAUL'S FUNERAL as if she were watching another person perform a role. She stood very straight, nodding and smiling, murmuring "Thank you for coming," to everyone she saw. "She's being so strong," she could hear them whispering to one another. "I just don't know how she's holding up."

The Catholic Mass felt muted and distant, as if Anne was watching the proceedings through a stained-glass window. The church was full of friends, her parents' neighbors, and a section of pews for Paul's partners and associates from the law firm. Several rows in the front were filled with Lorellis, all in black, most weeping throughout the Mass.

It all went by in a daze. "Lord have mercy," intoned the priest; the people repeated it back in a weak echo. The burnished coffin lay in front of the church, closed, with a large spray of yellow roses resting on top. These, like the rose the maître d' had given Anne the night of his murder, were crisp and scentless.

Suddenly the service was over. Everyone stood. The pallbearers escorted the coffin out. Anne's father took her arm and led her out a side door toward the long, black limousine idling behind the hearse.

During the fifteen-minute ride to the cemetery Anne said nothing, just looked out the window and watched the neighborhoods go by. Bill Madison stared out the window as well, his usually cheerful Irish face drooping and sad. Virginia sat erect, her back not touching the seat, her hands folded over her square, black leather purse. Molly and Clark were in the car behind her. Anne looked back through the rear window and saw the long line of cars following them down Old Dominion Drive, their headlights on. It registered somewhere in her mind that this was a funeral. But what she could not understand was that it was *Paul's* funeral.

At the cemetery, after the final blessing and the sign of the cross, Anne stood with her head bowed for a moment more, thinking of Paul's face after the explosion of the gun, as he slid against the tree that night in Georgetown.

It hadn't been pain as much as surprise, she thought, and anger, rage at the muggers, and then a choking kind of fury at this thing that had torn up his chest. And then he had lost consciousness.

Anne's father was standing, his smooth face lined with concern, his shaggy eyebrows down, his arm extended. It was over. The limousine was waiting again. She couldn't stand it any longer.

Anne broke from the cluster of solemn faces and walked quickly over the bumpy ground, away from the green canvas tent stretching over Paul's new grave. Behind her she sensed people looking at one another, unsure of whether to follow or not. Then she heard the familiar sound of Molly's running feet.

"Can I help?" Molly asked, slipping her arm through Anne's as if they were old ladies.

"Just walk with me for a minute," Anne muttered. "I need some space. I hate to make everyone wait. We'll go back in just a second."

"They can wait," Molly said. "You do whatever you need to do."

They walked between the gray rows of graves, slowing down as they got farther from the cluster of people. Anne looked at the smooth stone markers. Some were pink, polished marble with black veins. Others were pebbled white and shiny black. "Janet Gaskins Carstone," read one. "Beloved Wife and Mother. 'How precious to the Lord is the death of His saints.'" Janet had been sixty-two.

Here was another, a double-wide: "Oliver Getty Wilkins" and "Eunice Smith Wilkins." "Beloved Parents: Together Forever." Oliver had been gone since 1952; he had died when he was forty-one. *Maybe an accident,* thought Anne. Eunice's side of the plot looked freshly dug, though it was a year old. She had died when she was eighty-four. *All those years without him. Didn't Eunice ever remarry? Did she live with her children at the end? Did she even remember life with Oliver? Had she called him Ollie?*

Anne's thoughts were flitting like the small birds she had seen lighting on the thin branches of a dead tree near Paul's grave. Molly was still quiet. Anne walked a few more steps and looked at a plain gray stone. Here was Linda Scott Carstens, June 12, 1948–October 15, 1995. Her epitaph: "I did the best I could." The stone was a simple block, no decorations or plantings. No "cherished wife" or "beloved mother."

What was Linda like, Anne wondered. *Let's see, forty-seven years old.* First Anne imagined a single, career government worker, probably a secretary to a midlevel bureaucrat, no nonsense, no humor, no car, just riding the Metro to and from the District every day, reading her newspaper, carrying her umbrella if the weather was cloudy, prim and tidy . . . then the vision changed to a middle-aged housewife, griping about footprints on her just-vacuumed plush carpet, harassing her children about undone homework, serving up tasteless, well-balanced meals each evening exactly at six, doing her best so meticulously that everyone had hated her. And when she had died her husband had put her favorite phrase on her headstone and left off everything else.

"I did the best I could." Maybe it was meant to be noble, a tribute to a lifetime of effort, but to Anne it just sounded whiny. And where did it get you, anyway?

Inside Anne there was a whine as well. *I've always done the best I could. Lived up to everyone's expectations, put others first, and out of nowhere my husband gets killed. It's not fair.*

She turned around. Molly heeled and turned with her like a well-trained guide dog. In the distance Anne saw a woman she didn't know, standing at the edge of the gathering of mourners. Not far from her was a tall, slender man in a trenchcoat—the detective who had questioned her the night of Paul's death. *What is he doing here?* Anne thought.

Her eyes moved back toward the woman, who was looking toward Anne and Molly, staring, really, but Anne couldn't make out her features. She was swathed in a sweeping black coat, her eyes covered by a pair of wrap sunglasses, her head covered by a big black hat, though Anne could see dark hair pulled into some sort of a twist at the nape of her long neck.

As they got back to Paul's grave, people were standing in clumps, talking quietly. Paul's brother's wife, Angelica, approached Anne, both gray-gloved hands extended, her fake-fur hat a bit askew. "Are you all right?" she asked. "We're so worried about you. But you just gotta know that Paul's up in heaven right now, looking down on us, already a saint. He always did the best he could."

SEVEN

"Would you like some coffee or tea, or something cold to drink, Detective Hogan?" Anne asked. She wasn't sure how one entertained a homicide detective in one's home. Tom Hogan wasn't there for tea, but she needed some. Holding a cup would give her something to do with her hands.

Tom Hogan looked up from the notepad resting on his knees. "No, thank you, Mrs. Lorelli," he said. "I don't care for anything, but please, get yourself something if you'd like. And please, call me Tom."

Anne flicked a speck of lint off her gray wool pants. "No, no, I don't need anything," she said.

Tom looked at her without speaking. He knew a file-full of facts about Anne Lorelli and her deceased husband, the type of information he gathered in every case. Now, after the funeral, he needed to dig a little further.

He saw now how her eyes looked larger than they had on the night of the crime, the planes of her face were more finely cut than before. He saw, too, how the waist of her pants seemed too large. Her belt was hooked into a new notch. Not uncommon; most women like Anne

Lorelli lost weight quickly after a shock like this. Her shoes were suede flats, her earrings heavy gold-and-pearl clusters. Her thick, shoulder-length blond hair was brushed back from her face and held in place by a black velvet headband.

Tom's work had taught him not to caricature people; doing so made you miss important details. But before he became a detective he would have dismissed Anne Lorelli as a photo from a Talbots' catalogue, the sort of woman who had once been the sort of girl who didn't interest him much.

"I know we've been over some of this already, Mrs. Lorelli," Tom said, "and I'm sorry, because I know it's all very painful to you. But for us to do our work and apprehend the men who committed this crime, I have to ask you again to remember every detail you can from the evening of your husband's murder."

She looked at the ceiling. "Go ahead."

He shifted. Anne looked at him and saw how his tall frame was too long for the armchair, just as Paul's had been. His green eyes never left her face. Anne had noticed that even good listeners who watch intently break eye contact when *they* are speaking, but Tom Hogan's gaze remained fixed on her even while he spoke. It was disconcerting.

Tom cleared his throat. "Let me give you some context for what's happened here. You probably know what the murder rate has been like in the District for a long time.

"Most of our homicides happen east of Sixteenth Street. Most of them are drug-related; 90 percent of the perpetrators are young, black men, a lot of them teenagers. Eighty percent of the murders are committed with firearms. Victims who aren't part of the drug or gang scene have been rare.

"We've been worried, though, over the past few years, because there has been an increase in robbery killings. Arbitrary murders of innocent people, members of the general population. We've had thirteen this year, most of them in the Georgetown area and off Dupont Circle. Most of those were robberies and carjackings, and a few people were killed after being forced to use their ATM cards to withdraw cash.

"So, I am sorry, but this crime fits that pattern. It appears that you and your husband were in the wrong place at the wrong time."

Anne closed her eyes. So it was dessert that had killed Paul. This matter-of-fact investigator was telling her that if they had skipped the raspberries and crème caramel and come out of the restaurant twenty minutes earlier, Paul might still be alive. Or what if they had had a second cup of coffee while those muggers were lurking in the shadows? Would that mean that the couple who had been at the corner table would have left first, and another woman would now be a widow instead of Anne?

"We've actually had little to go on," Tom continued. "No witnesses besides yourself. We've combed through a lot of people we talk to now and then about street crimes like this, people who usually seem to know about these sorts of things. No one's talking. But we're working with the physical evidence we have and pursuing a few other leads that may turn up something of value.

"But also, in a case like this we'd be negligent if we didn't consider other scenarios besides a simple robbery motive," Tom concluded, still looking at Anne directly. She had to know that the victim's family were never far from the detectives' list of suspects, even when the crime seemed fairly straightforward. Particularly when physical evidence was lacking, Tom tended to think in terms of what he didn't see, the pieces of the puzzle that weren't even in the box.

"So I'll need to ask you some more questions. Some of them may seem a bit shocking, but they're just standard considerations, however remote, that we have to look into."

"Go ahead," Anne said.

"Do you have any reason to suspect your husband had any involvement with illegal drugs?"

"I don't really know what you're going after," Anne said, after a pause. "Paul and I were married for ten years, and I knew him for almost two years before that. He's never been involved with any drugs, in any way. We've never even known anyone involved with drugs. It was never an issue that came up, except, you know, in political discussions about crack babies and narcotics enforcement and things like that . . ." She trailed off. Tom Hogan's steady gaze made her nervous, as if she had something to hide.

"All right," Tom said. "So your husband was not a drug user. Do you have any reason to believe he was involved in the sale or distribution of illegal drugs?"

"No," Anne said, frowning. "Certainly not."

"Did he abuse alcohol at all?"

Anne shook her head again. She and Paul drank as did most people she knew: wine with meals, or beer at a cookout, or occasional gin-and-tonics in the summertime, at the beach.

But Paul didn't drink to excess. Abuse of alcohol would have stood in the way of everything he strove for, his schoolwork, his law career, their social standing, the future he had plotted so neatly that Anne sometimes imagined it like the diagram of a constellation, lines drawn point to point to point, Paul's stars rising like the upward curve of Orion's belt on a clear winter night . . . and Paul had seemed wary of anything that might make him lose control. Control was big for him.

"No," she said.

"I'm just a little curious," he said. "The hospital lab reports show that Mr. Lorelli's blood alcohol level was .10; that's right at the legal limit for driving."

Anne sat back in her seat, her eyebrows drawn together. This didn't sound like much of a murder investigation. It sounded rude and invasive and unfair. "Who's on trial here?" she said. "I mean, Paul was the victim, right? He had an aperitif, some wine with dinner, some champagne afterward—he was a big, healthy, man. That wouldn't be enough to affect him very much. And what does that have to do with finding out who killed him?"

"I'm sorry," Tom said smoothly. "Again, please understand that we have to look at every angle here. I don't mean to offend you. These are the routine type of questions I have to ask in order to determine if there were people your husband might have known who would have any reason to come after him, or if your husband might have had any instabilities or addictions of any kind. I know it might seem callous, but these are the sort of things we have to ascertain."

He jotted a few things in his notebook and went on. "Did you notice any unusual behaviors on your husband's part in the weeks or months prior to his death? Any changes in patterns? Working late?"

"Paul always worked late," Anne said. "Before he made partner he worked late so he could make partner. After he made partner, he worked as late as ever."

"What time did he usually get home?"

"An early night would be 8:30 or so. I'd always have dinner ready—" She stopped. The detective didn't care whether she made dinner or not. "Most nights were about nine or ten. During big cases it was usually midnight. Sometimes he'd just sleep at the office. He had clothes and toiletries and things there in case he needed them."

Tom Hogan nodded and scribbled something in his notebook.

"This may seem unconnected to the evening of your husband's death," he said, "but we would be negligent if we didn't try to pursue any possible scenario, if we did not assume that there's more to this case than meets the eye."

Anne paused. She felt like there was more than met the eye. Not in terms of the case itself, but her response to Paul's death had baffled her. She felt a shred of relief mixed with her shock and sorrow, something she could admit to no one.

In the nights she had lain awake since the shooting, she had thought less about Paul's murder than the few years that had preceded it, the growing sense of panic that all was not well. Paul had always worked long hours—this detective should know that was true about any good attorney in Washington—but in the past year, Anne had welcomed those absences. And when Paul was home, he passed into some smooth, distant mode. Anne recognized it. It was the same way he treated his parents, but with much more polish on it. Like a thick layer of polyurethane over varnished wood. Through the gloss, the finish underneath looked almost perfect; you couldn't even see the scuff marks.

SHE COULD ALMOST CIRCLE the day on the calendar that Paul had shifted gears. He had been in the middle of a big case. He treated her politely and deferentially in public and without any passion in private. That had been all right with Anne. She didn't care much for passion any more. *Maybe later,* she kept thinking. *After*—After, she didn't know what.

And that loss of their passion confused her almost as much as losing Paul. The whole thing didn't make any sense. All she knew was that she felt guilty, relieved, and bereaved, all at once, and she wasn't supposed to feel the first two. And there was no one she could tell. Partially because she couldn't make any sense of it herself, and partially because no one would understand. Even Molly.

Molly's loves and hates were so simple. She and Clark had their ups and downs, but there were no masks or masquerades. Over the years, Anne had begun to feel like she and Paul were playing roles, and in the familiarity of the play, she had forgotten the reality.

When she had first met Paul, it had been so different, her feelings so vibrant, her connection with him so sure. Anne and Molly were living then in an old Tudor row house on Q Street with two other friends. Since graduation from college, Anne had worked as a legislative correspondent at the Capitol Hill offices of Fred Nolan, the congressman from her district.

Anne enjoyed her work. It was always so busy, the sense of energy and importance so high, and yet in some ways it felt like college. The Hill was like a small campus; the older office buildings there seemed like a school, with their unpretentious brown doors off the wide halls, bells ringing for votes, the intrigue as thick as high school when the rumors flew that some former homecoming queen was getting together with some former senior class president . . . except all of it, the romance, the power plays, the media spotlight, played out against the backdrop of real legislation for the nation.

At the time after-work events sponsored by various lobbies were a staple of Anne's dinner diet. One evening Rosemary Ringer, who worked for a congressman from Louisiana, invited Anne to come with her to a reception sponsored by the National Shrimp Board.

A long, linen-covered table was spread with steaming silver cauldrons and chilled crystal bowls. There was jambalaya, shrimp Creole, shrimp étouffée, shrimp salad, baby shrimp, Cajun shrimp, jumbo shrimp—shrimp so abundant that the effect was intoxicating. Even among the members of Congress and lobbyists attending, there was little pretense of moving, shaking, or networking. Shrimp was the great leveler, and everyone simply parked next to the buffet table and gorged themselves unabashedly.

Anne had been contemplating packing her purse with ice to bring home shrimp for Molly when a friend of Rosemary's appeared with a tall, handsome man by his side.

"Hey, Hunter, how are you?" Rosemary said to her friend. "Do you know Anne Madison? Anne and I are getting drunk on shrimp!"

"No, hi, Anne," Hunter said. "This is Paul Lorelli. He's in law school at Georgetown, and I thought maybe some shrimp would cheer him up tonight."

Rosemary had extended a fishy hand toward Paul. "Well, it's certainly cheering us up," she giggled. Anne looked at Rosemary sharply, checking the goblet in her friend's hand. It really was just Perrier in there.

She wiped her hand on a napkin and extended it to Paul. "How do you do?" she had said formally, wondering where in the world that 1950s phrase had come from. It was probably a reaction against Rosemary's shrimp intoxication.

Paul had taken her hand and smiled, and Anne suddenly saw just how handsome he really was. His eyes were incredible. "I do well, Miss Madison," he said, teasing, echoing her cotillion language. "May I call you Anne, or should I wait until we know one another better?"

In the end they had all eaten more shrimp together and then gone out for coffee at a Capitol Hill hangout. Rosemary had sobered up after her second cup of cappuccino. And much later that night, as Anne was home in bed, she thought about how Paul had looked at her, even as they sat at the table at Bullfeathers, how his eyes had lingered over her.

Sometimes that assessing look from men was annoying and proprietary, but with Paul, Anne had felt the opposite, a sense that he somehow recognized something about her . . . she couldn't define it. But as she lay in bed and watched the streetlights on Q Street filter through the narrow blinds, she couldn't go to sleep.

She could hear Molly in the bathroom, singing a Van Morrison song as she prepared for bed. "It's a marvelous night for a moondance," Molly was warbling, without much regard for key or for the fact that anyone might be trying to sleep in the house. "A marvelous night for romance . . ."

Anne stretched and turned on her side, holding her pillow. And every time she thought about Paul Lorelli's eyes on her face, his deep voice saying, "or should I wait until we know one another better?" she smiled into the darkness.

AND EVEN NOW, more than a decade later, Anne smiled as she remembered. Why couldn't it have stayed like that? She missed the old days, the time when the biggest decision on her agenda was what to wear to work the next day, when one never knew what surprise the evening might bring. She missed the old Paul, the old warmth before he had become so cold.

Tom Hogan was watching Anne as she thought. "I'm sorry," she said, realizing with a start that she had been staring off into some point in the corner of the ceiling, smiling and watching the dust particles float through the air. You could only see them if you didn't look for them, if you fixed your eyes vaguely on the whole area at once. It was like looking into one of those Magic Eye picture books.

"I'm sorry," she repeated. "I was just thinking back, back about Paul when I first knew him."

"I know this is really hard," Tom said. "I'm sorry to have to ask you these questions. Did you notice any unusual phone calls, or unusual charges on your phone bill?"

"Oh," Anne said, "Paul always paid the bills. I never even looked at the statements. I'm sorry. I guess they'd be in a file . . ."

Tom Hogan looked at her like she was twelve years old. She could tell he didn't think much of women who didn't pay their own bills, let alone not even look at them.

But she thought, too, of those times that the phone had rung and she had picked it up to find no one there. It hadn't been enough to make a pattern. "It's probably just kids," Paul had said, "messing with the phone while their parents are out."

Tom Hogan was waiting. "So," he said, "phone calls? Unusual

spending? Did your husband seem preoccupied? Any concerns over people following him? Changes in sleeping or eating habits?"

It was too much. Anne looked up at Tom. Couldn't this wait until later? "No," she said, shutting off, her blue eyes cold and remote. "No. I can't think of anything."

EIGHT

Two weeks later, Molly O'Kelley walked out on her front porch. Boaz, her golden retriever, stood at full alert at the picket fence, monitoring the neighborhood boys gliding by on their skateboards. Ruth, the cocker spaniel, was gleaning the last bits of dog chow from the bowl on the porch.

Clark and the kids were at a soccer game, and Molly had invited Anne to come for lunch. Since Paul's funeral they had talked every day on the phone, but Anne had seemed distant, in a faraway fog where Molly couldn't reach her. She knew that grief did different things to people, but she wasn't quite sure what it was doing to Anne.

She had on a pair of ancient blue jeans, an old Princeton sweatshirt of Clark's, and a pair of Birkenstocks with orange socks. Her hair was skewered on top of her head, perilously secured with one of five-year-old Amelia's blue barrettes, dark wisps falling around her high cheekbones and angular face. Somehow Molly could scrounge from her family's closets and still look, if not good, then at least eccentric.

She went down the three front steps and walked through the yard, snapping off a dead twig here, shuffling through some leaves there.

From nowhere a phrase popped into her head. *"Time, time, and half a time."* She couldn't remember what it was from—probably some long-forgotten college literature course—but it stirred in her like the elusive smell of old, damp leaves kicked up on a walk through the forest. Maybe it was *Beowulf* or something. *Time, time, and half a time.* It was haunting. How could she tow Anne through the deep waters of this strange time?

Already she had seen other friends' odd reactions to Paul's murder. She had taken Anne to the grocery store a week ago, and in the produce section they had run into an acquaintance.

The woman, Pat somebody, knew. Everyone in the D.C. area knew. Paul's picture and the description of the anniversary night murder had been all over the local news and in the *Washington Post* and the *Washington Times*. As soon as Pat recognized Anne, she had stuffed a huge bunch of spinach leaves in a plastic bag and reached for a fastener to twist it shut.

"Hi, Anne," she had said vivaciously, lightly tossing the bundle in her cart, turning to leave. "How are you?" Molly had stared at her, disbelieving. The spinach leaves she had stuffed in the plastic bag were spotted and withered.

Stuck in the stare, Pat had continued, feverishly. "The store's packed tonight, isn't it? It always gets this way when it looks like it's going to snow. Of course it's way too early to snow. I guess people are trained to run out to the store whenever it clouds over when the weather's a little cold. Milk, eggs, bread, you know. Well, I'd better get going."

Anne's blue eyes had clouded too. Molly got angry. "What do you mean, how are we? How would you be if your husband had just been killed? Don't you have the decency to at least say you're sorry or something?"

Pat fluttered, totally flummoxed. "I am sorry," she said. "I really do have to go." She turned and rolled toward the checkout lanes. A long shopping list scrawled on the back of an envelope and the withered spinach were the only items in her cart.

Anne looked at Molly and reached past the spinach leaves and garlic bulbs for a bouquet of fresh parsley. "She's sorry? Why'd you make her say that?" she asked. "She didn't do it!"

"I know," Molly said. "But I just cannot believe how people can be so insensitive. Does she really think we can just stand here and chat about the weather?"

"It's not as unusual as you think," Anne said. "People don't know what to say, so they don't say anything. Or they act like I've got some contagious disease; if they spend time with me, maybe their husbands will get shot too."

Molly had thought about that later. Did she feel that way? She let her imagination play over the scene of Paul's murder, the men emerging from the shadowed trees, the sight of the gun, and the twist of the gut. What if it had been Clark? Some years ago an aide to an Alabama senator had been murdered a few blocks from the Capitol, walking to a corner store for a cup of coffee. The senator had later pushed through an assault-weapons bill.

But Molly couldn't make it personal. It hadn't been Clark. It had been another senate aide. It hadn't been Clark. It had been Paul.

She looked at her watch. It was a few minutes before noon, and Anne would drive up right at the stroke of the hour. She went back inside to finish putting lunch together.

She had been infatuated lately with Latin food, with unexplained longings for chili peppers and cilantro, and earlier that morning had assembled pupusas: cornmeal pockets of pork, cheese, and spices. Then she had dumped tomatoes, cilantro, a jalapeño pepper, brown sugar, ginger, and lime juice into the Cuisinart and pulsed everything together. She kept dipping a soup spoon into the salsa, testing, adding more of this and that until she realized with horror that she had eaten almost half of it.

What she hadn't consumed was now in a green pottery bowl; she set it on the long farm table in the kitchen. She cut a fresh lime into wedges and set out plates and silverware. It was noon. Anne would step up on the porch within the next sixty seconds.

Ruth and Boaz started barking. Molly heard the slam of a car door, and then Anne's voice talking to the dogs. She treated them with the same unusual abandon that she did Molly's children, except she talked to the dogs in a higher falsetto. "Hello, Boaz!" Molly heard her say. "You are the most wonderful male dog in North America! You put other dogs to shame! You are a prince among dogs!

"And Ruth! Your fur is looking especially nice today! Have you had your ears done? They're so curly, so beautiful!"

Affirmed, the dogs lay down on the porch. Anne opened the door. "Come on in the kitchen," Molly called.

She and Anne hugged and sat down to attack the pupusas. "How are you doing?" Molly asked.

"I don't know," Anne said. "Any other questions?

"I'm okay," she went on after a moment. "Most people have been so nice, bringing food and sending notes and flowers. I've written a million thank-you notes.

"But everybody else can just go on with their lives. I mean, you still have kids and laundry and soccer matches. Clark still goes to work. I don't know how to plug back in.

"My parents have been great. Dad's gone through everything, and financially I'm okay. I don't have to work right now unless I want to. But I have no idea what I'd do anyway."

"What about writing?" Molly asked. "You've put that on the back burner for so long. What about your children's stories?"

"Right," Anne said sarcastically. "The kids' market is so easy to break into. There are plenty of really talented people out there. I can't compete with them."

"Why not?" Molly said, shrugging. "You can do it."

Anne just shook her head.

"You know what I've been doing? I feel most comfortable when I'm by myself, but in a crowd. So I've been going to museums, art galleries, exhibitions . . .

"I can stand in front of a painting at the Corcoran and talk about brushstrokes or lighting technique with the person next to me, and it feels good. I'm connecting, but the focus isn't on me and what happened."

"Where have you gone?" asked Molly.

"You name it," said Anne. "The Capitol. The White House. Mount Vernon. We used to laugh at all those people with cameras riding around on the Tour-Mobile. Pretty soon I'll be a regular."

"Why haven't you told me about all this touristy stuff?" Molly asked. "I'll come with you one day while the kids are in school."

"I went on the tour of the FBI," Anne went on. "Remember how we wanted to do that when we were kids? I went to the top of the Washington Monument. The last time we did that was at midnight the summer after junior year. I hooked up with two fourth-grade classes at the National Aquarium. Did you know that the killer whale there has lived in captivity for ten years?

"Oh, and don't get me started on the zoo! There's a new baby zebra. The cheetahs run every day at ten. They train the elephants at eleven. The prairie-dog colony is doing well."

Molly stared at Anne. She was sounding more animated than she had in a long time. Manic, even. It was a good sign. It used to be that she would get going in these tirades, Molly would join in, and they would both laugh for hours. She hadn't heard any word-torrents from Anne since Paul's death—or, actually, for a long while before that.

"Maybe this obsessive attendance at public attractions is good therapy," Molly said. "I mean, Washington is the right place for this type of thing. If you don't mind repeating now and then, you could keep this up for years. And you could extend out toward Baltimore. Manassas. Richmond. Have you done any battlefields? Circuses? Meetings of the Edgar Allan Poe Society? Poetry readings at local bookstores?"

"I haven't gotten that desperate yet," said Anne dryly. "Give me another few months. I still have the Washington Cathedral. The Building Museum. The East Wing. The Nixon papers at the National Archives: forty million pages! Now, that could take some time. I've got time."

She took a swallow of water. "I even went to Arlington Cemetery," she said.

"You're kidding," Molly said. "Wasn't that depressing?"

"No," Anne said. "I can't explain it, but it's like I'm on automatic pilot; I don't feel much of anything. I went there trying to make myself feel something. To me it was a lot of white headstones in rows on the hills."

"I don't understand," Molly said. "If Clark died, I would die—"

"No, you wouldn't. But you would hurt, you would feel. I don't. The only thing that gets to me is when I remember the old times, how things used to be. But when I think of the last year or two, it's like Paul was a stranger. It's like a stranger died."

"Why?" Molly asked. "What was going on between you for things to come to that?"

"Nothing," Anne said, shaking her head. "And that's all I feel now. Nothing."

"Well, you shouldn't be too hard on yourself—" Molly said.

"I'm not," Anne interrupted. She stood to take her dishes to the sink. "Somebody told me that the best way to deal with bad stuff is to face right into it. Maybe I'm repressing everything; that's why I feel so dull. Maybe I need CPR, you know, or when they put those electric paddles on your heart to jump-start it again. The shock almost kills you, but then you come back to life.

"So I thought as long as I'm on this roll of compulsive touring, I should go to the Holocaust Museum. That's murder on the biggest scale you can imagine. If that doesn't shock me into feeling something, I don't know what would."

"Do you want me to go with you?" Molly asked, taken aback.

"No," Anne said. "I want to go alone."

NINE

INCREDIBLE, ANNE THOUGHT, as she pulled her black Volvo between the white lines on the dark pavement. *A parking space!* The small lot next to the Tidal Basin was almost always full. But here was this space, waiting for her. Free.

Across the waters of the Tidal Basin she could see the white columns of the Jefferson Memorial. Sea gulls wheeled in the sky. The air was crisp, the trees brilliant bursts of orange and red, their leaves reflected in the pool's cool waters. A flotilla of blue plastic paddleboats were roped, huddled together near the refreshment kiosk, which was closed until spring.

She got out and walked across the path toward Fifteenth Street, her leather purse slung over her shoulder and her hands stuck deep in her jacket pockets.

When the Holocaust Memorial Museum opened in 1993, Anne had read about it in the *Washington Post*. The architect had escaped from Hitler's Germany as a child; the building he designed had captured more attention than the exhibitions themselves.

Anne could see why. She felt quieted, disturbed even as she crossed the uneven red-brick plaza to the museum's entrance. A few golden leaves skittered across her path in a quick gust of wind. Before her was a heavy piece of black bronze, shaped roughly like a house turned upside down.

Ahead was its companion piece, perhaps an abstract tree, or a person—Anne couldn't tell. She hated modern art. So hard to define. Was it subtle and evocative, a work of genius, or was it just a piece of twisted bronze? She didn't know the right answer, and she couldn't decide on her own. At any rate, it was something broken.

Anne entered the museum. She felt small. The walls were red brick, four stories high, the floors silver pockmarked steel, the girders and beams dark gray. It felt like a prison, or something industrial, something skewed.

She went to the admission desk, where she got a same-day entrance ticket from a jovial old man with bushy eyebrows. "There you are," he said. "Do you need help finding where to go? Are you warm enough? You can take your coat to the coat-check, if you'd like." His expansiveness made her shy. Was he a survivor? He acted like he belonged here.

She walked hesitantly toward the elevators for the main exhibition. The silver doors slid open on the top floor of the museum, and before Anne was a huge, wall-sized photo of American troops standing over the charred corpses of Nazi victims. An immense, curved black wall read starkly in deeply cut letters: THE HOLOCAUST.

Anne took a breath and began walking. One wasn't free to wander at will; the route was set by the construction of the exhibit. The images bombarded her from left and right. Here were old newsreels, with hearty choruses of Germans singing patriotic songs. Adolf Hitler smiled and waved to cheering crowds the night he was appointed chancellor of Germany.

"The terror begins," read a photo caption of storm troopers

restraining a huge German shepherd. Somehow the fact that the muscular dog was muzzled made him more menacing than if he'd been free. Swastikas were everywhere, piles of Jewish authors' books burning. "Where books are burned, in the end people will be burned," a German Jew had written.

Then came the "science" of Aryan supremacy. Anne saw pictures of people having their noses measured with pointed metal calipers, their hair color recorded, their eyeshades matched and noted on long, closely typed lists. The Nazis loved recordkeeping. It was a short step from the lists—Aryan or alien?—to the sterilization of "inferior" races.

Here was a young blond girl with braids, her arm straight and proud, stretched in the Nazi salute. And *Kristallnacht*, when Torahs and synagogues were desecrated, Jewish shops smashed. German soldiers swore oaths of loyalty to Adolf Hitler. And down the slippery slope the Nazi millstone tumbled until it rolled over Poland in 1939.

Anne gazed at a wall-sized set of sepia photos. Here were the mass executions of Polish teachers, writers, politicians, and priests. In one, five bound men stood in front of a brick wall, waiting for the firing squad. In another, anonymous, helmeted German soldiers, thick-coated and belted at the waist, fired into a blurred huddle of people.

In some of the photos, though, the faces were clear. A weary yet defiant Pole stood with his hands behind his head, hating his captors. A priest wearing a white collar stood with both hands loosely by his sides, his eyes steady on his killer.

And here was a balding man with deep dimples, a striped bow tie, a vest, jacket, and thick round glasses. His eyebrows were up, his face frozen—now for more than half a century—in an expression somewhere between supplication and a smile.

Anne saw herself the night of Paul's murder, her eyebrows up, apologizing to the animals who were robbing them that she couldn't get her pearls off properly. This man looked the same. It was as if he could not conceive of the horror happening, so it would not happen.

The picture to his right showed a ditch filled with corpses. It had happened.

She walked on. Here was a photo of a naked eight-year-old boy who was mentally retarded. The Nazis had administered a lethal injection. Operation T-4. Elimination of the handicapped.

But individual executions, needle by needle or bullet by bullet, were too inefficient for the grandeur of the Nazi vision. Soon came the ghettos, the camps, the crematoriums.

There were four high towers in the museum, echoes of the immense guard towers at Auschwitz. Anne stood in one. Three stories high, it was filled with hundreds of photographs of the people of Eishishok, a small Jewish town that had flourished for nine hundred years in what became Lithuania.

Anne looked up, to the left, to the right. The photos were mounted all the way to the ceiling, even where no one could see. Light shone down from a skylight in the roof.

Anne could almost hear the stories the photos told. A bride and groom sat side by side. A young man, casually graceful, leaned to light his girlfriend's cigarette. A little boy in a sailor suit stood proudly on a chair. A small girl posed high in her father's arms, her arm draped around her daddy's neck, the collar and cuffs of her little plaid dress starched crisp and white.

And here was a picture of two young women, one blond, the other brunette, arm in arm. The photo was blurred. They had been walking quickly, laughing, caught in the moment. Anne smiled; it was easy to do in this tower of life. The picture reminded her of herself and Molly.

She walked on through the tower and back to the horror.

More killings. Babi Yar. The Warsaw Ghetto uprising. Here was an actual old railroad car, one of the hundreds used to transport Jews to Poland's six killing centers.

Anne stood in the car's dim confine. The air was dusty, the smell more potent than if there had been vast volumes of words posted on its wooden walls. Anne sensed the real people who had once pressed in this space, their flesh so close that none could sit.

As she went further, here were the actual possessions people had brought with them to the concentration camps. Anne saw hundreds of old umbrellas, their spokes spindly and worn. Prayer shawls that had been ripped from Jews who would soon be dead. Artificial legs. Combs. Scissors. Razors. Toothbrushes. The intimate articles of everyday life—no need for them in the grave.

And then she came to a vast pile of shoes: men's leather lace-ups, sandals, high heels, hundreds and hundreds of shoes, preserved as a shrine, their dusty aroma filling the air half a century after their owners had been unloaded from the cattle cars, stripped, and herded to their deaths. The crematoriums spared no flesh or bone. But here were the shoes, the shoes of those who had never come home.

Anne thought of Paul's wingtips and loafers at home in their closet, perched on his shoe rack, polished and durable as the day he died. She didn't know what to do with them now.

Then came Auschwitz. *Arbeit Macht Frie*—work makes freedom—read the replica of the sign that had hung over the entrance to the infamous Nazi camp.

Here were the voices of Auschwitz, tapes of ordinary men and women who had survived, telling fragments of their stories, overlapping, endless, never stopping.

"They were sorting us, some on one side, some on the other," said a woman. "We didn't know what was happening. I asked about my grandparents. Someone said, 'Oh, if they're with the children, they'll be all right. The soldiers won't hurt the children.' I never saw any of them again."

"We were naked," another woman remembered. "If they saw anybody pregnant, they took them out."

Anne walked on, dazed. By now she had the strange feeling that she no longer existed, that there were only the strands of stories braided together into one huge story before her. Nothing in her experience tied to the surreal scenes before her. Even the horror of Paul's murder did not connect with the spectacles of the exhibit. He was just one. Here there were millions.

The exhibition path took her again through the Tower of Faces. Now she was on a lower level, with hundreds of new pictures, though if she looked up where the wall went up past the catwalk upstairs, she could almost see Molly and Anne, the two friends walking.

But here, in a terse caption, was the end of the story of Eishishok. A mobile killing squad arrived in the little town in September 1941. The town's four thousand Jews were taken into confinement. The men were shot one day, women and children the next. Within forty-eight hours, nine hundred years of Jewish life and culture ceased to exist.

Anne shook her head. She was dimly aware of other people in the exhibit, but they were not important. She hurried on, now to a section devoted to rescuers, the "righteous among the nations," as they were called, the heroes who risked and gave their lives to save Jews.

Then came the death marches, the great tide of liberation, the Nuremberg trials, the new state of Israel. Anne saw an amphitheater whose walls were made with stone from Jerusalem, where again, survivors told their stories.

She didn't want to hear any more. Already it had been too easy to imagine stories from the photos she had seen. That dimpled Polish man with the bow tie, half-smiling, thinking that civilized people don't execute one another; the priest calmly staring down the long barrel of the Nazi rifle; the people who had suffocated, naked, and then been incinerated, lost in smoke, now only their shoes and umbrellas left behind. The two friends in the Tower of Faces, hurrying toward their future, laughing as they walked, unaware that it would all end one September day in 1941.

As Anne left the exhibit, she came to a large, six-sided open room. She could smell candles burning. White steps led down to a hexagon of rose-colored marble in the floor. There were white ledges cut in the stone where a few people sat quietly.

The five walls angling out from this entrance were inlaid with black panels inscribed with the names of Nazi killing camps. Sobibor. Treblinka. Belzec. Auschwitz-Birkenau. Majdnek. Bergen Belsen. Small candles flickered in front of each. On each of the front walls were what looked like quotes from the Bible. In the center, to the right, there was an eternal flame. Above it an Old Testament passage was carved in the wall:

"Only guard yourself and guard your soul carefully, lest you forget the things your eyes saw, and lest these things depart your heart all the days of your life. And you shall make them known to your children, and to your children's children."

Anne looked up. At the rooftop was a six-sided skylight. She could see triangles of blue sky.

Just then a class of teenagers clambered into the room, straggling in cliques and clumps. Anne walked down the few steps and sat down on the ledge to her right.

The kids looked like they were about fourteen or fifteen. Maintaining quiet respect seemed impossible, their noisy irreverence almost inescapable.

The man sitting on the ledge to Anne's right turned toward her. "They will appreciate this later," he said, pointing toward the kids. One of the teachers was escorting a boy out for climbing over the restraining wall and trying to beat out the eternal flame with his notebook.

Anne watched the teenagers. Several were giggling now, pointing at another girl, who was sitting quietly and staring at the candles. "I don't know," Anne responded. "Maybe the museum should have an age requirement for entrance. Or a maturity test, or something."

She turned toward the man, realizing, with a start, that he was a priest, draped in a billowing black cassock. He had white hair, pale, smooth skin, shaggy white eyebrows, and startling blue eyes. They met hers as if he and Anne were conspirators at a party, talking about the guests.

He laughed. "How many of us would fail the maturity test?" he asked. His English was precise, though heavily accented. "And who would administer it? Some bureaucrat sitting at a little table, checking off responses, using old metal calipers, maybe, typing a long list?"

Anne smiled too. "I guess this isn't the place to talk about lists and tests, is it?" she said. She thought of all the Nazi inventories she had just seen, people deemed fit and unfit. "I'm sorry. I remember being in middle school. It's amazing anyone grows out of it."

Her breath felt stale. Anne turned away and began fishing in her purse for a piece of gum, or a mint, or something.

The priest reached into his pocket and pulled out an old-fashioned white tin. "Would you like a peppermint?" he asked. He flipped the lid open and extended the box toward her.

"Thank you," she said. He took one for himself and slid the tin back in his pocket.

"What do you think of the museum?" he asked. Most of the teenagers were already milling out.

Anne exhaled. "It's overwhelming," she said.

"I have not seen it before," the man said. "It is very good. People have to see." He gestured toward the few teenagers who were still hanging around. "Most of them don't seem to care, but they will not forget what they have seen. Later it will come back to make them think. This museum is a witness—so it never happens again."

Anne frowned. "I just don't see how it could ever happen again," she said. "I mean, people are much more aware than they used to be. They're much more tolerant. They would never line up behind a Hitler."

The priest smiled at her again. "It is interesting that you think that," he said. "But I don't believe human nature has changed in fifty years. It has not changed in thousands of years. Tolerance is a feeble restraint when people's passions run amok. The same thing happens today. Think of Bosnia, or Rwanda, or the Sudan."

Anne blinked a few times and started to pull her purse toward her. She hadn't come for a lecture. The priest put out his arm. "Please forgive me," he said. "I did not mean to offend you. Please tell me your name. I am Father Kowalski." He extended his hand toward her.

Anne smiled. "I'm sorry," she said. "I'm Anne Lorelli."

"Why are you sorry?" Father Kowalski said, smiling again. "I asked you to forgive me."

She shook her head. "I guess I'm not used to people asking for forgiveness. It was nothing. And I say I'm sorry a lot, I guess. It's a habit."

"I have noticed that a lot of women in America have that habit," Father Kowalski said. Something about the way he talked reminded Anne for a moment of Yul Brynner in *The King and I*. Then she wondered how such a crazy thought had come into her head.

"Particularly in the South," he continued. "People tell me that Washington is a southern city, even though it is where it is. I like to listen to how people talk, and I hear many women apologize even when someone else has wronged them. I was in an elevator, and I stepped on a woman's foot. It was clumsy of me. But before I could even say anything, the woman said, 'Oh, please excuse me.' But I had stepped right on her foot!"

For the second time that day Anne thought of herself apologizing to her husband's murderers.

"Where are you from?" she asked.

"I am from Poland," he said. "From Krakow."

"Do you live here now?"

"I am visiting my sister. She lives in Washington. I have not been well, and so my colleagues at the seminary where I teach sent me on a little vacation. Or maybe they just wanted to get rid of me for a few months." He smiled.

"Are you feeling better?" Anne asked.

"My sister takes good care of me. I have rested, I eat well, I take long walks. And I enjoy the museums here."

"I do, too," Anne said. "There are so many wonderful things to see here."

"Are you a tourist?" he asked.

"No," she said. "I've just had a lot of time on my hands lately, and I like to come out and be with people."

"Why?" he asked.

It was an innocuous question, but so invasive. However in this place, Anne felt more inclined to answer it than if she had been at the grocery store.

"I have had a hard time, Father," she said. "I come to the museums as a diversion, I guess."

He waited.

She looked down at the floor, with its patterns of light reflected from the skylight above. "My husband was killed just a few weeks ago," she said. "We were out to dinner to celebrate our anniversary, and afterward we were mugged, and then my husband was shot."

Father Kowalski leaned toward her and took both of her hands in his, holding them firmly. His eyebrows were down, his eyes on hers. "I have heard about your case on the television," he said.

Anne sat rigidly, unsure of what to do. She had never held a stranger's hand before. But he had taken hold of her so naturally, so reflexively; it was like he had the authority.

He's a priest, she told herself. *It's okay.*

"I'm sorry," she said. "I'm not Catholic." Then she flushed. What did that have to do with anything?

He smiled, his hand firm on hers, the conspiratorial look in his eyes again. "You are sorry you are not Catholic?" he asked.

"No," Anne said. "I mean—"

"Tell me more," he said. "What have you done since your husband died? Do you have children? Do you have family?"

"We didn't have children. We were married ten years, but we had decided to wait to have children—" *Oh, no,* Anne thought. Priests didn't like birth control. "Anyway, my family has been wonderful, and my friends have been so kind. It's just that— "

She squinted as she looked across the room toward the flame. It was quiet now. No one else had entered the room since the teenagers had left. The priest still held her hands.

"What?" he asked.

She continued to look at the flame. "It's just that I don't know what to do now. I don't know what to think. My husband is gone. I'm still in shock. It's like I think and think, and I realize I don't even know how to think. I feel so overwhelmed."

Tears stung her eyes now, but she didn't care. It felt good to talk to this priest she didn't know. Maybe that was why Catholics went to confession. It was cheaper than going to a psychiatrist.

"My friends think I need time to grieve. My parents think I should move to a new house and redecorate and then take a part-time job at an antique shop, something to keep myself busy.

"My best friend told me to keep a journal, to try to get inside and find myself. She thinks this is a time for me to look within and get to know myself in a new way, that all my life I've just been how other people have wanted me to be.

"That's easy for her to say; Molly always knows exactly what she thinks. She would never apologize in an elevator if you stepped on her foot," Anne concluded, wondering what was wrong with her brain today. Everything was just flowing out, no coherent connections. It must have been the exhibition.

Father Kowalski laughed and withdrew his hand to fish in his pocket. He drew out the peppermints again and a big white handkerchief.

Anne took a mint, and then, less readily, the handkerchief. It seemed so old-fashioned, and she had never understood the etiquette of handkerchiefs. Was she supposed to dry her eyes and blow her nose on this man's hankie, then give it back so he could carry it wadded in his pocket, wet with a stranger's tears?

"Thank you," she said. She dried her eyes and blew her nose. The priest drew her hands into his again.

"Have you ever suffered before?" he asked.

What an odd question. Anne thought immediately of her sophomore year in college, but then cleared her mind. As a result, she answered more frankly than usual.

"I'm not sure I'm suffering now," she said. "I mean, I'm not suffering like people here suffered." She nodded toward the candles in the front. "I just don't know what to do."

"Maybe," he said, "you do not know what to do because you do not know who you are."

She waited. He said nothing.

"Okay," she said. "How do people find out who they are?"

"Not by looking within, like your friend says," he said. "You have to look outside yourself."

"How?" she said. "I'm not going to become Catholic, you know. My husband's family are Catholics, and I can't see how it's done anything for them."

He laughed and shrugged a little. "It is not always trustworthy to judge the Lord by His followers," he said.

"I'm sorry," she said. "I'm not sure they're really His followers. Their faith doesn't seem to affect their behavior very much. But I didn't mean to be facetious."

"You were not," he said. "But I have an idea. Would you be willing to talk again? I have to meet my sister in just a few minutes, and I do not want to keep her waiting. But I would like to see you again; we could talk some more. I would like to listen, is what I mean. Maybe it would help for you to have a friend who didn't know you before your husband's death."

Anne paused, feeling vaguely disappointed, as if she were being stood up. Then she felt a spark of liberation. She might as well grab for it. She had never taken up with anyone she had met alone in a public place, but he was a *priest*, after all.

"I think you're right," she said. "I would like to meet again. You've been very kind to listen to me."

He nodded. They both stood up, a bit awkwardly. Anne smoothed her jacket, the handkerchief still balled in her fist.

"Let us meet here, in the Hall of Remembrance, on Thursday morning at eleven," Father Kowalski said. "I will be right here."

Anne nodded, thinking they should exchange phone numbers, in case something came up. But maybe priests didn't do that.

He smiled at her. She held up his handkerchief, her eyebrows up. "But what about this?" she asked.

"Oh," he grinned. "You can bring that on Thursday. You will wash it?"

TEN

As time went by, Tom Hogan didn't expect Anne Lorelli to be much help regarding her husband's case. In Tom's experience, if there was a dark side to be discovered about the victim, his colleagues would have a clearer understanding of it than his wife. Based on the interviews he'd conducted right after the murder, Tom thought he'd better stop by Paul's law practice and chat in depth with one of his cronies.

In his own way, Randolph Percey had missed Paul Lorelli since his law partner's death. He had stopped by Paul's office to say good-bye on the Friday of the mugging, and then on Sunday there was his dead friend's picture in the paper. And on that Monday Paul's office was empty, his appointment book lying open on his desk, and a raincoat he had left behind still hanging on the back of his office door. It seemed impossible.

Randolph had taken to Paul when Paul first started at Hagen and Hortsen. Some men of Randolphs age and mind-set took care to surround themselves with younger, beautiful women and older, unattractive men so as to compare better with the competition. But Randolph had noticed that while the women appreciated money and what it bought, they stuck around longer if they didn't feel that they were in a geriatric ward. Better to travel in circles where the friends were fit and the money still flowed.

Randolph's first two ex-wives had each left to make way for the newest ex-to-be; he and his current wife were living separately. But he remained on cordial terms with all of them, partially because he was generous in his divorce settlements, and partially because, for all his sophistication and expensive habits, Randolph Percey maintained a bizarre sense of guilelessness that drew people to him. Not that he wouldn't lie, steal, lust, and cheat given the opportunity, but it was as though he had no clue that anyone might be offended by such behaviors.

He was about six feet tall, with broad shoulders and a straight Roman nose, his backswept hair mostly silver. He took care to dress well, but his best feature was his steady blue gaze that made women feel as if he really cared and men feel that he was really listening to them.

Randolph did care, and he did listen. He defied a quick stereotyping, even though he seemed like a hot-tubber from the early eighties, caught in a time warp that had made him belatedly aware of the bad news most of his contemporaries had soberly absorbed years earlier: drugs, alcohol, smoking, and promiscuous sex were all bad for one's physical and moral health.

He had been drawn to Paul Lorelli. Paul worked hard, as did all the younger lawyers in the firm, but he seemed driven by some unusual interior demon. Though he was ambitious, it wasn't ambition that propelled him. Though he was smart, it wasn't the thrill of the legal chase. It was as if Paul Lorelli was compelled by some inner insecurity, and he had to prove himself to the world. And in that, maybe it was a fatherly concern that made Randolph want to counsel Paul Lorelli with some particularly useless advice: *Lighten up!*

But Randolph had not spent much time puzzling over Paul Lorelli's personality. The guy had some quirks, but Randolph enjoyed taking Paul out for a drink or two or three after they left the office, or for dinner with whoever Randolph was seeing and perhaps one of her friends. Paul never invited his wife for those little get-togethers, and that was fine with Randolph. He had met Anne at firm functions. She was attractive and cordial, but uptight.

Now, sitting at his massive mahogany desk, Randolph tapped his fingertips on its polished surface as he looked at Tom Hogan and Otis Jefferson, the two detectives sitting in the leather chairs opposite him.

"We understand from several of your colleagues that you spent a good deal of time with Mr. Lorelli outside the office," Tom Hogan said. "How would you describe your relationship?"

"I don't know how you'd define a good deal of time," Randolph said. "We worked together; that meant some long hours here. Occasionally we'd have dinner out, go get a drink after work, that type of thing."

"How long had you known Mr. Lorelli?"

Randolph paused. "You can check as to when he joined the firm," he said. "I knew Paul from when he first came. I don't know, a number of years."

"Did you notice any changes in Mr. Lorelli in the time immediately prior to his murder?" Tom asked.

"Well, I would be lying to you if I said there was no change in Paul," Randolph said. "But it didn't happen just before Paul's death. Almost two years ago, I guess, we handled a sexual harassment case. We often represent corporations when they're sued.

"At any rate, Paul was working on this case, a woman who sued her supervisor and her company, claiming that she had been passed over for promotion because she didn't respond to the sexual advances of her boss, one of the company VPs.

"It wasn't a particularly unusual suit. But what was unusual about it was that we lost. Maybe Paul missed something, or lost his concentration, I don't know, but the jury ruled for the plaintiff. She got big bucks, the whole thing. Paul really took it personally. He kept talking about it, kept making personal remarks about the woman, that she was a Hitchcock sort of ice queen who had masterminded this scam for money—it was pretty irrational.

"He'd fight the case over and over in conversations. I kept telling him, just let it go. But he wouldn't. It's like it was eating him up inside. He was furious. He started drinking more. Before, we'd go out, he'd have a beer, and that would be it. But after that case, he'd have two or three hard drinks. Nothing too extreme. And he got more moody, more edgy. It actually made him more fun to be around—he was a little more of a risktaker, and I like that in a person."

Tom looked up from his notes. "Was there anyone he might have tried to get even with, so to speak, in regard to all this? Anyone he might have pursued who could have turned on him?"

Randolph shrugged. "It wasn't like he was out to get anybody. He was just mad about it. The plaintiff wasn't someone he would go after, anyway—she was a young, attractive woman, blond hair, blue eyes, just like his wife, and she ended up moving out of town soon after the verdict. What happened was that Paul allowed himself to get obsessed with that one loss, even though he'd had plenty of victories over the years."

THE DAY AFTER HER TRIP to the Holocaust Museum, Anne stopped by Molly's house.

Molly was in the kitchen. "Look at me," she said to Anne. "I used to have an exciting life. Remember? And now every time you see me, I'm in the kitchen, slaving over some simmering pot on the stove. All I do is cook, feed, and wash dishes. How did it come to this?"

"Remain calm," Anne said.

"Here," Molly said, jabbing a soupspoon in Anne's direction. "Try this."

Anne dipped into the big pot and tasted. "I don't know," she said. "Maybe it needs more pepper, or Tabasco, or something. Something to add some zip to it." She went over to the sink and washed her spoon.

Molly dipped her spoon back into the pot again without washing it, flipping her dark hair back over her shoulder as she did so. "You're right," she said. "Some things just aren't meant to be low-fat. Clark wants us to eat more low-fat meals, and I found this recipe for poached chicken in white-bean chili. It sounds okay, but I should have known. It just isn't the same as a big pot of beef. It's too bland.

"Some low-fat things are all right," she continued. "I can live with low-fat sour cream, or cream cheese. But life is too short to go total non-fat. Have you tasted non-fat mayonnaise? What's it made of? Twenty years from now they're going to find out it causes cancer.

"And all those magazines in the grocery store checkout line, with those perky headlines like 'Short on fat, but long on flavor!' And they always want you to squeeze fresh lemon juice on everything. I love lemons, but I don't think they're going to save this chili."

Molly took another spoonful from the pot. "What this needs is some fat. Maybe if we fried some bacon and threw it in."

"Yeah, or there's always the ultimate secret weapon," Anne said. "Heavy cream."

"That's it," Molly said. "If we put some cream in here and a little cayenne pepper and some more salt, we can rescue it. We just won't tell anyone. Do you think Clark will be able to tell the difference? Probably. It'll taste too good to be lean."

Upstairs there was a crash, and then the sound of crying, like the pause between lightning and thunder.

"I'm coming," Molly shouted toward the ceiling, wiping her hands on her pants. "Amelia has a little friend over," she said. "One of her buddies from kindergarten. I hope they don't kill each other up there."

After the children's crisis was resolved, Anne told Molly about her strange conversation with Father Kowalski.

"Interesting," Molly said. "A priest from Poland." Her green eyes looked far away, and Anne remembered when they went to Europe together after their senior year of college, and Molly barely slept. She didn't want to use up time sleeping when she could be having experiences. She ate every kind of food they were offered, drank everything with abandon, talked with everyone: old ladies on trains, children in parks, other Americans they met in the hostels.

And the men! The men in Europe had loved Molly, especially the French and the Italians. Although come to think of it, the men in Italy had loved Anne, too, and they had loved those two obese, ugly women from Germany who had traveled with them to Florence . . . *Forget the men from Italy,* Anne thought.

But there was a restless part of Molly that Anne saw every once in a while, the person who wanted to have adventures in Tibet and was instead now burping a Tupperware container to put in her refrigerator, which was decorated with children's watercolor paintings, PTA newsletters, and reminders about dentist appointments. Molly loved her family passionately, but sometimes Anne saw a faraway passion in her eyes.

"So," Molly said, bringing Anne back from her own faraway thoughts, "this priest says you find yourself outside of self. I'm not sure I agree with that, but maybe in your case he has a point. You've got to do something! If you get moving a little bit, you'll get an idea of what to do. You know: you can't steer a parked car.

"Since you're into all these tourist attractions anyway, why don't you become a professional sightseer and write articles for travel magazines? Or volunteer somewhere. Do that inner-city tutoring thing we talked about."

Anne stiffened. She hadn't told Molly what Paul had said about the tutoring, just before he was shot. She had hated his snobby attitude about it, but she would hate it even more if he had been right, that she never would decide to do it, or anything else for that matter. She resisted when Molly tried to push her into things, but she depended on it. Just like she had depended on Paul to make her choices for her.

She sighed again. The fact was, aside from her new habit of touring D.C. and the fact she'd met Father Kowalski, nothing had changed. Paul had known that much about her: here she was, still just waffling along.

ELEVEN

TWO DAYS LATER, Anne returned to the Holocaust Museum. She sat in the Hall of Remembrance and watched as Father Kowalski swept down the steps in his cassock. He looked older than Anne remembered him, but he moved with a smooth sort of grace, his arms swinging free, his face open . . . Anne couldn't define it, but it was like he was at home in his body. A funny thought for a priest.

"Good morning, Anne," he said. "You are well today?"

She smiled, enjoying the warmth of his face. "Yes, Father," she said. "How are you? I've brought your handkerchief." She had washed it in Woolite and carefully ironed it into a sharpened square. She had also stuck some Kleenex in her purse, just in case.

"Ah," he said. "Thank you. And I have something for you. My sister sent it to you." He handed her a small parcel wrapped in white tissue paper, tied with a thin satin ribbon. She opened it carefully. Inside was a white handkerchief with a border of yellow flowers, embroidered with tiny stitches.

"Oh!" said Anne. "It's beautiful! Your sister didn't have to do that!"

"Of course not," said the priest. "She wanted to do it. I told her a little bit about you. I hope you don't mind. She is a wise person, and I thought she might understand some things that I cannot, since I am not a woman."

"What is your sister's name?" Anne asked. "How did she come to live in Washington?"

"She is Danuta," Father Kowalski said. "A good Polish name. She came to America after the war. I stayed in Poland and became a priest."

"Why did she come here?" Anne asked.

"She could not stay in Poland. It was too painful for her. Like you, she lost her husband. Danuta felt she could start over in America."

Anne was silent for a moment, not wanting to press too far, but then remembered how she hated it when people clammed up as soon as they found out Paul had been killed. "Did her husband die in World War II?" she asked.

"He died during the war. An SS officer shot him in our home. We were all young back then, still teenagers. He and Danuta had only been married a short while."

"Oh!" Anne said. "How horrible!"

"It was horrible," he said, and then he was silent for a moment. Then he shook his head and reached into his pocket, pulling out a little card with an address and phone number written on it in feathery blue handwriting. "Here is where we live," he said. "Danuta would very much like to meet you. She wanted you to have this so you could call her sometime and perhaps come to tea. You could give her a call whenever you like."

Anne smiled at him.

"That would be very nice," she said. "Thank you—"

"Good," he broke in, "now tell me what you have been thinking. When we talked the other day, you said you didn't know what to do. What were you doing before?"

"Well, I made things run smoothly at home," Anne said. "I did a little writing. And I did some volunteer work with the Junior League."

"Oh?" Father Kowalski said. "Someone told me that the Junior League does very good work with a battered women's shelter in Washington."

Anne looked down. "The League has a lot of programs. I never felt comfortable with things like that. I sold Junior League stationery."

Father Kowalski didn't say anything, and then Anne felt ridiculous. She kept talking.

"My husband was gone a lot. He worked long hours. I was drifting, I guess. I felt like I was waiting for something to happen."

"Now it has happened," said Father Kowalski.

Anne didn't say anything.

"Have the police apprehended the men who shot your husband?" he asked.

"No. They're working on the case, but there aren't very many clues. The muggers got away. It was just a random thing, a robbery that got violent. We could have been anyone."

"To me," he said gently, "the older I get, the more I see that nothing is random. This is an awful thing, but God allowed it to happen to you and your husband."

"Why would God allow something like that?" Anne asked. "Paul hadn't done anything to Him. They had a very cordial relationship. They left each other alone."

"No one can answer why God allows evil," Father Kowalski said. "That's the question people ask in this museum. Where was God? Why did He allow six million Jews—and five million others—to be killed?

"It is a mystery why such things happen," he went on. "But you can't explore the mystery until you acknowledge the anger. Maybe the first thing you need to do is allow yourself to be angry. Are you angry because your husband was killed? Angry with God? It is all right. He can handle honest rage. But you don't seem to be a person who permits herself to be angry.

"If you don't mind my asking," he continued, "tell me about when you were a young girl. What did you want to be when you grew up?"

Anne smiled in spite of what he had said about anger. *What did you want to be when you grew up?* The phrase sounded so quaint, yet so pleasing, on the lips of this Polish priest.

"When I was little," she said, "I wanted to be an actress. And when I was about fourteen, I wanted to be a writer. I wanted to write great stories that would move people, take them on journeys to places they had never been. And then for a while I wanted to be a teacher.

"But then I wasn't sure. I majored in English in college, and then after I graduated I worked as an aide to a congressman.

"And then I met Paul, and after we got married I still worked for a couple years, but then my congressman retired . . . and then I kind of drifted."

"And what about your family?" he asked.

"I'm an only child. My father is a businessman. From the time I was a little girl he was always an entrepreneur, setting up small businesses here and there. Then he started a hazardous waste disposal company that did very well.

"Just before I graduated from high school my parents moved to a much bigger house. My mother really came into her own then. She had always been a perfectionist. But when they moved she had the whole backdrop to make everything just right. The big house, the beautiful gardens, the club, and the Martha Stewart–type parties."

"What is Martha Stewart?" Father Kowalski asked.

"Never mind," said Anne.

"Anyway, I grew up thinking I had to do things just right; if I had a report card with all A's and one B, my mother would focus on the B. Never any congratulations for the A's. Those were expected. My mother watched everything I ate; she lived in fear that I would get fat in high school or college. Appearances are very important to her.

"I mean, my parents are wonderful. They've been so generous and so kind to me with everything that's happened. But we're not a huggy, warm kind of family. My dad is always a little preoccupied, thinking about his business or investments or things like that. But he and I are much closer than my mother and I are. She's a very reserved person."

"Are you like your mother?" asked Father Kowalski.

"Well, yes, but I don't take after her as much as I would have if I hadn't gone away to college and then lived with my best friend after we graduated. Molly has always made me come out of myself more. I've always lived up to other people's expectations; she's driven by her own expectations."

"It is an interesting thing," said Father Kowalski. "Some people define themselves by other people, as you say. Some people define themselves by looking within—like your friend. And some people define themselves by looking without, to something beyond other people."

"Isn't there a fourth category?" Anne said. "People who never determine who they are, but instead just react to what happens around them."

"That's really the same as defining yourself by others," he said. "Identity—and the motivation to act—either comes from within oneself or from outside oneself. If it is defined outside, it is either through other people and events, or, in the way that I believe, from finding one's identity and determining one's action in relation to who God is. We lose self to find self."

"I thought about that, not quite in those terms, when I went through the exhibits here," Anne said, wanting to divert the conversation a little. "The Holocaust made that so clear. Some people went along with the flow, like all those Germans who cheered Hitler on because the rest of the crowd was yelling so loud. Other people became the rescuers who risked their lives to save Jews. They didn't compromise."

"Sometimes if I'm honest it makes me afraid," Anne said, looking at the eternal flame as she spoke. "I'm afraid that I would have been a compromiser, that I wouldn't have had the guts to stand against the tide.

"I can just see Molly in an underground resistance group, hiding Jews in her house or something," she said. "But I see myself going along with the crowd. There's a picture in the exhibit here of a blond girl raising her arm in the Nazi salute. I'm afraid that would have been me."

Father Kowalski was silent for a moment. "That is a sobering thought. But perhaps the fact that you worry about that makes it less likely that it would be the case.

"But—" he said, and then he stopped. "What will help you right now?" he continued abruptly. "What will help you go forward after your husband's death?"

"That's the problem," Anne said. "There's nothing in front of me, no great moral dilemma that demands a choice. I'm not good at choices. But there's not even a crowd all shouting something. There's just me.

"Molly thinks I should throw myself into something, like writing or volunteering in an inner-city program that tutors underprivileged children."

"Well," Father Kowalski said, leaning back and stretching his arms above his head. Anne could hear his joints crack. "That might be good to pursue. It is good to give yourself to those who cannot give anything to you.

"Except," he said, now leaning forward and looking straight in her eyes, "if you teach little children in the city, you will find that they will give far more to you than you give to them.

"It would be hard to go wrong helping the poor," he concluded. He winked at her.

"I know," Anne said, nodding reluctantly. "And I know it's a lot better than selling fancy stationery."

TWELVE

IT WAS A CLEAR FALL DAY. Anne took in the familiar views of the Kennedy Center on the left and the Lincoln Memorial on the right as she drove over the Roosevelt Bridge. A jet followed the turns of the Potomac as it skimmed, barely overhead, toward National Airport. On the hill in the far distance toward the left, Anne could see the towers of the National Cathedral standing tall on Mount Saint Alban.

Some people called Washington a cold city, a transitional town where few had roots. Others said it was divided turf for two disparate populations. First were the politicians, diplomats, lawyers, and lobbyists who lived in Northwest and put their progeny in private schools. Second were the disenfranchised District dwellers whose government was bankrupt and couldn't provide for proper trash or snow removal, whose public schools bristled with metal detectors, yet were still the sites of regular shootings.

But Anne's spirits lifted, as they always did, at the vistas of this capital city she loved. She had been born just a few blocks away in Foggy Bottom, and though she had grown up in the suburbs, she could still drive these familiar boulevards of federal Washington and pick memories like flowers: the fifth-grade field trip to the Museum of Natural History, when Russell Barker had tried to climb up on the African elephant; high school explorations of Georgetown's cafés; a cherry blossom breakfast picnic by the Tidal Basin, when Paul had first told her he loved her.

And besides the memories, there was still a backyard feeling to Washington. In restaurants, Anne often ran into people she knew. She could open the *Washington Post* and read snippets about old friends from college who were now rising in the ranks of government service.

But now, as the bridge dumped her onto Constitution Avenue, she realized that her Washington experience had always been confined to certain sectors of the city, and within a few miles she would cross over into unknown territory.

She cruised onto Constitution Avenue and past the Vietnam Veterans' Memorial and the Washington Monument. There was the back of the White House sitting serenely in the distance. Anne passed the Smithsonians, the art galleries, the Canadian embassy, and turned left toward Union Station.

Behind the white-columned train station, the neighborhood began to change. The streets were littered, the walls scrawled with graffiti. Anne's stomach tightened. She glanced down at the directions in her hand. She had gotten them from Jordan Taylor, the woman in charge of the learning center at the Jubilee Community Church.

JORDAN HAD BEEN VERY matter-of-fact on the phone. She had a low, authoritative voice, and Anne had imagined her in her fifties, maybe, the top button of her sensible shirt fastened tight, a severe, gray-clad woman creating order out of chaos in the inner city.

"We've been here seven years," she had told Anne. "This is a very tough part of the city. Every kid we work with knows at least one person who's been killed. They've had to get under their beds at night when there's shooting in the street.

"But there's so much that's good too. The church has built a real community here. And the kids have so much potential. We have a school, kindergarten through eighth grade—we want to expand, but we don't have the resources to do that yet. The after-school program is for three-year-olds right through high school. That's what we need volunteers for. What age group are you interested in, Anne?"

Anne had never even thought about older kids. White suburban high-schoolers were intimidating enough; she couldn't imagine relating with inner-city teenagers. "Uh," she said. "I had been thinking about five- or six-year-olds. I used to tell stories in an after-school program for that age group."

"All right," Jordan said, as if she was taking notes. "You know, the church and the learning center are a haven for these kids. They need to be able to count on us. So, if you decide to tutor, I would want you to be here for at least a year's commitment. I can't have people dropping in and out of these kids' lives. That happens too much to them already."

On the phone, Anne had paused at that. *But,* she thought, *I haven't committed yet. I need to see this place. And the way this woman is talking, I probably won't make her cut anyway.*

"I understand," Anne had said to Jordan. "So many things are up in the air for me right now, it may not be the right time for me to take this on."

"Then why are you calling about the program?" Jordan asked.

"It was recommended to me," Anne said after a pause. That made it sound like a restaurant. She hesitated and then spoke more bluntly than she usually did. "I lost my husband in September," she said. "I'm trying to start over. I want to help somebody else. I don't usually do things like this."

"I can tell," Jordan said.

No padding with this woman, is there? Anne thought. Then Jordan surprised her.

"I'm sorry about your husband," she said. "Why don't you come and visit us and see if this is a place for you? We would be glad to have you any time. We're not going anywhere, if you know what I mean."

So now Anne was going to them. She could still see the Capitol dome in the distance, but she'd never seen it from this direction before. She felt like she was entering a foreign country. Teenagers on the corner watched her drive by. *Border guards,* Anne thought. *I should have a passport.*

As she got closer to the learning center, the neighborhood was mostly row houses, some boarded up. Men sat on stoops, drinking out of paper bags, squinting in the morning sun, and looking with dull interest at the gleaming black Volvo.

Anne wished she had brought Molly or Clark or someone with her. Every news report she had ever heard about drive-by shootings and street gang gun battles starting scrolling through her mind, like archival video footage. She kept feeling the automatic lock button with her left hand, reassuring herself that, yes, the car doors were secure.

There was no mistaking the church. It stood next to a weed-and-glass-littered vacant lot, a neat four-story old house with a turret on its right front corner. Its walls were old stone, its front doors bright red, and Anne could hear the shouts of little children playing in its walled courtyard. "Jubilee Community Church," read a small sign to the left of the front doors.

She pulled up to the curb. A young black man wearing a white shirt and a blue tie, carrying a bookbag, was just crossing the street, heading toward the church. *If he's going there, he's probably okay,* Anne thought.

He looks like a teacher. She lowered her car window six inches. "Excuse me," she called. "Is it all right to park here?"

He turned toward her with a big grin, quickly sizing up her situation. "Sure," he drawled. "You go right ahead and park your car there. That's a nice car. It won't be there when you get back, but you go right ahead."

Anne froze.

"Hey, I'm sorry," he said. "I'm just teasing with you. You can park there. You coming to the church?"

"No," Anne said, a defiant spark igniting somewhere inside her. "I'm here to buy crack cocaine."

She paused. "Just teasing!"

He looked up at the sky, laughed, and came to the car door. "I'm LaVon Webb," he said. "I've been coming to church here for years. Now I go to college at night; I help with the kids during the day."

Anne stood up, forcing herself not to check the Volvo's locks again. "I'm Anne Lorelli. I'm thinking about tutoring here, and I want to find out more about your program."

"That's great," he said. "Come on in."

They went up the steep cement steps together and through the red doors. Anne saw a large room full of folding chairs on her left and a narrow staircase going up to her right. "That's our sanctuary," LaVon said, nodding to the left. "We have our church services in here, but we're so crowded now in the school that we use it for classes during the day. Most of the classes are upstairs. If you wait right here, I'll get Miss Jordan for you. You want to hang up your coat?"

"Thanks," Anne said. She walked into the big room. At the front, over a fireplace, was a large wall hanging of a dark-skinned Jesus, His arms outstretched. There was also an electric piano, a set of drums, and lots of pieces of heavy black sound equipment, their cords snaking all over the front of the room. A Styrofoam cup sat on top of one of the speakers. Light streamed through a large, barred bay window.

There was a sound behind her. A woman about Anne's age came through the entrance. She was tall and black, with dangling earrings and curly jet-black hair cascading down her shoulders. She wore a beige cotton sweater, a flowing skirt, a wide leather belt around her narrow waist, and tan, calf-high boots. She moved toward Anne, her hand outstretched.

"Hi, Anne, I'm Jordan Taylor," she said. "We're so glad you came. Can I get you some coffee?"

Anne shook the firm hand, her former vision of the ironclad gray woman disappearing like smoke into the fireplace and up the chimney, right past the African Jesus. "Thank you," she said. "No coffee, thanks."

"I thought I could take you on a tour and show you everything, and then if you have questions, we can talk about them at the end," Jordan said. "I have a meeting with some people from a foundation later. We're always trying to get more funding—so we won't have much time. But we'll move fast."

Anne nodded. She imagined Jordan Taylor did everything fast.

"Come," Jordan said.

"This is our sanctuary. We're really crowded on Sunday mornings and during the week as well; we use this room for all kinds of things. We've started an aerobics class. Some of our women don't tend to take good care of their bodies. So three evenings a week we've got exercise class in here. Sometimes on Sunday mornings you can still smell the sweat."

They swept through a door at the back of the room. "Here's our kitchen. The kindergartners meet in here."

Anne looked down at the miniature tables and chairs filled with little children. The smell was just like she remembered from her own childhood: aromas of peanut butter and jelly, fat waxy crayons, Elmer's glue. Two women were cutting construction paper into the shapes of five-point stars. The children were gluing glitter to them. "They're doing a module on outer space," said Jordan.

A tiny girl with enormous dark eyes grinned at Anne and held up a sticky piece of paper. She had golden glitter on both hands and a glow on her face as well. "Stars!" she said to Anne.

Anne smiled at her as they continued on through a back hallway through office areas and up the steep staircase. The upstairs halls were narrow and cramped; Jordan opened doors like compartments in a ship's hold. "Here's LaVon's class," she said. "LaVon tutors kids who need some extra help. He's not yet certified to teach, but he's working toward it, and we really appreciate his help."

"Hey, Anne!" LaVon said, turning toward her as if he had known her all his life. He motioned to his students. There were about ten of them, boys wearing neat blue pants, white shirts, and blue ties. The girls wore blue-plaid jumpers and white blouses; the uniforms made them look like Catholic schoolchildren.

The kids pushed back their chairs and stood. LaVon nodded. "Good morning, Miss Anne," the children recited in a singsong, all together. "Welcome to our classroom."

Anne smiled, overwhelmed by their formal welcome. "Good morning," she said. "Thank you for having me."

The students sat down. A little girl tugged urgently on Anne's sleeve. She had five tight, fat, black braids sticking out at random angles from her scalp, secured with bright pink barrettes. "Miss Anne!" she whispered, pointing up at Anne's head. "That be your real hair?"

Jordan led Anne up a staircase to the top floor and opened the door to a little library. The room was part of the front turret of the church building, its walls light yellow and its carpeting dark green. A tree with a broad trunk was painted on one wall, its leaves and branches twining up onto the ceiling. A wooden bunkbed was built against the same wall, the top bunk covered with a bright bedspread and bolstered with soft pillows. Beneath it were several beanbags and a shelf full of picture books.

The adjacent walls were lined, floor to ceiling, with more book-shelves. A globe stood on a pedestal next to the far window, which was a big bay, unbarred—it was four stories up. The window seat was thickly cushioned with pillows. A big rocking chair sat nearby.

"Oh!" Anne said out loud, feeling the power of this room. She could envision a child sitting on the flowered cushion, leaning against the side of the bay window, reading stories of faraway lands, dreaming a little and looking out the window toward the blue skies above.

But even as Anne gazed out the big window, she realized that the view looking down was nothing but the barren blocks of some of the meanest streets in Washington. The room felt like a castle turret, a magical tower, but not like the fairy tales where the princess was held captive within its tall walls. Here, the princess came to be set free.

Jordan led Anne through six more classrooms, and in spite of her-self, Anne felt drawn to this lively school. The draw was in the details: the red-apple nametags decorating a bulletin board, all bearing names like Latisha, Rwandina, Shekina Rose, Chanelle, Zenetria; the roomful of donated computers, with kids picking their way across the key-boards, proud of their prowess.

Then there was the health clinic, the job center, the Habitat for Humanity offices, with desks and staff people crammed haphazardly, working hard. In everything, from the sticky stars to the old-fashioned school uniforms, she felt a brimming sense of potential, of purpose, of things being done well, of hope. *I'd like to be part of this,* Anne thought.

"I want you to see the neighborhood," Jordan said.

They went down the stairs. Jordan stopped in the kitchen to get a big black plastic garbage bag. Anne opened her purse to get out her car keys.

"No," Jordan said. "We'll walk."

She grinned at Anne. "It's not like we hide in the church, like it's a fortress or something. I live here. This is my neighborhood."

They turned right out of the church's front door and walked. Jordan waved at people sitting on the stoops and picked up paper and litter off the sidewalk even as she talked. "I'll give you the *Reader's Digest* version of things," she said.

"My husband and I moved here seven years ago. Michael had been the youth pastor of a suburban church, but then we felt like we wanted to serve the poor. We realized we had a mission field in our own backyard—the inner city. But we didn't want to just come in and out of this neighborhood. After all, Jesus didn't commute to earth. He lived here.

"So we felt we had to do the same, so the gospel would be real to the people we're trying to reach. We moved in. For the first year we renovated our row house and taught a kids' Bible club. Michael played basketball with the men in the neighborhood. The people here thought we were narcotics agents. The police thought we were dope dealers. No one could figure why two black professionals would choose to live here.

"But anyway, we built some relationships, a community of people to start a church, and then our denomination brought in a man named Leonard Sims to serve as the senior pastor. Gary Williams, a man who lived in this community and made it out—that's unusual—came back to help his old neighborhood. And gradually we've seen changes over the years. It's tough work, but with some of the kids, in particular, we've seen great progress."

A slight, elderly man wearing suspenders over a T-shirt and a pair of suit pants opened a sagging screen door. "Hello, Miss Jordan!" he called.

"How are you today, Mr. Morgan?" Jordan said, climbing the stoop to shake his hand. "How's your wife doing? Is she feeling any better?"

"No, she's having a real hard time," the man said. "But she said to tell you thank you for bringing over those muffins."

"You're welcome," Jordan said. She came down the steps, bent to pick up a beer bottle, and threw it in her trash bag.

"This neighborhood matches the typical center-city statistics across the country," she continued, in a voice that suggested to Anne that she had presented this information many times before. "The infant mortality rate here is thirty-five per thousand. That's higher than in a lot of third-world nations. Most of the family units here are dependent on welfare.

"In 95 percent of them, the father isn't in the home. There might be men in and out, but there's not a biological father in the picture. Welfare has created a couple generations of dependence, and crack and alcohol have stripped people's ability to help themselves.

"The people here need real hope, and the church offers that. And they need practical help. That's why we have the job center, the learning center, the health clinic, and why we do the Habitat program that helps to provide low-cost housing they can own."

As they walked, passing boarded-up homes and burned-out shells, occasionally Anne would see a neat, newly painted home with fresh white trim, a refurbished roof, clean windows. They all had brightly painted front doors. Pink, turquoise, yellow; the one in front of them now was a brilliant blue. "I can see what a difference the Habitat project makes," she said, pointing at the fresh paint and the lace curtains at the windows.

"Jackie Jones and her daughter live there," Jordan said. "Jackie's doing what we want to do more of. We helped her set up a little business, right here in the neighborhood. It's down the street.

"There aren't exactly any major grocery-store chains in this neighborhood. But people here don't have cars, so they can't drive out to the suburbs to pick up groceries. We wanted to put in a market with fair prices and fresh food. Jackie's done a great job with that.

"We've had people from HUD come and see what we're about here, and the mayor. Jack Kemp spoke at the dedication of our church building, and we've had a lot of media interest over the years. People are blown away when they see the potential."

They rounded a corner and came back to the church. Jordan looked at her watch. "I need to go," she said. "Do you have any questions? I've just given you an overview, but you can get a feel for what we're trying to do here. The tutoring program is in the church; you wouldn't be out in the neighborhood. And most of the kids you'd be working with have been in the church since they were babies. They're pretty well behaved. It's not like you'd be starting from ground zero."

"Well," Anne said awkwardly, "what kind of requirements do you have for your tutors? Do they need to be part of your religious belief, or, uh, denomination?" She realized she had no idea what denomination the church was.

"Let me be clear," Jordan said. Anne couldn't imagine her being anything else.

"This is a Christian school. Our programs are rooted in the belief that truth exists, that God has set physical and moral absolutes.

"Everyone talks about values today, but values shift according to popular opinion. Moral codes don't shift. Like the Ten Commandments. If kids aren't taught these codes, then they end up with no respect for human life. No conscience.

"And if someone has no conscience—no inner restraint—there's no amount of outer restraint that can control his behavior. It'd take a police state. There's a whole lost generation out there. But we're trying to get to the younger ones, and train them over the long run.

"Anyway," Jordan concluded, "I'm running on about that, can't help it, but the point is, this is a Christian school, not a public institution, and so things are run according to biblically rooted beliefs."

"Well—" deferred Anne, but then Jordan continued.

"You know, Anne, I see a role for you here. We have a number of white volunteers who come in, and we appreciate that. I can tell you would love these kids. That's what they need most. You could read to them, you could tell them stories, since you've done that before. Storytelling is a great way to engage their imaginations.

"We're not asking you to teach these kids theology. We'll take care of that. We do ask that you show respect for our world-view, that you not undermine what we're teaching them about God. But I'm sure you wouldn't do that.

"So if you'd like to come, we'd love to have you. What I've learned over the years living here—and at times it's been really rough—is that we've received so much more than we've given."

Just like Father Kowalski said, Anne thought.

"Well," she said to Jordan, "I appreciate your frankness, sort of. But I'd like to help here."

"So then you'll tutor?" Jordan asked, glancing at her watch.

"Can I call you?" Anne asked. "I'm sorry, I just can't decide right away. I need time to think about it."

Jordan smiled at her. "Okay. But don't think about it too much. Just come and do it."

She waited while Anne unlocked the Volvo and got herself strapped in. "Do you know your way back home?" Jordan asked.

"I think so," Anne said.

"Good," Jordan said. "Just reverse the directions I gave you. Otherwise you're going to end up on some streets where you don't want to be."

THIRTEEN

THE NEXT MORNING ANNE headed toward a more familiar destination: the National Gallery of Art. An old friend who was a docent there had gotten Anne a ticket to the Johannes Vermeer exhibition at the west wing.

"Right now this is the best-kept secret in Washington," she'd told Anne. "It just opened. People don't realize yet that this kind of exhibition has never been put together in the last three hundred years. It's going to the Hague in February. By Christmas people will be camping out on the sidewalk to get tickets."

The exhibit was small, just twenty-one paintings. Johannes Vermeer had painted in the mid-seventeenth century. He'd been regarded as an excellent but not unusual Dutch painter until the middle of the nineteenth century, when the invention of photography revealed his extraordinary three-dimensional vision, his almost supernatural manipulation of pigment, brush, and canvas.

Most of the scenes in this collection were life's ordinary events illumined by the light of a window. There were also street vistas and a few religious themes. Anne loved the quiet, contemplative quality of the domestic scenes: A woman writes a letter while her maid stands in the background. A teacher instructs a girl during her music lesson. A girl gazes directly at the painter, her expression fresh as the moment. *It's like a photograph*, Anne thought. Somehow Vermeer had known how to seize the second and preserve it for centuries.

She walked on. Against a far wall was a large painting from a later period after the artist's religious conversion: *The Allegory of Faith*. A woman in a blue-and-white satin gown rested her foot upon a globe, her hand on her breast and her eyes staring upward at a glass orb suspended from the ceiling from a blue ribbon. On a table next to her sat a chalice, a crucifix, and an open Bible. Behind the woman was a large painting of the crucifixion of Christ. On the floor lay an apple and a snake crushed by a cornerstone.

Anne recognized the biblical symbols, but the painting seemed less powerful because it was so explicit. *Why spell everything out?* she thought. *The snake equals Satan, the apple equals temptation, yes, there's the cross and the crucifix, and the woman is so pure, looking upward with wonder toward the sphere. It's like a formula. Art moves more when there's more mystery.*

Beside her a man was whispering to his wife, something about perspective and how Vermeer had used strings and a pin to find the vanishing point in the paintings; the pinhole was still visible on a few of them. Anne looked. There it was, a tiny hole in the canvas.

She moved to a different wall. Here was another of the domestic scenes. "Woman with a pearl necklace," read the caption.

The young woman was blond, her hair ribboned and tucked in a bun, her saffron jacket trimmed with fur. She stood in profile to the viewer, facing a window opposite her, a window hung with a rich golden curtain. Light suffused the wall to her right with a translucent glow and illumined the girl's left hand, her face, her pearls.

She had been caught in the moment, like so many other Vermeer women, the golden glow overwhelming the dark table before her. Even though she was still, holding the long pearl necklace about her neck aloft in her two hands, her forearms up, there was a sense of active engagement. It was as if the girl was seeing something the viewer could not.

Anne thought of a painting of the Annunciation she had seen with Molly years ago in Italy. In it, the Virgin Mary had stood before a window, her eyes aglow in wonder, overcome by the light of an angel only she could see, an angel telling her that she would give birth to the Christ.

Anne stepped closer. There was a dark chair in the foreground of the painting, a cloth over part of the table, and something on the wall opposite the woman, the wall that was not lit by the window's light. Anne stepped closer still and realized it was a small mirror mounted adjacent to the window.

Oh, she thought, disappointed. *So she's not embraced by the light; she's engrossed by her reflection.* Vermeer's meaning was enigmatic, though. It was hard to believe the woman was overwhelmed by her own image rather than the light flooding the window. The force of the light was so intense, the mirror so small and secondary.

Anne sighed. She couldn't figure it out. But it did something to her, something that made a strange lump come into her throat. She stared at it for a long time. She thought again of the night of Paul's murder, of her own thick strands of gleaming pearls, ripped from her throat by a dark hand, bouncing across the brick walkway while Paul's blood flowed.

Just then two women with strong perfume jostled just behind Anne.

"This one is nice," said one. "I like it better than the painting of the lady with the red hat."

"Oh, that reminds me," said the other. "I forgot to tell you I'm getting the whole kitchen redone. I told Ross I've wanted an authentic Dutch kitchen my whole life, you know, with copper pots and real Dutch tiles imported from Holland, Michigan. He said, 'Honey, you go right ahead, do whatever you want, just don't bug me about it.' It's going to be all blue and white, and I'm going to have a tulip border around the ceiling . . ."

She was still talking as they jiggled away toward the next painting. *Imported from Holland, Michigan?* Anne thought.

She moved in a different direction from the two women and went into the next room of the exhibit, nodding at the guard who stood in attendance at the doorway, took another hour to drink in the paintings, then came, grudgingly, to the end.

At the exit were tasteful warnings that you could not reenter the exhibit once you had left. Anne paused for a moment—were there any paintings that she had to see again? This was it for the next three hundred years. She beat back the need to go back through the exhibit rooms, envisioning herself compulsively viewing and reviewing the paintings, circling back through the rooms again and again like a crazy person until the guards finally escorted her out in handcuffs. She squared her shoulders and left.

She took the escalator downstairs to the underground passage connecting the west wing of the gallery with the east wing, where there was a gift shop, bookstore, and café.

Across from the café was a large window stretching from floor to ceiling, lined with green plants at its base. You couldn't see through it—it faced a concrete wall—but if you looked up, you could see a bit of the walkway above, the paved area up on the street level. Several triangular skylights poked up through the street, and a fountain flowed around them and then down past the underground window below, creating a captured waterfall.

Anne bought a cappuccino. She sat down at a small plastic table with a faux-marble top and sipped the hot coffee through its foamy milk, watching the people go by.

A young woman pushed a stroller stuffed with a bulky blond toddler, asleep. She stared at the café menu as if wondering if she dared stop and get something for herself while her baby dozed. A cluster of Japanese tourists posed in front of the waterfall as a man took their picture. A man with a goatee sat at the next table reading a thick Vermeer catalog with a glossy cover.

Anne thought again about Vermeer's woman with the pearls, the mirror, and the window. *Father Kowalski would like it,* she thought. *Is she looking out toward the light, or is she looking in at herself in the little brown mirror?*

She stared at the window before her, the rushing water, the restraining glass.

Five black children stood there now, enchanted by the waterfall as well. One of the girls held a blue helium balloon on a slender ribbon, but she lost hold of it when a boy jostled her arm. The balloon rose about five feet to the top of the waterfall window and hung there, wafting up and down with the breezes of the vented air, just out of the children's reach, its blue sphere diaphanous against the light of the sunlit glass.

The scene was like the Vermeer paintings, Anne thought, the faces illumined by the light from the top of the window. But here the action was moving too fast for a sense of quiet contemplation. Anne watched the laughing children jumping up and down, their arms reaching up, the blue balloon just out of reach, framed against the glass waterfall.

Transfixed, she took her last sip of coffee.

She thought of Paul on their anniversary night. He'd said she would never go to the inner city. Enough of his contempt, she thought. Enough of her own paralysis over the years. It was time to do something, anything, and the most obvious step was to tutor.

I'll do it, she thought.

FOURTEEN

ANNE SAT ON THE CUSHIONED window seat of the yellow turret at the learning center. Her blond hair was tied back in a ponytail with a blue satin ribbon, and she wore some long silver earrings Molly had given her, along with a denim shirt and jeans. She had felt excited when she arrived at the Jubilee church, but now, looking at the children before her, she felt totally out of place.

She had talked with Jordan Taylor about her idea of doing a series of connected stories for the children. "Over the past few years all those books on virtues have been so popular," she had said. "I thought it would be good for these kids to have stories for their age level, each one focusing on a different character trait, mostly positive, but maybe some negative ones too."

Jordan had nodded. "That's a great idea," she said. "Your only problem might be that you'll have to translate quite a bit for these children. They're growing up in a different culture than the suburban kids whose parents read to them from *The Book of Virtues* every night."

Today's story was rather general. Anne had jotted notes at home, the outline for a tale about how good character was more important than physical beauty.

In spite of her preparations, however, she wasn't sure she could deliver. The children were sitting in a semicircle before her, giggling and nudging one another. "Keep your hands to yourself!" one little girl shouted, pushing the boy to her right.

"You started it!" he yelled, placing both hands on her chest and shoving her backwards so she keeled over in a heap. "Hey!" another girl said, hitting the boy over the head with a Dr. Seuss book she grabbed off a shelf. "You leave her alone!"

"Uh, children, please!" Anne called out helplessly, watching the neat semicircle mutate into a mass of shoving, shouting bodies. "Children!"

"OW!" someone cried as they all ignored Anne, pushing each other wildly.

Jordan Taylor appeared in the open doorway. "All right!" she thundered. "That's enough! Jawan! Latisha! Quiet! Get back in your circle!"

The shoving stopped immediately. "Thank you," Anne mouthed to Jordan, feeling ridiculous. She took a deep breath and began.

"Once upon a time, in a faraway land," she said, "there was a beautiful princess who lived in a castle. Her hair was long and golden"—*no,* she thought, looking at the brown faces in front of her—"Her hair was long and black, curling around her shoulders and cascading past her waist and down to her feet.

"Her name was Princess Yasmine, and her father was king over all the land." Anne smiled at the children, laughing to herself how these fairy-tale phrases lurked in one's subconscious, just waiting for an opportunity to be released.

"Princess Yasmine was known for her beauty in all the neighboring kingdoms, especially for her long, amazing hair that swirled around her as she walked, like a dark, magical cape."

A little girl on the floor giggled. "Just like Pocahontas!" she burst out.

And I thought these kids were deprived, Anne thought. *I guess Disney is everywhere.*

"That's right," Anne said to the group. "Except Princess Yasmine's hair was even longer, even stronger, even more beautiful, than the swirling hair of Pocahontas.

"Princess Yasmine was engaged to be married to the good prince from a nearby kingdom. His name was Prince Yosef."

A little girl raised her hand. "What's engaged?" she asked.

Anne stopped. This was what Jordan had meant about translation.

"Engaged means that you promise you're going to marry someone, and you tell all your friends, and you plan a wedding," Anne said. She hurried on, realizing that there probably weren't a whole lot of weddings in this neighborhood. "Anyway, so Princess Yasmine was going to marry the good Prince Yosef.

"But an evil sorcerer had admired the princess's beauty and wanted her for his own. So he locked her in a castle tower from which no one could escape.

"Then he captured Prince Yosef and locked him in the twin tower of the same castle. Through the window in her tower, Princess Yasmine could see Prince Yosef as he paced back and forth, back and forth in his narrow, round cell.

"'Ha ha!' the sorcerer said to the princess. 'Unless your prince can escape within three days, you will be mine—and your prince will be my captive forever. Your beauty shall belong to me alone!'

"There was no way for the prince to escape. Yasmine wept as the time rushed by . . . the sun set and the moon rose as the first day passed into night. And then the second day came and went. By the moonlight of the last night, Yasmine could see her prince, still pacing.

"She wept as she paced back and forth in her own dark tower. Her hair, braided in a long tail as strong and thick as a mighty rope, trailed behind her as she walked. Suddenly, Princess Yasmine had an idea. She reached around her shoulder and lifted her heavy hair in her hands, pulling the braid, feeling its supple strength.

"She looked across the divide. If only there was a way to cut the hair-rope from her head, she thought. I could divide the braid into three parts, tie them together, end to end . . . I could throw it to Prince Yosef, and it would be long enough for him to climb down from his window.

"She tried to pull her hair from her head. Its roots were too deep, the pain too great. She had no knife, no tools, no way to cut her hair.

"Then, in the dark hour before the dawn, Yasmine heard a scratching noise. She could barely see, but a stone in the tower wall jiggled, and began to move. A small gray mouse poked out his head.

"'Oh, Princess,' said the little mouse. 'My brothers and sisters and I are so sad that you are captive here. We want to help you. But what can we do?'

"'Thank you, small friend,' said Princess Yasmine. 'Your kindness is large when hope seems so small.'"

Anne paused.

"Princess Yasmine was wise," she said. "She knew that even though there seemed to be no hope, sometimes little things can make a big difference. So she said to the mouse, 'Tell me what you can do.'

"'Well,' said the mouse. 'I can sing songs. I can eat cheese. I can climb through tiny tunnels in the castle.'"

Anne looked at the children. "There was one more thing the mouse could do," she said. "Do you know what it was?"

The little girl in the front nodded, her eyes big. "Are mice like rats?" she asked.

Oh, no, Anne thought. Rats had never even entered her mind.

She nodded. "Well, yes, but mice are smaller, and, uh, cuter and nicer."

"One time when I was littler, this big rat got into my brother's bed," the little girl continued. "My mama screamed and got a broom. But you know how he got in our room?" she asked Anne matter-of-factly. Anne just shook her head no.

"He chewed through the wall like it was paper!" the girl said triumphantly. "So if mice are like rats, they can chew!"

"Well, yes," Anne said slowly. "Right! Mice can chew.

"So, uh, the mouse said to Princess Yasmine, 'I can chew!'

"Princess Yasmine looked at the little furry mouse. 'What is your name?' she asked.

"'I am Raphael,'" said the mouse. "'I have seventeen brothers and sisters, and we are all named after famous artists.'"

Anne paused. Where had that come from? The mouse was getting out of hand.

"'Well, Raphael,' said the princess. 'Could you do me a big favor? If I lie down on the floor, could you and your brothers and sisters very carefully chew the braid off my head? Then I can use it as a rope to help rescue Prince Yosef.'

"'Oh, yes, Princess!' said Raphael the mouse. He squeaked three times, and suddenly a swarm of little brown mice popped up through the loose stone in the wall.

"The princess lay down on the cold stone floor. The mice surrounded her.

"Raphael raised his right paw. 'Mice!' he shouted. 'Let the chewing begin!'

"The mice began to gnaw. Yasmine felt nothing but the gentle pressure of their tiny paws as they moved through her long mane, snipping carefully around the crown of her head like tiny hairdressers.

"In just a few moments, Raphael raised his paw again. 'Mice!' he shouted. 'Splendid work!'

"Yasmine sat up. There, in the moonlight, her thick, long braid stretched like a rope. Her head felt light. She touched her scalp and felt only tiny bristles. Her heart sank. She knew she had sacrificed her beauty for her prince . . . but it was the only way to save him."

Anne sped up her pace. As she did so, the story got more modern.

"Yasmine called quietly across the night air to the twin tower. 'Prince Yosef!'

"'My own true love!' he called back. 'Even if I am a prisoner forever, I shall always love only you, my own beautiful Yasmine! I shall think of you always, your glorious raven hair dancing through my dreams.'

"Yasmine cleared her throat. 'That's lovely, my darling, but I have something for you,' she called. 'A rope! I shall toss it and you can use it to climb down and break the sorcerer's spell!'

"'A rope?' the prince called. 'Where did you get a rope?'

"'Behold, my prince, it is my own glorious raven hair that I have sacrificed to rescue you,' Yasmine said sadly. 'So please stop asking questions and get ready to catch the rope so we can get out of here.'

"So," Anne said, "the princess aimed carefully and gently tossed the hair-rope through the prince's open tower window. The prince caught it. The mice cheered. The prince fastened the rope on a nail in the window and quickly climbed down the tower. He confronted the sorcerer in the castle.

"'How can you be free? Impossible!' shouted the sorcerer, twirling his dark mustache in frustration.

"'Not impossible!' shouted the prince. 'My own true love has sacrificed her hair to save me. For her true loveliness is the far deeper beauty of the soul that a toad like you could never understand.'

"The sorcerer looked at the long, shining rope. 'Princess Yasmine cut her hair?' he asked the prince. 'She's not beautiful anymore?'

"'No,' said the prince, 'but she is all the more glorious to me because of her sacrifice.'

"The sorcerer raised an eyebrow. 'Well, if she's not beautiful any-more, then you can have her,' he said. 'I'm outta here.'

"The sorcerer was never seen again. Prince Yosef freed Princess Yasmine from the tower, kissing her shorn head tenderly. They got mar-ried, and Raphael the mouse and his brothers and sisters sang in their wedding. And they always kept the hair-rope hanging on the castle wall, so that all in the kingdom would know that true beauty is a matter of the character of the heart, not the hair on one's head.

"And they lived happily ever after," Anne concluded.

The children were looking at her closely. Several were frowning. "I don't get it," said one little boy. "Why didn't she call the police?"

"Oh, don't be stupid, thatta good story!" the little girl next to him said. She smiled at Anne. "I liked when the mice helped her. When are you coming back?"

AFTER ANNE DISMISSED the group, the same girl pulled on Anne's sleeve. She was small and sturdy, with long, curly eyelashes, her hair smoothed back in a tight ponytail, and tiny gold balls in her pierced ears. "Miss Anne," she said. "I like your story. I use to have beautiful long hair but I never made a rope out of it. And then my friend cut it off!"

Anne knelt next to her. "Please tell me your name," she said.

"I told you at the beginning, when you first came in," the girl replied.

"I'm sorry," Anne said solemnly, "I know you did. But I learned so many new names today that I didn't remember them all. If you tell me again, I promise I'll remember your name forever and ever."

"I got to think about it," the little girl said seriously. She went over to the window and looked out over the rooftops, her lip out, her brow furrowed in mock contemplation. She turned back to Anne.

"All right," she said. "Sherah. Sherah Loutangia Jones. Isn't that a beautiful name? Mama says it's a name nobody can ever forget. How could you forget a name like that?"

"I don't know," Anne said, laughing. "Sherah Loutangia Jones, thank you for coming to my class today."

"Miss Anne," said Sherah, "can you walk me to my mama's store? It's right down the street."

Anne hesitated. She didn't feel comfortable cruising the neighborhood, but how could she tell that to a five-year-old? "Well, I'd love to do that," she said. "Maybe Miss Jordan could come with us too. Does your mama's store have ice cream? Maybe if I buy us some ice cream, you can forget I forgot your name, Sherah Loutangia Jones."

Sherah grinned and stuck out her hand. "Come on!"

For all her efficiency, Jordan Taylor turned out to be the kind of woman who could be bribed with ice cream.

Within five minutes, Anne, Jordan, and Sherah were walking down the sunny side of the street. It was a clear day, with just a hint of the melancholy feel of autumn that rode the crisp breezes to even this concrete floor of the city.

"Sherah is one of the brightest kids in the program," Jordan said to Anne as Sherah hopped and skittered, running on ahead of them. "And Jackie's an incredible person. She's come up from a horrible situation, where she was abusing drugs and taking abuse from Sherah's father. Then she started coming to church, she went through a detox program, she worked hard and got a job, and then a Habitat house, and then a few months ago she opened the little market.

"At first she wanted to call it the Black Market, you know, as sort of a joke but also to show that it was black-owned, but we all decided that wasn't a great idea. Other people were suggesting these basic names, like the Corner Market or Jackie's Grocery, but Jackie really wanted it to be something that pointed to what God had done in her life."

"Here," she said. The market had a bright pink front door and a large, hand-painted sign that read, "Daily Bread," with green vines and grapes painted around the lettering. Heavy grillwork protected the windows.

They went in, and Anne was reminded of old-fashioned markets at remote beach towns, or of Thelma's old ice-cream market in Great Falls—the aisles were narrow, the shelves crowded, and the options limited.

But the fruits and vegetables were fresh, and everywhere one looked were hand-cut construction paper stars calling attention to prices or pointing out specials. Sherah pointed them out. "I make those," she said proudly. Then, louder, "Mama! I brang my new friend Miss Anne to see you. She wants some ice cream."

Jackie Jones emerged from somewhere in the back of the store and extended her hand to Anne. "Hey, Anne," she said, smiling and reaching with her other arm to embrace Sherah's. She was a tall black woman with a big smile and shoulder-length coiled hair. Even as she stood there, her shoulders and legs were moving slightly, as if to the rhythm of an inner music only she could hear.

"How was school today?" she asked Sherah.

"Oh, Mama, Miss Anne tell us a story about a princess in a castle and the singing mice chewed off her long beautiful hair so she could excape!"

Jordan Taylor laughed. She turned to Sherah.

"What did you learn from the story?"

Sherah paused for a moment, jiggling from one foot to the other with the same inner pulse that stirred her mother.

"I learn that girls are smarter than boys."

Anne sputtered. *What about true beauty being more than skin deep? I'm poisoning the minds of young girls, turning them off to men before they even hit puberty—although maybe that's not a bad idea.*

115

Jackie laughed. "Well, sometimes that's true. It just depends on *which* girl, or *which* boy, you're talking about.

"Why don't you go to the freezer case in the back and choose some ice-cream bars for you and Miss Jordan and Miss Anne and me?"

"I'm sorry," Anne said. "That really wasn't the point—"

"Don't worry about it," said Jackie. "The way her mind works, in the middle of the night she'll come and tap me on the shoulder and wake me out of a dead sleep and a good dream to tell me some great truth she learned from your story.

"Besides, most of the men I meet aren't exactly geniuses." She nodded toward Jordan. "With the exception of Jordan's husband, of course, and a few others I can think of.

"Are you married?"

Sherah returned from the back of the store, carefully clasping a bouquet of Nutty Buddies. She passed them out solemnly, and everyone peeled their cones. Sherah ate hers as she hopped on one foot on the black and white tiles to the rear of the store and back.

"I was married," Anne said plainly. "My husband died in September."

"Was he sick?" asked Jackie.

"No," Anne said. Something about the way Jackie talked made it simple to be simple. "We were mugged, and he was shot."

"Anne's just started with us," Jordan told Jackie. "She's doing some new things, starting over a little bit, since her husband died."

Jackie looked at Anne for a moment. "I'm sorry you lost your husband," she said. "Starting over's hard. My husband was shot too. Not quite the same, though. He owed some drug money, and he got shot in the face.

"For me, though, it was a new beginning. We had no life before, just crack and booze. When Sherah was born she was so tiny, she almost died. They said they would take her away, but she kind of slipped through the cracks of the system, and they forgot to take her away. And

I said to myself, I've got to stop this stuff, I've got to get help, I've got to take care of my girl and pull myself together. I actually prayed, 'You please do something, I can't do it on my own, I'm going down.'

"Then Vernon got shot. It's not like God answered my prayer that way. I don't think God set Vernon up. He brought it on himself. But after Vernon passed, things started to turn around. The church people came and brought food and helped get Vernon buried. I felt this little bit of hope that maybe I could get out of the pit. They took care of Sherah while I went to the program.

"I got clean, and then that hope started to grow. It was like someone took a veil off my eyes, or somebody washed the windows, and I shook my head and said, 'Where have I been? Oh, Lord, where have I been?'

"And I prayed all the time, 'Help me make it every day. Help me take care of my girl. Help me!' And it's been like I feel this hand on my shoulder, someone saying in this voice so quiet I have to be quiet to hear Him, 'I am here.' Over and over, I feel Him: 'I am here.'"

Anne felt tears prick the back of her eyes, like at the Vermeer exhibit.

"It's like you had a real before and after," she said, her usual reserve melted by Jackie's honesty. "You knew what you wanted to change. I was going along, living what looked like a nice life, Paul gets killed. That pulled the veil off for me, too. But for me, I realized I didn't know where I had been or where I was going."

"Well, at least you're consistent," Jackie said, grinning.

"I'm going to check on Sherah," Jordan said. "It's too quiet back there. She must be getting into something."

Jackie licked the last of her Nutty Buddy, tossed the paper in the trash can behind the counter, and reached out for Anne's hand with the same unconscious movement that Father Kowalski had used in the Holocaust Museum. Her hand was warm, firm, strong.

"Hey," Jackie said. "I think I know what you mean. Nobody in their right mind would want to go through drugs and detox, but at least the goal is clear. Stay clean. Pretty basic. After that, all the everyday choices can look pretty complicated.

"But what I know is that whatever those choices happen to be, the point is, God is with us. He knows who you are, where you are, even when you don't. He is with you. You hold onto that, day by day, and the rest of the story comes clear, bit by bit."

LATER, ANNE DROVE SLOWLY toward home, the voices from the learning center replaying in her mind. She kept thinking about Jackie and the quiet voice, the hand on the shoulder. "I am here." What would that feel like?

She got to McLean and decided to stop by her parents' house. After the disorder of the city, her mother's gleaming white kitchen looked more lovely than usual. Anne and her mother sat in the breakfast room and shared a pot of steaming mint tea. Still thinking about Jackie and the children, Anne forgot to keep her defenses up. It was a mistake. Her mother was on the warpath, in her usual understated way.

"I think it's commendable that you're trying to reach out to those less fortunate than you," Virginia said to her daughter, emptying half a packet of Equal into her cup. She crisply folded the blue package and stirred her tea clockwise, four times. She wore a white sweater, trim white pants, and her gray-blond hair was freshly cut, its razored layers resting perfectly on the back of her neck.

"But there are so many other things you could do," Virginia continued. "I'm sure this church in the city needs money. You could send a donation and designate it for the learning center. Or you could do some of that correspondence coursework through the League, where you help an adult in another state improve his or her literacy."

In her mind's ear, Anne could just hear Jordan Taylor's response to her mother's suggestions. She consequently found herself defending the very thing she'd doubted herself.

"Mother, if I do something like that, no one will ever see my face. It's easy to write a check; it keeps you at a distance. All my life I've kept things like this at a distance. Don't you think it's good for me to get out and try some new things? I've been in a rut."

"I'd never say you've been in a rut, Anne," her mother shot back. "And I'm all for new things. But not just for the sake of doing something new. This tutoring program seems like an overreaction. It's extreme. There are so many other things you could do. You don't have to go to a high-crime area. It's not safe."

Anne felt one of the flashes of anger that seemed to be coming more readily over the last few weeks.

"Mother!" she exclaimed. "All my life I've been safe. I've always been careful. And then what happens? I'm having a lovely, normal dinner with my husband, and suddenly I'm not safe. There's a gun in my face. Nothing is safe anymore."

"Well," Virginia said evenly. "No one doubts that you've been through a terrible ordeal. But that's no excuse to go off half-cocked into things you know nothing about. This tutoring program is more for someone like Molly than you."

Anne drained her cup in silence and banged it down just a little too hard on the saucer. She wished Molly was here or Jordan Taylor or someone who wasn't under her mother's spell the way Anne was. With just a few well-chosen words, her mother had always known how to squelch her.

Her conversation with Father Kowalski came into her mind.

"Helping the poor may not be on your list of approved charitable activities," she said to Virginia, hoping that her words were dispassionate and noble and realizing, too late, that she just sounded snotty.

"But it's a lot better than selling stationery for bored white women to send each other little thank-you notes after their latest little dinner parties."

FIFTEEN

Tom Hogan and Otis Jefferson were back in Randolph Percey's office. "We're sorry to have to take up more of your time," Otis was saying to Randolph, "but we have a few more questions for you about Paul Lorelli."

"All right," Randolph said.

"Did you ever travel out of town with Mr. Lorelli?" Tom asked.

"Well, we went out of town on business occasionally, and personally, we went to my beach place in Bethany a couple of times."

Tom nodded. A friend in D.C.'s check-and-fraud unit had called in a favor and gotten Tom a stack of credit-card statements of charges to Paul Lorelli. Though the Lorellis shared several credit cards, about two years ago Paul had set up a separate Visa account in his name only. The statements came to a post office box address in D.C., and it was clear to Tom that Anne Lorelli was unaware of that personal account's existence.

Tom had found that the statements included several transactions from Bethany Beach. There were charges to various restaurants in the beach town last July and two other weekends in May and April. Tom already knew from Anne Lorelli where she had been on those weekends.

Paul, she said, had been traveling on firm business. Tom didn't feel like he needed to trouble Randolph Percey about the other miscellaneous receipts from Annapolis, and Charlottesville, and Baltimore. Most were from restaurants and hotels within fifty to one hundred miles from D.C.—with the exception of the batch from Bermuda.

"Were you with Mr. Lorelli in Bethany on the weekend of May 12?" Tom asked.

"Yes," Randolph said after a moment's figuring. "A couple of us went there for a getaway. Went out and did some deep-sea fishing. Didn't catch much of anything."

Tom nodded.

"How about the weekend of July 7?" he asked. "Were you with Mr. Lorelli that weekend as well?"

"No," he said. "I gave Paul the key and told him to go ahead and enjoy the place. I was here in D.C. I'd have to check my calendar if you want to know exactly what I was doing."

"No need for that, Mr. Percey," said Otis. "Did Mr. Lorelli travel to your beach property alone?"

"I don't know if he traveled alone or not," Randolph said. "I assume he drove his car."

"Well, yes, it appears that he did," Tom said. "We have some gas charges from that particular weekend. Looks like he filled up on Friday evening at a Mobile station in Ellendale, Maryland. That's right on the way to the beach, isn't it, Mr. Percey?"

"Yes, it is," Randolph said. "I've gotten three speeding tickets there. I can never remember to slow down when I hit those little towns, and they always have cops there, you know, lurking in parking lanes like sharks, just waiting for people like me. That town's whole budget is probably dependent on speeding tickets. I'm just glad to do my share to help 'em out."

"That's kind of you," Tom said dryly. "Of course you know that in a murder investigation it's our duty to shuffle through quite a bit of the deceased's paperwork, just to see if we can find anything of use toward solving the crime. It seems that on Friday night, July 7, Mr. Lorelli had reservations at a restaurant in Bethany. Sedona. Do you know it?"

"I eat there whenever I can," Randolph said. "You wouldn't expect it of a beach restaurant, but they've got great fresh game—elk, venison, you name it. Have you ever had ostrich? You'd think it would taste like poultry, but it's more like beef, except leaner. Makes sense. You know how much exercise ostriches get . . . but yeah, Sedona, it's great."

"Well, on the evening of July 9, apparently after he got his gas in Ellendale and then arrived in Bethany, Mr. Lorelli ate at Sedona. He billed $120 to his Visa there."

"Well, Paul liked to eat well," Randolph said. "He probably had cocktails, appetizers, a good bottle of wine, the chef's special for the evening, dessert, coffee, a glass of port, a nice tip—"

"Still, wouldn't you think that's a lot for one person to spend?" Tom pressed. He could tell this Percey guy was going to tell them whatever he knew. But he wanted to string him along, just for fun. It was his job's only perk.

"I had the people at Sedona fax me a copy of their menu from last summer," Tom continued. "Unless he was a sumo wrestler, there's no way Paul Lorelli could eat that much food alone—although we should note that Sedona's not known for its big portions. But his reservations that night were for two."

Randolph nodded.

"Mrs. Lorelli tells me she was out of town that weekend. She and a friend went to Richmond for a birthday party for an old college room-mate. Do you have any idea who Mr. Lorelli's guest might have been that evening at Sedona—or the following night over in Rehoboth at a restaurant called Lala Land? I have the waiters' descriptions, but I thought I'd ask you."

"I have an idea," Randolph said. "But aren't you guys supposed to figure all this out for yourselves?"

Tom smiled. He liked this guy in spite of himself.

"Well, Mr. Percey," he said. "Isn't it your duty as a D.C. resident"—Randolph lived in a big federal-style house on N Street—"to help support your city's beleaguered homicide squad? Why don't you save us a couple of steps here and tell us what you know, especially since you didn't the first time we interviewed you."

Randolph smiled. "You didn't ask me about this the first time," he said. "I don't tend to volunteer information. I just respond to direct questions. It's a lawyer's habit.

"Are you sure I can't offer you gentlemen some coffee?" he continued. He pushed a button on his phone. "Nancy, can you bring in a coffee tray, please?"

"She'll be here in just a minute," he told Tom and Otis. He ignored the detectives for a moment and looked out his big office window overlooking K Street, drumming his fingers on the desk. "I'll need to go in a few minutes," he said. "I'm sorry, but I'm supposed to meet a client at Red Sage for lunch, and I need to review the file before I go."

There was a tap on the office door, and Randolph's assistant entered, balancing a heavy tray with silver coffee service, linen napkins, and cream-colored coffee mugs emblazoned with Hagen and Hortsen's logo. She poured coffee for each of them and left.

"All right," Randolph Percey said. He took a swallow of coffee.

"Her name is Maria," he continued. "Maria something Garcia. She and Paul had been seeing each other for about a year, maybe more, I don't know. I met her last fall. Paul and I were working on a case in Boston, and on the day the verdict came in, and we won, we were both kind of over the top. It'd been high stress, and it was time for a big celebration. That night we took all the staff out to dinner.

"The next morning the staff came back to D.C., but Paul and I stayed to unwind. We played some golf in the morning, and then I had a friend take the shuttle up from D.C., and Paul suggested that this friend of his come up, too. So she did.

"I was shocked when I met Maria. She was tall, with long, black hair, very sexy, knew exactly what she thought about everything, but at the same time was a lot of fun. And she was Latin. I shouldn't have been surprised. When men mess around, they either go for a younger clone of their wives, or they do a 180. Maria was the exact opposite of Paul's wife."

"Was Mr. Lorelli secretive about the relationship?" Tom asked.

"Well, in the beginning he was pretty discreet about it. He knew he could trust me with it—and he made sure that Maria was only on the scene in out-of-the-way places. Like Boston or Bethany. Never in any public place in D.C. But as time went on, he got a little more blatant about it. He said his wife was so preoccupied, she wouldn't notice anything."

"What about other occasions when you saw Maria?" Tom asked.

"Like I said, a few times, out of town. Party weekends, getaway-type things. And then for a while I was dating someone who liked to cook and entertain, so we had Paul over a couple of times, and he brought Maria."

"Did they ever spend the night?"

Randolph paused. "I can't see how things like that have anything to do with your investigation," he said. "Do you think Anne got jealous and had him knocked off?"

Tom just looked at him. It was hard for him to imagine Anne getting mixed up with all this. She seemed so naive, so oblivious to the dark side. The more he found out about Paul Lorelli, the more of a scumbag the guy seemed to be. He didn't mind at all that Paul had gotten plugged.

"Okay," Randolph said. "They did spend the night in one of my guest rooms, probably three different times. I didn't spy on them or anything, so I don't know anything about their habits or private conversations. I just gave them clean towels and toothbrushes and let them be."

"Do you know anything about Maria's background, where she lives, what she does for a living?" Otis asked.

Randolph shook his head. "No. The conversations we had were more on the surface. We didn't really get into history or background or soul-searching issues. I do remember that she was from Peru, because I remember some conversation about terrorism, and she talked about the Shining Path, and how violent Peru had been in the eighties, and how President Fujimoro had really cracked down there."

"Do you know if Maria had any connections in Peru or Colombia with any illegal organizations?" Tom asked. "Any drug connections? Could Mr. Lorelli have gotten involved in drug use or trafficking of any kind?" The way things were going, Tom thought, he'd bet money that Paul Lorelli had not been the victim of a random mugging, but had gotten himself tangled up in some D.C. drug operation. Maybe he owed somebody money or drugs and had gotten hit as a result.

"I don't know what kind of connections Maria had or didn't have," Randolph said, shaking his head. "I've told you what I know about what you've asked, but I have no knowledge of any kind about drug involvement. If Paul was dabbling in that, he certainly didn't tell me, and I didn't see any evidence of it." He looked at his fat gold Rolex. "I'm sorry, I really do need to go—but I'd be glad to answer any more questions later on, at your convenience."

The detectives stood in unison. "Thank you, Mr. Percey," Tom said. "We appreciate your time. We may need to contact you again. Your secretary told us that you don't have any travel plans for the next several weeks. We'd appreciate it if you *would* stay in town, or let us know of your whereabouts, just in case we need you."

Randolph stood as well and shook the men's hands. "Of course," he said. "Nancy will show you out."

"Oh," said Tom. "One last question. When was the last time you saw Maria?"

Randolph stared out the window. "Not for a month, or probably two months, before Paul's death." He shook his head. But then a picture came into his mind.

"Oh," he said. "I did see her once after Paul died, just for a second. I didn't talk to her. It was at Paul's funeral, at the cemetery. I saw her from a distance, dressed in black, wearing a big black hat. It was stupid of her to come there, but she had a right to mourn too, I guess. I guess she couldn't help herself."

SIXTEEN

As Anne continued to volunteer at the Jubilee learning center, she found that the weekly hour-long commitment she had at first expected could not be contained. Soon she wondered how she had ever thought an hour would be enough. She started driving to the center several times a week to tell stories. But the stories became less important as she learned the children's names, began to understand their personalities, and spent more time with them after her sessions. They were as alert and imaginative as the kids she had taught at the McLean Community Center, and Anne felt ashamed of herself for ever assuming otherwise.

As the weather outside grew crisper and colder, the church building felt warm and cozy, a haven, Anne thought, as much for herself these days as for the children.

Sherah Loutangia Jones was still her favorite, and today, after story time, Anne had offered to help one of the other volunteers draw and cut out life-size drawings of the children. They were down in the main sanctuary area with a big roll of butcher paper. Each child would lie down on the paper, and Anne would trace around him or her with a brown crayon. Then they'd cut out the outline, and the kids could color on clothes, hair, and accessories.

Anne knelt down. "Okay, Sherah," she said. "You have to lie still." Sherah shrieked and giggled, thrashing her arms and legs on the paper. "I can't," she gasped. "It tickles!"

"How can paper tickle you?" Anne said sternly. "You lie there quietly, or we won't be able to trace around you, and you won't be able to color yourself."

"Color myself!" Sherah repeated, giggling again. "I'm already colored! I heard somebody say that once."

"Well, that's an old expression that somebody who didn't know any better might have used," Anne said smoothly. "We're all colored; some are lighter, some are darker, some are in-between. It's not a big deal."

She put her hand on Sherah's middle to hold her in place and began to draw around her torso, then her arms and legs. Sherah lay quietly, barely breathing. "You're doing a great job holding still," Anne said. "Just a minute more."

"I want you to draw me holding a book, okay, Miss Anne? I love books."

"Okay," Anne said. "Just let me get your body done first."

Sherah was silent for a moment. "Miss Anne, what happens after you eat food? Where does it go?"

Anne paused, the brown crayon in her hand. "Well, let's see. What have you eaten lately?"

"I had two peanut-butter crackers and some apple juice at snack time," Sherah said.

"Okay. So you chew up the cracker and drink the juice, right? And then it goes from your mouth, down your throat, and into your belly," Anne said, lightly tracing the path on Sherah's body, while she laughed. "Then it, uh, goes into your intestines, right?"

"Intestines!"

"Right, intestines. And the vitamins and good things from the food are pulled out of the food and absorbed into your body to help you be strong and healthy. And then what's left moves on through and comes out when you go to the bathroom."

Anne paused. It was pitiful, really, how much she didn't really know about anatomy. Where *did* food go? What would it be like if you never forgot anything, if you remembered everything you were ever taught in high school and college?

Sherah was giggling again. "Okay," she said. "Have you finished? I want to color myself. I want to be pink!"

SEVENTEEN

ON THANKSGIVING MORNING, Anne felt a little awkward about attending her first worship service in the Jubilee church. But as she entered the sanctuary, the five-year-olds ran to her right away, shouting "Miss Anne," and hugging her hard, holding her hand.

That's the great thing about children, Anne thought. *These kids don't evaluate you for a year before they decide to be your friend. They just love you because you come.*

Such abandon seemed to be a gift of the young; Anne hoped their mothers would receive her as openly.

She sat in the back row of plastic chairs, next to Sherah and Jackie Jones, and watched Jordan Taylor's husband, Michael, standing up at the electric piano, his head thrown back and his voice pouring out, his hands moving all over the keyboard, freedom flowing from his every move.

Music, Anne thought. *I forgot about music.* At home her CDs were stacked neatly in their tower next to the sound system; she hadn't listened to music in so long—long before Paul was shot. It had seemed like too much trouble to put the disks in the player.

Anne hadn't been to a church service in a long time either. Paul's funeral certainly didn't count. But there was something in the movement of the service, the way the people responded so freely, the music flowed so boldly, that both compelled and repelled her. She was far from the naked emotion of it all—the raised hands and the shouts and the loud amens—but on the other hand, the spontaneity drew her. Just so long as it was clear that no one expected her to raise her hands, she could enjoy the old hymns belted out in new arrangements on the electric piano, the whoosh of the cymbals, and the beat of the drums.

Reverend Sims, a soft-spoken man with a short, graying beard and deep dimples, spoke with a restrained passion as if he were yoked yet free, preaching about the Lord's blessings. Anne listened to his torrent of words, her mind full of pilgrims and pumpkins, and felt a little drowsy as the morning sun shone through the big, barred windows of the makeshift sanctuary.

Where am I? she thought. *A year ago Paul was alive. And now here I am sitting in the city holding hands with a little black girl.* She didn't know where her connection with this church would lead. But it felt good today, with the earnest celebration of thanks, the sun in the window, and Sherah sitting next to her wiggling with excitement.

After the sermon, Reverend Sims invited the children forward to share their blessings. "You kids come on up front here, and you tell us what you're thankful for," he said. "Well, not just what you're thankful for, but Who you're thankful to. All the good gifts that we enjoy, our friends, our families, all the stuff, all the stuffing, it all comes from God."

Next to Anne, Sherah shot up from her chair and ran to the front of the room, toward the old fireplace and the wall hanging of Jesus. One by one, other kids followed.

Reverend Sims held the microphone for the children. "And what are you thankful to God for?" he asked a small, wiry boy. The boy took the microphone and scratched his head. "I'm thankful to God for turkey today," he said confidently. "We're gonna have turkey."

A little girl came forward. "I thank God for my mama."

Anne watched as Sherah jiggled and jostled and waited her turn. Jackie Jones rolled her eyes toward Anne. "Sometimes she thanks God for the entire inventory of our store," she said. "Piece by piece by piece."

Sherah took the microphone. "I thank God today," she said, "for my friend who tells us stories, Miss Anne!" Sherah danced back toward Anne, and Leonard Sims took back the mike. "We're glad you could be with us today, Anne," he said. "You come back and worship with us any time."

Jackie grinned at Anne, and Anne took Sherah onto her lap, hugging her compact body. *I don't think I'm here to worship,* she thought. *But I do thank God for this little girl.*

As ANNE DROVE FROM the Jubilee church to Molly's house, the streets were quiet, most of the leaves off the trees, the skies heavy with clouds that seemed to promise snow. Anne had always loved Thanksgiving. It was such a cozy holiday, without the hype and pressure that usually made Christmas an exercise in list-making rather than a celebration.

She tried to recall last Thanksgiving. She shook her head. Into her mind came another memory, one from a few years after she and Paul were married. Her parents had been in Europe, and Paul grudgingly agreed to take Anne to his parents' home for the holiday.

Anne had never felt so claustrophobic. The house was filled with too much furniture, too many people, too much noise. The kitchen was too small. After a few hours, she was amazed when dinner actually went on the table in the cramped dining room filled with too many chairs, too much linen, old pieces of Italian glassware everywhere.

At the time Anne considered herself a person without prejudice—a thesis, she realized, that had not been tested much. But as the day wore on, she recognized that, yes, she did have an entrenched bias. It was against red sauce. She couldn't help it. If Italians wanted to live in America, they should stick to turkey and gravy. Tomatoes had nothing to do with Thanksgiving.

She had tried to hide her distaste, but Paul saw it, and it fueled his own anger and embarrassment. As they sat down at the crowded table, Paul was simmering. His father, enamored of any electric device—lamp timers, microwaves, blenders, electric can openers, salad shooters, whatever—had ceremonially brought out the electric knife to preside over the carving of the overcooked bird.

At that point Paul had broken, his usual reserve in pieces. "Dad!" he had hissed. "All that does is shred the turkey!"

A pause.

"You don't need to make such a big deal of it!" Paul had said again, his voice shaking. "Just take a regular carving knife and cut the bird!"

Sal had cast a withering glance at Paul and began buzzing, buzzing, over the turkey's large breast. Anne, frozen, watched as shreds of dry, white flesh started flying over the table, raining down on people's plates like unwanted manna.

Sal buzzed on, implacably. Ignoring the turkey storm, Celia asked for a pile of plates to make the serving easier. "Everybody, pass to your right, okay?" Paul, his face dark red, left the table. Anne smiled helplessly at everyone and obediently passed her littered plate to the right.

They had left for home soon after the meal was over.

Anne tried to make light of it in the car. "It's just the way your family is," she had said. "It was just a meal. I don't know why you're taking it so personally. It wasn't like you were being presented somewhere."

"That's nice for you to say," Paul had said, furious, gripping the wheel. "You *were* presented. You needn't make those kinds of comparisons. Miss Debutante comes to Philly to be pelted with shreds of turkey meat."

He had shaken his head a few times, and Anne had wondered why he was bringing up something as remote as her being a deb. It was just part of how she had grown up, how her parents were. Paul had always seemed to appreciate that. She knew that there was a lot he didn't appreciate about his own family; she could see why.

"But why should your family's behavior make a wedge between *us?*" Anne had asked. "We're building our own life together, apart from them. It doesn't make sense for you to be so angry."

Paul had not responded, and Anne had retreated, looking out the car window into the darkness of I-95. Finally, as they passed Baltimore, he took her hand, apparently having willed himself back into good humor. "I shouldn't have lost control like that," he said. They had not celebrated a holiday with his family since.

AH, WELL, ANNE THOUGHT. *And where were we last Thanksgiving?*

For a moment she couldn't recall, but then it occurred to her that a year ago she and Paul had been at her parents' house along with several other couples. It had been an understated, lovely event about which she remembered absolutely nothing.

She was glad today to be with Molly and Clark and the kids and the miscellaneous strays they had picked up for the day. The chaos there would feel comforting, much warmer than the crystal sterility of her parents' drawing room.

She pulled up to the O'Kelleys' curb, crunching on the piles of leaves there, and went into the house. Molly was, of course, in the kitchen. Anne found her beating her oven-mitted hands on her green-and-white-striped apron.

"I can't believe I did this," she was crying. "How many turkeys have

I cooked in my life? I've never let this happen before! Look at this! He's perfectly roasted, almost done, I worked so hard to get all those bay leaves and sprigs of rosemary slid perfectly under his skin, but I forgot and left the little bag with the giblets and neck and heart and liver and who knows what else inside his body! I wondered why I couldn't stuff more stuffing in!"

"Well, it's good we found this out now rather than while you were serving," Anne said. "It always tends to bother people when they find organ meats in a Baggie at the table."

Through the kitchen window toward the backyard, she could see most of the dinner guests running with the children, playing hide-and-seek. In the family room, the television was droning, the comforting sound of football noises blending with other people's conversations. Anne could hear Clark holding forth about Senator Wiggins's latest snafu, in which the aged statesman had inadvertently gotten his gold cuff link caught in a wire protruding from the push-bar in a hotel's revolving door.

A local television anchor was waiting to interview the senator in the lobby. Unable to extract himself gracefully, Wiggins automatically reverted to campaign mode and had gone around and around and around in the revolving door, smiling, waving with his free hand to everyone in the lobby and on the street, while the camera crew filmed the whole thing for the six o'clock news.

"This is not a big deal, really," Anne said to Molly, picking up the long, honed butcher knife lying on the cutting board. "All we have to do is perform a little surgery here. Is the patient ready?"

Holding both sides of the roasting pan, Molly carefully hoisted the huge bird and presented its rear end to Anne. "The patient feels no pain," she said.

"Excellent," said Anne. "But why don't you turn him around?"

She began spooning dressing out of the turkey's cavity, then poked around inside with a pair of tongs and withdrew the bag holding the giblets.

Anne stuffed the stuffing back in the big bird. Molly returned the turkey to the oven.

"Great," Molly said. "I'm not going to mess with that bag. I don't think anybody really needs giblets in their gravy anyway, do you?"

"I've never met anyone under the age of seventy who likes giblets at all," said Anne.

"That's true. But giblets just seem like one of those Thanksgiving things you have to do even if you really hate them. Kind of like pretending that it's a fun family outing to go chop down your own Christmas tree when it's really just a lot of work and arguing out in the cold."

"Right, or in the summer, those pick-your-own-berry places," Anne said. "It's hot, there are a million bugs, you're sweating, the bushes are scratchy, but it's supposed to be a fun thing to be out there in the fields, filling your own basket."

"It's funny how things get overrated," Molly said. "There's some secret conspiracy out there shamelessly manipulating everyone to hold up certain things like that for laud. Like Cuban cigars. Or colonic spas. Or opera. I mean, if you tell someone you went to the opera last night, *Aida* or something, they'll always swoon, oh, how divine, because there's an unspoken rule that opera is sacred.

"I'm sorry, I do love the music, but there's just not enough action. These people get themselves into their own problems, and then they keep mooning about everything, and then they die in the end. I would much rather listen to the music on my own while I'm doing something else than spend three hours and four intermissions watching overacting by overweight characters I don't care about."

She paused. "Or caviar! Who *really* likes little salty fish eggs?"

"Oh, I don't know about that one," said Anne. "I love the way they pop when you bite down on them."

"Don't interrupt me when I'm raving," said Molly. She looked at the kitchen clock and wiped her hands on her apron. "I think we've got about forty-five minutes before we'll put things on the table. Let's go sit down with people for a while. Do you want a glass of wine or something? Are you doing okay?"

Anne smiled at Molly. "I'm doing fine," she said.

MUCH LATER THAT Thanksgiving night, Anne slumped on the O'Kelleys' flowered sofa, crunched between Clark and Molly. They had lit a fire in the fireplace. The other guests were gone, the kids were in bed, and Clark's sister and her husband, visiting from New Jersey, were sprawled on the carpet in front of the fire. So were Ruth and Boaz, their paws twitching as they dreamed dog-dreams.

"So," Clark was saying, "why is it that the human brain remembers all the insignificant things you'd rather forget and forgets the important information that just might come in handy?"

"Brain sludge," Molly said. "There's a whole generation of us who remember every single word to the theme song of *Gilligan's Island*—"

"Right," Clark broke in, "'a thr-ee hou-r tour.' And then there's everyone's favorite, *The Beverly Hillbillies*. 'The first thing you know, old Jed's a millionaire,'" he sang, "'the kin folks said—'"

"'Jed, move away from there!'" everyone shouted.

"Or," Clark's sister, Polly, said, "those words that get stuck in your head. One time when I was about four years old Great-uncle Wilbert pointed to a stop sign and told me that the word 'stop' was 'pots' backward. Here I am thirty years later, and every single time I pull up to a stop sign all I can see is POTS. Great-uncle Wilbert's been dead for years, and that's all I remember about him. POTS!"

"And then you forget things you used to know," Molly said. "The other day I was in Old Town with Maggie Merriweather, and she was looking at French antiques, and she was interested in this set of chairs over in the corner of the shop behind some other furniture. So I kind of climbed over the other things so I could see the tags on the chairs.

"'What are they?' she asks. And I'm there looking at the tag and my mind goes totally blank because I haven't really focused on Roman numerals in a long time. So I'm staring at this tag, brain-dead, and she says 'What are they?' again, so I just say to her, 'They're Louis X-Vees.'"

"X-Vees?" Anne said. "You're kidding. It's not like XV is a hard one, not like Ls and Cs and Ms and things."

"Well, I'm sorry," Molly said with mock offense. "When you have three small children, your brain cells die at a faster rate, and the cells I had Roman numerals stored in died a long time ago."

"Well," Clark said, standing and stretching. "It's almost X-I-I o'clock, and I think we should all go into the kitchen and eat turkey sandwiches with lots of salt and pepper and mayonnaise. It's an O'Kelley family tradition, begun long ago by Great-uncle Wilbert."

"That sounds great," Anne said, "but I really need to get home."

"Don't be ridiculous," Molly said, standing up and throwing a wadded paper napkin into the fire. "It's late and I don't want you driving home now. Just stay here. You're having lunch tomorrow with your friend the priest, right? You'll be closer to his apartment if you stay here. You've got a toothbrush here. Scott and Polly are in the guest room, but you can sleep with Amelia in her bed."

"I'm not sleeping with a five-year-old," Anne said. "She wiggles too much."

"You are staying here, period," Molly said. "No one leaves my house at midnight to go sleep in an empty house."

"It won't be empty if I'm in it," Anne said. "Besides, I know the drill here. You'll all be up until two eating turkey sandwiches. The only way for anyone to get any sleep at your house would be to go to an empty house."

Clark sank down on the couch next to Anne and put his arm around her shoulders. "You have to stay here," he said seriously, looking deep into her eyes. "I don't want you going out into the night alone. Stay with us."

Anne looked at the circle of friends, heard the throbbing of Kenny G in the background, and felt the soft warmth of the fire. She put her head on Clark's shoulder. "I was just waiting for *you* to ask," she said, smiling and raising her eyebrows at Molly. "Thank you."

AT MIDNIGHT, A CAR sat in front of Anne's brick town house in McLean, its lights off, its engine running. The woman at the steering wheel looked up at the house's dark windows. *Is Anne asleep?* she wondered. *Or is she there? She usually sleeps with a few lights on. And it looks like her car isn't in the garage.*

Maria remembered the only time she had been in the town house. Anne had been at the Greenbrier on a long weekend with her parents. Paul had been "too busy" at work to get away; he had encouraged Anne to go ahead and enjoy herself without him.

The first night Anne was gone, Maria and Paul had driven up to Annapolis for dinner, and then late in the evening, he had brought her to his home.

She remembered the garage door sliding up, Paul's hand on her back, the way in which she'd explored the house, looking over the orderly rooms, the heavy, silver-framed photos, the expensive vases, the faceted crystal, the whole house furnished, it seemed, by wedding gifts and family heirlooms.

Paul hadn't shown much interest when she asked about all the things. "She doesn't choose much," he had said shortly. He never called Anne by name when he talked to Maria. "Most of this came from her parents."

Three days later, just before Anne was to come home, Maria had watched while Paul had taken the house apart as if it were a crime scene, furiously washing sheets, pillowcases, vacuuming everywhere, and plucking long, black hairs from the shower drain with a pair of tweezers. He had opened the windows and let the breezes blow, then brought in big bouquets of freesia and other fragrant flowers for Anne's homecoming, so that no scent of Maria remained. It had been humiliating.

The lighter popped out of the dashboard, and Maria lit a cigarette. That had been the only time they had been together at Paul's house. It was too risky, he said.

But now Maria wished that she had left a telltale hair on Anne's pillow, or some of her scent on Anne's clothes hanging so neatly on their padded hangers, or a lipstick smear on one of the Waterford wineglasses—some piece of physical evidence that would shock the complacency of this bland blond woman she had never met, this woman who seemed content with her lovely things and her distant relationship with her husband, this woman who was so stupid as to think that such appearances were enough for a man like Paul Lorelli. Who did she think she was?

But now Paul was gone, and the memories of their nights together were like smoke lost in the dark. Maria had come too far to be impractical, but sometimes the luxury of telling this woman the extent of her husband's betrayal danced in her mind like a shadowy fantasy.

It would be so satisfying to tell her everything and watch the shock play over her face, the recognition that Maria had owned something in Paul Lorelli that Anne had never realized existed.

Maria sighed. She liked to squelch her enemies, but that particular fantasy would never come true. It would be too dangerous. But it was still fun to toy with, now and then. She stubbed out her cigarette and eased the car away from the curb. It looked like Anne Lorelli wasn't coming home tonight anyway.

AT MOLLY AND CLARK'S house, Anne stood in a borrowed night-gown looking down on Amelia in her double bed, her little body spread-eagled in the middle, her hair tossed as if she had been in a windstorm, her arm flung around V'Albert, the big, soft, white stuffed bear Anne had given her last Valentine's Day.

"Okay," Anne said. "If she starts wiggling, though, I'm going to come and get in bed with you and Clark." She gave Molly a quick hug; Molly's hair smelled like smoke from the fireplace. "Thanks for a great day," Anne said. "Sleep well."

"You too," said Molly, gently scooping Amelia from the middle and placing her on the side of the bed. "We'll see you in the morning." She snapped off the light.

Anne climbed under Amelia's plump yellow comforter and lay back on the soft pillow, gazing up at the ceiling, which was pasted with hundreds of stars, glow-in-the-dark constellations that Clark had arranged, working as meticulously as if his daughter's bedroom ceiling were the subject of some Senate committee hearing.

The stars glowed faintly, and they looked so real that Anne could pick out Cassiopeia and Orion, with the strange sensation that she might as well be outside on a clear winter night, but instead was warm and sleepy, inside, on a sheltered Thanksgiving evening.

Next to her, Amelia mumbled something in her sleep and clutched V'Albert tighter. Anne smoothed the child's soft hair away from her face and stared up into the shining stars above, cozy in the warmth of the day and its embraces. *Thank you,* she thought.

EIGHTEEN

The next morning, as she climbed into the Volvo, Anne waved good-bye to Amelia. "Thank you for letting me sleep in your bed," she called. "You take good care of your mom and dad. Don't let your brother and sister eat all the leftover turkey."

"I have to save some for V'Albert," said Amelia, still clutching the huge bear. V'Albert loves turkey."

"That's good," said Anne. "You'd better go get inside now. You don't have any shoes on." She waved and pulled away toward Danuta's apartment.

Later, Anne sat with Danuta and Father Kowalski, wondering how she was going to digest lunch—soup, mashed potatoes, pork chops, carrot salad, and cake—on top of everything she had eaten yesterday. *That's the problem,* she thought. *You stretch your stomach one day, and then it's clamoring for more the next, refusing to go back to its normal size.*

The bouquet of big yellow chrysanthemums Anne had brought sat in the center of the old table. Outside the apartment's picture window, a few late leaves fluttered to the ground in a gust of cold wind. "Anne, would you like more tea?" Danuta asked, holding up the teapot. "Jozef?"

"No, thank you," said Anne. "I'm sorry, this has been delicious, but I am absolutely full."

"We always eat our big meal in the middle of the day," Father Kowalski said. "In the evening we have a little bread and fruit and cheese."

Anne pointed at an old black-and-white photograph of a young couple that was hanging on the dining room wall. "I've been looking at this picture all through lunch," she said to Danuta. "The woman looks so much like you. Is she a sister?"

Danuta smiled and poured herself a cup of tea. "No," she said. "It's my mother. When I was younger, I did look much like her. That picture was taken soon after she and our father were married."

"They made a beautiful couple," Anne said. The woman looked so strong, yet with a smile tucked around the corners of her mouth, as if she knew a private joke too good to share.

"They were beautiful," Danuta said. "We lost them in the war. Now that I'm in this part of my life, it seems so strange that my mother never grew old. I'm older than my mother. She died in her early forties."

"Oh, I'm so sorry," Anne said.

Danuta looked at Anne. "We lost almost everyone, all swept away by the Nazis. I was seventeen years old when it started."

She stared at the old picture.

"In 1939 we lived in Krakow, in the south of Poland. It was a beautiful, golden, ancient city, the center for the artists and writers of Poland. Jozef was fifteen. Our parents were both teachers. My mother taught little children, and my father was a professor of history at the Jagiellonian University.

"In the late summer of 1939, we heard little bits of news from Germany, about what was happening there, and how skirmishes between the Germans and the Polish border guards were growing more frequent. It seemed like war was coming."

She stopped and looked toward Anne.

"Oh, please, go on," Anne said. "I know it must be hard to talk about. But I love hearing stories from back then. My father was in the army, but he never talks about it."

"Well," Danuta said, "For me, it is good to talk about it now and then.

"I remember when the war began. It was the first day of September. Everyone was listening to the radio, and the Polish president read a proclamation: the Germans had crossed our borders, and we were going to fight them off.

"But it was impossible. By September 6 Krakow fell to the Germans. A week later Poland was an occupied nation.

"The new government was run by a Nazi named Hans Frank. He set up his headquarters in Krakow, in our Wawel Castle. After the war we would discover that his orders were to eliminate every trace of Polish culture.

"But we didn't know that. It's funny how you can cling to any shred of normalcy even as the world is falling apart around you. My brother and I still played games and fought and teased, and my friends and I still flirted and gossiped and told secrets. I had a boyfriend, Jerzy. We had been special friends for as long as I could remember. But we both wanted to go to university before we got married.

"Then the noose around all of our necks got tighter.

"The people of influence in our city—some of the businessmen, the political leaders, the priests who people looked up to—were taken out to the square and shot right there. We stayed home as much as we could, as if the Nazis would forget about us if they didn't see us.

"They did not forget. One evening there was the sound of boots in the street, and SS officers came to our front door. They called for my father: 'Pawel Kowalski! You are to come with us.' He was to report to a work camp.

"They let my father pack a little bag—my mother stuffed it with everything she could think of. The soldiers shouted for him to hurry. We all ran to him and kissed him on his cheeks and hugged him, and then the soldiers took him away.

"We would never see him again, but we didn't know that then.

"Most Poles were very anti-Semitic. So a lot of our people cheered the Germans on when the anti-Jewish policies began. They didn't know the Nazis would just as soon kill all the Poles too.

"But there were some Poles who felt differently about the Jews. People like my parents. As things got worse and worse for the Jews—they were rounded up, put in the ghetto, shot on the streets—my mother's concern was for the Jewish children. She had a special bond with little children. She didn't talk down to them. She drew them out, even the shyest ones.

"So when it seemed clear that even the Jewish children would not be spared, she was horrified."

"What year was that?" Anne asked, as Danuta stopped and took a sip of tea.

"It was still early in the war," Danuta said. "Jerzy and I weren't married yet. I remember one night Mama tiptoed into my little bedroom. I was still awake, lying there thinking about the war and Jerzy and all my dreams that might not ever come true, and then my mother came and sat on the edge of my bed.

"'Danuta,' she said in her quiet voice. There was a full moon that night, I remember, so I could just barely see her in the shadows. She had long, golden-brown hair, thick and heavy—she looked so young, people used to tease us about being sisters. At night she wore her hair in a long braid down her back, hanging down over her ivory nightgown. She was my mother, so I didn't think much about her age, but when I look back on it, she was only forty years old then.

"'Are you awake?' she asked.

"'Yes, Mama,' I said.

"She patted my leg under the sheet. 'I cannot stop thinking about the children,' she said. 'The Jewish children. I know you will understand what I'm going to say to you.

"'We have to help the children. If they are not saved, there will be no new generation to carry on for the Jews. We are to love our neighbors as ourselves. Will God forgive us if we turn away from those who are so helpless?'

"I sat up in the bed and put my arms around my knees. I loved children; I knew I wanted lots of them with Jerzy. I wanted to be just like my mother. But I was afraid.

"'What if they find out?' I asked. I meant the Nazis. We had already seen a whole family we knew, hanging in the marketplace, the mother and the father and the children. They had signs around their necks: *This is what happens to Poles who help Jews.*

"'Danuta,' my mother said. 'It's too far gone. You know what could happen if they find out. But that's not the right question.' She had her arms around my shoulders now, looking at me in the dark.

"'The right question for us is, what do we do?' my mother said. 'The Germans force us to make a terrible choice. We can obey the Nazis and ignore the Jewish children, and we'll be safe. Maybe. Or we can obey God and help the children, and we'll be in danger. Probably. But it's not like the choice will go away if we close our eyes and pretend these insufferable things are not happening. They are happening.

"'So it's very logical. We have to choose. Would you rather disobey God or the Nazis? Would you rather risk losing your life or losing your soul?'

"Sitting in my bed in Krakow that night, the full moon rising like it had every month of my life, my mother's warm arms around me, I felt my stomach clench with fear.

"And yet my heart swelled with love for my mother. She prided herself on being logical, but I knew the truth. It was not logic alone that compelled her. She knew that if we were to continue being the kind of people we had always been, we had to help the children. To turn away would change us forever.

"But it was also my mother's heart, her passion, her irresistible instincts, that were drawing her—and us—into the whirlwind. She had to help the children.

"And so we did."

I would have been too terrified to take that risk, Anne thought. *I would have just sat on my hands, scared to death of the Nazis.*

"It began in small ways," Danuta continued.

"A Jewish woman had done a lot of sewing for my mother, and they had struck up a friendship over the years. One day, out of nowhere, a German officer was standing at our back door. He had two little boys with him, maybe six and eight years old.

"My heart turned over when I saw him, but after the doors were closed and the blinds were shut, he spoke to us in perfect Polish. He was a member of the underground and had somehow gotten a German uniform, and he was bringing us the two children of my mother's seamstress.

"We knew it could be a trap, but our instincts said to trust him. When I tell the story now, it sounds surprising that such things were possible. The Nazis were so thorough. How could someone wearing a stolen uniform bring Jewish children to our home? But the Nazis were still human, and they had a lot on their hands, and so now and then we could outsmart them. And, now and then we were lucky.

"The underground agent put on regular clothes and buried the uniform in a little satchel in our garden—he would come back for it later. He disappeared, and now we had these two beautiful little boys to take care of. Their names were Jan and David. We had built a false wall behind the wardrobe in my parents' bedroom, and we went through a lot of practice drills. The boys got so they could hide in just a few seconds. For them it was like a game. We always kept all the doors locked, the curtains drawn.

"We had a big, tall house, and so we were able to construct other hiding places up in the attic and down in the cellar. More Jewish children came to us, and we helped to get some of them spirited out of the area through the underground. Some ended up in Catholic boarding schools; their parents died in the camps, but those children survived the war.

"And we had a few adults with us as well. Some of the Jews were able to survive for a while because they were fair-haired and blue-eyed. Some got false ID papers and new names.

"One was a girl named Ruth Hirsch. She became Biruta Barski, my 'cousin' who was living with us. We schooled her in the Catholic faith; sometimes the Nazis drilled people they suspected of passing as Gentiles with questions about Holy Communion or the Blessed Virgin.

"So time went on. Sometimes we felt that we would all be found out and killed. Other times we had hope, hope against all hope that the war would play itself out, that normal life would return.

"But that was not to be.

"Because of the war, Jerzy and I decided to go ahead and get married. We had a little wedding; we didn't want to call attention to ourselves. On our wedding night, our friends who were hiding in our home gave us little presents. Biruta gave us an embroidered handkerchief. Jan and David gave us a polished brown acorn they had found, and they sang us a funny song. It was a sweet time.

"Jerzy and I lived on the top floor of my mother's home. There certainly wasn't much privacy. But we were in love, and we were working hard, together, on something we believed in. Even though we slept lightly at night, always listening for the Nazi boots on our doorstep, we slept peacefully. There is no better sleep than the sleep of a clean conscience.

"Then it happened.

"A young woman, one of the members of the underground, was caught by the Nazis. She was carrying a book that listed all the people like us who were part of the network of rescuers. Carrying information like that was absolutely against our regulations. We don't know why she had it with her, but when the Nazis found that book, it was all over for us.

"We heard the sound of boots on the street, and the German shepherds barking and barking in front of our house, their teeth flashing like they were going to tear us apart.

"The troops came storming in, and they put us all in one room—Jerzy and my mother and Jozef and Biruta and me. They still didn't know Biruta was Jewish. One of them stood guard over us while the rest swarmed through our house like demons, breaking down walls, tearing open cupboards, crashing axes into closets upstairs. We could hear screams and shooting and then silence. We didn't see what had happened. I don't think I could have stood it. It was bad enough to hear it.

"But then it got worse. We were all there, standing in a little huddle, and the SS officer in charge was walking around us, around and around, with his hands behind his back. And then he stopped in front of me and slapped me across the face with his gloved hand.

"'Polish whore,' he shouted. 'You are a Polish whore who loves Jews. If you love Jews so much we can send you to where all the Jews are going.' And he slapped me again. Then Jerzy pulled me back and got in front of me and said to the officer, very calm but very angry, his words shooting out like he was spitting, 'You keep your dirty Nazi hands off my wife.'

"And the officer just took his gun from his hip and shot Jerzy right in the side of the head. Jerzy crashed down to the floor. There was blood everywhere, spurting out of his head like a fountain, running in rivers across my mother's parlor floor. It was like someone blew a candle out. He was gone instantly."

Danuta stopped and looked out of the dining room window.

"Oh!" Anne breathed, her eyelids fluttering, thinking of the sudden explosion of the gun on the night of Paul's murder. "How horrible!"

Danuta nodded. "Yes. Still, it was a mercy that he went so quickly." She cleared her throat and continued.

"They took us out of the room and left Jerzy just lying there dead on the floor. We were in shock, just numbly holding on to one another; we knew they were going to shoot us in the street. But just when you were sure of something the Germans would do, they would surprise you. They looked us over. Jozef was a tall, skinny kid, but he, all of us, we were still in pretty good shape, in spite of the war. And my mother and Biruta and I were all blond-haired and blue-eyed.

"One of the officers came up to me and touched my hair. '*Goldene Haar!*' he said. He went back to the first officer, and then they came back to us. 'We are not unreasonable people,' he said. 'You are young and strong; we will send you someplace else. They need strong workers there. *Arbeit macht frei.*'

"The next thing we knew, we were in Auschwitz. They sent Jozef off with the men, and Biruta and my mother and I were processed. They took all our clothes, shaved our heads and all of our body hair, and sent us to the showers. The real showers—not the gas. We were naked and shivering, and they gave us dirty gray dresses with holes in them. Then we were sent to Barracks 8.

"Within a few weeks the flesh disappeared from our cheeks, our arms, our breasts. Our bellies were bloated with starvation. We had only a few hundred calories a day. We dreamed constantly of food.

"Every day the camp chimneys pulsed smoke into the sky, constantly burning, raining ashes on all of us, the foul smell of burning flesh, the transports of Jews who arrived and minutes later were nothing but smoke churning from the chimneys.

"We were sent to work detail. Mama was smart, and she told Biruta and me to say that we were skilled seamstresses. We didn't know much, but the threat of death does much to loosen one's fingers. The commandant's wife couldn't get enough fancy gowns and dresses, and she liked what we did. So her friends, the other officers' wives, started using us too.

"It was so ironic—I would look over at Biruta, sitting at a sewing machine. The Nazis still didn't know she was Jewish, but there she was, a thread in her mouth, her eyebrows puckering with concentration, and I would think how beautiful she was, and how it was a few little things, some nimble fingers and a sewing machine, that stood between her and the ovens.

"We heard terrible stories in the camp. The SS officer would stand where the trains full of Jews let out, impeccable in his spotless uniform, with his polished riding crop by his side. He would use it to point people either to the left or the right, as if he were God Himself on Judgment Day. To the left meant death. The right meant life. For a while, at least.

"One Jewish woman got off the train with her mother and her two young sons. Old people and children under twelve were automatically sent to the left. People who could work were sent to the right.

"The woman thought they were all coming to work camp. The officer in charge immediately waved her younger son to the left. Then he paused over her older son. The boy was tall for his age. 'He must be more than twelve,' the officer said thoughtfully to the woman. 'He's a big boy.'

"'Oh, no,' she said. In fact, the boy was twelve, but she hoped to spare him from work too difficult for him.

"'All right,' the officer said. 'To the left, then.'

"The woman felt relieved. The officer waved her and her mother to the right; they were both still young enough to work hard. 'Sir,' the woman said, 'may my mother go with my children? She can take care of them while I am at work.'

"'Very well,' the officer said again. 'To the left, then.'

"It was only later that the woman found out that she had condemned her older son and her mother to the gas chamber."

"Oh!" Anne said, leaning back in her chair. "It's unimaginable—"

Danuta shook her head. "Even for me, sometimes I cannot believe it all really happened. But these things happened every day.

"Auschwitz was an ocean of mud, a swamp of excrement. The Nazis knew we were their slaves if they could keep us smeared in dirt, starved, and sick. But even as they tried to degrade us by keeping us in filth, we would do all we could to keep clean.

"Around us some daughters stole bread from their own mothers; people preyed on one another. But my mother and Biruta and I pledged that we would lift one another up when we fell down in the mud, that we would save one another, if at all possible, but that we would not commit suicide to do so.

"Even in the despair, the unexpected sometimes occurred. One day we heard of a group of Polish Jewish prisoners who came to Auschwitz from Bergen-Belsen. They were taken to Crematorium 2 and ordered to undress.

"One was a beautiful young dancer. She removed her clothes slowly, suggestively, and when she was done, she flung her skirt on the head of the SS sergeant. He fumbled, blinded by the thin material. She grabbed his revolver and shot him twice. The other women attacked the Nazis with their bare hands. In the end, all were gassed. The SS sergeant died as well.

"We kept going. Mama was growing weaker. At one point during a roll call the senior female SS officer—a demon woman who was hanged after the war for her crimes—slashed Mama with her whip, a leather riding whip inlaid with colored beads. Mama was so weak that when the infection came, she had nothing to fight it.

"In the end she was lying in the bunk where the three of us slept each night, fading away with a killing fever.

"'We did what was right,' she whispered to Biruta and me. We had become as close as sisters; I never thought of Biruta otherwise. 'I am happy in that. I have no regrets. We have run a good race in this awful place.'

"Mama could barely speak, but she was using everything left inside of her to utter those last words. It was fitting. She was as logical—and passionate—as ever. Her thin eyelashes fluttered, and she spoke to me directly. 'Never forget that I love you,' she whispered. 'Never forget, we must always choose life—until God lets us go. *He is letting me go.*'

"And then she died, right there in the rotting straw of that bunk in that stinking death camp. I could not even weep. I looked at Biruta, and we clasped one another tightly. The women all around bowed their heads in respect. My mother had been well loved. And then the roll call sounded, and we straightened our backs and went out to the Nazis. It was what my mother would have wanted.

"Finally, the end came. I cannot describe for you the confusion at the end of the war. Biruta and I were like skeletons, dead women walking, yet somehow we survived.

"After liberation, we found Jozef. You cannot imagine our joy. Eventually, we went back to our home.

"It was all torn up, but it was still standing. Most of the furniture and things were gone, stripped, but there were still brown smears on the parlor floor where Jerzy had died. We went upstairs, and we could see bloodstains where the hiding places had been.

"But I went to one place the Nazis had not found. In one of the kitchen cabinets, my mother had made a special compartment about the size of a shoe box. It was behind a false back of the cabinet where she stored ant killer and mousetraps and things like that. She had even set a trap there as if we had mice, and so maybe the Nazis hadn't looked much there, not wanting to stick their hands in and get them caught in a trap.

"I found the secret panel, and I opened it. It was where my mother had hidden her jewels. One by one, we had sold off most of the pieces during the war. Some of my grandmother's diamonds had even been used as bribes to save Jewish children. There was only one piece left, and as I stuck my hand into the hiding place, I could feel it was still there.

"I pulled it out, gently. It was a perfect strand of pearls, the most exquisite of the jewelry. We had saved it for the last because it was the best, and because my mother could not bear to part with it. It was still there!

"I felt the old pearls, as smooth and unmarred as if the war had never happened. Attached to the clasp by a little thread was a tiny note, written in my mother's firm handwriting: *For Danuta, when this is all over. Never forget, I will always love you. And never forget, you must always choose life!*

"I broke down then and I cried, torrents of tears that I had never cried at Auschwitz, the tears I could not cry when Jerzy was shot, rivers of sorrow for my parents, my husband, the children . . . all of them so beautiful, each one a rare pearl, all dead, destroyed for nothing. I wept oceans that day. And I decided the only revenge for me was to keep on living, to press on in the fullest way I could; to lose myself in the despair would be to grant the Nazis some victory in my life. And that I would not allow.

"So we started over, trying to clean up the wreckage of Krakow and the wreckage of our lives. Jozef went on to study for the priesthood.

"I got work as a secretary in a manufacturing plant. Biruta lived with me until she found a cousin and a brother, who had survived as well. They eventually went to Israel. To this day we are like sisters.

"Soon I met an American soldier. Joe Waters.

"I grew to care a lot for Joe. He wasn't dramatic or passionate like Jerzy, but he gave me the space and protection I needed to grow again. He asked me to marry him and to come to America. I will always love Poland. But Krakow was too painful for me. And Jozef had gone into the Church. He had his family, if you will.

"Joe died six years ago. We had two sons—it was a miracle that I could have children, I had been so starved in Auschwitz. And don't you know I named them Jan and David in honor of those two little boys we lost in Krakow. I always wanted a girl, a girl I could raise up like my mother raised me, but that wasn't to be.

"In 1982 the Holocaust Memorial Museum in Jerusalem, Yad Vashem, honored me and Jozef for our work during the war. We went to Jerusalem and planted our trees on the Avenue of the Righteous. It was a great honor.

"When I look back, though, we had to do what we did, or we would no longer be who we were. Not to choose would be to choose. And the choice was, we could either obey God or the Nazis. In spite of everything that happened, so horrible, we made the right choice.

"When we went to Jerusalem, Joe and Jozef and I went on a little tour around Israel, retracing the steps of the life of Christ.

"One day we went to the Sea of Galilee. It's right in the basin of some hills so that if the winds pick up just right, storms can begin very suddenly.

"We read in Saint Mark where Jesus was out on a boat on the Sea of Galilee with His disciples. Suddenly a storm came out of nowhere. Jesus was sleeping. The disciples woke Him up. 'Don't you care that we're drowning?' they screamed. (You know, that wasn't quite true, they weren't drowning yet.)

"But Jesus got up and spoke quietly to the wind and the waves, and the storm stilled. Then He said to His disciples, 'Why are you still afraid? Do you still have no faith?'

"And Jozef and I talked about the winds that had whipped through our own lives, the storms we had endured. We'll never know why those terrible things happened. But we did feel some comfort that we had not been alone during the storm. Jesus had been in the boat with us. He can calm the storm, but He doesn't always choose to do it right away. But when the horrors come, He is with us."

Danuta paused and sipped her cold tea. The sudden silence was like the breaking of a spell. Anne remembered to take a breath. Danuta's eyes had lost the faraway look they had had during her story, and Anne realized with a start that the last part of what Danuta had said had been directed at her.

It's the same thing Jackie Jones said, she thought, her mind reeling. *He is with us.* She looked out the window of Danuta's apartment. *Is He?*

NINETEEN

TWO WEEKS LATER, Tom Hogan got out of his car and walked toward the yellow banner of police tape rippling in the wind. Eastlake Gardens—it had no lake and no gardens—was a housing project in southeast D.C., a series of rectangles of low-rise apartments facing littered concrete courtyards. Though he hadn't been there recently, it was familiar turf to Tom and most of the detectives he worked with, site of frequent shootings, gang warfare, and random incidents of domestic violence.

So here was a familiar sight: the fluttering yellow tape marked an area in the center of the courtyard square, where the corpse of a young black man was spread-eagled, face up.

A group of neighborhood kids stood in front of the tape, shuffling their feet in the cold. A uniformed officer drank coffee from a Styrofoam cup, watching the kids, while a detective jotted notes.

"Hey, Tom," the cop called. Tom looked. This was the guy who had called him.

"Thanks for getting hold of me," he said.

"Right," the cop said. "I thought this might be one of your guys from the Lorelli case. It looks like he's missing part of his ear. Hard to tell, though, because now he's missing part of his head, too. Don't you just hate when that happens? Ruined this kid's entire day."

Tom raised an eyebrow. Unless the case involved a child, the uniforms always made light of crime scenes. There was too much stress otherwise. They had seen too many stiffened bodies lying in alleys, shattered in cars, plugged on the sidewalks of D.C. The only way to deal with the carnage was to joke about it.

Tom ducked under the tape and looked at the body. It was an African-American male, maybe about twenty years old. He lay on his back on the gritty ground, his right eye open and gazing at the cold sky, a clouded red hole where his left eye had been. The bullet had shattered the back of his skull, whose contents had leaked onto the pavement.

Whoever had shot him had probably known him, Tom thought. No sign of flight, and the shooter had gotten right up close. It seemed, too, like the shooter had been about the same height as the victim. The medical examiner would have to see, but it looked to Tom like the bullet had gone pretty evenly right in through the eye and out through the back of the head, no angle of entry up or down. And the killer was confident, taking his man down in the middle of the night right in the middle of the complex. Dozens of people had probably heard, and possibly seen, the shooting. Tom's experience in these communities told him that few, if any, would talk about it.

A thick gold earring was still in the kid's right ear. It looked like his ragged left lobe had healed from where it had once been torn.

"How many kids in this city are missing part of an ear?" the cop asked Tom. "Probably a few."

"Any identifying information?" Tom asked.

"Nothing," the cop said. "No wallet, no Boy Scout ID card, no nothing."

Tom sighed. The medical examiner's white van had arrived, and technicians were unloading a collapsible gurney. "We'll run his prints."

TWENTY

Tom Hogan had an errand to run in McLean, so it wasn't too far out of his way to go to Anne Lorelli's home after he finished at headquarters. Anne looked less than pleased when she opened her front door to let him in. She had a newspaper under her arm and a mug of tea in her hand.

"Can I help you?" she asked. "Is something wrong?"

"I'm sorry to trouble you," Tom said. He should have just called her. "There's been a development that may have a bearing on your case."

"Oh?" Anne said. "Won't you come in?"

They sat in the same chairs as they had when Tom had questioned her right after the funeral. He wondered if Anne herself had had any questions about her husband, if she had rifled through any underwear drawers or checked any files, wondering if her husband's murder was something more than a mugging. He doubted it. She seemed so complacent. He hated complacency.

Tom told Anne about the body in the housing project. "I need you to come to the morgue to identify if this is the man who shot your husband," he said flatly. "Normally we would never do this. Normally you would just look at photos. But this guy didn't have a wallet on him, no cute little Kodak photo album in his pocket. We haven't even been able to identify him, so we have no family to contact, and so there's no one to give us any pictures of him when he was alive.

"We took pictures of the body, but they didn't turn out. All they look like is a dead guy. You can't distinguish his features at all.

"So I need you to come to the morgue," he repeated. "You're the only one who can tell us if this is the same man who shot your husband. It's highly unorthodox, but lately in D.C. a lot of stuff we do is highly unorthodox."

Anne looked at him in disbelief. "I'm sorry, but you've got to be kidding," she said slowly. "That night it was dark. I couldn't really see the guy; the only detail was the torn ear. My husband was killed. Isn't that enough? Why do I have to get pulled into things like going to look at some dead guy I don't even know?"

Tom leaned toward her. "I know this is very difficult," he said, brushing his hand straight back through his hair, which was so fine that it all fell back exactly where it had been before. "But the fact is, you were the victim of a crime. There's nothing we can do to erase that. And the wrong done you didn't just end the night of the shooting. It goes on, even as we find the men who did it and bring them to justice. If and when that happens, you'll need to testify in court. That will be very difficult too.

"I'm really sorry this happened to you, but it's not like we can just deal with it without bothering you any more. We need to solve this case, and that means that you may have to put yourself into some situations that are difficult."

He looked at Anne. He felt for her, but her helplessness irritated him, igniting a perverse spark that wanted her to realize that life could be ugly, that, yes, even nice people from McLean could have their lives turned upside down and scattered on the sidewalk—and then you had to deal with the mess. People like Anne Lorelli made him mad. It was as if they were addicted to control, and if anything happened outside the parameters of the addiction, they just went into denial.

"Well?" he asked. "It will help us if we know that this guy in the morgue is the same man who shot your husband."

Anne looked up. "How will it help? It's not like he's quite able to tell you where the other guy is. It seems to me that you *want* me to go to the morgue, you want to rock my boat a little."

He seemed to assume she was too weak to handle whatever was at the morgue. He was like Paul, telling her she'd never be able to tutor at the learning center. It made her mad. "Well, I'll be happy to go," Anne said defiantly. "I've been doing a lot of sightseeing lately, but I just haven't made it to the morgue yet."

"Okay," Tom said, ignoring her sarcasm. "Thank you. We'll do it tomorrow. I'll take you there if you can meet me at police headquarters at noon."

THE MORGUE WAS IN southeast Washington, near D.C. General Hospital. As they drove toward it, Tom turned to Anne. "You may need to prepare yourself," he said. "Have you ever been to a morgue before?"

Anne shook her head. "No," she said. "Most people haven't."

He smiled as he pulled the car around a broken-down bus in the street. "That's true," he said. "It's not exactly a Washington tourist attraction."

"That could be an idea," Anne said, her nervousness making her chatty. "You know, they used to have that Washington scandal tour, where a bus would take people to the spot where that congressman drove his car, with the exotic dancer in the front seat, right into the Tidal Basin. Or the town house on Capitol Hill where some senator had some assignation with some woman, or the spot on the Capitol steps where Congressman What's-his-name and his wife enjoyed marital relations."

"Yeah," Tom said. "Or they could have the morgue tour, or the drive-by shootings tour, the crack-house tour. It's like there are two Washingtons. There's the one that all the tourists come to see, and then there's the other Washington that's falling apart.

"You know, there was an article in the *Washington Post* about this morgue we're going to see. The mayor came with a bunch of aides and media people. You know what he said? 'The dead need to be treated with dignity even though they're dead.'

"Okay, I mean, that's a no-brainer, we're all for the dead being treated with dignity. But what this morgue needs is about three million dollars' worth of renovations. But the mayor doesn't have that, because the city is bankrupt. It's not like dignity comes free."

"How can you deal with dead people all the time?" Anne asked abruptly.

"It's like anything else," Tom said. "You get used to it. You start looking at things clinically. Dead bodies are fascinating, actually, because they can tell you so much not only about the way a person died, but how he lived. You know, you can examine the liver and see signs of alcohol abuse, or the lungs and see what smoking did to them, or look at calluses on their hands or elbows, and you can tell what repetitive actions a person had done most of his life.

"Or tan lines, or stomach contents, or hair. A blood or urine test will tell you if someone has used drugs or alcohol within a certain recent time period. But you test somebody's hair, and you can see if he's a habitual, longtime user.

"Anyway, I like the problem solving of the whole thing, the reconstruction of who did what to whom. The only thing that skews it, though, is that human behavior has gotten so skewed. It used to be that even with crimes of passion, you could figure out motivations. Now some of these kids popping each other off defy that. It's like they're totally random in why they do what they do.

"But for the most part, though, I guess the crimes still boil down to basic human drives—greed, jealousy, rage. The basics."

Before, he said the mugging was random, Anne thought. *Now it's just random greed. Some kids wanted what Paul had, and they killed him to get it.* She changed the subject.

"Do you have family in the area?" she asked Tom Hogan.

He looked back at her. He had been staring at the traffic as he drove, his mind still clicking away on what he needed to pursue about Paul Lorelli. But it didn't seem useful to question Anne; it was clear she was oblivious to some of her husband's basic human drives.

"My parents are in Pennsylvania," he said. "I have a brother in Reston and two sisters in North Carolina. My wife and my son were killed a few years ago. They were visiting my wife's parents, and their plane went down. The FAA still doesn't know what caused that crash."

"Oh, I'm so sorry," said Anne. "I didn't realize—" She stopped. She hadn't realized that Tom Hogan could have been married. He seemed so businesslike, so focused, so unemotional. *What would you expect?* she said to herself. *He's a detective working on a case; it's not like you're on a date or something.*

"I'm sorry," she said again. "That must have been a terrible shock for you."

"It was," he said.

They rode in silence for some time. Tom pulled into the morgue parking lot. "Just brace yourself," he said. "Take shallow breaths. Don't look around. We'll just do the ID and then go."

They came into the morgue's main room, and Anne's stomach heaved. There was a heavy, foul smell that stuck in her throat, along with the dim smell of something that reminded her of ninth-grade biology class, when she and Molly had had to dissect long-dead frogs.

Tom looked down at her. She hadn't realized he was so tall. "Are you all right?" he asked. She nodded, even as she watched three cockroaches crawl across a stainless steel autopsy table. Her eyes flicked to a stack of plastic receptacles about the size of Chinese carryout containers. Each was labeled with black marker scrawl: Brain. Brain. Brain. On top of the stack was a plastic plate with a half-eaten sandwich and a long dill pickle on it. A cockroach was marching up the tile wall toward the plate.

"Just stand here for a second," Tom said. "I'll be right back." He headed toward the far end of the room, where several people were standing. Anne looked down at the floor. At intervals were drains, some of which were clogged with thick, red fluid.

Anne closed her eyes and tried to think about the Chesapeake Bay or Skyline Drive or the Swiss Alps—anywhere but here.

Tom came back with a young technician in tow. "Okay," he said. "Our man is in the freezer."

They came to the freezer.

"All right," said the technician. "You come right on in. We got fifty-nine bodies in here. Some of them have been here for a while. We got a backlog—folk that nobody has claimed, so usually what we do is go ahead and put them in the crematorium after the waiting period is over, but the crematorium's been broken for about a month now, so the folk in here are starting to pile up."

Shivering already, Anne looked around the freezer. It was lined with gurneys that looked like body-length metal shelving on wheels, four tiers high, with sheet-wrapped bodies lying on each. They were tied and tagged at the feet, scrawled with numbers written with a black marker. *If I see any half-eaten sandwiches on any of these, I'm going to throw up,* Anne thought.

"Okay," said the technician. "You need Mr. 59190-10, if my paperwork is right. He's right over here."

Anne followed Tom and the other man, as in a dream, over to a

168

single gurney that sat near the middle of the room. The technician pulled back the plastic that had covered the corpse's face.

Anne closed her eyes for a moment, then looked down at the dead man in the cooler. It was as if her thoughts and emotions were frozen as well. This was ridiculous. She felt a spark of anger also. Why in the world was she having to do this? But it was too cold for the anger to ignite, and then she just felt dead, too.

The man's face was dark ash, flat-looking, with gray undertones, his lips the same color as his face, both his eyelids closed, the left one a bit sunken. Anne stared, remembering the torn earlobe, and there it was, but otherwise there was nothing, really, that connected with the night of Paul's shooting, except this guy was dead and so was Paul.

She looked up at Tom and smoothed back a piece of hair that had fallen over her eyes. Her arm was shaking. "It's like I told you before," she said. "When my husband was shot it was dark. I was terrified. I don't remember anything about the guy's face, except that his earlobe was ragged, like someone had torn an earring from it and then it had healed roughly without being stitched up. Just like this here." She gestured down at the corpse without looking at it.

"Otherwise I can't identify this person. He's black, he's the right age, he's got the ear thing, but I didn't notice anything more about him that night, and I sure can't tell anything else about him now."

"Okay," Tom said. "You aren't positive this was the guy, but you aren't saying that it's not the guy."

Anne paused, her frozen brain working its way through his double negatives. "Right."

TWENTY-ONE

LATER, TOM HOGAN ESCORTED Anne out of the building. She was still shaking. "Are you going to be all right?" he asked.

Anne frowned and said nothing. She felt like she'd never get the smell of the morgue out of her hair.

"Are you okay?" Tom repeated. "You can stay here for a while if you need to."

"No, I can't," Anne said, her teeth clenched. "I have to go to my tutoring session."

"Tutoring?" Tom said, smiling in a falsely interested way that made Anne seethe. It was like he was humoring her. "What kind of class are you taking?" he asked.

Anne looked up at him. *I really despise the way you put me down,* she thought.

"Basket weaving," she said cheerfully, taking her headband off, flipping her hair back, and then smoothing the band back in place. "It's really been great for me. It's a new form of therapy for crime victims."

Tom just looked at her, his eyebrows furrowed, and then Anne regretted her sarcastic tone. It had been a luxury. "I'm sorry," she said.

"I don't know why I'm so ugly today. This whole thing," she jerked her head toward the morgue, "has really gotten to me."

Then Tom got mad. "Of course it has," he exploded. He kept his voice down, but his green eyes were cold as he spoke deliberately to Anne, each sentence an indictment. "It would get to anyone. I have never seen anything like your response to this crime. I've never seen anyone like you. You hold everything inside—real, normal emotions that real people have in response to crime and violence and life—and then you let it come out every once in a while for a moment, then you smooth everything over like nothing's happened.

"You know what that's called? It's passive-aggressive. You've got all this anger inside, and it comes out in strange little aggressive ways, just for a second. You attack and then you retreat like nothing happened. Were you like this before this happened to you?"

Anne stared at him, unbelieving and absolutely furious. "Wait a minute," she said, clenching her teeth. "You are way out of line. You are not my therapist. You are a detective who is supposed to be investigating this case. It's not your job to roll all over me because I don't happen to be your type of person.

"You've got the guy who mugged us, right? Hard to tell—he's dead. I know he's dead; you made me go in there to see him, all blown away. Was that part of my shock therapy? Just bill me.

"But otherwise, just find that other guy and wrap up this case and leave me alone. Everything's upside down for me, and I don't need people like you who I don't even know making it worse."

Her voice was trembling. She stopped and pulled her keys out of the side flap of her leather purse, then remembered, too late, that her car was back at police headquarters, where she'd met Tom. She looked around wildly. A miracle! There was a yellow cab, cruising down the street. She waved her arms up and down. It stopped.

"So if you'll excuse me," she said to Tom, her voice still shaking,

"I have to go to my tutoring session. I have a class of five-year-olds at the Jubilee Community Church who are waiting for me. And they'll actually be happy to see me, just like I'm sure you'll be happy to see me go."

She ripped open the cab's rear door and climbed in. The driver turned toward her, smiling, his arm over the seat. He wore a turban and nodded enthusiastically when she gave him the church address, but he evidently didn't speak enough English to make conversation. *Thank God for that*, Anne thought as the cab screeched away from the curb. She hated being late, and she was late, and she hated Tom Hogan for making her angry and making her late, and she hated this whole thing for ever happening. *I will not think about this any more right now. Maybe later.*

She took some deep breaths, willing herself to let it all flow away.

AT THE LEARNING CENTER, LaVon Webb was sitting with Anne's kids in the turret, the group clustered around him while he read to them from a big picture book. Anne stood outside the doorway and looked at him, his face dark against the warm light of the bay window. She thought about the young black man lying in the morgue freezer. She looked up and down the corridor, hearing the voices from different classrooms, little kids learning about computers and science and geography. She shook her head.

Just then Sherah turned and saw her. "Miss Anne!" she shouted. "We were worrying about you! You never been late before!"

Anne came into the yellow room, put her purse on the top bunk, and went over to the kids in the circle. "LaVon, thanks so much for filling in," she said. "Do you want to keep going? I can just sit here and listen too." *That would be an absolute pleasure today*, she thought. She couldn't even remember what story she had planned to tell the kids.

"Oh, no, Miss Anne," Sherah said, rolling her eyes at LaVon. "You let him go back to math class or wherever he came from. He skips pages and his book's not as good as your stories."

"Well," said LaVon. "You just wait 'til I get you in math." He grinned at Sherah and got up. "Anne, you can have them."

Anne sat on the cushioned window seat, her mind blank. She looked at the kids in front of her.

"You know what?" she said brightly. "My brain is on vacation today, and so we're going to have a special treat. Instead of my telling you a story, today you get to tell stories to me!"

She looked expectantly around the semicircle, her eyebrows up. They weren't buying it. A little boy named Jawan politely raised his hand.

"Yes, Jawan?" Anne chirped. "Do you want to tell the first story?"

"Nope," he said. "Forget it. You're the one who's supposed to tell the stories."

Anne sighed. "Doesn't anyone want to tell one?"

They all just looked up at her, shaking their heads solemnly from side to side. Even Sherah.

"Okay," Anne said, giving up. "I'll tell a story. But you may not like it."

"Once upon a time, long ago," she began, "the king and queen of a faraway land set out to sea with their six children, twin boys and four girls. Day by day the warm winds blew, and the ship sailed to the east.

"But then one day the skies grew dark and a great storm arose.

"Queen Prunella and King Prospero huddled with their children belowdecks. 'Children,' the good king shouted. 'If we must abandon ship, remember this: we are not far from an island. The sailors say there is a great lighthouse there. If we should get separated, steer for the lighthouse.'

"'Yes, Father,' the children chimed.

"Soon the ship began to sink. Prince Hatwink got into one life raft with two of the young princesses; Prince Fredrik got into the other with the other two sisters. They lashed the rafts together.

"The winds eventually calmed, and the children fell asleep.

"A few hours later, while it was still dark, Prince Hatwink awoke. He heard the faint sound of music and singing and the crash of breakers on a beach.

"He sat up in the raft, rubbed his eyes, and looked toward the sound. He saw what looked like the glow of a big light in the distance.

"He called to his brother in the other raft. 'Fredrik, do you hear the music?'

"'I do,' his brother responded. 'And I see what looks like a big bonfire.'

"'Father told us to steer toward the lighthouse,' said Prince Hatwink. 'He didn't say anything about a fire.'

"He looked in the distance, way to the left of the fire, and saw a faint glimmer of a small, steady light. He blinked. Could it be the lighthouse? It looked so small. The fire looked so bright.

"The royal princesses slept on, and the two boys paddled toward the lights. As they got closer, the music was rollicking. They could smell the aroma of roasting meats. Their empty stomachs rumbled.

"Prince Hatwink looked to the north, and the small, steady light shone on.

"'I think we must paddle to the north,' he said to his brother. 'The lighthouse is that way.'

"'No,' said Prince Fredrik. 'I'm going toward the bonfire.'

"'No!' Prince Hatwink shouted—and then there was a chopping noise in the dark, as Fredrik loosed his raft from his brother's and rowed furiously away, toward the south.

"Hatwink knew he couldn't catch his brother. He paddled toward the small light to the north.

"Eventually morning began to dawn. Prince Hatwink could make out the outlines of a tall brick lighthouse.

"He brought the small lifeboat into shore and woke up his sisters. The children got out of the boat and into the warm water lapping gently on fine, white sand.

"King Prospero was on the beach, waiting for them. 'Ah,' he shouted. 'You are safe!'

"Prince Hatwink ran to his father's arms. 'Thank God you followed my instructions,' King Prospero sobbed.

"'Some of the life rafts didn't steer toward the lighthouse. They headed toward the other end of the island. There was a band of pirates there. They had made a great party, trying to draw us toward them. But then they robbed and killed those who were lured by the light of their fire.'

"The king paused and opened his arms wide toward the two young princesses, who were running toward him. 'But where are the other two girls?' he asked Prince Hatwink. 'And where is Prince Fredrik?'"

ANNE STOPPED. The kids were all looking up at her, their mouths slightly open.

"So where was Prince Fredrik?" asked a little boy named Jarren.

"Well," said Anne, "You tell me. What did he do?"

"He rowed toward the pirates and the party," Jarren said.

"That's right," Anne said. "He disobeyed his father. He suffered the consequences." She stopped. She sounded so dour. So conservative.

"So did he get killed?" the boy asked.

"Yes," Anne said plainly. "He got killed by the pirates."

"Was that a consequence?" Jarren asked. "What's a consequence?"

"It's like if your mom tells you not to play with matches," Anne said, "and you disobey. And a fire starts. And your house burns down. Those bad things are consequences of playing with matches."

Another kid piped up. "My big brother went to a party once, and he didn't come home. He got shot at the party. Was that a consequence?"

"Well," Anne said, thrown, "sometimes people break the rules, and bad things happen as a result. And sometimes bad things happen for no obvious reason. Sometimes people are just in the wrong place at the wrong time."

She trailed off. She had nothing to give these kids. Jordan Taylor and the others had figured out all the right answers, the carefully reasoned responses for any tough issue. All Anne felt was a vague sense of confusion.

"I'm sorry," she faltered, "but today I'm just not feeling very well. I think I need to go. I'm sure I'll feel better next time, and I'll have a really good story for you then."

She wanted to creep away, but the next thing she knew, Sherah was pulling on her sleeve. "I'm sorry you don't feel good, Miss Anne," she said, "but can you walk me to my mama's store? Maybe some ice cream will make you feel better."

AT THE STORE, Sherah disappeared into the back room to play, and Anne found herself sitting behind the front counter, sipping a Diet Coke and talking with Jackie Jones. She told Jackie about the morgue.

"Wooh," Jackie said, taking a long swallow of Coke. "I know that must have been bad. I had to ID my parents. And Vernon. It's awful."

"Well," Anne said, humbled, "I shouldn't have been so upset by it, but I've never done anything like that in my life. And I feel like that detective enjoyed putting me through it, like it was a little exercise for his entertainment. I don't think he likes me."

"Why wouldn't he like you?"

"I don't know," Anne said, staring off toward the shelves near the store's ceiling, where Jackie stocked mousetraps and roach killer. "You know how sometimes people don't really know you, they just seem to judge you and decide what you're like based on what you look like?"

Jackie stared at Anne, a huge grin on her face. "Are you kidding?" she asked. "You ever been black?"

Anne's hand flew over her mouth. "Oh, I'm sorry," she said. "That's not what I meant."

"Why are you saying you're sorry?" Jackie asked. "I know you weren't talking about color. But I do know how you feel, if you're talking about people sizing you up by looking at you. I've lived all my life in this neighborhood, but you should see what it's like to step out of here sometimes and feel people judge you because of the color of your skin, not by who you are inside."

Anne thought about what she had meant, how she felt like Tom Hogan dismissed her because she dressed a certain way and had a certain lifestyle and didn't know how much her phone bill was each month. *Why does he get under my skin?* she thought. *I think it's because I think he thinks I'm stupid. Maybe he's right.*

"Jackie," Anne said. "How do you deal with that? I mean, don't you get angry when people judge you without knowing you?"

"I used to be angry all the time," Jackie said. "I didn't know what to do with it. If I stopped and thought about stuff, I would feel all these things filling up inside of me, nowhere to put them, and that's part of why I was always doing drugs. It made everything go far away; it blurred the edges.

"Or depending on what I was doing, sometimes a good high would make me feel like I could handle anything, like I was Tiger Woman, just let me at 'em, whoever they are, and I'll come out on top. And then I'd come down, and the feelings would be worse than ever, so then I'd have to do some more stuff, just to get away again. It never ended."

"But what do you do with those feelings now?" Anne asked. "Did they go away after you went through the, uh, program?"

"No," Jackie said. "That's one thing I learned. Those feelings are always going to be there. Life's a mess. That doesn't change. What changed was me and how I deal with the mess and the feelings. And I didn't change myself, you know, like I got into the power of positive thinking or something. Jesus changed me."

Anne drew back and took a sip of Diet Coke. She liked Jackie. She was refreshing. But she hated it when Jackie talked about Jesus. It made Anne so uncomfortable. Most people she knew, if they talked about religion at all, referred to a Higher Power, or used vague New Age terms straight from the bestseller list.

Or they talked about angels: angels protecting them in car accidents or on the ski slope or surrounding their homes when the security system was on the blink. Angels had become acceptable in the last few years. But it seemed so invasive, so rude, to talk about Jesus.

But Jackie didn't care.

"The thing is," she went on, "Jesus saved me from myself. I was locked up so tight I couldn't escape, and He set me free. He saved me from my sins by dying on the cross. He rose from the dead. He gave me eternal life so I can live forever. And then to top it off, He helps me live every day down here in this mess by the power of the Holy Spirit!" She started swaying with her inner music, and her face looked far away.

Anne smiled in spite of herself. She had never seen anyone so happy to have religion. It wasn't a social cause or a political posture or a self-help device. Jackie Jones just loved Jesus. And in that, ever so slightly, Anne envied her abandon.

TWENTY-TWO

ANNE WOKE SLOWLY the next morning. She lay still as the wave of her dream receded and swept back into the ocean of sleep, depositing her on the warm shore of her bed, her blond hair strewn on the pillow and the white cotton sheets pulled up to her chin.

She opened her eyes and focused on the big Chippendale mirror opposite the bed. If the angle was just right, she could see the reflection of the print hanging on the wall above her head, a soft watercolor of magnolia blossoms.

What a frustrating dream, she thought. In it, she had been at Jackie Jones's store, counting cans of vegetables, going up and down the narrow aisles, the manicured white tip of her fingernail precisely tapping the ridged edge of each can, noting the paper labels' pictures of yellow corn and hominy and the green beans chopped on the diagonal into neat one-inch lengths.

Then she came to the end of the aisle, where Jackie had arranged an immense pyramid of Campbell's soup cans. Anne knelt on the floor, counting the bottom row, and then worked her way up, past tomato and cream of mushroom and chicken alphabet and old-fashioned vegetable, up almost to the very top of the triangle—and then Tom Hogan came through the front door. Anne heard the bells on the door tinkle as he entered. He took a big gun out of his pocket and left it on the front counter. Then he came to Anne, who was standing on her tiptoes, gently tapping each red-and-white label as she counted. "I've got to get it right," she said.

And then Tom had shouted at her.

"Anne!"

And she had jumped and turned, her arm brushing against the top of the pyramid, and the rows of cans wobbled and crashed to the ground, rolling over the black and white squares of the floor, under the shelves, into the corners.

In her dream Anne had started to pick up the cans, but every time she put one back in the pile, it would fall off and crash into another. She couldn't get them into order. And Tom Hogan just stood there, eating a Nutty Buddy, and then Jackie Jones picked up Tom's gun and started firing at the cans like she was at target practice. Anne had just kept trying to pick up cans, but finally they had all been blasted to pieces, and then Tom Hogan finished his Nutty Buddy and told her it was all just a dream, and she thought he meant that Paul's murder was a dream, and that had made her feel confused, because she wasn't sure she really wanted Paul to come back, and that had made her feel so guilty. Then she realized, no, Paul was really dead, but the can-counting episode was just a dream, and for some reason that was a comfort. And then she woke up and was guilty all over again.

Anne stretched and looked out the big window next to the bed. *Why am I dreaming about Tom Hogan?* she thought. *What day is it? Saturday.* The skies outside looked full and gray, pregnant with snow.

She got out of bed and rummaged in the big closet. Her warm blue robe was in the laundry, but the one Paul had gotten her last spring was hanging on a fat hanger near the back, along with some cocktail dresses and knit suits she rarely wore. The robe was heavy, white terrycloth, with the blue-and-white Ritz Carlton lion logo stitched on the top pocket. Paul had gone to the Ritz in Rancho Mirage for a conference and brought back matching robes for the two of them. Anne hadn't worn hers. It had been too heavy for the spring and summer, and then she had forgotten about it. It would feel good today.

She put it on and walked into the master bath, tying the belt around her waist, and then felt something in the right front pocket. She fished it out. It was a small cigarette lighter, slender, in a brushed-gold finish, with script initials engraved in the center, like a monogram: MLG.

Anne stared at the heavy gold rectangle in her hand. She opened it, flicked it with some difficulty, and a small flame leapt up, difficult to see in the bright lights of the white-tiled bathroom.

Her stomach clenched, and then she deliberately walked to Paul's side of the long, double-sinked counter, opened his medicine cabinet, and shoved the lighter in, next to the shaving cream and razor that she still had not thrown away. She slammed the mirrored door. She would not think about the lighter now. She brushed and flossed her teeth. And then she took off the big robe and stuffed it into the bathroom's too-small trash can.

By 10:00, THE SNOW had started. Big, lazy, lacy flakes settled on the brick patio in Anne's backyard and clustered on the holly trees by the front bay window. Anne had put on a pair of jeans and a big red Christmas sweater. Her hair was pulled back in a ponytail, and she had stuck a big gold bow with silver stars in it for fun; she knew Molly's children would like it. She had pulled out candles of bayberry and cinnamon, and those holiday smells had compelled her to the sound system, where she found the Christmas CDs—mostly George Winston piano arrangements and an old Mel Torme holiday collection that she knew Molly loved, even though Mel Torme gave Anne the willies.

Anne's father had come by the night before and helped her get the Christmas tree set up in its stand. It was a Frasier fir, full and straight, with silver-blue undersides to its short-needled branches. Its fragrance made Anne nostalgic for Christmases long ago, when the magic was still real.

She pulled out boxes of ornaments, all the matching balls that Paul had bought, those uniform, polished golden globes, exactly enough to ensure the precise and symmetrical decoration of a nine-foot Christmas tree. And then there were the cardboard boxes of the old ornaments Anne loved best: the red crocheted stocking that had hung on the pet parakeet's cage when she was five, the lumpy Santa Claus she had made from salt-and-flour dough when she was nine, the star-spangled photo-ornaments of each of Molly's children when they were babies, the Charles Dickens *Christmas Carol* advent calendar whose numbered doors had counted down the days for many a Christmas past.

Every year she rediscovered them all, amazed that frail cardboard hinges could open the doors of memory, that old red yarn could become a fragile rope-bridge, swaying delicately over the deep gulf of the decades, linking the child-Anne of long-ago Christmases to the Anne of Christmas present.

This year Anne stared at the ornaments for a long time, thinking how strange it was, too, that the old dough from her childhood had survived another year, and that her husband's handsome flesh and bone had not.

A few minutes later there was the sound of wild honking outside. Anne went to the front door. The O'Kelleys' car was idling in the driveway. Molly had gotten out and was standing with her head through the open window of the driver's side, kissing Clark good-bye. One of her purple gloves had fallen out of her pocket onto the new snow.

Molly turned and bounded up the brick steps toward Anne.

"Be careful," Anne called, waving at Clark. "Those are getting slippery."

"Don't worry," Molly said, putting her booted heel right on a patch of ice. Her foot went out from under her, and she grabbed hard for the black iron railing lining the steps and managed to stay upright, swinging and swaying on the rail.

"Oh!" she shouted. "That reminds me. I forgot the soup." She edged carefully back to the van, retrieved her purple glove, and Clark handed her a black cauldron through the window. Holding its handles with two potholders, she inched back toward the front door.

"Clark and the kids are going to the mall at Tyson's," she said. "That'll give us time to decorate your tree before they come back for lunch, and they can buy all the Mommy presents without me around. I'm hoping for great stuff. Here, I'll just put the soup in the kitchen on the stove."

They were about halfway through decorating the tree and halfway through Anne's account of her trip to the morgue, when the doorbell chimed.

"That can't be Clark and the kids," Molly said. "It'll take them much longer to choose my presents. They'll have to argue about each one for a while."

Anne went toward the front door. She had a star garland draped around her neck and some silver glitter in her hair, but it was probably just a UPS delivery person. She unlocked the door and swung it open, and there was Tom Hogan, snow in his brown hair, his hands in his pockets, and his collar turned up against the cold.

"Uhhh," Anne said, searching in her brain for something more gracious to say. She did not want to see Tom Hogan after yesterday's blowup, and here he was, invading her space.

"Uhhh," she repeated, then said the first thing that popped in her mind. "Do you want me to go to the morgue again?"

"No," Tom said. "Their freezer broke down last night. Today they're probably storing people in the parking lot if it's cold enough. Which it seems to be. I think we can skip the morgue for a while." He waited.

Anne said nothing, imagining gurneys lined up in the morgue parking lot, with the snow gently drifting down on unfeeling faces.

Tom coughed. "Do you think I might be able to step inside for a moment? It's really cold out here, and your steps are a broken leg waiting to happen." He smiled, and Anne warmed toward him. If he had come to torment her some more, he would have been more serious.

"I'm sorry," she said. "Please, come in."

She ushered him into the foyer and took his long trenchcoat. He wiped his shoes on the doormat there and then slipped them off and placed them next to Molly's boots, which were drying on a thick towel near a heat vent.

Anne looked at him for a moment, her eyebrows up. How long was he planning to stay? Then she remembered the basics. "Please, come into the living room," she said. "We're just decorating the Christmas tree. This is my friend, Molly O'Kelley. Molly, this is Detective Tom Hogan. You've heard me mention Mr. Hogan; he's one of the investigators working on Paul's case."

Molly appeared from behind the tree, some sap and needles stuck in her hair. She had slipped two of the biggest gold ornaments into her pierced ears while Anne was answering the door. They bobbled gently around her shoulders as she moved toward Tom, her right arm stretched out toward him. "Hi, Detective Hogan, it's great to meet you. Anne has told me about you. We certainly appreciate everything you're doing to solve Paul's case."

Tom grinned and shook Molly's hand. "I'm glad to meet you," he said. "Please, call me Tom."

Anne, meanwhile, had remembered that she was wearing the silver star garland like a jaunty neck decoration and was trying to remove it surreptitiously before Tom turned his attention back to her. *Why is he here?* she thought.

Tom turned toward her just as she got the loop of the star garland stuck on her ponytail. "Oh, that's nice, Anne. You look like Santa Lucia," Molly said helpfully. "All you need are some candles."

Anne ripped the garland from her hair. "Well, Tom, it's a surprise to see you today. How can I help you? Would you care for some tea?"

"Or cocoa?" Molly added. "Or a nice cup of arsenic? What is it like investigating all those murders? I remember reading in the paper about you and the Taft investigation and those nice young boys putting arsenic in their mom's milkshake."

"Molly," Anne said, shooting eye-daggers toward her friend. Molly hated conventional interaction about the weather and the Redskins and other normal topics. She had an incredible ability to dredge inappropriate details from the past to jump-start more eccentric conversations. Anne was just glad she hadn't yet finished telling Molly about yelling at Tom after the morgue visit; Molly would have brought that into the conversation by the third sentence.

"I'm sure Detective Hogan is very busy," she said primly. "He's probably just stopped by on official business. We don't really need to quiz him about heavy metal toxins. Now, please, Tom, may I get you a cup of tea? Coffee?" She paused. "Cyanide?"

She couldn't help it. Something about the combination of Molly, Tom, and the Christmas tree made her feel out of control.

Tom stared at her. Molly stood slightly behind him, her golden ear-globes dangling, her eyes dancing, egging Anne on.

"Cyanide would be just fine, thank you," Tom said. "Anne, the reason I'm here is that I need to apologize to you."

Molly's eyebrows shot up. Anne could tell she was getting dangerous.

"Molly," she said. "Listen, would you mind just giving us a few minutes?"

"Oh, sure," Molly said. "I'll just go downstairs and, uh, put some things in the dryer. If you need me I'll be listening on the stairs. Just kidding!"

Tom looked behind him and sank into one of the blue wingbacks. Anne did the same.

"I'm sorry about yesterday," he said. "I was very unprofessional with you. You had been through a difficult experience, and I certainly had no right to engage in personal matters. I'm very sorry."

Anne sat for a moment. She didn't know what to say. "I appreciate your coming here," she said. "It's very kind of you to apologize. I'm sorry I got so upset. I rarely lose my temper like that."

"Well," Tom said. "If I respond to that, we might get into the same discussion all over again. Maybe you should allow yourself to get mad more often—but that's really none of my business.

"You know," he continued, "there are some victims' support groups in the area, and it might be good for you to plug into something like that. It may be that things are going to get worse for you before they get better."

"How can they get any worse?" Anne muttered. "I mean, I know eventually testifying in court will be horrible, but at least that might bring some closure to all this . . ." She trailed off.

Tom nodded. He wanted to plant some seeds with her, but he could see that she wasn't going to anticipate any new revelations this case might bring.

"Well," he said. "I really don't want to take up any more of your time. You have company. But I did want to let you know I'm sorry for my behavior yesterday. It won't happen again."

Anne looked at him, thinking how soothing, how foreign, such an apology was. *That's the thing about me,* she thought. *I'll forgive anything if someone just tells me he's sorry. Maybe that's why I say 'I'm sorry' so much. I just want to hear it.*

Paul had rarely apologized for anything. Early on in their relationship, if they had a difference, he would just smooth it over with a joke or a dozen roses. Later, when the polite tension began to crack, he would just leave the room, or hang up the phone, and appear hours later without apology or explanation. And so they would continue on. In her darker flights of fancy, Anne had sometimes thought she was like a ghoul from an old horror movie, staggering along, decaying yet refusing to lie down and die, except that she took care to look good. She shook her head slightly, then realized with a start that Tom Hogan was staring at her.

"Why is it that people don't apologize more often?" she asked Tom abruptly. She could sense Molly lurking on the stairs, dying to come out on that one. "I can't remember the last time someone really apologized to me."

"Didn't your husband ever say he was sorry?" Tom asked, then bit his tongue.

"For what?" Anne asked inanely.

The doorbell rang again. "I'll get it," Molly chimed from the hallway. She opened the door and Clark and the kids poured in, sounding like a crowd far larger than four. "Mommy!" shrieked Amelia, "You won't believe what we got for you!"

"Shhhh," seven-year-old Lincoln shouted. "It's a secret! If you tell, we'll put you out in the forest and wolves will eat you!"

"Lincoln!" Molly sputtered. "Where did you hear something like that?"

"From Dad," Lincoln said.

"Anne!" Amelia shouted. She ran into the living room, her pink plastic boots making a wet trail on the pale carpet. Anne opened her arms wide and scooped her up. "We got you some presents too! Mommy gave us a list! I love your bow!"

"That's wonderful," Anne told Amelia. "I want lots of really big presents. Huge. Enormous. Gigantic."

Clark had taken off his shoes and was striding into the room, his hand extended in his best Capitol Hill style.

"Hi," he said to Tom Hogan. "I'm Clark O'Kelley. I go with the living Christmas tree here." He gestured toward Molly, who had augmented the golden ornaments in her ears by draping a holly-crown around her head.

"Clark, this is Detective Tom Hogan," Anne said. "He just stopped by to correct some details of, uh, police procedure."

"Great," Clark said. "Listen, is lunch ready? The mall was packed, and the kids are starving, and I'm going to die if I don't eat. Is the tree done?"

"Does it look done?" Molly asked. "We've been working on it, okay, but it's not like we have to finish it at a certain time, you know."

"Especially if you've spent half the time decorating yourselves," Clark said. "Tom, why don't you stay for lunch? We're having this German sausage soup that's sort of a tradition with us, and some herb bread—we've got plenty."

"Great idea!" Molly said.

"I really shouldn't," Tom said. "I just planned to stop by for a minute. I've got a lot to do, and the snow looks like it's getting worse. I should get home."

Anne thought about going home to an empty home. She had done it too much herself lately, and it didn't seem right for Tom to do it with the snow falling and Christmas coming. "No," she said, surprising herself. "Please do stay with us. We'd love to have you. Just stay for a while and have some hot soup. It only has a little arsenic in it."

FIVE HOURS LATER, Anne stood with Tom on the brick walkway in front of the town house. As darkness had fallen, it had gotten colder. The snowflakes were still falling, but they were tiny now, and fine, like points of glittering confetti in the streetlight. The Christmas tree glowed in the big front bay window, its tiny white lights reflected in the glass, the window panes dark mirrors in the night.

"Thank you for coming," Anne said, not quite knowing what to think. At the lunch table, it was as if Tom had decided to put aside his investigator role. She had imagined him opening his wallet, taking out the police ID, and leaving it on the table. *Like my dream,* she thought, *when he left his gun on the counter.* Then he had eaten three bowls of soup. He and Clark had argued about the space program, waxed eloquent on fly-fishing, and had harassed Molly whenever she deserved it. Amelia had spent much of the afternoon trying to climb up on Tom's back while he helped finish decorating the tree. *Did Amelia ever climb on Paul's back?* she wondered, and then stopped herself, horrified.

"Thank you for all your help," she said again. "You've been most kind."

"Well," he said. "Thank you. I certainly didn't realize this would turn into an all-day visit. Good thing I wasn't working overtime. Not that D.C. could pay me if I was."

"Oh," Anne said lightly. "You could put this afternoon down as part of your continuing investigation. You know."

Tom looked down at Anne in the swirling glint of snowflakes. She still had some stars from the garland stuck in her hair, but she didn't realize it. Her eyes looked a much darker blue than usual.

The clues in this case don't add up, he thought. *There's more than meets the eye here.* And in spite of her appearances, it was the same with Anne Lorelli.

"Thank you again for today and for your help yesterday," he said. "I'll be in touch with you if anything else comes up."

"Wonderful," Anne said, her mind suddenly flipping back to the dill pickle on the plastic plate on top of the containers of brains at the morgue. "Thank you again for the lovely time at the morgue. Do call me when you can get clearance for us to visit the sewage treatment plant!"

TWENTY-THREE

A FEW DAYS LATER, Tom Hogan sat in a side room at police headquarters, watching quietly as the young girl in front of him wept into her arms, head down over the laminated table. A policewoman walked the perimeter of the room, gently rocking the infant the girl had brought with her.

How is it that women just know how to rock and sway with a kid, Tom wondered briefly. He had first given the baby to Toby Jackson, a three-hundred-pound investigator who had eleven grandchildren of his own. Tom had figured that Toby would be comforting, or at least soft, so the baby could rest while her mother got control of herself. But Toby's seismic jiggles had only annoyed the infant, and he had gratefully given her over to a female colleague, who was now walking and pacing with just the right touch. It was a hip-related thing, Tom thought. His wife had done the same thing with their baby.

He waited for the girl to calm down, handing her fresh tissues whenever she lifted her head. He couldn't remember the last time something like this had happened. Occasionally he'd get a suspect who'd go over the top during questioning and admit to a killing he wasn't even under investigation for, but rarely did a female witness come in like this, ready to talk.

Usually the women behind the men in the gang wars kept quiet. They had seen how witnesses in upcoming cases got blown away, usually just before they were to testify. But there was something different about this girl. She had brought with her a bag, her baby, a bruised and bloody face, and she was angry. She was ready to talk and ready to get out of town. Tom admired her nerve.

She was a smart kid, too. She had made it clear what she wanted and how much she was willing to do. Tom wasn't sure they'd get any information that would be useful or admissible in court later, but he was intrigued. If she had anything, they could sequester her locally until trial, and after that all she wanted was a bus ticket to a little town in rural North Carolina, where she said she had an aunt who could take her in.

The girl stopped crying and lifted her head. "All right," she said. "I'm gonna talk with you today, and you can use this to do whatever you need to do. You see that baby there?"

Tom nodded. The baby had fallen asleep in the officer's capable arms.

"She's the most important thing now. I'm not gonna have her grow up here in this place. No more. No more."

Tom nodded again, reaching into his pocket. "All right," he said. "Would you like something to eat?"

He slid a Snickers bar across the table, and she unwrapped it. "Thank you," she said. She was fifteen, she had told him, with short, almost shaved hair sculpting what had been a beautiful face, with dark eyes and high cheekbones. But one eye was swollen nearly shut; there were large welts on her cheeks and deep bruises on her throat. She was short, probably about 5 foot 2 inches, and still a little chunky with the weight the baby had left on her. Her name was Tynia; she called the infant Tynelle.

"I've seen a lot," she said. "I never talked to police before, ever. But now I'm here for this baby.

"You know that boy you found dead in Eastlake Gardens?" she asked Tom.

"Yes," said Tom. Eastlake Gardens was the housing project where the torn-eared corpse had been found.

"I know who did that boy. So do a lot of other folk. He's my baby's daddy, called Jerome Brown."

"Why did he do it?" Tom asked.

"Jerome's got a terrible temper. That dead boy is somebody's cousin from Baltimore. He started hanging around with Jerome awhile ago. He's called Lobe, because of his ear. Lobe's not so smart, you know, and he came over one day and started looking at me in a way that made Jerome go crazy. So that night Jerome went over to Eastlake and blew him away, you know, through the eye so everybody would know not to look at his woman."

Tom looked down at his yellow pad. "So your boyfriend shot this Lobe guy because of you?"

"Well, sort of," said Tynia, licking her lips. "You got any more candy bars?"

Tom got up and went over to the door. Toby Jackson was lumbering by. "Toby!" he called. "Can you get us a couple of Snickers and a big cup of coffee for me? What do you want to drink, Tynia?" he called back over his shoulder.

"Coke!" she responded.

"You heard the lady," Tom smiled at Toby. "Thanks."

Toby shuffled away toward the snack room, mumbling, "I get relieved of baby-sitting so I can be a waitress?"

Tom looked back to Tynia. "'Sort of,' you say. What else? How'd you get beat up?"

"Well, last night Jerome came back real late, and he'd been out drinking and doing some stuff, you know, with some guys, and when he came back, he was over the top. I wasn't very smart, I was joking, and I said, 'So'd you shoot anybody tonight, anybody who ever looked at me for too long?' Something like that. And Jerome freaked out. I've seen him mad before. I've seen him hit people; he's hit me, but not like this. He was crazy. He was beating me, kicking me, screaming as if I'd done it with Lobe.

"And then the baby was crying. And he went over to where she was, and he picked her up by her little feet, and he went to the window and opened it with one hand and held her out over the street with the other, and he stopped screaming. He got real quiet. That was the scariest part of all, just him talking real quiet, and his eyes all dead like a vampire or something. And he said, 'You listen and you never look at anybody ever again or I'll kill you and I'll drop this baby right out the window.'

"And Tynelle was screaming and screaming, and I had blood running down my face and I couldn't get to her, like in a bad dream when you want to run but you can't move."

Tom exhaled.

Tynia blew her nose on a Kleenex. "So I said to Jerome, 'Okay, okay, anything, just get my baby inside the window.' But inside myself I was saying never again if I have to die is that going to happen to my baby.

"So I came here."

She paused, and suddenly Tom realized there was something more.

Her voice went on, the emotion drained. "Jerome killed Lobe. But he and Lobe killed that white guy awhile ago, down in Georgetown."

"How do you know that?" Tom asked.

"Jerome was already mad at Lobe before he looked at me," she said. "Jerome said Lobe was one dumb kid, that he lost a bunch of money when they killed that guy."

"Why do you say that?" Tom asked. "The man was robbed that night—"

"Yeah, and they got his watch, and Lobe broke the lady's pearls," Tynia said without much interest.

Tom's interest sparked. Those details had not been released by the police. She would have known them only if she had been there that night or if one of the perpetrators had told her.

"But Jerome was mad because they were paid to do it," she said to Tom matter-of-factly. "They weren't just out hustling some cash. It was a hit, with a big-time payment."

"You're saying it was a contract murder?" Tom asked, the hair on the back of his neck prickling. "Why?"

"Jerome told me. He didn't know who the customer was, but some guy came to him one day and set up the job. Not somebody we know. He gave him some money up front. And when it was over, even though it got screwed up, he gave them some more money to get out of town for a while. But they went through the money right away and came back."

Tom flipped his pad to a new page and prepared to start asking questions in a more orderly fashion. Just then the baby woke up and started to cry. Tynia's attention moved away from him and toward the infant.

"Wait," he said. "Why did you say Jerome was mad at Lobe for losing money on the job? If it was a paid hit, like you're telling me, it didn't get messed up. The guy got killed."

The baby quieted for a moment, the policewomen clucking over her softly. "Because," Tynia said, "they didn't get paid the rest of the money. It did get messed up. Lobe got dumb, crazy; he got mad and shot the *husband*."

She looked at Tom like he was dense. "Don't you get it? The hit was supposed to be on the *wife*."

TWENTY-FOUR

ALL RIGHT, TOM THOUGHT. *One thing at a time.* He wasn't going to tell Anne about Tynia's testimony until he had a chance to check it out. He didn't want Anne to freak out, and the first thing he needed her to do was to identify Jerome Brown. Then he'd move to the next step, though he didn't like where it looked like it was going to lead him. A few more explorations into Paul Lorelli's financial papers, and, once he found her, a nice, intimate conversation with Maria Garcia—who had moved and left no forwarding address—and it might all come together. And then he'd have to tell Anne. But for now, one thing at a time.

"You don't need to feel any sense of alarm," he said, turning toward Anne. *Well,* he thought, *maybe you do need to be alarmed, but not about this.* They were at D.C. police headquarters, looking through a one-way window into the dark, boxlike room the police used for lineups.

"Okay," Tom continued, "we'll just take it slow, one man at a time. You take as much time as you need. We can see them, but they can't see us. The window's a reverse mirror. And they can't hear us unless I've got the microphone turned on."

"Okay," Anne said. Her stomach was in a knot. She had seen police lineups in movies and on television reruns; her mind refused to accept the fact that this one was real. Surreal.

Tom flipped the mike on. "All right, I think we're ready to begin. Ma'am, you were witness to a homicide in the District of Columbia on September 8. We ask you to look at the stage. Do you see anyone there who was involved in the crime that night?"

Suddenly a spotlight flipped on, shining on the men who stood at the front of the room. They all wore similar, nondescript shirts and pants, each with a big shield around his neck with a number on it. They were all the same height, but a knee-high partition blocked Anne's view of their feet. She realized that some could be standing on boxes or something to even them out.

Anne looked at the first man on the far left of the stage. His hair was short. He wore a gold loop in one ear, and he rocked back and forth a little bit as he stood in the spotlight.

He seemed too innocuous, not like the monster in the night that she remembered.

She looked at the next man. He was dressed identically to the first, and wore a gold loop in his ear as well. But he was built differently, with huge, muscled arms that strained against the fabric of his shirt.

He looked like he spent more time working out than prowling the streets; Anne remembered what she'd read about inmates and gyms in prison. This guy had probably spent a good deal of the last few years behind bars, pumping iron every day. She knew the mugger hadn't been that enormous.

Number three seemed shorter than the man who'd accosted them. Four was too thin. Five's nose seemed too narrow, and he looked too old. Six looked too friendly.

She got to the end of the line. The last young man was a variation on the same theme as all the others. Anne scanned his face, looking for some clue, and then her heart sank. She had expected she would recognize the man who had been in the background the night Paul was shot, and yet now these men in front of her were blending together in her mind, nothing remarkable about them. Nothing to connect them to the terror of Paul's murder. *It's hopeless,* she thought.

She looked up at Tom Hogan. "I'm sorry," she quavered. "I just can't tell about these men. Do you have any more?"

Even as she said that, she envisioned herself standing in this lineup room for weeks, staring at row after row of young men until the city's black male population was exhausted and so was she. It was hopeless.

Tom looked down. He could see that she was on the edge of panic. It happened about half the time when witnesses came in for IDs.

"We're in no hurry here," he said soothingly. "Look at them again, one by one. Don't feel anxious. These guys have all the time in the world. Let your mind think back to the night your husband was shot, and just look these men over, slowly. Do you want them to do anything?"

"Like what?" Anne faltered. "Do they sing?"

"Yeah, they do show tunes," Tom said dryly. "No, if you want them to say something or turn around or whatever, they can do that for you."

"Let me just look again," Anne muttered.

She stared at the stage. They all looked as unremarkable as ever. She thought back to the night of the murder. The minutes went by.

"Could you have them turn?" Anne asked Tom.

"All of you, please turn to the right," Tom said. The men on the stage rotated.

"Now to the left," he said, watching as one of the men, who was actually a young policeman who fit Anne's description, nearly fell off the box he was standing on to make him the same height as the suspect.

"Thank you," Tom said to the group.

They turned back toward the light. The first man in line was getting antsy, shuffling a little and jerking his head with irritation. Tom could tell he was getting dangerous. That happened regularly in lineups with these young guys who had absolutely no self-control. They lived on the streets with guns in their hands, popping people off whenever they got mad. In custody they had no guns, but that didn't mean they developed any self-control. Number one was mad now, and he'd probably start yelling in a minute, even though that was going to hurt his chances to blend in with the others.

Tom looked at Anne. *Come on,* he thought. *Come on.*

The first man jerked his head a few more times, like an angry horse in a stall, and then he stared directly into the spotlight, defiant. And then he smiled.

Anne jumped back and grabbed Tom's arm, hard. "Oh!" she cried, feeling bile rise up in her throat, her mind going back to the darkness under the Whitehurst Freeway, the soft, pleasant voice of the man who spoke from the shadows so quietly. *"If you don't take them off, we can do it for you, you know."* And then he had smiled, the horror of that smile on the smooth young face with the empty eyes of a killer.

"Oh!" she cried again, gripping Tom's arm with her left hand, her right hand now cupped over her mouth. "That's him!"

"Are you certain?" Tom said. Procedure required that he ask that. But he could feel her fingernails in his arm, and he knew that she was sure. Thank God. Anne's identification meant that Jerome Brown would not be back on the streets anytime soon.

TWENTY-FIVE

I CANNOT BELIEVE THIS!" Clark O'Kelley shouted in his best voice of righteous indignation as Anne's Volvo crawled along the Dulles Airport access road. "I mean, I am fully resigned to the fact that National Airport has been under construction for the past several light-years. I can accept that. It is such a ridiculous airport. It is in the middle of the city. It deserves to always be under construction.

"When I am dead of old age and my relatives are flying into town for my funeral—for which Senator Wiggins *will* deliver the eulogy, believe me, even though he will be approximately 160 years old by then—National Airport will *still* be under construction. What else would anyone expect?

"But why in the world is Dulles Airport *also* under construction? This is immoral! It's unethical! It's ruining my Christmas vacation, which hasn't even started yet!"

"Clark!" Molly shouted from the backseat, where she was trying to wrestle her carry-on suitcase shut. "Stop! This is not a personal affront to you. This is our tax dollars at work to make a bigger, better airport for the future!"

Anne laughed as she inched the Volvo up a few more feet. Clark and Lincoln occupied the front seat, with Molly, Amelia, and Scarlett packed in the back. The traffic stretched interminably into the distance, where Anne could see a long line of cars standing still in the departure lane that led up to the airport terminal.

Construction cranes were everywhere. Huge piles of dirty snow towered at intervals on pavement streaked with red Virginia mud. The bare, girder ribs of the new terminal's curved skeleton stretched like a dinosaur carcass in the distance.

The O'Kelleys were flying to Miami for what might be a last Christmas with the family matriarch. Molly's grandmother, known to all as Baba, was eighty-eight now and in declining health, though she still loved to get into shouting matches with anyone who would take her on, waving her cane and blasting away about one nation with tobacco and guns for all.

"There!" Molly gasped from the backseat. "Got it!" She patted her bulging leather satchel. Amelia, who had been staring out the window at the clay-clodded snow mounds, suddenly spoke up.

"Is Baba going to die soon?" she asked.

"Well," Molly said, "honey, everybody dies sooner or later. Baba has had a long, full life, and at some point she is going to die. No one knows when. But you have to promise me that you won't run up to her first thing and ask her when she's going to die. Wait at least until everyone has said hello."

Clark took off his round glasses and polished them on his shirt, looking sideways past Lincoln toward Anne. "The last time we visited Baba, Amelia went right up to her, hugging her knees, saying, 'Oh, Baba, when are you going to die? You're so old!' Not the most comforting greeting in the world."

"Okay, Mama," Amelia said to Molly. "I'll wait."

The Volvo edged forward a few more inches. Clark looked at his watch and started drumming the side window with his fingertips. "You know, Anne, if you don't mind, I think we'd better go into the parking lot. It'll be quicker than waiting in the departure line for the terminal. It's not moving, and I don't think our plane is going to wait for us. In fact, if they know all the O'Kelleys are coming, it'll probably try to leave early without us. You don't need to come in, but if you could just drop us in the parking lot, that would be great."

"Oh, no," Anne said. "I'll come in with you. I can help you with luggage. It's fine."

She pulled into the left lane and toward the short-term parking. Eventually they found a baggage cart, snaked through the lines, checked their big suitcases, and headed for their gate. Anne went through the security checkpoint with the O'Kelleys; everyone boarded the mobile lounge headed for the midfield terminal.

"I like these things better than the airplane," Scarlett proclaimed. Anne smiled. She remembered when she was a little girl, how these mobile lounges—like wide subway cars on wheels—were as exotic a part of traveling to faraway places as boarding the airplane itself.

Anne and the O'Kelleys walked into the midfield terminal. Amelia clutched Anne by the hand. At the gate, a flight attendant stood at the Jetway entrance, a hand-held microphone in her hand.

"Welcome to American Airlines jetliner service to Miami, Florida, with continuing service to Lima, Peru," she said in a cheerful yet distant voice, as if she was thinking about something altogether different than her falsely hearty welcome of the passengers she had to cram onto this overbooked flight to Miami.

"At this time we'd like to ask our first-class passengers to board as well as anyone traveling with small children or anyone needing a little extra assistance."

Parked with Amelia for a moment, Anne stared absently as the first-class passengers shuffled forward. There was the usual assortment of businessmen and a young man with his hair in a slicked-back pony-tail who looked vaguely familiar, traveling with someone with a brief-case who looked like a business manager, a tanned older couple in resort wear, and then a woman about her own age with long, black hair twisted at the nape of her neck, thick black sunglasses, a long rope of pearls, an expensive leather bag over her shoulder. Anne gripped Amelia's hand hard. The woman seemed familiar; seeing her made Anne's stomach turn over. Where was she from?

"Ow, Anne, you're hurting my hand!" Amelia yelled, looking up at Anne reproachfully. "What are you doing?"

At the sound of Amelia's voice, the black-haired woman turned toward them. Anne couldn't see her eyes because of the sunglasses, but she thought she saw an odd start of recognition, and then the woman turned quickly away.

"Anne!" Amelia shouted again.

"Oh!" Anne said. "Honey, I'm sorry. I didn't mean to squeeze you so hard. I thought I saw someone I knew." She leaned down and hugged Amelia. "Have a great time in Florida. Tell Baba hello for me!"

She straightened, embraced Molly, Clark, and the others in a flurry of hugging, and watched as they gathered their stuff and moved into the clump of people waiting for the summons for ordinary passengers.

Then Molly turned back toward her. "Thank you so much for bringing us," she called softly, catching Anne's eye. "We love you. Have a great Christmas! We'll be back soon!"

Anne nodded, her eyes suddenly full of tears. She watched in a blur as the black-haired woman gave her ticket stub to the flight attendant. She walked through the doorway toward the jet, then stopped and turned back for one more second. She looked directly toward Anne, raised her eyebrows for a moment, then turned and walked onto the Jetway.

WHILE ANNE DROVE SLOWLY away from Dulles, her mind in a fog, Tom Hogan was back at police headquarters. He and Otis Jefferson had spent the morning with a witness who had put most of the pieces of the Lorelli case into place—and now Tom needed to talk with Anne. Reporters were all over the developments in this story. Depending on how many leaks there were, parts of it would be in the *Washington Post* by tomorrow. He had to get to Anne first.

Tom sipped some coffee from a Styrofoam cup, looked at his watch, and called Anne. No answer at her home; he left a terse message and wondered where he might find her. He called directory assistance, silently cursing the new computerized Bell Atlantic system, and got Clark and Molly O'Kelley's Arlington number.

No answer there, just a message in Molly's voice saying Merry Christmas and that they'd be out of town until the 27th.

That's stupid, Tom thought automatically. *Nothing like advertising to burglars that there's no one home.* He left another short message, just in case they called in, and tapped the gray phone on his forehead. He remembered that Anne's parents lived in McLean and thought for a minute, *What was her maiden name? Something Founding Fathers-ish . . . Jefferson? No. Adams? No. Madison.*

There were only two Madisons in McLean, and Tom got Virginia Madison on his first call. "Oh, Detective Hogan," Anne's mother said in a polite, distant voice. "Yes, Anne has mentioned you to us. How can I help you?"

She sounded eager to get off the phone, and Tom imagined her standing in a solarium somewhere, tapping a manicured nail on a marble-topped table, anxious to get to the luncheon at the club on time.

"Yes, please, Mrs. Madison," he said in his best detective voice. "I need to contact your daughter right away, and I've been unable to locate her. I'm wondering if you might know how I can reach her at the moment."

"Is anything wrong?" Virginia Madison asked. "Is Anne all right?"

"I'm sure she's fine," Tom said. "I just need to contact her regarding some developments in her case that it would be best for her to know sooner rather than later."

"I see," Mrs. Madison said coolly.

She paused for a moment. "Well, Anne doesn't have a very pressing schedule, but I do believe she does have a standing commitment on Fridays around this time. She tutors at that—" she paused, as if the concept was utterly distasteful to her, "uh, learning center a couple times a week. Perhaps you're aware of her work there? I believe it's in an area of Washington where you gentlemen on the police force are called rather frequently."

Tom raised his eyebrows. Just talking to Anne's mother for forty-five seconds made him understand Anne in a whole new way.

"Would you happen to know the name of the, uh, learning center?" he asked, echoing her.

"Oh, no, I'm sorry," she responded. "I never can remember its name."

He paused.

"Well, thank you so much for your help, Mrs. Madison. If you should talk to Anne before I've reached her, please do ask her to give me a call at police headquarters. Thank you."

Tom hung up, willing his brain to bring up the name of the learning center. Anne had mentioned it in passing, that time she was so angry.

His brain obliged. "Jubilee Community Church," it said.

ANNE WALKED UP THE narrow stairway toward her turret in the learning center. As she had driven away from Dulles Airport, she had closed and locked the closet in her brain that held the image of the dark-haired woman.

I'll think about it later, she thought. *I've gotten really good at this.*

Scarlett O'Hara would be proud. She remembered when she first read *Gone with the Wind*, as a young girl, she had wondered why there were so many things that Scarlett said she would just think about later. Now she knew.

The doorway to her turret was covered with a big construction-paper manger scene, the star of Bethlehem shining down on a straw-thatched roof, chunky cows, horses, and several three-humped camels gathered with shepherds and wise men around the baby Jesus.

Anne had borrowed a Bible from Jordan Taylor. She hadn't opened a Bible since the days of childhood Sunday school, and then later, in high school, when she had to read the Book of Job for a world literature class.

She hesitantly flipped open the New Testament and found the beginning of Matthew's Gospel, skimming through the first two chapters. This looked good. *Angels, Mary, Joseph, wise men, the star, let's see, oh, no, here's King Herod, killing all the boys who were two years old and under . . .*

Anne skimmed back up the page; she would read just through the part where the wise men brought gold, frankincense, and myrrh. No need to get into the slaughter of the babies.

She tapped lightly on the door and walked in. LaVon was sitting in a circle with the kids; they seemed to be playing "I spy" while they waited for Anne. The room was draped with silver garlands, and gold and silver stars plastered the ceiling. "Miss Anne!" Sherah shouted.

Anne knelt and hugged Sherah, then the rest of the girls and most of the boys. They were gyrating with excitement; there was to be a Christmas party after Anne's class.

"Okay," Anne said. "Today instead of telling you a story, I'm going to read the story of the birth of Baby Jesus."

Sherah danced up and down, buzzing in Anne's ear. "Miss Anne!" she said. "We got a present for you! Wait 'til you see it!"

"Shhhhhhh!" said another little girl. "We gotta wait 'til after, at the party. Let's hear the Bible story."

Anne laughed and went over to the window, the heavy Bible in her hand, her finger stuck in the beginning of Matthew. The kids settled down on the carpet, two of them on LaVon's lap. "I'll stay for this, Anne," he said. "Can't hear the Christmas story too much."

Anne perched on the window seat and smoothed out the pages of the big Bible on her lap. "Now the birth of Jesus Christ was as follows," she began.

There was a quick double tap on the door, and Jordan Taylor came in. She didn't smile, and Anne couldn't read her face. "Excuse me," she said. "Anne, there are some men downstairs who need to talk with you."

Anne looked at her, her eyebrows up. Jordan's eyes were steady on hers. "One is Mr. Hogan," she said.

"Oh," Anne said, smiling as she remembered being with Tom Hogan outside her town house in the dark, the snow swirling around him, after he had helped to decorate her Christmas tree.

"Anne?" Jordan said.

Anne looked down at the Bible. If Tom Hogan was here, of all places, it was probably something official.

She stood, offering the Bible to LaVon. "Could you continue here?" she asked. "Please excuse me, everyone. I'll be back in just a little bit."

Tom Hogan and Otis Jefferson were waiting in the sanctuary area downstairs. Anne slowed down when she saw them, her smile evolving into a question. Their faces held no good answer.

"We're very sorry to interrupt you here, Anne," Tom said formally. "But it's imperative that we speak with you. Mrs. Taylor has given us her office, if you could come with us, please."

He put his hand in the small of her back, steering her toward Jordan Taylor's crowded office. He and Otis pulled three folding chairs into a little circle and pointed Anne toward one.

"Please, have a seat," said Otis Jefferson.

"Anne," Tom began. "You're aware of some of the progress in our investigation to date, with the deceased teenager who actually fired the murder weapon, the accomplice you were able to identify for us in the lineup."

He stopped. Anne waited. His police language sounded so stiff, so formal.

Tom looked directly into her eyes, connecting with her for just a moment like he had outside her town house.

"I'm very sorry," he said slowly. "You need to brace yourself for some bad news. It's better that you hear what I need to tell you now, rather than read it in the newspaper."

Anne stopped breathing.

"Things have taken an ugly turn," he said. "I can fill you in on all of the evidence if you'd like, but right now we need to tell you where the investigation has led to date."

Tom paused, took a breath, and then let her have it straight.

"Your husband had been involved in an extramarital affair for approximately eighteen months prior to his death. I don't know—perhaps this isn't really a surprise to you.

"You may recall from our interviews with you that we had asked for access to your financial records, particularly any transactions or developments from the past year or so. If you recall, your husband took out an extensive new life-insurance policy on you about a year ago."

Tom hadn't meant for Anne to respond, but she did so automatically.

"Well, yes, I remember," she said. "I mean, he had substantial coverage in case of accidental death, and I remember he said we should do the same for me. So he jacked up my policy; I remember having the bloodwork and the physical for it."

"Well," Tom said, "as you may remember, that policy insured your life for $300,000, with the proviso that if you died accidentally, it would be tripled."

Anne sat on the folding chair, clutching her hands in her lap. She was holding her muscles so tensely that the small of her back ached horribly.

"That's nearly a million dollars," Tom said quietly. "That information, combined with Mr. Lorelli's romantic involvement, caused us concern. But it didn't fit with what happened on the night of your husband's death. Until we received testimony from someone who was involved with the suspect, Jerome Brown.

"We interviewed Mr. Brown after you identified him in the lineup. In return for some things we were able to offer him, he told us he was hired by a Latino gang member called Luis. The deal had been a contract murder on a lady, he said, with a retainer up front, the rest of the payment to be delivered after the job was complete.

"Jerome was told the hit was to take place next to the waterfront in Georgetown. He was given a description of the woman, even down to what she would be wearing the night of the murder. They were to take the husband's wallet but leave him alone.

"Jerome said that his partner—the man with the torn ear, who was called Lobe—messed up the whole thing. According to Jerome, they were taking a bonus up front, the watch and the pearls, before the hit, and then the husband got mad, and then Lobe lost his temper, and he shot the husband.

"Then some people came along the path, and Jerome and his partner ran away. So they didn't shoot the wife. And they didn't collect the rest of their payment."

Tom Hogan and Otis Jefferson had talked to Luis Rojas, who had hired Jerome Brown, only that morning. He had turned out to be a slick kid who spoke quietly and carried himself more like a stock portfolio manager than a hood. Thanks to connections in Colombia and Peru, the Latino gangs did a booming drug business in D.C., and Luis seemed to handle more of the business end of the gang's activity, leaving the dirty work to others.

Luis had told Tom and Otis enough for them to piece together the plot. Tom marveled that the perpetrators had thought they could pull it off. It was as if they thought the cops would be too dumb to put it all together. At any rate, in order to distance themselves from the actual crime, they had had to involve too many people, people who were only too happy to talk once Paul Lorelli was dead.

Luis had first been contacted by a man named José Montero. Montero was part-owner of two Latino restaurants in the city, a shady character investigators had long suspected of laundering drug money. They had never launched a full investigation, though, because of lack of funds and too many other concerns, like the constant supply of new homicide cases. Evidently Montero had given Luis the down payment and the identifying information to pass on regarding the hit, making it clear that he himself was not the customer.

"One time he slipped, though," Luis told Tom, "and he said something about 'Maria.' I didn't think much of it, that's a common name, probably not a real name, but it stayed in my mind because of her being a woman, that's kind of unusual, you know? Then one time I'm on the street, and I see Montero walking into his place with a woman, this woman with long black hair down to her waist, long legs—I always notice the legs—I thought, yeah, I see why Montero doesn't mind doing a little business for her."

TOM PAUSED AS HE came to his conclusion. Anne was looking at him, her face upturned and frozen like someone crouched beneath the curl of a huge, dark wave. He knew of no way to tell her but to tell her.

"I'm sorry," he said again. "It appears that the events of the night of your husband's death were not a random mugging. Jerome Brown and his accomplice were hired that night. They were hired to carry out a contract murder. They were hired by the woman Mr. Lorelli was seeing, evidently with his complicity. And they were hired, with money from Mr. Lorelli's private account, to kill you."

The wave crashed, and Tom could see Anne swept under, so tossed she did not know which way was up. She made a gagging sound, and Tom leaned toward her. Otis Jefferson lunged out of the room to get a glass of water.

Usually in a situation like this, the victim went right into denial, anger that such an allegation could even be made against his or her spouse. But Tom could tell that Anne had no such illusions. What he had told her meshed too well with the things she had locked away to think about another day.

"How could Paul?" she asked, her hand over her mouth. "What did I do?" She couldn't finish the sentence. Tom waited for a moment. He should have known Anne would blame herself. He plowed ahead.

"I know there's nothing I can say that can begin to address this," he said. "It's horrible. Your husband seems to have had a sociopathic personality."

Anne didn't say anything, and Tom hurried on.

"Sociopathy isn't classified as a mental illness. I've read a lot on it. It's like a character disorder. It comes from the lack of a normal human conscience.

"Most sociopaths function normally in society. They're successful, particularly in professions where the lack of conscience is an asset. They don't usually kill. But they're able to kill without guilt if killing becomes expedient."

Anne stared at Tom. She couldn't absorb what he was saying. It was so dark. But other dark pictures were in her mind.

"Who is the woman?" she asked.

Tom paused for a moment.

"Her name is Maria Luisa Garcia," he said carefully. "Ms. Garcia is a Peruvian national. She married a U.S. citizen seven years ago, an older man who died in a boating accident three years ago. In fact, we're going to open an investigation into his death, because now the circumstances seem rather curious to us. He left her financially well off, but Ms. Garcia seems to have had at one point a nasty cocaine habit that ate up some of her finances.

"At any rate, we have a subpoena for her to testify, and we'll pick her up today. We're not sure how she and your husband met, although we have talked to one of his colleagues at the firm who did know Ms. Garcia."

"Randolph Percey, right?" Anne said, shaking her head and holding her temples. "I should have known."

"Mr. Percey knew about the affair," Tom said. "But it's clear to us he had no idea about any criminal conspiracy."

"I'm thankful for small favors," Anne said bitterly.

Otis Jefferson returned with a cup of cool water, and she drank it, staring into the gray side panel of Jordan Taylor's steel desk.

Her mind moved back to the night of the shooting. She remembered Paul's phone call to her before he left his office: "What are you going to wear for dinner this evening?" At the time she had thought his query odd. Was he was getting her a corsage or something? She remembered the darkness under the Whitehurst Freeway. She remembered Paul's preoccupation as they left the restaurant—he had checked his watch like he was heading to an appointment, not just a stroll by the river.

And then, when the muggers appeared, she had been too overwhelmed by her own fear to notice what Paul was doing. But now, in slow motion, the images came back from the rest of the crime. Paul had handed over his wallet readily enough. Now she knew why it had been his *old* wallet.

But then he had been surprised. Surprised when the muggers demanded his watch. And then outraged when they called for her pearls. Anne remembered his anger toward *her* for cooperating and trying to take them off. Then his last cry, that NO! of fury. Had it come not from a sense of protection, as she had thought, but instead an outrageous greed that had blazed out of control and led to Paul's death rather than her own?

Anne stood, her brain whirling. Tom and Otis stood, too. "I've got to go," she said. "I've got to get out of here."

"No," Tom said. "We will take you wherever you need to go. Or can we call someone for you? Could Molly come get you?"

"Molly's out of town," Anne said dully.

"Oh, that's right," Tom said.

"She's on a plane to Miami," Anne continued, and then the raised eyebrows of the woman on the Jetway came into Anne's mind, as did the glimpse of the tall, dark woman in the distance at Paul's funeral, as did the smooth golden lighter with its brushed script initials, resting hidden and heavy in her fluffy Ritz bathrobe pocket all those months, that lighter that Anne had slammed into Paul's medicine cabinet so it could go ahead and mate with his razor. MLG.

"What was her name again?" Anne asked Tom.

He knew who she meant.

"Maria Luisa Garcia," he said quietly.

"Your subpoena won't do much good," Anne said. "She's on a Miami flight that's bound for Peru."

TWENTY-SIX

ANNE STUMBLED DOWN THE steps of the Jubilee church, her keys jangling in her hand. She threw herself into the Volvo, turned the key in the ignition, jammed the car into gear, and pressed her foot to the accelerator. She could see Tom and the other detective running toward their car to follow her, but she didn't care.

She drove as fast as she could toward Danuta's apartment. She felt like she had nowhere else to go. Molly was gone. She certainly couldn't drop this news on her mother just yet. And any other friends Anne could think of came up seriously short to the challenge at hand.

She clipped across Washington, stopping briefly at some red lights, speeding through others, accelerating toward Rock Creek Park, her mind a stone.

At Danuta's apartment building she pulled into the circular drive-way, punched her flasher switch, and left the Volvo there, gesturing wildly to the doorman, shouting that she had an emergency, and she needed to get in right away. He seemed so taken with her extremity that he let her right into the building rather than have her wait and be admitted by phone from Danuta's apartment.

Anne found the stairway and ran up four flights. At Danuta's brown door she knocked hard, three times, quickly. There was nothing, then the sound of footsteps, heavier than Danuta's, and then the door swung open.

A tall man with dark hair and bright blue eyes, about ten years older than Anne, stood with his hand on the doorknob, his eyebrows up.

"May I help you?" he asked.

"Oh," Anne said, her breath coming fast and her chest aching. "Excuse me. I'm sorry, I'm having an emergency. Is Danuta here? I'm a friend of hers."

"Oh?" the man said. Anne could see him assessing her blotchy face and wild hair and deciding to take pity on her.

"Please come in," he said. "I'm Jan Waters. Danuta's son. I live outside Philadelphia; came to take Mom and Uncle Jozef home with me for Christmas with the family. Mom's not here, I'm sorry. She went out to get her hair done. She just left. It might be awhile."

"Do you know where she gets her hair done?" Anne asked desperately, clutching her purse against her chest, vaguely surprised that Jan had no Polish accent and was not a little Jewish boy from World War II. Then it dawned on her that, of course, he didn't have an accent; he was an American, born after the war was over, born when Danuta had started a new life in the United States.

Jan shook his head slowly, looking at Anne with concern. "No, I really don't. She took a taxi. It's probably not far from here, but I have no idea."

Anne looked past the foyer where they were standing toward the living room of the apartment. "Is Father Kowalski here?" she asked.

"No," Jan said. "He's gone too. I took him over to the Holocaust Museum about twenty minutes ago. He was going to a lecture, some sort of seminar. They were going to have a speaker, and then a panel, and Uncle Jozef is on the panel."

"He's at the museum?" Anne echoed.

Jan nodded, looking at his watch. "Yeah. The seminar was supposed to start at three."

Anne jerked her head toward her own thin wrist. It was five after.

"Thank you," she said. "I'm sorry, I really do need to find him. I'll look for him there. Thank you!"

AT THE HOLOCAUST MUSEUM, the men at the information desk looked Anne over with the same concern as had Jan Waters. "Please," she said, "it's an emergency. I need to find Father Kowalski. He's participating in a seminar in the museum, I don't know where."

"Here," said an old man with gold wire-rimmed glasses and a shiny bald head. "I'll take you downstairs to the lecture hall. There's just one program going on right now; he must be there."

At the hall the man eased open the big doors and motioned to Anne that she could stick her head in. She spotted Father Kowalski immediately; he was at the front, his black cassock gathered around him. The bald man gave her a pen and the back of a program. Anne scribbled a note. The man took it to the priest. Father Kowalski whispered something to the man next to him, then stood and came toward Anne.

"Oh, thank you!" Anne exclaimed to the bald man, and then looked to Father Kowalski. "I'm sorry to interrupt you, but—" her voice trailed off. *But what?*

"But I had to," she concluded.

He put out his arm toward her. "Come," he said.

Anne wasn't sure where they could go, but she didn't want to spend time looking for a lounge. Near the central hall of the museum was an open room with black nooks, almost like study carrels, or confessional booths.

She pulled Father Kowalski toward one of the booths. It was outfitted with two benches and headphones and video screens for watching newsreels about World War II. There were no other people around.

Anne sat down. Father Kowalski sat next to her, waiting.

She took Danuta's handkerchief from her purse, and then told him, as best she could, where the police investigation of Paul's murder had led.

"I don't even know what to feel," she cried. "I can look back and see the distance creeping, growing, between Paul and me. I don't even know if I loved him anymore. I just wanted him to leave me alone.

"I just made do. It was like I'd rather limp along than go back and have a doctor rebreak the bone so it could be set properly.

"And so Paul did leave me alone. There were clues I could have picked up on that he was having an affair. Of course there were, but it was like I was on automatic pilot. I just kept going along, never thinking a lot because I might have to deal with something that hurt too much.

"And now this! It would be one thing if it was just an affair. I can't believe I'm even saying that. But he was trying to have me killed! Murdered right in front of him! How could I live with someone and never even realize he was looking at me every day and smiling at me and holding doors open for me and all the time figuring out just how to have me killed!"

She broke off in ragged, choking sobs, feeling nauseated, thinking of the gun in their faces that night, of Paul's protective arm draped around her, the stinking liar standing there and waiting for her to be executed right in front of him. Like Tom had said, a person without any feeling, no conscience at all . . .

Father Kowalski took her hand quietly, letting her cry, letting her shake with rage and disbelief.

"You don't understand," she said. "All my life, I've done the right thing. Not like I've given to the poor and helped the sick, not how you would define the right thing, but I've been what my parents expected. I did well in school, I've been a good girl, a good daughter, a good wife, always helping make everything smooth for everyone. It's not my fault that Paul hated his parents or that he was so obsessive about climbing the ladder. What did I ever do that he would turn on me like a cold-blooded killer? What did I do to deserve this? If God is so merciful, why would He allow me to be betrayed like this?"

Father Kowalski was quiet for a moment, then said softly, "You are still alive."

Anne stopped. She had been so frightened—in retrospect—and shamed and nauseated and angry—that she had forgotten for a moment how the story had ended. Paul was dead. She was not.

"I am not a trained counselor," Father Kowalski said. "I do not know how you can digest this terrible news, how you can make it a part of you for your health, not for your detriment."

"How could this be for my health?" Anne cried, her pain and anger overcoming her usual default to be polite at all costs. "How can you even say that? This is horrible!"

"It is horrible," Father Kowalski repeated. "But it has happened. Your husband went the wrong way. He chose to do evil. He almost killed you. But you are here, alive, and so you must choose life out of his death. Otherwise you will flounder for the rest of your life in the pool of your own self-pity. You will be like so many American women who have been wounded by one thing or another and refuse to heal, spending the rest of your life in therapy and becoming a professional victim."

Anne's eyes stung with fresh tears. How could he be so harsh, this old Polish priest who didn't understand—but then reason took over. *He's been through torture you can't quite imagine,* she thought. *Be careful.*

"Let's sit quietly for a minute," he said. Anne held the wet hand-kerchief in a ball in her fist, her mind a swirl of dark thoughts, tears pricking her eyes as pictures of Paul and that foreign woman filled her mind, the memories of the gun in the dark. She felt so small, so afraid, so hungry for Molly or even her mother, someone more familiar, more normal, more American than this Polish priest. *Why did I even bother to come here,* she thought.

"I want to tell you something that may be of help," Father Kowalski said. "You may not find it helpful today or tomorrow, but there is truth in this story for you, I think."

Anne said nothing. She just sat and let her mind swirl.

"Danuta told you a little bit about our time at Auschwitz," he said. "So you understand, a little bit, about what it felt like to try to survive in that place. I knew of a woman who came there. She was young and strong, and so she was not sent to the gas and the crematorium. She was put on a work detail.

"In the camps, most women stopped having their time of the month. The Nazis put something in the food so as not to be bothered with the possibility of pregnancy. So this young woman did not think about it much that her monthly flow had ceased, nor did she notice much when she felt tired and ill. Everyone felt tired and ill in the camps.

"But as time went on, it dawned on the woman that she was pregnant. It seemed impossible that she had not miscarried, given the starvation and the torment of her life in Auschwitz. But she knew. She was pregnant by her husband; they had been together just before she was taken by the Nazis to the camp.

"To be pregnant in Auschwitz was a death sentence. The Nazis had no use for infants or their mothers and routinely sent them to the ovens. But sometimes pregnancy was hard to detect. Almost all the women's bellies were swollen—with hunger.

"So the pregnancy went on. The woman did not know what to do. She knew that if and when the baby was born, it would be killed, and herself as well.

"There was a doctor in the women's section of the camp, a Jewish woman who had practiced obstetrics in her native Hungary. Dr. Mengele had set the woman up to run a primitive hospital ward in Auschwitz; it was also a playground for his gruesome medical experiments. At any rate, this Jewish doctor examined the woman and estimated that she was in her fifth month.

"The doctor was a principled and compassionate woman. She understood that the Nazis' most horrific torture was not physical abuse, but the choiceless choices they presented their victims. For a pregnant woman at Auschwitz, the choice was excruciating, for only if the baby perished did the woman have a chance to survive. As a result of that impossible dilemma, the doctor had become a clandestine abortionist at Auschwitz, weeping as she destroyed fetuses so that their mothers' lives might be saved.

"The woman understood the moral complexity of the problem, and how the doctor had arrived at her choice. But something within her would not allow her to go forward with a procedure that would end her baby's life. It made no sense, but she clung to this life inside, if only because it was the last connection with her husband. She wept and prayed and cried in the nights. She knew that birthing the child would only mean its death and her own—but she could not help herself.

"Time went on. The woman kept working on her detail. She somehow stayed on her feet during roll calls. She ate her tiny ration of food each day, and somehow the baby grew inside her. The other women stood in front of her, casually, when the Nazis were looking. They bound her belly with an old strip of cloth under her shapeless gray prison dress.

"Finally, as things turned out, it came time for her to deliver in the middle of the night. The doctor managed to get to the woman and helped her deliver her firstborn child, a son. The doctor severed the umbilical cord with a razor smuggled from the hospital.

"The woman lay back in the bloody straw, exhausted. The doctor laid her son on her chest, wrapped in a little square of cloth another woman had torn from her prison dress.

"The other prisoners had tried to keep watch, but what could they do? Suddenly an SS officer was standing at the bunk, his face cold with the most dangerous kind of fury. The doctor stepped back; the woman lay holding her son.

"The officer said nothing, as if he was considering and rejecting, various forms of torture for them. Then he looked down over the tiny infant, a perfect boy.

"'What a beautiful son,' he said. 'Beautiful for a Polish pig.'

He paused.

"'Shall I kill him, or will you?'

"All around the bunk the women prisoners sucked in their breath, a silent *no* of terror.

"'Come now,' the officer said in a pleasant voice. 'We can't have little babies in this camp. This is a work camp. Shall I kill him, or will you? Which do you prefer?'

"The woman who had just given birth felt faint, her thighs smeared with blood, her head swirling with fatigue, her heart ripping in fear. She looked into the officer's face and saw the strange glitter in his eyes, the dark, empty eyes of a sadist."

"'No,' she whispered. 'No. No.'

"She held the child close to her chest and kissed the wet top of his head. He had a tiny, perfect swirl of brown hair, just like his father. 'No,' she said again, and then she felt a rushing tiredness come over her, drawing her into a vacuum. She held her baby tight, waiting for the bullet in her head. And then she lost consciousness.

"The next thing the woman knew, it was early in the morning, in the dim gray before the dawn. She had fainted and then passed into a deep, deep sleep. Her baby was gone. She was alive. Miraculously, the doctor was alive as well; she was standing above her, her hand on her shoulder.

"'My baby!' the woman whispered. The doctor shook her head. 'He is gone,' she said.

"And that was as much as the woman ever knew.

"The woman survived Auschwitz. As the years passed she saw her son everywhere, his brown hair flying high in the arc of a playground swing. She saw him in line at an ice-cream store, his eyebrows furrowed as he tried to decide between chocolate and strawberry. She would see him in a group of young men laughing on a street corner, or as she got older, perhaps in a car passing hers on the highway—a glimpse of a strange yet familiar face in the rearview mirror, speeding by, and then he would be gone.

"She knew he *was* gone, but there was always a thin strand of hope woven somewhere deep within her that he had survived, even though she knew it was impossible. But none of the women in the barracks that night of his birth, nor the doctor, ever told the woman what had happened to her son. It was a contract of silence that was never broken."

"Oh!" Anne cried, tears in her eyes and her hand over her mouth. "What an impossible choice!"

"What happened in the camp was not necessarily the choice," Father Kowalski said. "The choice for her has been how she has responded to that crime every day of her life since."

"Oh!" Anne cried again. She felt more nauseated than ever. "The horror!"

"The horror," Father Kowalski echoed, nodding slowly. He stared into nowhere for a moment and then turned to look at Anne straight on.

"That baby in Auschwitz was my nephew," he said plainly. "That woman was Danuta."

TWENTY-SEVEN

ANNE PUT HER HAND OVER her mouth again, feeling that she might vomit. *Danuta.* How could it be? Danuta was out getting her hair done. Danuta had a son who was taking her home for Christmas. It didn't make sense. She thought of Danuta's story the day after Thanksgiving, the calm telling of a terrible tale, yet her voice was so steady, her face unlined, her eyes clear, her spirit gentle.

From her story that day Anne had thought there was more than enough to warrant bitterness. And yet Danuta had left out the very worst of all.

Why?

It made her angry. Everything made her angry today, but now she felt no freedom to be angry, no outlet for anything from her own situation, so clouded and confused by the terrible story from Auschwitz. Why had she ever connected with this priest? His stories were too strange, too inaccessible, too dusty, like the dim smell of all those shabby shoes in the exhibits upstairs.

She stood up. She really felt like she might throw up. Where was a bathroom in this place?

She left the carrel, the handkerchief pressed to her mouth, and walked out of the dark room. Outside was the entrance to the Hall of Remembrance, the sunlight shining in. She walked toward the hall and sat down to the left of the steps, looking toward the eternal flame and the flickering candles in front of the carved names of the death camps. Maybe if she could just sit in here for a moment. She sighed.

I hate all this, she thought. Paul. He was worse than those muggers from the city, his evil hiding behind his handsome face. He *was* a sociopath. He thought he could operate by a different standard from everyone else, like those Nazis with their polished riding crops, looking like a good man, a decent man, all the while planning her extermination as if it were an appointment on his calendar, a day in court. For money.

She shook her head back and forth, looking down. The hall was empty, but for once she didn't care if anyone was watching her or not. Her mind was a hurricane, churning with the twisting winds of Danuta's terrible story, Paul's betrayal, and, worst of all, her own dull sense, yet sharp fear, that she had no idea of where to go from here.

Nothing.

Where was God? Where was He? What was He doing while people betrayed one another to the death? She thought of Father Kowalski's words, how Danuta had chosen, every day of her life, how to respond to the crime done to her.

I hate that too, Anne thought. Why should God put Danuta in that position, having to try to "choose life," to do what her mother would do, when the choices were so narrow, when her mother and father and husband and child all died, died, died. *I hate it all.*

Anne stared at the eternal flame at the front of the room, feeling like she had nowhere to turn, nowhere to go. Her eyes lifted up above the eternal flame to the words carved in the soaring right front wall. They were from the Old Testament:

"I call heaven and earth to witness this day: I have put before you life and death, blessing and curse. Choose life—that you and your off-spring shall live. Deuteronomy 30:19.

Why are you doing this to me? she thought. *It's ridiculous! First, Danuta's story that made me cry, her mother talking about saving the Jewish children, I will always love you, the pearls—and now the missing link of that story, choosing life all over again. If You want us to choose life, why didn't You save that baby?*

But then Anne thought again of what Danuta's mother had said, that losing one's life and losing one's soul were not the same thing.

She thought, too, of what Danuta's story had stirred within her. Buried under years of normal life, it seemed like a murky dream. Anne usually suppressed it, pushed it back into the muddy waters if it ever threatened to surface, but she entered into it now, venturing into the swamp just a few mental steps, yet perched on the ledge of the hall, her hands holding her knees, rocking a bit back and forth and remembering, remembering, her blue eyes narrowing. Back in college, it was that date so many of her friends had envied, that blond, green-eyed fraternity president who'd asked Anne to one of the biggest parties of the semester. And then, so much later that night, the sour smell of alcohol on his breath, the dark car, her own struggles, then one hand across her mouth, the other ripping at her clothes, the grinding violation . . . and then, weeks later in some doctor's office, her terror come true, the fear of what her parents would think, the disruption in the scheduled flow of her life, the forms, the receptionist's reassuring voice: *We help college girls like you more often than you might think.* The appointment, that one small spark lost in the shadows, so small, so quick, no one would know.

One choice—it need not dictate the rest of her life so that she made no more.

I'm sorry, she thought. *I'm sorry.* She didn't know what she was referring to, just a load of sludge she now felt on her shoulders, a weight of sadness in her chest, a sour taste in her own mouth.

I'm sorry, she thought again. *Maybe I'm not the victim here. Maybe I've gone with the flow so often that I've let the tide pull me to the wrong destinations. I thought I was always in the right. I'm sorry.*

She looked up at the flame again, unsure why tears were in her eyes. She thought of Paul, of the past. It hurt.

And then a voice came to her mind. *Never forget, I will always love you.* But it wasn't the voice of Danuta's mother. It was a far more powerful voice, so beyond in its strangeness, yet so strangely known.

Anne sat on the steps, conquered, violated, overwhelmed—and finally willing to accept the Stranger.

I love You, she thought.

TWENTY-EIGHT

ANNE SAT ON THE STEPS for what seemed like a long time, her eyes wet as the tide receded and the storm was spent. She was thinking nothing and everything all at once. She looked up occasionally at the writing on the wall, turning the words over in her mind.

She looked down at her hands like she had never seen them before, stretching her naked fingers in the light. She no longer wore her wedding ring and the big diamond solitaire Paul had given her when they became engaged. She had taken them off and locked them in the safety-deposit box after she found Maria Luisa Garcia's gold cigarette lighter in the Ritz bathrobe pocket. Now Anne carefully examined her trimmed cuticles, the neat ovals of her fingernails with their young-moon crescents of white.

She looked down at her feet encased in their slim, black leather loafers and thought of the miles she had traveled to reach this day. She sighed, expelling old air she had kept inside her chest for a long, long time. She opened her mouth and breathed deep, taking in a breath so strong and new it made her dizzy.

As she did so she became aware for the first time in a very long time that she was hungry and thirsty. Her mind turned to warm places and simmering pots of fragrant stew served with hot, buttered loaves and a rich Brie cheese, the tinkling of ice cubes in a long, tall glass crowned with a slender wedge of lemon.

As she sat staring at the flame, there was the sound of a throat clearing in the doorway to the Hall of Remembrance. Anne turned reluctantly.

Father Kowalski stood on the top step, his hands clasped before him at his waist, expectant, as if he was ready to celebrate the Mass, his eyes searching for something in Anne's eyes. Then it was as if he saw it. He relaxed.

Behind him was Tom Hogan, who looked anything but relaxed.

Anne stood and brushed herself off.

She started to tell him she was sorry. But then she stopped herself. "I'm all right, Father," she said. "I needed some time alone."

Father Kowalski reached toward her as he had the day he first met her. He squeezed her hands briefly and then turned back toward Tom.

"Mr. Hogan has been following you," he said. "He's very concerned about you."

"You shouldn't have bolted like that," Tom said to Anne. "We followed you here, but then Otis took the car and went back to headquarters. We radioed about Ms. Garcia and the plane to Miami and Lima. Agents in Miami should have been able to intercept her. The plane had a layover there before it left for Lima."

"If it is all right with you, Anne," Father Kowalski said, "I will return to the seminar. You come first, of course, but if you are all right, and your friend is here with you now, the speaker is probably finishing and it is time for the panel. I will go back; I would not want to let them down."

"Oh, of course, please do," Anne said. "Thank you. I don't know why, but what you told me helped me more than you know."

"It was an odd sort of helping," he said, "but it seemed the right story to tell."

Anne looked down at Danuta's handkerchief in her hands. The story inside her was like a razor blade. It was sharp, but would not cut her unless she turned the wrong way. It was as if its honed edge had wounded someone else so she could heal.

"Father," she said, "can you tell Danuta what has happened and that I was looking for her?"

"Of course," Father Kowalski said. "I will tell her to call you after Christmas, when we come back from Jan's house."

He turned to go, then turned back toward Anne, taking both her hands in his, a great light in his blue eyes. "Merry Christmas, Anne," he said. "Don't forget what we celebrate. *Emmanuel. God is with us.* That is the great miracle."

"Thank you, Father," Anne said again.

He released her hands and walked up the steps, his black cassock swirling behind him. Anne looked up at Tom, who was watching her with an expression she could not read.

"What are you doing now?" she asked

He paused, thinking of a few good ways to answer her.

"I just wanted to make sure you didn't come to any harm," he said. "The way you tore out of the learning center, we were worried. People have done strange things. We've had people who've jumped off Key Bridge; it's not very high, but it'll do it. I didn't know what you'd do, but I wanted to take care of you. I had no idea you'd end up coming to confession in the Holocaust Museum with a Polish priest."

"Well, if part of your official duty is to protect me now, then I really do need you," Anne said. "I have to go and tell my parents about all this. I cannot tell them on my own. They will not understand. Something like this is absolutely foreign to anything they've ever experienced. I can't explain it to them. You need to do it."

Tom remembered Virginia Madison's icy tones on the phone.

"I can do that," he said. "But I don't have a car. You'd need to take me."

"Where did I park?" Anne asked, suddenly realizing she had no idea where she had left the Volvo.

"You don't remember?" Tom asked. "You double-parked on Fourteenth Street. You left your flashers on. You would have been towed in a heartbeat, but we were right behind you, to the rescue. I put your car over in the lot near the Tidal Basin."

"How did you move it?" Anne asked.

"You left the keys in the ignition," Tom said. "The car was still running."

Anne shook her head. All her life she had never left a car unlocked, never gotten a parking ticket, never had a moving violation, and today she was like a crazy woman, jumping out of her car and leaving it running. She didn't even remember how she got to the museum.

"Thank you," she said. "But can you come with me to my parents' house?"

"I can do that if that's what you need," Tom said. "I think Otis has things under control back at headquarters."

"Can we go somewhere else first?" Anne asked. "I need to walk around for a while and get my head together before we break this to my mom and dad."

"That's fine," Tom said. "Do you want to get a cup of coffee?"

"I want to go to the zoo," Anne said.

"The zoo?" Tom echoed.

"Yeah, the zoo," Anne said defiantly. "I want to walk around. I want to look at animals. I have always found the zoo very therapeutic, and I have had what you just might call a very bad day, and I want to reassure myself that all is well with the animal kingdom, even if the human kingdom is falling apart all around me."

Tom looked at her. Her hair was a mess, her eyes were red, and her nose was blotchy. She had never looked better to him.

"It's December," he said helpfully. "The zoo probably isn't even open."

"I know what month it is," Anne said. "The zoo is open every day except Christmas. They have buildings, remember? The animals are all warm and cozy over there, except the polar bear, and he doesn't want to be. It's not even that cold out anyway. Just humor me. We won't be there that long. Then we can go to my parents."

THE NATIONAL ZOO WAS about to close, and there were few visitors strolling its walkways. Tom and Anne parked near the Rock Creek entrance and walked up the hill toward the lion and tiger exhibits. The lions' enclosure was a large, outdoor, semicircular, terraced habitat.

Anne and Tom stood at a waist-high concrete wall topped by a short railing. Beyond that was a narrow strip planted with ivy, and then a steep drop to a wide moat filled with green water. At the far edge of the moat was a nine-foot concrete wall, and then three long, grassy tiers rising up, progressively smaller like the layers of a wedding cake. The male lion was on the highest tier, lying on the winter grass with his head erect, his huge paws placed precisely side by side. He stared away into invisible distant savannahs imprinted in his genes, indifferent to their presence. Occasionally the tip of his long tail twitched.

"Remember that woman who climbed over the wall last spring?" Anne asked suddenly.

Tom remembered the case well. It had been one of the more unusual investigations of the year.

In the dawn hours of the first Saturday in March, a young woman had flung her leg over the waist-high wall, climbed down into the moat, swum across the cold, dark water, and climbed up the concrete

235

wall to the first tier of the lions' den. Two African lions were there to greet her: a 300-pound female named Asha and a 450-pound male named Tana.

Zoo officials explained later that the two lions had been born in captivity and were quite well fed, usually consuming "a prepared diet akin to dog or cat food."

"Right," one of Tom's colleagues had said when that quote hit the newspapers. "The big kitties usually eat Friskies, but they just couldn't help themselves when a hot breakfast climbed over their wall."

When zoo workers arrived for work, Tana and Asha seemed agitated. There were pools of blood in the matted grass, and the remains of a dismembered human body lay on the first tier of the lions' den. It was a woman. Her hands and forearms had been devoured, so fingerprint identification was not an option.

Eventually the woman had been identified as a mentally ill military veteran from Little Rock, and her case had made official Washington go a little crazy, too. After all, the D.C. premiere of *The Lion King* had been held at the National Zoo. And now here was a little reminder that these animals were not the noble-talking Simbas of Disney lore, but beasts who, given the chance, would eat human flesh without a thought, right in the middle of the civilized city while the Metro trains ran on time and the flags flew briskly over the White House lawn.

For his part, Tom had thought again how you just couldn't make up anything as bizarre as what actually happened in Washington. Like the time a year or two ago when a man committed suicide by crashing his small plane into the first floor of the White House. Hopefully the Secret Service had beefed up their defense on what allegedly had been the highest-security airspace in the world.

And then there was the case more recently when a Marine was arrested as he tried to scale the White House fence. Reeking of alcohol, he had explained to police that he had thought he was climbing over the fence to his barracks at Quantico—forty-five miles away—just trying to get to his bunk without being noticed.

Oops.

The cliché's true, Tom thought. *Real life is always stranger than fiction.*

After the lions ate part of the homeless woman, zoo officials had sequestered them. Curious visitors, held back from the enclosure by yellow police tape, could hear the lions roaring, their full-throated bellows shaking the walkways as their keepers timidly tried to bring them back to their bland and balanced diet of vet-approved kibble.

Since then security had been tightened and sophisticated surveillance cameras installed. They were pointed toward Tom and Anne now, just like at an ATM.

"The woman the lions ate was trying to commit suicide, right?" Anne said. "I mean, that's a pretty creative way to go. Or do you think she just thought she could be friends with the lions, those big, pretty cats. We're all part of the circle of life, you know?"

"She had a history of depression, schizophrenia, and delusional thinking," Tom said. "Her psychiatric records said that she thought she was Jesus Christ's sister. She was mentally ill."

Anne looked at the lion, which was now staring at them, flicking his tail. "Like Paul?" she said. "He was mentally ill, too, right? You know, the sociopath I married who tried to kill me. I hate when that happens."

"If it helps you to make light of all this, then go ahead and do it," Tom said. "Your husband wasn't mentally ill in the sense that he had no responsibility for what he did. He was a total sleazeball. I'm really sorry. It looks like he was the kind of person who wanted what he wanted and saw no reason to let anything or anyone stand in his way. It wasn't anything about you."

"That's reassuring," Anne said. "I just happened to be the wife he was cheating on and the wife he decided to kill. You're right, I won't take that personally." She paused. "If you ever get tired of police work, you could go into counseling. You really have a knack for ministering to hurting people in their hour of need."

"I'll keep that in mind," Tom said, returning her tone. "I'm sure it pays better than homicide investigation. But I'll give you this little insight for free. You're doing better than you were when I first met you. At least now you're dealing with it. Before you were suppressing everything. It's better to know the truth and deal with it than pretend everything is lovely and keep polishing the pickle forks. It's never lovely. This is real life, and it's a mess."

"Wait until you meet my mother," Anne said. "She is the princess of pickle forks, the matriarch of manipulation, the sovereign of suppression. She has never met a problem she couldn't ignore."

"Then I can't wait to watch her ignore me," Tom said. "Can we go now?"

"I guess so," Anne said. "It's time to face the lions."

TWENTY-NINE

SEVERAL HOURS LATER, Anne sat on the beige linen sofa in her parents' formal living room. This morning, when she had taken Clark and Molly and the kids to the airport, seemed light-years ago. She herself had traveled immeasurable distances to get to this evening.

Before Tom began his rather clinical recitation of Paul's plot, Anne's mother had insisted that they have something to drink, and she had served them appetizers left over from a small dinner party the Madisons had given the night before.

Anne sat, absently petting her parents' dog's fluffy head and munching hors d'oeuvres from a silver tray as if it were a social occasion, listening for the second time to the blow-by-blow of Paul's murder-for-hire plot. For the rest of her life she would never again be able to stomach such things as melon wrapped in prosciutto, scallops with mustard-cream sauce, and spinach-stuffed phyllo pastry triangles, for those flavors were forever linked to the tale of Paul's betrayal. But on this night she sat and ate them as if she could not get enough.

After Tom finished, her father had sworn and paced the room, his usually bland face red and blotched with anger. Her mother's face did not change, though the muscles in her jaw tightened, and there was even more precision in her speech than usual.

"Thank you, Detective," Virginia said in the awkward silence after Tom concluded. "I'm sure you must need to get back to headquarters."

She stood and moved toward the foyer. It was clear that she could not wait to get Tom and his ugly revelations out of her beautiful home. Anne half-expected her to say "shoo," and sweep Tom out the front door with a broom, but Virginia Madison did not say things like "shoo," and the maid was the only one in the home who wielded a broom. Tom followed Virginia toward the door.

"Anne," said Virginia as Anne started to get her coat along with Tom's. "You've had such an upsetting day. Wouldn't you like to spend the night here tonight?"

Anne thought for a moment. She was exhausted. It would be so easy to crawl into the warm bed in her spacious old room upstairs, to draw back into the cocoon. Even though this house was a minefield of invisible explosive devices, at least it was familiar turf. Everything else about this day had sent her to foreign soil.

She looked over at Tom and remembered he had no car. Something new inside her clicked into gear.

"Thank you, Mother," she said as crisply as she could muster, trying to rally, but feeling more wilted than witty. "Tom's car is at police headquarters, so I'd better find a way for him to get back there. We can talk more about all this tomorrow. Thank you."

Tom shook hands with her father, who had removed himself into his silent mode and was, as far as Anne could tell, either planning to have Paul exhumed and shot or masterminding his next stock deal. It had always been hard to tell if he was thinking about business or pleasure.

Bill Madison gave Anne a hug and kissed her gently on the cheek. "I love you, honey," he said. "I'm so glad you're all right." He looked away for a moment, and his face became preoccupied again. "Don't worry, Anne," he said absently, giving her a final squeeze. "I'll take care of everything."

"Thanks, Dad," Anne said. "But isn't it a little late for that?"

He looked down at her with surprise, then glanced at his gold watch. "Oh, of course, you're right," he said. "It's nearly 9:30."

He ushered Anne out the door, with Tom following. She looked up at Tom. "That's not quite what I meant," she said. "He lives on his own planet sometimes."

"Well," Tom said. "I can understand that, given the way your mother is. Excuse me if this could be construed as disrespectful, but next time you ask me to talk to your mother I'll have to beg off with a preferable appointment—like a double root canal or a barium enema."

"She can have that effect sometimes," Anne said, "but really, she has her good points."

"No, no," Tom said. "Please don't interrupt. I was just getting to what I must say. Please, please, you have to forgive me again for ever having accused you of being remote in any way. I had no idea of the type of home you came from. I had no idea what your mother was like. She makes Catherine the Great look like Mother Teresa."

They were standing by Anne's Volvo, parked in her parents' circular drive in front of the house. "Now, wait a minute," Anne said tiredly. "There's no reason to attack my mother—" but then Tom interrupted again.

"It's amazing you're as normal as you are," he went on. "She had absolutely no human compassion. It's like she blamed *me* for the fact that your husband tried to have you killed. It was my fault for finding it out. She liked it much better when Paul's intentions were buried with him and everyone could mourn the brilliant young life so cruelly cut short. And then it's like she blamed you for allowing the whole thing to happen. You should have nipped the affair in the bud, and then it wouldn't have escalated."

"Can't win," Anne said. "She trained me from the time I was a little girl not to rock the boat, then blames me on this one for not rocking the boat."

She paused and shook her head, then continued.

"You know, I think I liked you better when you were a tight-lipped detective. Remember? You were so professional and removed, and I only knew how you felt by the way you lifted your eyebrows in disdain whenever I said anything. How did it get to the point where you felt like you could yell at me outside the morgue? And then how in the world did we get to the place where I'm standing outside my parents' house with you and you're freely trashing me, my mom, the dog—"

"I didn't say anything about the dog. But I will if you'd like. I don't see why people bother to have those decorator dogs. Why have a dog whose name no one can pronounce? What's a Dijon, anyway? It sounds like mustard."

"*Bichon*," Anne said, laughing. "Bichon Frise. Not like Grey Poupon. They're expensive dogs."

"Of course they are. But that's not a real dog. It looks like a curly white throw pillow with eyes. I'll take a real, manly dog any day. Those poofy dogs should all be stuffed and made into bedroom accessories."

"Watch out. I love that dog, and I love my parents, too. Lay off. They're all I have."

"I'm sorry," Tom said. "I shouldn't be so judgmental. But your parents are not all you have. You have Molly and Clark and that priest and lots of friends—"

"Tom," Anne said, "could you just take me home? I can't think about anything else today. I am absolutely, totally tired. You can use my car to get wherever you need to go. Just get it back to me tomorrow. But I am too exhausted now to do anything but go home."

"Okay," Tom said, taking the car keys from her and unlocking the front passenger door of the Volvo. "But I didn't get to finish my sentence."

"What sentence?" she asked. "The one about who I have?" She waited, suddenly as compliant as a sleepy child.

You have me, he had wanted to say. But that sounded ridiculous. "Never mind," he said. "Let's go."

Anne swung herself slowly into the Volvo. "You can tell me tomorrow," she mumbled tiredly. "That's a suspended sentence."

He closed her door gently and looked back up at the Madisons' big house resting so gracefully on the hill, a huge wreath on the Palladian window over the entrance. Rows of single white candles shone with false welcome in all the other front windows. Tom shook his head. Then he got into the driver's seat and looked over at Anne. She had folded her scarf into a small, neat pillow and put it between her head and the car window. She was already asleep.

THIRTY

ANNE WOKE LATE THE next morning, emerging slowly from a sleep so deep she could not move. Her body lay still as her mind, recalled from its distant voyage, extended its languid mass like a jellyfish pulsing through the waters of the sea, and then reassumed its brainlike shape inside her head.

Anne stretched too, smiling a little, the soft pillowcase against her cheek. *What was I happy about?* she thought. And then, with a shock, she remembered the events of the day before. *I wasn't happy about anything,* she corrected herself. *That peaceful feeling must have come from a dream.* Yesterday's nightmare had been the reality. Paul's betrayal.

But then it came back to her again, that elusive sense of something set right, a slim tether of hope holding fast to something she could not see, a conviction to choose well in the decision now before her every day of her life. She felt Father Kowalski gripping her hands again, his rich Polish voice saying, *Emmanuel. God with us.*

LATER THAT MORNING Anne called Jackie Jones. It seemed odd to her to call this new friend with grim news she wasn't planning to share firsthand with many old friends. But she knew that Jackie would understand. She did. Anne told her about Paul's murder plot and then about her experience in the museum. Anne couldn't put that encounter into the same terms Jackie used, but she wanted her to know about it.

Jackie dismissed Paul with a snort. She seemed unimpressed by the violence of his intentions.

"Well, girl," she said. "Your husband sure got what he had coming. The Lord protected you on that one."

"Well," Anne said, "A few weeks ago I wouldn't have known what you were talking about, but now I feel like He is with me. That's so new for me. I just hope this feeling never goes away."

"Are you crazy?" Jackie said, snorting again. "Of course that nice warm feeling will go away. I think God gives us those feelings in the beginning just to encourage us and get us going while we start living new. But later on you won't feel that way, so you might as well prepare yourself now. It's still real. It'll always be real. But it won't always feel real. That's where you've just got to believe and hang onto Him with your faith, because He doesn't always give us sight."

BY NOON A FEW DAYS later, Christmas Day, Anne was sitting with her parents by the big stone fireplace in the Madisons' family room. They had had a late brunch, just the three of them, and sat sipping coffee and watching the fire crackle and glow. It felt to Anne like the peaceful tides of long-ago Christmases, before the undercurrent had gotten quite so cold and strong.

While they were opening presents, Anne had hugged her mother after she unwrapped a gift box holding a bulky Christmas sweater. As she did so Virginia had apologized, in her own way, for her coldness toward Tom Hogan.

"Your father told me I should have treated him more kindly," she told Anne. "I'm sorry if I didn't welcome him with open arms, but he wasn't exactly bringing good news."

"Right," Anne's father interjected from across the room. He was fiddling with a portable CD player he had gotten for Virginia to use while she gardened. "Nothing like shooting the messenger."

They had not spoken about Paul. Anne realized she couldn't remember much about last Christmas morning, nor did she want to try to resurrect any memories about it. Better to leave Paul buried and move on.

But then, rather extraordinarily, she had felt drawn to call the Lorellis. Paul's plot had made the A-section of the *Philadelphia Inquirer*, and Anne felt that whatever their idiosyncrasies, the Lorellis didn't deserve the shame their son had brought them.

"I called Paul's parents this morning," Anne said. Her mother's thin eyebrows shot up.

"What in the world did you say to them?" she asked.

"I told them Merry Christmas," Anne responded. "I kept it short. I said that I knew the whole thing about Paul was a huge shock to everyone, and that my heart went out to them to discover this about their son. I know we won't see much of each other again, but I just felt drawn to let them know I was thinking of them.

"You'd be surprised," she continued, smiling at her mother. "They were very gracious. In their own way, of course." Celia Lorelli had simply cried into the phone, nonstop, with Sal on the extension saying, for once, very little.

Virginia shook her head and returned the grin. "Well, I must say, Anne, no one would argue that you've changed a lot over the past few months. Before you never would have voluntarily called Celia in a thousand years."

"That's true," Anne responded. "I did take the liberty of telling them you'd be checking in with them every month or so, and that you'd love it if they'd come visit you for three weeks in February and bring Aunt Ellie and the poodle with them. Hope you don't mind."

She paused for a beat or two. "Just kidding!"

She stood up and stretched. Things were going pretty well. Might as well rock the boat a little more. She pulled down the sleeves of the new sweater; it was woven of heavy cotton, festooned with Christmas stockings going down each sleeve and a huge green fir tree on the front decorated with red-and-green plaid grosgrain bows. It made her feel like a walking yule log, but she had put it on to please her mother.

"Mother, Dad," Anne said. "I need to go on a little errand."

"On Christmas?" her father interjected. "What, you need to go to the 7-11 and get some bread and milk?"

"Right," Anne said. "No, I need to go to the city. I want to give Sherah and Jackie their Christmas presents, and it would be really special to do it today."

"Who are Sherah and Jackie?" Virginia asked. "What kind of name is Sherah?"

"I've mentioned them to you before," Anne said, gritting her teeth. "They're part of the community at the learning center where I tutor. They've become friends."

"Well, Anne, I can't imagine your going down into that part of the city today."

"I do it all the time, remember? Besides, on Christmas the gangs have a cease-fire."

"It's nothing to joke about, Anne," Virginia said, but then, to Anne's surprise, her father interrupted.

"Why don't I go with you?" he said good-naturedly. "I'm sure we won't be that long, Virginia, and that way you can get things together for the open house tonight."

ANNE AND BILL PARKED at the curb in front of Jackie's row house. Anne had told her dad about the church, the learning center, and the neighborhood in far more passionate detail than she usually would have. Bill had listened and nodded. Then, as they rapped on Jackie's blue front door, he drew his coat around himself and smiled as if he was on the front step of the White House.

Jackie drew the bright door open. She was wearing a red satin dress, her hair in dreadlocks wrapped with shining gold thread.

"Come on in!" she shouted. "Merry Christmas!" Sherah was behind her in a green dress, jumping up and down with excitement, and they all hugged tight, like sisters. *What's happened?* Anne thought. *Some threshold has been crossed. Jackie's threshold.*

"Jackie, Sherah," she said, pulling her father into the small living room, where a thin pine tree tipped sideways in the corner, "I want you to meet my father. This is Bill Madison."

Jackie pumped Bill's hand enthusiastically, and then Sherah looked at Bill carefully, her eyebrows drawn together. "Miss Anne," she said. "This is your daddy?"

"Yes," said Anne, laughing. "What, did you think I didn't have a dad?"

"No," Sherah said solemnly. "I didn't know anyone as old as you had a daddy. Mama doesn't have a daddy."

"Anne, Bill," Jackie broke in, "can I get you some punch? We're having a few neighbors over later, and I made some cranberry-juice-and-ginger-ale punch. It's not bad."

"I'd love some," Bill Madison said. "Thank you so much."

"We brought just a few things for you," Anne said, putting their packages down near the leaning tree in the living room as Jackie went into the small kitchen.

"Oh!" Sherah exclaimed. "Mama!"

Jackie came back with four glasses of red punch. "Okay, yes, honey," she said. "You've been pretty patient, for at least thirty or forty seconds now. You can go ahead and open them."

Sherah started with the big one, ripping open its shiny wrapping paper. As she opened the box, her eyes widened. She reached within and pulled out the doll inside, holding her gently next to her heart. The doll had dark skin and kinky hair; she came with several changes of clothes, a book, and other accessories.

Sherah looked up, Christmas wonder on her smooth face.

"Her name is Addie," Anne said. "I thought you might like her."

"Oh, Miss Anne," Sherah said, "She's beautiful! She looks like me!"

Jackie laughed. "You can see how my girl doesn't have much problem with feeling good about herself," she said to Bill Madison.

"That's good," Bill said. "Kids need that as they grow older. Especially girls, I think."

Anne watched her dad, realizing that she had underestimated him for a long time. It was true he had been preoccupied for years, but, she thought, *I haven't even tried to connect with him. The way Mom is has made me pull away from Dad. I forgot how nice he is.*

"Anne," Jackie said, "we have something for you, too." She pulled an oblong package from under the tree, then turned to Bill Madison. "I'm sorry we don't have anything for you, but we didn't know you were coming. You'll have to come back, won't you?"

"I'd like that," Bill said.

"I would too," Anne added, catching her dad's eye. She took the package and opened it. Inside was a worn paperback Bible, dog-eared and full of underlining.

"It's not the most beautiful present you've ever gotten, I'm sure," Jackie said to her, grinning. "But I was thinking about you and about what you said you've been thinking about since you found out about your husband. It's my Bible. It's helped me through some real rough times. I want you to have it."

"Oh, no," Anne said reflexively. "It's yours. You'll need it—"

"I'll get a new one," Jackie said. "You need it. Take it!"

LATER, AS ANNE AND BILL drove back toward Virginia, the streets were empty, with a closed-down, holiday feeling that was rare in Washington. As they came to Constitution Avenue, they could see the national Christmas tree off to the right on the ellipse on the back side of the White House. Just opposite, at the entrance to the Washington Monument, Anne's dad surprised her. "Let's pull in here for a minute," he said.

Bill eased into a spot and looked up at the white monument, its fifty flags flying in the brisk December breeze. "Anne," he said quietly. "I need to talk to you about your mother, and I suppose now is as good a time as any."

Something in his tone frightened Anne. She looked away for a moment, up at the soaring white obelisk. She saw the mark about halfway up where the color of the stone changed. She remembered when she was a little girl how her dad had told her that it was a watermark from the biggest flood the world had known since Noah.

It was in fact the place where construction on the monument had ceased during the years of the Civil War. When building had resumed, the original stone could not be matched. But Anne hadn't known that then; she remembered her awe as a young girl that the floodwaters had ever reached so high.

"What is it, Dad?" she asked.

"I've been meaning to talk to you about this for sometime," Bill said. "Everything you've been through over the last few months has been so hard, so I wanted to wait. But now I see how difficult things can be with your mother—"

"*Now* you see?" Anne interrupted. "She has been difficult ever since

I've known her. I've felt the need to walk on eggshells around her ever since I could walk."

"I know that, honey," he said. "We can come back to that, okay? Let me explain something to you. I'm just going to tell you, okay?"

"Does that mean I'm supposed to brace myself?" Anne asked.

"Yes," Bill Madison said.

"What we have never told you is that you once had an older brother," he continued. "When your mom and I were married, she was pregnant. I'm sure we would have gotten married even if that wasn't the case. We really were in love, and so you might say that her situation just caused us to move a little faster.

"She didn't want anyone to suspect anything, so we eloped and she concocted this whole story about the romance of it all, how we just couldn't wait, we had to run off for a private wedding to affirm our love. Back in those days your mom was a very good storyteller, and our parents bought it. They had a big party for us when we got back, and all their friends came and brought great presents, and your grandmother passed it off to her friends that it was just a madcap case of irresistible young love, that sort of thing.

"Anyway, as things turned out, the baby was late. He was a big, lazy boy, and I guess he just liked being comfortable and cozy inside your mom, because he was about three, almost four weeks late. Your mom was so uncomfortable, physically; she looked like a big, overblown cabbage rose. But she was glad he was so late. It helped appearances.

"Neither of us had suspected how much we would love this child. He was strong and sturdy—a happy baby. We were just kids back then; we played with him and took him everywhere, to the beach, camping, picnics, you name it. Your mother bloomed even more. She loved being a mom."

Anne made a little choking sound, but her father kept talking, now looking out the window, away from her.

"His name was William Jr. When he was a little less than a year old, your mom put him down in the playpen one afternoon to play and hopefully to fall asleep while she did some laundry. I was at work.

"Your mom was down in the basement of the house where we lived then, and the washing machine started acting up. One of its hoses was cracked, or something, and water was leaking out. So your mom ended up being in the basement for a long time, trying to deal with the hose. She didn't worry about the baby; she had left him in the playpen a thousand times before. She knew he couldn't climb out.

"When she finally got the washing machine straightened out, she went back upstairs. The playpen was in the living room, and it was quiet in there. She thought that was good; the baby had fallen asleep. She went in to check on him.

"Somebody had given us a crib toy—an elasticized cord with plastic toys strung on it at intervals. It connected at each end to the corners of the playpen; you saw a lot of those sort of toys in the 1950s.

"When your mom went in to check on William, she found him twisted up in that toy, with the cord wound tightly around his neck. He was blue. He was already dead then, but your mom didn't believe it. When the ambulance arrived, the medics couldn't get her to let go of the baby. It was as if she had lost her mind."

Tears were streaming down Anne's father's face, but he kept talking. "It was awful," he said. "I had never felt that kind of pain. But it wasn't just that I had lost Will. As the weeks went by, it was clear to me that I had lost your mother as well. At first I thought that when she got over the shock she would be like she was before—that young girl so full of life. Everything was like an adventure for her before. But even when she got out of the hospital, and she seemed like she was calm again, the old Virginia was gone. She had become like she is today.

"She took all the baby pictures of Will out of the house, all his clothes, all his toys, everything. She forbade anyone to ever speak his name. It was as if the pain was so great, the only way she could deal with it was to pretend he never existed.

"I didn't quite know what to do. I spent more time at the office. I began to build up some business plans; it was therapeutic for me. I wanted to have more children right away, I knew we could never replace Will, but I felt that we could still build a family.

"But your mother wouldn't hear of it. It was like she had been so deeply wounded she would not risk that kind of loss and pain again. Eventually she seemed all right to people who knew her superficially. She really got into social things—entertaining, gardening—things she could control and make look beautiful.

"But she kept everyone at arm's length. Including me. Finally she told me that I had to go and get a vasectomy, she didn't want the risk of any more children. By that point I was so worried about her, I went ahead and did it.

"A few years went by. Things seemed okay on the surface, so we never dipped beneath the surface. There was a distance between us, but we functioned. Lots of marriages break up under that kind of stress. But I loved your mother, and I was not going to let this situation beat us. I don't like to lose.

"Eventually I got this crazy idea. I was thinking about that old phrase, you know, when God closes a door, He opens a window. I thought, let's open a window here. So I went to Doctor Murphy and had my vasectomy reversed.

"I doubted that anything would really happen, but I felt like if it did, it was a sign from God that this new child was truly meant to be, and I felt like it was the only hope of healing for your mother. And the miracle did happen. You were conceived.

"Your mother was mystified. She called Dr. Murphy, but he didn't break our little pact of silence. He was very sympathetic. He told her, 'Well, Virginia, sometimes these things happen. A vasectomy is 99 percent effective, but you know, nothing's 100 percent. I guess Bill's just a very virile guy.'

"Your mother did not laugh.

"Anyway, you were born, and you were the most beautiful girl in the whole world. I loved you so much it hurt. And your mother loved you too, of course. But I could see in her face this fear mixed with her love, the fear of coming too close and losing too much. She insisted that you never know anything about Will. And she always kept you at a bit of a distance. And she maintained very strict control over herself."

Bill Madison blotted his eyes with a handkerchief and blew his nose. He looked at Anne. "I know that's a truckload of stuff to dump on you. You should have always known about Will. I should have insisted things be different. But now you know, and you can see why your mother's the way she is. Inside, she's terrified of life and what it can do to people. So she distances herself. But she loves you very much."

Anne looked at her dad, shocked, thinking of his years of pain, the deadly playpen, an older brother who was forever a baby. At the same time, she looked at her dad and saw a young man mourning the loss of his boy, yet so irrepressibly trying to save his wife. She thought of the tiny faucet inside her father, opened so life could flow again.

Overwhelmed, Anne said the first thing that came to her mind: "Thank you, Dad."

JUST BEFORE THEY GOT BACK to the Madisons' home, Anne's father turned toward her again. "Don't talk with your mother about what I told you," he said. "Not today, anyway. You'll know the right time to bring it up. Just keep in mind that when you do, she'll kill me."

"Dad," Anne said, "Given my situation, that's not funny."

"Oh, honey, I'm sorry," he said. "You know I'm just kidding. Just a figure of speech."

"I know," Anne said. "The rest of my life people won't be able to talk normally around me, terrified they'll step on my toes. What am I going to do?"

"I don't know," Bill said, turning into the Madisons' driveway. "Marry the cop."

"What?" Anne sputtered. "No one is talking about marrying the cop. No one is even talking about dating the cop. He's not a cop anyway, he's a homicide detective. He was assigned to my case. That's all. It's a professional situation."

"Sorry," Bill said dryly. "Didn't mean to strike a nerve." He pushed the garage-door remote control, and he and Anne went in the back door through the mudroom and into the big kitchen. Virginia was standing at the island, arranging a tray of cold hors d'oeuvres.

"Hi," she said. "I'm so glad you're back safely. Bill, you'd better change clothes; people will start coming in an hour or so. Anne, that detective called for you. I told him to call back later."

Bill raised his eyebrows at Anne and went over to kiss his wife on the cheek.

THE OPEN HOUSE WAS underway when Molly called Anne from Florida.

"Hi," she said. "I just wanted to say Merry Christmas. Everyone here sends their love."

"Thanks," Anne said. She walked with the phone into the big pantry, where it was quieter, and shut the door. "How's Baba?"

"She and Clark are playing backgammon," Molly said. "Clark's in depression because she's beaten him three times."

"Molly," Anne said. "I need to tell you something. Are you sitting down?"

Anne could remember few times over the course of their friendship that Molly had been rendered speechless, but this was one of them. After Anne finished a quick summary of Paul's affair and the murder-for-hire plot, Molly said little. Just "Oh, Anne," over and over, and then, "I am so sorry. I cannot believe it."

"I can't either," Anne said. "But it happened. I hate to shock you like this on Christmas, but there's no way around it. It's been in the papers up here. I'm famous as the 'attractive blond wife' who was the intended victim."

"Oh, Anne," Molly said.

"Well, we'll talk more about it all when you come back," Anne said.

"Oh, Anne," Molly repeated.

"You should be here," Anne said. "My parents are having a party, and all the neighbors are gathered, lots of sons-in-law and grandkids and things, too. None of them know what to say to me. What can they say? 'Merry Christmas, I just love your sweater, and oh, I'm so sorry your husband cheated on you and tried to have you killed—'"

"This is absolutely the weirdest thing that has ever happened in the entire history of the known universe," Molly said suddenly, having finally regained the power of speech. "But perhaps I understate."

Then Anne could hear a commotion in the background and the familiar sound of Amelia shouting. "Oh," Molly said. "Back to normal life here. Baba just beat Clark at backgammon again. He's challenged her to arm wrestling now. You know, if the old lady beats you in brains, go for brawn. That's my guy."

"Well, thanks for calling," Anne said. "Give my love to everyone. Tell Clark about what happened as best you can. Call me when you get back."

"I will," Molly said. "It's amazing. It sounds like you're really handling this well."

"Thank you," Anne said. "There's something going on inside of me that's new. I'll tell you about it when you get back."

Anne hung up the phone, and it rang again almost immediately. It was Tom Hogan.

"Hi, Anne," he said. "I talked with your mother earlier and she suggested I call back later. I told her 'Merry Christmas,' and she said 'thank you.' I took that as a good sign. I think she's really warming up to me. How's the dog?"

"Did you call just to harass me," Anne said, "or do you have more bad news about my case?" Tom sounded unusually ebullient; sometimes Christmas had that effect on people. Maybe he had gotten into the eggnog or something.

"I called to harass you with good news," he responded cheerfully. "I'm over at my brother's house in Reston; we're about to sit down for Christmas dinner. So I'll be brief. I just wanted to let you know about some confidential information about your case."

"What now?" Anne asked, her stomach churning suddenly.

"Oh, this is about me," Tom said reassuringly. "Nothing to worry about."

"What are you talking about?" Anne asked, starting to get impatient. "What kind of confidential information? What good news?"

"Well," Tom said. "It seems that over the course of the investigation, I've developed a personal attachment to the intended victim that could violate the standards of police professionalism."

"A personal attachment?" Anne echoed.

"Yes," Tom said affably. "I thought you should be the first to know. Don't tell anyone. We don't want to mess up your case when it comes to court. Well, I see that the turkey here is just about ready to go on the table. I have to go. Merry Christmas, Anne. I'll be in touch. Give your mother a kiss from me. Kiss the dog too."

"Good-bye," Anne said slowly, shaking her head. She stared for a while up at the boxes of raisin bran that lined the pantry's top shelf, then smiled and came out, cradling the phone in her hands.

Suddenly Bill Madison came into the kitchen, a Waterford ice bucket in his hands. "We need more ice," he said, then stopped when he caught sight of Anne fondling the phone.

"Who was that?" he asked.

"Oh," she said, winking at her dad. "It was the cop."

THIRTY-ONE

H ELLO, ANNE?" Danuta said as Anne picked up the phone two days after Christmas. "How are you? We're back from Jan's house."

"Danuta!" Anne said. "Did you have a nice Christmas?"

"Oh, yes," Danuta said. "It was good to be with the grandchildren, and I was so glad Jozef could see everyone again."

She paused. "Anne, Jozef told me he told you about my story from Auschwitz."

"Yes," Anne said hesitantly. She should have known Danuta would bring it up right away. *It must be nice to be Danuta and to be so free, without the weight of hidden layers of secrets.*

"He told me also about your husband," Danuta continued. "I was so sorry to hear that you had been hurt like that. If Jozef thought my story could help you, I'm glad he told you."

"Thank you," Anne said.

"Don't feel shy about it," Danuta said, reading her mind. "If you ever want to talk more about it, just let me know. But the reason I am calling is, I want to invite you for dinner on New Year's Eve. Jozef and I are going to have a quiet evening, no fireworks or dancing or

261

paper hats, and we would like to have you and a friend, if you like, join us."

"Oh," Anne said, thinking how fitting it would be that she end this strange year with these new, unlikely friends. What would make it even more fitting would be if she brought Jackie and Sherah, but she immediately rejected that idea. No, what would be even more perfect in its strangeness would be to invite Tom.

"That is so kind of you," Anne said. "I would love to come. And I would like to bring someone. That's very kind of you. Father Kowalski has met him. Tom Hogan."

"Oh, is he the detective?" Danuta asked. "Certainly. We would be happy to have him."

It was seven o'clock on New Year's Eve. Danuta and Anne sat at the kitchen table in Danuta's apartment. Dinner was in the oven, and Tom and Father Kowalski were hunched over a small table in the living room, playing chess, the priest regarding the chessboard benevolently, Tom scowling and jiggling his foot with concentration.

Outside, the bare trees were still, the sharp air crackling with cold. Anne sipped a hot cup of tea. Danuta gently closed the oven door and sat down with her, smoothing out her apron.

"How are you feeling?" Danuta asked. "This has been quite a year for you. You're probably glad to see it end."

"You know," Anne said, "I was thinking about that on the way here, and to be honest, I feel better than I have in a long time.

"A year ago Paul and I were at one of his law partners' homes for a big New Year's Eve party. It was a gorgeous home and a lovely party, but all I really remember is that I had a headache. We went home kind of early, and then on New Year's Day, Paul was gone for most of the day.

He said he went into the office to catch up on some work while it was quiet there. But now I know that was a lie."

"Do you feel like you can forgive Paul for what he did to you?" Danuta asked.

Anne shrugged her shoulders. "That's moot, isn't it?" she said. "How could I forgive him if he's not here anymore?"

"Well," Danuta said, waving her hand in the air as if to dismiss Paul altogether, "it is too late, so to speak, as far as he's concerned. That is his own problem.

"But I mean for you. If you don't forgive Paul, you'll end up with bitterness growing in you, like a tumor. You may not feel it today or tomorrow. It's too early to detect the cancer inside.

"But if you don't forgive, it will eventually grow, and it will eat away at you. I know. When I got out of Auschwitz, I felt like I was entitled to feel anything I wanted. I could be bitter or angry or moody or selfish—why should it matter? I was entitled. I was a victim. I was one of millions of victims of one of the greatest concentrations of evil in history. I felt like we all should have been issued official papers allowing us to feel or do whatever we wanted for the rest of our lives.

"But even those pictures in my head let me know that I was turning into a Nazi myself. I mean, the idea of issuing papers. Being granted a special dispensation. You know what I mean. What I began to discover was that if I didn't forgive, I would turn into my oppressors.

"It doesn't seem fair, does it? But the victim has to forgive, or she'll be victimized the rest of her life. That's the choice."

Danuta got up, turned down the gas flame under a pot simmering on the stove, and came back to the table.

"I heard a woman tell her story years ago," she continued. "Her name was Corrie ten Boom. Her name is on the displays that list the rescuers in the Holocaust Museum. She was from Holland. She and her family concealed Jews in a hiding place in their home. The Nazis found them out, and she and her sister were sent to a concentration camp in Germany.

"Her sister died there, and I think the rest of her family died during the war as well, but Corrie ten Boom survived.

"Many years ago she came to speak at a Presbyterian church in McLean, and Joe and I went to hear her story. She was in her eighties then, a big, square old lady with a gray bun.

"She told about when she was speaking at a church in Germany, right after the war was over.

"Afterward, a man made his way forward through the crowd to speak to her. She remembered him. He had been a guard at the very camp where she and her sister had suffered.

"But he did not remember her. He told her how fine her message on God's forgiveness had been. He said he had been a Nazi guard, but since the war he had come to faith. He said he knew God had forgiven his sins—but it would mean so much to know that a camp survivor could forgive him, too.

"He stuck out his hand and asked her to forgive him.

"Corrie ten Boom stood frozen, thinking of her dead sister. She remembered the shame of walking naked before the guards, the blows, the pain. She was a very holy woman, I think, but still, she could not forgive.

"She thought about how Christ said we are forgiven as we forgive those who trespass against us. She thought of the Holocaust survivors she had counseled since the war. She had seen that those who were able to forgive had begun to rebuild their lives. Those who had not forgiven suffered further.

"But still, she felt frozen. Then she told herself that forgiveness is not an emotion, but an act of the will. She told God, all I can do here is to lift my hand. You do the rest.

"And then Corrie ten Boom slowly lifted her hand to shake the former guard's hand. As she did so, she said, it was like an electric current passing from her shoulder, down her arm, and through their joined hands. As that happened, she was filled with peace. 'I forgive you!' she shouted.

Danuta looked at Anne. "I sat and listened to that simple, old woman that night with tears. Her journey was so similar to my own."

Anne sighed and shook her head. "I don't know," she said hesitantly. "That seems like such a hard point of view—"

"Hers was a very hard message," Danuta broke in. "But in the end, God's hardness is far kinder that the soft comfort others might give.

"It is the hardest thing in the world to forgive. But we must do it. If we extend, by our will, even that little bit that we are able, God will help us do the rest. And then the healing comes. And in that, your story is just beginning."

Suddenly Tom and Father Kowalski appeared at the kitchen door. "It smells really good in here," Tom said.

"Who won?" Anne asked.

"He did," Tom said. "I should have known that you can't beat a priest. He got me with his bishop."

"We members of the clergy have to stick together," said Father Kowalski, smiling at Anne.

MUCH LATER THAT NIGHT, as they came in to Anne's town house in McLean, Tom left his coat on as Anne hung hers up in the hall closet. She felt a surge of panic.

"Are you leaving?" Anne asked. "Wouldn't you like to sit by the fire for a while? It's not even midnight yet, and I refuse to celebrate New Year's alone. I'll have a nervous breakdown. No one should have the kind of year I've had and be alone on New Year's Eve."

"Hold on," Tom said. "No need to threaten me with nervous break-downs. I have a surprise for you. It's at your neighbor's. I'll be right back."

"Which neighbor?" Anne asked. "Since when do you know my neighbors? I don't even know my neighbors very well."

"Three doors down," Tom said. "The Bentons. Pam and Wilson. They're a great couple. I'll be right back."

He went out the front door, and Anne flicked the remote control for the gas logs in the fireplace, marveling, as she always did, at the miracle of instant fire. She went to the kitchen, filled her white teakettle with cool water, and set it to boil. She went upstairs to the master bathroom and stared at herself in the big mirror under the merciless bright lights. She brushed her smooth blond hair and ran a fluffy blush brush across her cheekbones, then brushed her teeth. She stared in the mirror a minute more, then walked deliberately to Paul's medicine cabinet. She pulled out his razor, the nearly full can of shaving cream, his tooth-brush, the things that still remained even though Paul was gone, the things she could not face and so had kept to deal with another day.

This is the day, she thought grimly. *Out with the old. In with the new.* She reached into the cabinet and took out the gold lighter, too, her nose wrinkling as if it smelled bad. *Happy new year, Paul,* she thought. Then she lifted up a white wicker trash can from the corner, looked over the pile of her dead husband's artifacts one last time, and swept them all into the trash.

Downstairs the doorbell rang. Tom was back.

Anne ran lightly down the stairs and let him in. His hair was falling a bit over his forehead, and he had a funny half-smile on his mouth. He was holding a big green gift box lightly secured with a large red bow.

"Come sit by the Christmas tree," he said, wriggling out of his over-coat and leaving it in a heap on the floor. Anne followed, and they sat down on the floor in front of the tree. He sat the green box before her. It was shaking a little bit.

"Merry Christmas!" Tom said. "This is a late present for you."

Anne reached out; it was suddenly clear to her that the box was mewing. She pulled the big satin bow, lifted off the lid, and immediately, the tiny kitten inside put its two wee front paws on the edge of the box, struggled over the edge, and crawled up onto Anne's lap. It was jet black, with heroic white whiskers and eyebrows sprouting erratically from its little face, a triangle of pure white on its dark chest, and half-moons of white on its stubby paws.

"Oh!" said Anne. The kitten fell off her lap into a wiggling heap on the floor, jumped up, and began bouncing sideways across the carpet.

"She's hallucinating," Tom said. "They do that; she's seeing invisible mice."

"Where did you get her?" Anne asked. "Is she really for me?"

"Of course," Tom said. "She's a present, get it? I got her from my neighbor, Sadie Miller. She had five kittens—well, no, Sadie didn't have five kittens, her cat did—and now she's giving them away. Not the cat. Sadie. I almost got you all five."

"Quintuplets," Anne said. "She is too cute. What's her name?"

"Well," Tom said. "I was going to let you name her, but then I thought you'd probably pick out some sissy name like Midnight or Princess or something, and so I'd better name her. I decided to call her Ruby."

"'Ruby' makes her sound like she should have a red beehive and be tending bar, with a little cigarette dangling out of her mouth," Anne said. The kitten wobbled in her direction and charged up her lap, its tiny claws digging into her skirt.

"That's why it's a perfect name for a cat for you to adopt," Tom said. "Against type."

"Ruby," Anne said, holding the warm kitten in the crook of her elbow and smoothing the tufted fur between her ears. "What am I going to do with you?"

The kitten looked up at her and cocked its head, its round green eyes open wide, with such a piquant expression on its little face that Anne laughed.

"I've got a litter box and food and stuff like that in the trunk of my car," Tom said. "I just thought I'd complicate your life a little."

Anne smiled again and leaned over the kitten's head. Ruby was purring now, her motor surprisingly loud for a cat so small.

"You've complicated my life ever since you got involved in Paul's case," Anne said.

"Well, now I'm not just involved with Paul's case," Tom said, moving slightly closer to Anne. She moved away a little. One of the Christmas tree branches poked her in the back. "Now I'm involved with you," he finished.

She looked up. Tom's green eyes were serious, but there was a little bit of a smile around the corners of his mouth. Suddenly the air in the room felt warm and languorous, the fire too bright, the rich fragrance of the Christmas tree too strong, the gravity of the moment pulling her toward Tom. Anne thought of Paul and everything that had come before, and it all seemed like remote, shadowy memories that were not flesh and blood.

I'm scared, Anne thought. *Why get involved? Why get hurt?* She thought of her father's strange story about her mother, how her mother had closed down for decades so she wouldn't feel pain. Then she thought about Danuta. *Danuta would say I must choose,* Anne thought. She shook her head a little, still stroking Ruby's furry head.

"What are you thinking?" Tom said. "Did my last line sound too stupid?"

"It was pretty stupid," Anne said, "but I like you anyway."

And then Tom leaned forward, across the gulf that was narrowing between them, and kissed her.

THIRTY-TWO

No, no, please, yes, no, thank you, Sherah!" Anne shouted incoherently, her hands fluttering in the air as she contemplated her kitten's early demise.

"Let's not hold the kitten up by her little neck. Her neck is getting longer and longer while you're doing that. In fact, I think she's going to turn into a giraffe. Please, now, STOP!" Anne didn't yell very often, but here she was, bellowing like a foghorn.

It was February 2, Groundhog Day, and having no groundhog, Anne had brought her kitten to the learning center as part of her storytelling time. But things were not going quite how she had anticipated. Ruby's fur was sticking straight out, and little wisps of it were shooting into the air like porcupine quills.

Sherah was even more excited than usual, her fat braids with their bright barrettes sticking straight out from her head. The cat was hissing at her whenever she could draw little choking breaths.

"Okay, that's it," said Anne, prying Sherah's fingers off Ruby and scooping her little cat into her lap. "Let's come together and have a story."

The children gathered around Anne as she perched on the window seat, Ruby in her lap. The kitten began to lick her paws with elaborate ceremony, pausing now and then to look out at Sherah with disdain.

Sherah giggled. "I wish I had a kitten," she said.

"Sherah, a kitten wouldn't last five minutes with you," Anne said. "You need to be more gentle."

"Why?" Sherah asked. "My mama told me cats have nine lives. That's lots."

"Not enough," Anne muttered.

"How many of you have ever seen a lion?" she asked the children.

"I have, on TV!" one boy shouted. "*Lion King!*" said someone else.

"But have you been to the zoo?" Anne asked the group. "You know, the zoo in Washington?"

The children shook their heads no.

"Well, you've seen pictures of lions or lions on TV," she continued. "Those pictures show you what a lion is like. But they're not the real thing.

"Or, like this cat," she said, picking Ruby up. "I can tell you that this cat is like a lion. She has paws, claws, whiskers, a long tail, and sharp teeth. She might be like a little lion, but she's not the real thing.

"Once I knew a girl who was scared of cats. But then she met a lion, and she was never afraid of cats again. Because once you've seen a lion, a cat is not enough.

"Anyway, today I want to tell you a story about a lion.

"Once upon a time, in a faraway land," she went on, "there lived a lion king who was old and wise. All of the animals of the forest and all the people who lived in the nearby village would come to him for advice.

"The lion king lived in a golden castle at the top of a silver, snow-capped mountain. In the castle courtyard was a deep well, filled with the clearest, coldest water in the world. All who made the difficult journey to the castle could drink from the lion's well, and they would be refreshed.

"But the lion's counsel was not easy, for he spoke in riddles. To some, his answers made no sense, and they would sadly leave the mountain, scratching their heads as they climbed back down the narrow path.

"One year a great trouble came to the people in the village. A huge, ugly dragon flew into their valley. "He would swoop down over the people's farms, snatch up their horses and cows, and take them away to his cave. He would fly over their crops and destroy them with a snort of his fiery breath.

"So the men and women of the village began to fight back. They sent spies at night to watch the dragon sleeping. They sent messengers out to find out what had happened in other lands that had been ravaged by dragons.

"The townspeople believed the only way they could fight against the dragon was by using dragon weapons.

"The dragon spewed fire from its mouth, so the people built an enormous fire-thrower. But their fiery arrows just bounced off the dragon's metal scales. The dragon could not be overcome by fire.

"Like a terrible snake, the dragon's fangs dripped a fatal poison. The warriors from the village went into the forest, picked the deadly mushrooms growing at the base of a dark tree, and ground the poisonous mushrooms into a fine, black powder. They sprinkled it in the dragon's drinking pool. But the dragon just drank the poisoned water, then vomited it back up toward the people. He could not be overcome with poison.

"Finally, in anger and frustration, the people stood at the entrance to the valley and screamed at the dragon in a mad passion of rage. The din was huge, the echoes of their ugly, murderous shouts filling the valley.

"But the dragon turned his gigantic, hideous body toward them and bellowed and roared back at them in a huge howl of hate so loud that the people ran away in terror. The dragon could not be overcome by hate.

"So the townspeople and all of the warriors who fought the dragon with his own weapons were defeated.

"Then, a young boy decided that he must act. He climbed the snowy, silver mountain of the lion king. He washed his face with cool water from the lion's well, entered the throne room, bowed down before the king, and asked for his wisdom.

"'What must I do, sir, to defeat the dragon?' the boy asked.

"The lion king shook his huge mane and looked down from his golden throne at the slender young boy. He loved him, for though he was small, he was valiant and courageous.

"'My son,' the great lion said in his deep, rich voice, 'you must overcome the snake with song.'

"The young boy made his way back down the mountain. He walked to the rocky valley at the base of the dark mountain where the dragon lived, a once-green glen now scorched by the dragon's fire, a once-swift river now clogged and muddy, its banks littered with bones. The townspeople followed behind the boy, but they kept their distance.

"The boy stood quietly before the dragon's cave. Eventually the dragon lumbered out of his lair, smoke billowing from his nostrils, his wicked claws sharp as razors, his narrow eyes cold with hate, poison dripping from his cruel mouth.

"The boy stood before him as if he had not a care in the world. He opened a sack on his back, drew out a bright red apple and a small sharp knife. He began to peel the shining apple, carefully cutting away the skin so it came away in one long piece, which fell to the bare ground in a graceful spiral. The dragon was so mystified that he did nothing, but stood still, breathing smoke.

"The boy ate the apple in small, neat bites, his eyes on the dragon's. He blotted his mouth with a handkerchief.

"And then the boy opened his mouth and began to sing. The boy had a voice like an angel. The power of the song flooded the valley, flowing like a river over the bare earth, soaring like a mighty wind through the land. The townspeople, listening from a distance, looked to the sky and thought they saw shining rainbows.

"The dragon stood still. He understood what the song meant better than any of the others who heard it. He hated the song. It burned his dragon bones. He had to get away from the song. He turned his huge body, his long, jagged tail scraping over the rocks. The ground shook as the dragon walked slowly back into his cave.

"The boy, meanwhile, continued singing, his sweet, high voice soaring into the skies. He waited until the dragon's tail disappeared into the yawning mouth of the cavern.

"And then the boy began to sing louder, sweeter, and higher still. Suddenly there was a sound like thunder, a crashing and tumbling that grew and grew as the rocks on the side of the mountain began to fall. The boy's singing had started an avalanche. The rocks crashed to the ground; dust filled the air.

"But finally, as the dust slowly cleared, the boy and the townspeople could see that the entrance to the dragon's cave had been destroyed and was now blocked by huge rocks.

"And from that day forward, no one could say that they ever saw the dragon again. But on still nights when the moon was full, they could hear the sound of bellowing deep beneath the earth of the dark mountain, and sometimes a red glow of dragon-fire would shine from crevices between the big boulders. Sometimes the earth would shake and swell.

"The people replanted their crops, and grass grew in the green valley again, and the waters of the swift river flowed clear. But when the mountain would rumble, the people would remember that they must always be on their guard, for the dragon might get loose again someday. But they lived in peace, for now they knew they had the power of the song."

"That's the weirdest story yet, Miss Anne," said a little boy named Damian. "Dragons aren't real, right?"

"No," said Anne. "Dragons aren't real. It's just a story. But there are things to think about from the story that are real."

"Yeah, I got part of that," Damian said. "It's like my mama always tells me, don't fight dirty."

"I like that story," Sherah said loyally. "Miss Anne, can I hold that cat again?"

"No, you may not," Anne said quickly.

"The only thing," Sherah continued inexorably, "is sometimes you use words I don't know."

Anne nodded. "I know I do sometimes, Sherah, but only every once in a while. You can figure out the words you don't know from how I use them in the story, right? You all are smart, and it's good to stretch your brains and make them work."

Sherah stuck her bottom lip out.

"My brain doesn't need stretching," she said. "It barely fits in my head like it is. That's why my pigtails are so tight."

THIRTY-THREE

AFTER THE STORYTELLING session was over, Anne and Sherah walked down the street toward Jackie Jones's market. The walk and Anne's visits with Jackie after the storytelling sessions had become a ritual. The store was only three blocks from the learning center, but it always took them a long time to get there, with Sherah jumping up and down, dawdling as she took pains not to step on any of the cracks in the sidewalk, stopping to talk with people they met along the way.

On nice days like today, when people were sitting out on their stoops, it could take an hour to get to the market. But Anne enjoyed the time with Sherah and the sense of community she felt from the once-threatening neighborhood. She never ventured more than a few blocks from the church, but within that radius, she was beginning to feel comfortable.

Anne had left Ruby in Jordan Taylor's office, laughing at the sight of Jordan sitting at her computer, a pencil stuck over one ear as she tried to design a summer-school curriculum, with the cat perched on the shoulder of her jacket like a furry epaulet.

It was a mild winter afternoon, the kind of day that comes to

Washington in the beginning of February, just to tease people weary of winter with a brief hint of spring. It had rained earlier, but now the sun was shining gently. *It feels so good to be outside with just a jacket on,* Anne thought, holding Sherah's bare hand as the little girl skipped and hopped down the stained sidewalk. *I'm ready for spring to come.*

"So, Sherah," Anne said, "if the groundhog comes out of his hole and sees his shadow today, that means six more weeks of winter."

"Which groundhog?" Sherah asked.

"*The* groundhog," Anne said.

"I never seen a groundhog in my whole life," Sherah said. "Maybe groundhogs aren't even real, like dragons."

Anne was just thinking how she really did need to get this kid to the zoo, when she saw, far ahead of them down the street, in the block where Jackie's corner store was, two teenage boys opening the pink door of The Daily Bread and going in.

"Oh, look!" Sherah cried out, pointing. "There's a rainbow in the street!"

Anne turned and looked past the littered curb. She could see the sun shining on a thin slick of oil on the asphalt. There was a rainbow of red and purple and green and blue in the glistening oil.

"You're right," she said. "That's from where the cars leave a film of oil on the street. We usually can't see it, but when it rains the water mixes with the oil, and then the sun shines on the puddles, and makes rainbows. A rainbow is a good sign. It means the rain is over. It means hope. This one also means that the street cleaners need to come and clean this street."

Sherah looked up at her and laughed. "Maybe we could clean the street. We could get brooms and mops and soap and make a big project—"

They stopped at the cross street and waited for a car to pass. Jackie's store was at the end of the next short block, on their side of the street.

Across the street from them, Anne now saw two more teenage boys walking the sidewalk at a quick pace.

At first she thought they might be LaVon and one of his friends. But as they got a little closer, their heads down, dark sunglasses on, their hands jammed in the pockets of their big jackets, she realized she'd never seen them before.

"Sherah," Anne asked, "Do you know those boys?"

Sherah looked toward them without much interest, evidently still thinking about oil stains and rainbows.

"Nope," she said. "Miss Anne, who was that little girl you told us about during story time who was scared of cats? I would never be scared of a cat. That little girl must have been a wimp."

Anne laughed.

"Yeah," she said. "That little girl was me. When I was about four years old, a cat scratched me pretty badly, and my mother made a big deal about how I should never go near cats again. So I was scared of cats.

"But then, when I was six or seven, a little older than you, my father took me to the zoo. We saw the tigers and lions at the zoo, and my dad told me all about lions, and I realized that a house cat was tiny, no big deal, compared to a lion. Once I saw the lions, I was never afraid of cats again.

"Now, if a *lion* got loose in the street, that would be something to be careful about. So, Sherah, if you ever see a lion, you don't tease it, right? You don't try to pick it up by its neck. A lion is so big you couldn't even reach up to its neck."

"Okay," Sherah said. "But I wouldn't be afraid of a lion. I would go right up to it and pet it. I would roar at it." She walked on, her feet stamping the sidewalk, her small hands clenched into claws. "Rrrrrrrrr! That's what I would say to the lion."

Anne looked up the street again.

The two boys were now crossing over toward Jackie's store, walking quicker now, not looking back. As they got to the market, Anne and Sherah were close enough to hear the bells on the door tinkle as one boy opened it.

The other teenager, the one wearing a baseball cap, reached into his jacket pocket and pulled something out. Something gray and angular.

Anne's stomach twisted. Alarms went off inside her gut. She remembered this feeling.

Not even stopping to think, she wheeled around, grabbed Sherah, and swung her onto her hip. She knew better than to try to talk Sherah into turning around. Too many questions. No time to reason with her.

Sherah weighed a ton. Anne ran as fast as she could, jiggling her on her hip, her arms aching, stomach heaving, back toward the learning center.

"Miss Anne!" Sherah kept shouting. "What are you doing?"

Anne just kept running, gasping for breath. She got to the church, put Sherah down and grabbed her hand, pulling her up the steep steps. "Come on, Sherah," she cried. "We've got to hurry. Emergency. I'll explain it to you later, okay?"

She stumbled down the narrow hall and pulled Sherah into Jordan's office, her chest heaving. LaVon was standing behind Jordan's chair, leaning over her and pointing at something on the computer screen.

"LaVon!" Anne gasped, pulling Sherah toward him. "Sherah, here, you stay with LaVon. Play with the cat. Jordan, you've got to come with me. Bring the phone."

Anne's face was wild. Jordan picked up the portable phone without a word and ran after her out of the office and into the sanctuary, where Michael Taylor and Elder Williams were messing with the sound equipment.

"Something's about to happen at Jackie's store!" Anne shouted. "Some guys with a gun are in there about to rob it or something. We've got to call 911! We've got to go back there and help her!"

IN THE MARKET, Jackie Jones was sitting on her tall stool, feet resting on its bottom rung, drinking straight from a liter bottle of Coke. A computer printout of her inventory was spread out in front of her, and she was preoccupied with the part she liked least about running this store, the paperwork.

So she didn't even look up when the second two teenagers entered the store. "Come on in," she said automatically, squinting over the columns of figures and vaguely remembering that there were two other customers somewhere in the back of the market as well. "Let me know if there's anything I can help you with."

The boys, guns drawn, shrugged at one another when she didn't look up and moved toward the back of the store.

Jackie frowned over the printout. *Where's all that baby food I thought I had in stock?* she thought.

In the back of the crowded market, the first two teenagers had been digging around for a while among the ice-cream bars in the freezer case.

The boys with the big jackets moved toward the back, walking lightly, both hands on their guns, police-style.

The boy who had chosen an ice-cream sandwich turned around first. He cursed when he saw the dealers bearing down on them.

"Time to pay up," said the teenager with the baseball cap.

"We didn't do it, man," said the kid with the ice-cream sandwich. "I swear we didn't do it. We cut a fair deal. It was K-Kaefel." He stuttered as he said it, all the while trying to reach toward his pocket for his own gun.

The exchange in the back of her store was not loud, but suddenly Jackie Jones sensed the tension. She put aside her inventory sheets. She came around the counter, past the first aisle, past the second, around the carefully stacked pyramid of Campbell's soup cans. She looked toward the end of that aisle, at the back of the store, and in a terrible second she saw what was happening.

"Thanks for that information," the teenager with the baseball cap said, smiling coldly at the boy with the ice-cream sandwich. "We sure appreciate your help." Then he gently squeezed the trigger of his automatic weapon at point-blank range, while his partner did the same to the other kid.

The two teenagers crashed backward across the freezer case, their blood and brain matter everywhere, as Jackie gasped in horror at the front of the store. "Oh, God!" she breathed.

She turned to run toward the door, even as the boys in the back wheeled around, took aim, and brought her down in a spray of bullets. They turned and ran out the back door of the store and into the alley.

ANNE WAS RUNNING down the middle of the street with Michael and Elder Williams. Jordan was back at the church making the 911 call. An explosion of gunfire erupted from the store.

"Get down! Get down! Get down!" Elder Williams screamed hoarsely. Michael pulled Anne toward the pavement at the curb and threw himself on top of her. Anne could feel him gasping, her own ragged breath tearing her chest, the dirty water from the gutter staining her clothes. Then, just a few seconds later, came the sound of a second burst of gunfire—and then, miraculously, the sound of sirens. *The police must have been right in the neighborhood,* Anne thought, even as there was now only silence from the market, and her terror increased.

Michael moved slowly off her and put out a hand, pulling her to her feet. Elder Williams was brushing off his pants, walking in a daze toward the market. Anne could see doors opening up and down the street, people gathering, shock on every face.

Anne stood up and walked toward the store, a little bit behind the others. At the door Michael stopped and turned back toward her. "Don't come in here," he said. "Don't come in here."

Anne kept moving forward, her hands clenched, pushing forward, pushing Michael, pushing through the door. Inside the store, at first all she could see was the huge pile of Campbell's soup cans that had toppled and fallen and rolled in every direction. And then, as she looked closer, she could see Jackie sprawled across the floor. Most of the soup cans were stained with her blood.

Anne turned, her hand over her mouth, tears streaming down her face. Blue-and-white District police cars were screeching up to the curb, lights flashing, radios crackling.

She moved away from the door, into the street, walking slowly at first, then jogging, running, sprinting as fast as she could back toward the church. People were pouring out of houses, walking toward the market as she ran the other way. When she got to the church, Jordan had the front door blocked and was holding kids back like an army sergeant, her face in anguish as she took in Anne's expression.

"Where's Sherah?" Anne gasped. "I've got to get to Sherah."

THIRTY-FOUR

ANNE BURST THROUGH THE door to Jordan's office. LaVon had pulled a paintbrush program up on the computer screen, and Sherah was sitting on his lap, her tongue stuck between her lips as she concentrated, clicking the mouse and creating an elaborate row of brightly colored flowers.

"Sherah!" Anne said, her voice shaking. LaVon's eyebrows went up. Anne shook her head slightly at his unspoken question. She came around the desk and took Sherah in her arms. "Listen," she said. "Why don't you come with me upstairs to the library, and we can read some books together?"

"Why?" Sherah asked. "I'm having fun here at the computer. I've never gotten to play with Miss Jordan's computer before."

"Well," Anne said, "She, uh, needs it back. You come upstairs with me. We can even bring the cat." Ruby was in the corner of Jordan's office, chewing on a rubber band.

"LaVon," said Anne, "Can you find Reverend Sims and see if he'll join us upstairs?"

"I called him already," LaVon said. "He's just down the street; he'll be here in a second."

THREE BLOCKS AWAY, Tom Hogan pulled up to the curb in front of The Daily Bread. He had recognized the name of the market when it came over the police radio. He had never met Jackie Jones, but Anne had told him about her, and Tom knew this was her store. He edged in the front door, exhaling when he saw the chaos inside. A policeman Tom knew was kneeling next to the woman in the pile of soup cans. He looked up at Tom. "Two down in the back," he said, "and this one here. They're all dead."

"Any IDs yet?" Tom asked.

"Not on the males," the cop said. "But the people out front all say this is a woman named Jackie Jones. She runs the store, lives just down the street."

"Thanks." Tom pushed the market door open and sprinted toward the Jubilee Community Church. He knew Anne was tutoring today.

In the church, about forty kids had already been gathered in the sanctuary. Jordan Taylor and the teachers had pulled together several long folding tables. Some kids were coloring, some were reading, and others sat in a corner watching a video on a portable VCR.

Parents were already starting to arrive, most of them talking quietly around the perimeter of the area where the children sat.

Jordan Taylor met Tom at the church front door. "What's happened?" she asked. Tom shook his head. "Ms. Jones is dead. There are two young men dead, too. I don't know if it was a robbery or a drug shooting or what. Does Ms. Jones have family other than her daughter?"

"Her husband and her parents are dead," Jordan said, leaning her head back against the wall and sighing deeply. "She has a sister. But we need to talk to Sherah first."

She led Tom up the staircase to the library turret and gently eased the door open.

Anne was sitting in the big, maple rocking chair with Sherah on her lap, rocking slowly back and forth. Leonard Sims sat in a chair next to them. He stood and came out to the hall. Jordan told him as much as she knew.

Reverend Sims came back into the library and knelt next to Sherah. Anne stopped rocking, waiting for what he had to say and hoping against all hope that Jackie was somehow still alive.

"Sherah," Reverend Sims said gently, "something very bad has happened."

"What?" Sherah said, her forehead wrinkling.

"There's been an accident, and your mama has been hurt," he said. "She's been hurt pretty badly."

"Is she at the store?" Sherah asked. "Can I go there and help her?"

"Well," Reverend Sims said. "She was at the store, but she's not there anymore. Some other people are taking care of her, some men from the ambulance. We can't go to where she is right now."

His eyes met Anne's, and then Anne knew for sure that Jackie was dead.

THREE DAYS LATER, everyone in the community gathered for Jackie Jones's funeral. The church sanctuary was full of folding chairs, and Anne watched from the back row as Jackie's neighbors and friends came together, weeping over the coffin. She knew some of them from the church, and there were others from the neighborhood. There were also a few friends who looked like they were part of Jackie's old life, who, even in the midst of their mourning, were jittery, high on something.

Anne went to the front to pay her respects, looking down at the closed casket and the vibrant photograph of Jackie resting on its lid, thinking of the bright, vital woman who had danced her way into Anne's life so unexpectedly.

A tall woman with Jackie's facial structure and build swayed in the front row during the funeral, moaning and sobbing loudly, clutching the arm of her companion, a younger man in his early twenties.

"That's Jackie's sister," Jordan whispered to Anne. "Kismet. She's big trouble. She and Jackie hadn't really talked in several years. Kismet gave Jackie a hard time for getting involved with the church. She said she felt like Jackie was looking down on her, judging her. Jackie was just doing what she had to do to stay straight, but Kismet told her she never would speak to her again. Now she's crying louder than anyone. She smells like she's been drinking."

Molly had come with Anne to the funeral and reception afterward. As they drove home, Anne told Molly what she had been thinking.

"You're not going to believe this. I'm thinking about doing something really, uh, different for me."

"You've been doing really different things ever since you started tutoring," Molly said. "I think it's great. You've met some wonderful people. Anybody can tell that those kids really love you."

"Molly, what I want to tell you is really different. I haven't told anyone else yet."

"Okay, I hear you. I'm waiting. You're going to run for public office. You're going to join the Olympic diving team. You're leaving to become a missionary to Tibet. What?"

"I've been thinking about adopting Sherah," Anne said.

"Whoa!" Molly said. "I wasn't thinking different enough."

"No, be serious," Anne said. "I need your help here. I never would have considered this before, but I keep thinking about what it would be like to raise her. I'd have to go through a lot of paperwork and a home study and all that, but people do it all the time."

"I can't believe it," Molly said. "You're serious. Do you have any idea what that would mean for you? It would totally turn your life upside down."

"I know it," Anne said. "I've tried to talk myself out of it, but it's like this compulsion inside of me. I don't know why. But I can't even think of her going into the foster care system. She doesn't have any mom or dad or significant next of kin, just that aunt who looks like she could care less. I don't know who has formal custody. There's a lot I need to find out. But I'm committed to that community for the long run, so she'd still be in touch with her friends and the church and everything, and I can provide for her. It would be good for me. And the bottom line is, I love her."

Molly's dark brows went down and her eyelashes fluttered, and she pulled a crumpled Kleenex from her trenchcoat. "That's wonderful," she said, honking her nose loudly and stuffing the tissue back into the pocket.

They sailed over the Roosevelt Bridge. "You've changed so much since, uh, the night of the shooting," Molly continued, looking out over the Potomac River toward the Kennedy Center and Georgetown. Ever since Molly had found out about Paul's betrayal, she had refused to utter his name. "A lot of that has come through this inner-city stuff. Who'd have ever thought—"

"Okay," Anne broke in, "let's not make it sound like I was a totally dysfunctional frozen white woman from the suburbs before, and now I've turned into Mother Teresa."

"I never said you've turned into Mother Teresa," Molly said, extracting a file from her huge leather purse and proceeding to attend to her fingernails. "But that other part about the frozen white woman is just about right."

"Okay, that's it, you're in time-out," Anne said. "I don't need this abuse right now. Go away and come back when you're nice."

"That's good," Molly said. "Have you been reading parenting books? You're already talking like a mother. Time-outs. I tried to put Lincoln in time-out for a month after he put the cat in the dryer, but Clark rescued him. Not the cat. Lincoln. You'll need time-outs if you're going to be the mother of a five-year-old."

"I'm not saying I'm going to be the mother of a five-year-old. Don't go too fast."

"Well, I'm behind you 100 percent," Molly said. "I don't know how easy it will be for a single white woman to adopt a black child—"

"That's what I need to find out," Anne said. "It may not be realistic."

"Hey," Molly said. "Can I be there when you tell your mother?"

"Shut up," Anne said pleasantly. "Why don't you go tell her for me?"

"Because I'm going to be busy that day," Molly said. "There are certain things I wouldn't mind facing alone. Like a herd of crazed, stampeding water buffalo. But that would be mere child's play compared to facing your mother."

"Thank you for your encouragement," Anne said.

TWO DAYS LATER, Anne sat in the Jubilee sanctuary with Jordan and Michael Taylor and Reverend Sims. Sherah had been staying with Elder Williams and his family for the past several nights, and she seemed to be doing okay.

"But," Anne was saying, "it seems like the sooner she gets into a more permanent situation, the sooner she can begin to deal with what's happened to her."

"Well," Jordan said, "there's something to be said for her being in a familiar environment near her home."

"Of course," Anne said, "but I'm serious about the idea of adopting Sherah. I could give her a secure home. Undivided attention. The resources for private school, and later on, for college."

She paused. "You all know that this is a very different step for me. I feel strongly about it. But I don't want to try to pursue it unless you all agree. You've known Sherah—and Jackie—a lot longer than I have."

"Anne," Leonard Sims said in his deep, rich voice. "I know you love

Sherah. She's a special little girl. I hear your love for her in what you're saying. But we need to consider all this very carefully."

"I'm with you on that," Anne said. "I am absolutely the last person in the world who would ever do anything impetuous in my whole life. That's why this idea to take Sherah into my home has to be taken seriously. It could only come from God, because I never do things like this."

Leonard laughed. "Don't underestimate the changes God can do in a person," he said. "I've seen you change a lot since you first started coming here. Don't presume you're too much for God. You're a cream puff as far as He's concerned."

"I object strenuously to that racist remark," Anne said, grinning at Reverend Sims.

He grinned back. "I know we all want the best for this little girl," he said. "I've seen a lot since this church started, but this is the worst thing yet. We've got to give her a good environment to grow in."

"I know I've got a long way to go," Anne said, "but I think I can provide her with an environment she can flourish in."

"I hear what you're saying, Anne," Jordan broke in. "And I'm so glad to hear you talk that way. But if you'll forgive me for being blunt, we can't mess around here. Sherah is not a kitten. You're talking about a lifetime commitment to another human being who is very different from you. This is not just a nice thing to do for a while."

"I knew you wouldn't mince words," Anne responded, trying not to become angry by reminding herself that Jordan's commitments were as sharp and clean as a razor dipped in Clorox. Jordan wanted the best for Sherah. There was nothing personal in what she was saying to Anne. Was there?

"I know she's not a kitten—" Anne went on, but then Jordan broke in.

"What do you know about interracial adoption?" she asked, her voice shaking a little. "Do you know about the cultural issues here? Do you know what it means to be poor and black? I know if you adopted her she wouldn't be poor anymore, but she'd still be black, and I don't think you've really connected at all with what it means to be black in America.

"Anne, you've come into this community and you've told your stories, and that's great. You've been wonderful with the kids, and we love you for it. But you haven't seen the tough side of the situation here—"

"Excuse me," Anne said. "I thought I saw something pretty tough the other day when Jackie died."

"That's just it," said Jordan. "Do you know what the murder rate is in the District of Columbia? Last year it broke another record. Every year, it just goes on and on and on. Do you know how hard it is for people's lives to really, actually, turn around? Michael and I have been here for years, and we're just scratching the surface. It's so frustrating. You beat your brains out, and people still fall off the rails. People still get killed for nothing. People still go back to drugs and alcohol. It's so slow and hard.

"You've come in here to tell stories to five-year-olds. Most of the kids in that class have been part of this church since they were babies. They're the cream of our crop. They have hope, they're respectful, they don't misbehave very much. Of course you love them. They're so easy!

"But that doesn't mean that they won't struggle later on. That doesn't mean they're not going to go the wrong way, no matter how nice you are and how hard you try."

Jordan kept going.

"And what in the world do you know, anyway, about grooming a black girl's hair or caring for African skin? Do you know that years ago the Association of Black Social Workers stood against transracial adoption, and ever since then most agencies haven't placed children of color with white families?

"And what about the more important issue? To us, it isn't as big a deal what color family a child goes to, it's more important that it be a two-parent family. The kids today aren't as concerned about cultural issues as they are for the basic needs that are met best in a two-parent family. You can't offer that."

"Jordan," Michael said, "why don't you tone it down a little—"

"And do you know what else?" Jordan went on, ignoring her husband. She stood up and began pacing in front of the fireplace. "Look at where you live. McLean. The richest community in the richest county in America. You're going to bring Sherah home there, right? Did you know that blacks adopted by whites develop most secure racial identities when their family's neighborhood is integrated? What kind of message are you giving this child if you choose not to live with people of her racial background?"

Anne stood up as well.

"Okay, Jordan," she said, her voice shaking, "I hear you! I wasn't saying I'm *going* to adopt her, I was just saying I *want* to adopt her. I came to you all to discuss it, not to subject myself to some diatribe against white people adopting black children. If we all agree it's not in her best interest, I won't pursue it. But you don't need to come after me with a sledgehammer!"

Jordan stood next to the fireplace, shaking her head, her lips in a straight line. "I'm sorry," she said coldly. "I guess it's just a question of what the best is, isn't it?"

Michael got up and came between his wife and Anne. "I think it'd be good if we all think about this," he said diplomatically. We need to have our act together, just in case Kismet decides she wants Sherah. One thing I know we all agree on is that *her* home environment wouldn't be healthy."

They all turned to go. "I'll walk you to your car, Anne," Leonard Sims said.

"Thank you," Anne said. And as they walked out the sanctuary doors, she thought how she had never realized that perhaps Jordan Taylor wanted to adopt Sherah even more than she did.

THIRTY-FIVE

Two weeks later, Anne was on her way to Dulles Airport. Father Kowalski's long visit to Washington had come to an end, and he was going back to Poland.

Dulles wasn't quite as busy as it had been on the day that Anne took the O'Kelleys there for their Christmas holiday, but as Anne and Father Kowalski and Danuta pulled into the parking area, the mud, cranes, and perpetual business of construction were still the same.

"Ah, well," Father Kowalski said, eyeing a huge, heavy tractor bleating an ear-shattering warning as it backed up onto the road, "This is part of the charm of America. Always so much going on, always developing, never still. I shall be glad to go back to Poland. I'm too old for all this. I was born for a life of quiet contemplation."

"Jozef!" Danuta admonished her brother. "You're talking like you're a hundred years old. Stop it."

"Some days I feel like I'm a hundred years old," he said, but his eyes were warm and twinkling. He patted his stomach under the black fabric of his cassock. "The other priests and the seminarians are going to see that you have fattened me up. They'll put me on a strict fast. You will have to send secret care packages full of chocolate-chip cookies and other contraband."

Anne laughed, but later, as they stood at the departure gate, she felt tears welling up in her eyes as she said good-bye to Father Kowalski. She could not imagine what her life would be like if she had not met this Polish priest. It frightened her that so much had hung on the slender coincidence that they would be sitting at the same time on the same step in the Hall of Remembrance. *What if?* she thought.

The flight attendant began calling row numbers for the flight to Warsaw. "Oh, Father," Anne said, overwhelmed, "thank you so much! You saved me! I don't know what would have happened if I hadn't met you!"

He hugged her gently. "I did not save you, Anne," he said, as she knew he would. "God has His strange ways. He weaves our lives together. If He had not used me, He would have brought another."

"But not another I would have liked so much," Anne said incoherently, bordering on the edge of panic, feeling like a child about to lose a parent.

"Ha!" Father Kowalski said. "You still have Danuta. She is not going anywhere, and she is far more understanding than I am."

Danuta hugged her brother, and for a second Anne saw them as they must have been long ago, before the war, a tall brother leaning down to embrace his sister, all their lives ahead of them, so full of promise.

Danuta brought her back to the present. "Who knows?" she said. "I might go somewhere. I might go to Las Vegas and become a nightclub singer. Don't assume I'm just going to sit around here because you're leaving."

Father Kowalski bent to get his bag. "Write me from Las Vegas," he said. "Send me a picture of you in your nightclub costume."

They laughed, and he moved toward the Jetway. Anne felt that sense of panic again. "Maybe we could go to Poland to visit him," she said to Danuta, who was waving enthusiastically. "I could be your escort, carry your bags, you know."

Danuta shrugged. "Who knows? Anything is possible."

Father Kowalski turned, his arm extended in a wave that looked like a blessing. And then he was gone.

"Oh, dear," Danuta said as she and Anne began the long walk back toward the car. "I always feel so deflated when family has to leave. I hope he'll be all right. It's such a long flight. But he seems to be doing better than when he arrived in the States back in October."

"He certainly does look well," Anne said. "You've done a great job fattening him up. He never even told me about the details of his illness. Is he going to be all right?"

"I didn't know he hadn't told you about his problem," Danuta said. "He has cancer. It's in remission, the doctor says. No one really knows when it'll come back, or how much time he has left. But what can you do? We've had a great visit together, but it is right that he go back to his seminary. The Church is his home. I just borrowed him for a few months."

Anne stared at Danuta in shock.

"I'm sorry, Anne," Danuta said. "I thought he told you. But since he didn't, you should know now. I wouldn't want you to be shocked later."

"You're right," Anne said slowly. It was about all she could say, but inside, she thought, *if I get any more bad news about anyone I care about, I absolutely will just go over the edge.* But she kept that thought to herself. She knew Danuta wouldn't go easy on her if she shared it.

LATER, AFTER THEY GOT back to Danuta's apartment, they were sitting at the small kitchen table, having a cup of tea. Anne told her friend about wanting to adopt Sherah.

"Oh, Anne," Danuta said. "I am so proud of you. You can never go wrong, helping the children."

Anne heard the echo of Danuta's mother's words across the decades.

"It's so unlike me to want to do something like this. I feel like I should charge ahead while I've got this conviction, so I don't lose my nerve. But I'm trying be realistic. Even though I can provide for her, it'd be better for her to be in a two-parent home."

"Well, Anne, do you think you'll ever marry again?" Danuta asked.

Anne blushed a little. "I don't know. I'm pretty delicate in that department, if you know what I mean. I didn't do so well marrying Paul. I look back at it now, and I don't even remember why I married him. It just seemed like the thing to do, and I drifted into it. I liked how he had chosen me. He seemed so sure about it. I didn't need to worry about choosing him.

"But given what happened, it's pretty scary to think about taking that chance again."

"In my case I knew I loved Jerzy," Danuta said, "and he was ripped away from me. So it was hard to think about risking my heart again. But then I found I could love again—if I took the risk." She paused and sipped her tea.

"What about Tom Hogan?" she asked. "It is clear he cares for you."

"Oh," Anne said awkwardly, feeling like she was sixteen years old. "He is so different from me; I never would have dreamed that we could get along. He feels like a fresh breeze, like a cold wind that stings your cheeks but feels so good when you breathe it down into your lungs."

What a metaphor, she thought. But it was true. There was something clean and freeing and bracing about Tom, and it felt good to her. "I'm not even going to guess what will happen with him," she said. "But I'm going to stick with it. I feel like if I try to protect myself from ever being hurt again, I might as well go live in a box."

"You've helped me see that. If I don't risk my heart, I'll end up like my mother. And I don't want to be like my mother," Anne concluded, feeling shy again. "I want to be like you."

"Oh, Anne, bless your heart," Danuta said, reaching across the table and clasping Anne's fingers in her own warm, strong hands. "I love you for that. I've not been a perfect mother—you can just call Jan or David and ask them—but I love you like the daughter I never had."

She looked deep into Anne's eyes. "You stay right here," she said. "I'll be right back."

She went out of the kitchen and Anne could hear her moving down the hall toward her bedroom. In a moment she came back, a black velvet box in her hands. "Anne," she said. "I had been planning to do this anyway, but what you've just said tells me now is the time."

Anne looked at the box, her heart starting to thump erratically.

"When I was young," Danuta continued, "my mother taught me that even the most precious gifts must be held lightly, with an open hand, not clenched tightly in a fist. She taught me how to pass things on, that the true gift remains for us only if we give it away.

"When I was a small girl, that didn't make sense. It was hard for me to share, let alone give away the things I loved. But then one day the little girl who lived next door to us was very sick.

"And I went up to my room, to my bed, where my favorite doll was propped against the white pillows. And I took that doll in my arms, and I ran down the stairs of my parents' house and up the stairs of our neighbors' house. I rapped on their door and asked to see my friend.

"I remember she was in her bed, lying against the pillows like a frail little doll herself. And I went over to her, put my doll in her hands, and gave it to her. And as soon as I did that, my heart felt so free and full. She was so overcome that she just lay there, hugging that doll with everything she had.

"I ran home and told my mother how I felt so good inside because it really was better to give than to receive.

"And I remember my mother smiling down at me and ruffling my pigtails with her hands. 'Oh, Danuta,' she said, laughing, 'I'm so very glad you agree with the Scriptures.' She had a tart tongue sometimes. And then she hugged me tight."

Danuta's eyes were faraway now, looking across the distant decades to her young, beautiful mother sitting in their home in Krakow, rumpling her hair. Then Danuta smiled and looked across the little table toward Anne.

"I know that you are the person who should have these next," she said, taking the velvet box in both hands and giving it to her like a gift of the Magi. "These are for you."

Anne carefully pried open the slender, hinged velvet lid, and there, resting gently on the black satin inside, fanned out in a heavy, gleaming strand, were Danuta's mother's pearls.

Anne put her hand over her mouth, her shoulders heaving, tears rolling down her cheeks. "I can't," she said. "It's too much." The enormity of the gift overwhelmed her. She didn't deserve Danuta's pearls. She hadn't suffered like Danuta had suffered.

"Take them!" Danuta said, her eyes bright with tears even as she smiled. "They're for you. Look, I put a note for you inside."

Anne looked down at the box. There was a tiny note inside, written in Danuta's feathery handwriting.

Never forget, I will always love you, it read. *And never forget, you must always choose life!*

"I kept the original note my mother wrote to me," Danuta said. "But now her message for me becomes mine to you. And later on, it will become your message to your daughter. And then to your daughter's daughter. It's like a contract we make with those who follow us, down through the generations."

Danuta paused.

"Take them," she said. "Here, let me put them on you."

Anne sobbed, then turned obediently to receive the gift, lifting her hair in the back so Danuta could fasten the heavy clasp around her neck.

"Ah," Danuta said. "Turn around. They are beautiful!"

Anne reached out again and hugged her friend. "Oh, Danuta," she said, her heart breaking loose, leaping and soaring inside of her. "Thank you!"

MUCH LATER, WHEN Anne got home, there was one message on her answering machine.

"Hi, Anne," Virginia Madison said briskly, "I don't know if your father told you that I'm going out of town for a few days. Caroline Harrison and I are going up to the Brandywine Valley to do some antiquing and go to the Wyeth museum and Winterthur, just to get out of town for a few days. February can be so dull, so we thought we'd give ourselves a little break. We're leaving tomorrow afternoon. I'll call you when I get back."

Whoa, Anne thought. *I hadn't exactly noticed that February was so dull. I'd better go ahead and talk to her before she leaves.*

The next day, Anne tapped on the back French doors leading into her parents' kitchen. She wore a denim jacket, a long-sleeved shirt, and a pair of jeans, her hair pulled back with a shiny gold clasp. Danuta's pearls hung gently under the soft, thick cotton of her white shirt. You couldn't see them on the outside, but she could feel them on the inside, and she needed their strength for this talk with her mother.

Anne tapped on the glass again. Through the paned doors she could see her mother's hanging bag neatly laid out next to the table. She knew from experience that every outfit would be carefully coordinated, all the right accessories packed in little matching jewel bags, her mother's leather shoes perfectly buffed, no detail left untended. Then she heard her mother's light footsteps on the back stairway that led into the kitchen, and Virginia unlocked the deadbolt and pulled the heavy door open.

"Why, Anne!" she said. "How are you? You should have called."

Anne stiffened. Her mother liked everything done decently and in order. One never just appeared at someone's home unannounced, even if it was one's parents' home. One phoned ahead and made a reservation.

"Hi, Mother," Anne said, coming in and putting her purse down on the gray speckled Corian of the kitchen island. "It looks like you're all ready to go. Can I help you do anything?"

"Oh, no, Anne," Virginia responded. "Caroline will be here in a while. Everything's under control."

Don't I know that, Anne thought grimly.

"Would you like some coffee?" Virginia asked. "I just brewed a fresh pot. I didn't sleep well last night, and I can't seem to wake up today. I was just going to have another cup."

"Oh, yes, please," Anne said.

A moment later they were sitting at the round glass table in the sunny breakfast area of the big kitchen. A huge spray of red gladiolas sprung from a heavy Limoges vase in the center of the table. Anne carefully poured cream in her coffee, gathered her strength, and began to speak.

"Mother, you know how involved I've gotten in the tutoring program at the learning center downtown."

"Yes," Virginia said. "I'm so glad you've enjoyed it, but I was thinking you might want to take up something else now. After what happened just a few blocks away! It simply isn't safe down there. The League has some great new service programs, you know."

"Mother, this is going to come as a big shock to you," Anne said, "but I called the Junior League in January and asked them to put me on the inactive list. I just don't have time now to go to meetings and keep up with that any more."

"How can you not have time?" Virginia asked. "You're not working. What do you do all week besides go to that learning center and hang out with Molly and those Polish people and that detective? And I certainly hope you aren't serious about that detective. You can do a lot better than that, Anne."

"Oh, really?" Anne said. "Better like that handsome, up-and-coming attorney, you remember, your former son-in-law who tried to have me killed?"

"Well, they haven't proved that, have they?" Virginia shot back. "We'll never know the truth. I think that detective and the others probably postulated all that about Paul's setting up a contract murder so they could clear a case from their books. You know how inefficient the D.C. police department is."

"Mother," Anne said, dumbfounded, "don't you read the newspapers? They arrested Maria Garcia, the woman Paul was having the affair with. She was trying to leave the country. She's in jail as we speak. When she finally talked, she blamed everything on Paul.

"To hear her tell it, he coerced her to set everything up, he blackmailed her with her past drug involvement, she was just a pawn in his plan to get me out of the way so they could live happily ever after and enjoy my life-insurance money along the way.

"She wasn't exactly a pawn—in fact, they exhumed her former husband, who died in an accident that they now know wasn't an accident, but that's another story—the fact is, it was a dirty, ugly plot from beginning to end, and Paul was part of it. The police didn't make it up—he did."

"Well," Virginia said, speechless for a moment. "But like I was saying, you have plenty of time to do the League and still keep up with other things."

"Oh, come on," Anne said. *She's like one of those dogs that absolutely refuses to unloose their jaws once they've clamped down on something*, she thought.

"I'm not here to give you an itinerary of my activities," she continued. "My not doing the League isn't a question of lack of time, anyway. It's a question of lack of interest.

"But I want to talk to you about something serious, and I'm afraid you're going to need to listen for a minute and not go on the attack right away. I want you to know what I'm thinking before you go on your trip."

"Well, maybe it should wait," Virginia said, changing tactics. "Maybe you should come and talk to your father and me together. He's over in Maryland today; he won't be home until about five o'clock. So perhaps it would be better to just wait until next week."

"I am not waiting," Anne said. "I will talk to Dad about this separately. He'll understand me a lot better on this than you will."

"There's no reason to start getting offensive, Anne," Virginia said.

"Better offensive than defensive, Mother," Anne said. "I've come here to tell you something. You can react to it however you want, but I am not here to react to you.

"You know the little girl Sherah, the one who's so special to me in the tutoring class," Anne continued. "It was her mother who was killed in that shootout. Her mother was a real friend to me. You remember my telling you about how horrible it all was. Or maybe you don't remember; maybe since it was ugly, you just suppressed it.

"Well, I feel a special bond with Sherah. I've had this feeling growing inside of me that maybe I should try to adopt her. She needs a good home, and I can provide one."

"Anne!" Virginia said, leaning back in her seat, her face blanching. Anne could never remember seeing her mother in such shock. Her voice was shrill. "Why in the world would you want to adopt a child?

Any child? Let alone a black one! Why? You're all by yourself. You don't have time to care for all the demands of a child."

"Oh?" Anne said. "A minute ago you thought I had all the time in the world."

"No, Anne, you really cannot even consider doing something like this," Virginia continued. "A child like that belongs with her own."

"Her own what?" Anne asked. "Her own people? Are you so shocked about this because she's black? I wouldn't think you'd become a racist at this point in your life."

"Let's not get ugly, Anne," Virginia said. "I am not a racist, and you know it. Her being black is not the point. But she comes from a very different world than yours. You're just being reactionary because of the shock of her mother's death. You've been dipping in and out of that learning center like it's a new hobby, but that doesn't mean you need to get in way over your head and adopt one of the children there. You don't know the first thing about being a mother, particularly to a minority child."

Anne struggled to hold her temper, and failed. "What I know about being a mother came from you," she said, her teeth clenched. "I learned what I know about nurturing by watching you, and then doing the opposite."

Her mother was silent for a moment. Anne saw Virginia's hand shake a little as she reached toward her coffee cup, and then she was ashamed of herself.

"I'm sorry," Anne said. "That was unkind." *But, I can't bring myself to say it's untrue.* She took a deep breath. "Some of what you're saying is right. I'm not unaware of the cultural issues here. Believe me, others have pointed them out to me.

"I'm not dead set on doing this, either. It may be better for Sherah to stay right there in her community. But if what's best for her is for me to take her and turn my neat little life upside down, then I'll do it. Even if you don't like it, you need to know about it. This is one of the healthiest things I've ever done in my life."

"Well, Anne," Virginia said, her mouth in a straight line and her face looking old. "I must say you have succeeded in ruining my day. I just hope you don't ruin your own life. But I need to get ready to go. Caroline will be here any minute." She started to reach out to clear Anne's coffee cup from the table.

"Mom!" Anne shouted, banging her hand flat on the thick glass, leaving a smeared palmprint and rattling the coffee cups. "Look at me! You are absolutely, totally already ready to go. Don't dismiss me like I'm someone trying to sell you something. I'm your daughter!"

Virginia looked across the wide, smooth space of the table between them and then stared at the perfect gladiolas like she had never seen them before. Then the phone rang.

"I needn't get it," Virginia said automatically. "I'll just let the answering machine pick up."

In spite of the tension between them—or perhaps because of it—Anne and her mother both sat silently, waiting irresistibly to see who it was. The phone rang four times and then the machine beeped and began recording.

"Hi, Mrs. Madison," came Molly's voice rather breathlessly. "I'm sorry to trouble you"—Molly knew her mother well, Anne thought—"I was calling to see if Anne had stopped by. There's a little bit of an emergency, but I guess I'll just keep looking for her."

Anne scrambled to her feet, almost knocking her chair over as she raced across the kitchen and grabbed the phone.

"Molly!" she shouted. "Molly! I'm here. What's going on?"

"Anne, listen," Molly said. "Jordan Taylor just called me; she's looking for you and got my number from somewhere. She wants you to come to the church. There's a problem with Sherah."

"What?" Anne said. "What happened?"

"Sherah was playing on the sidewalk in front of the church with some other kids awhile ago," Molly said, "and a car came by with her aunt, you know, that Kismet woman, and her boyfriend, and they just snatched her right up and stuffed her in the car, and they've taken her away.

"I don't know what the people at the church are going to do. But I told Jordan I'd find you and that we'd get there as fast as we can."

Anne's heart tightened. "Okay. I'll come right by to pick you up." She slammed down the phone and grabbed her purse and keys.

"Listen, Mother, I really am sorry if I offended you," she said dismissively. "I was way out of line on some things. We can pick up on all this later, okay? I've got to go. Sherah's been kidnapped."

She leaned down and kissed her mother on the cheek and ran out the French doors, leaving Virginia Madison alone in her big, perfect kitchen, staring vacantly at the empty coffee cups.

THIRTY-SIX

ANNE AND MOLLY RAN up the front steps of the Jubilee church, breathing hard, and bolted into the sanctuary. Clusters of people had already gathered: Jordan and Michael Taylor, Leonard Sims and his wife, Elder Williams and Ruth Williams, along with Elder Wilson, who in his former life had been a heavyweight wrestler. LaVon and two of his friends were in the corner, talking quietly, along with a few teachers from the learning center. In all, there were about twelve people, as well as Anne and Molly.

Jordan came right over to them.

"I'm so glad you came," she said. "Here's the deal. Sherah was playing out front, right in front of the church, with the Williams kids and a few others, and this big, broken-down, old wine-colored Lincoln comes cruising down the street and slows down next to the children. Then it stops.

"You know how all the kids here are trained not to talk to strangers or to get in a car with anyone unless we know about it, but then somebody in the car calls Sherah's name, and you know how curious she is, and she goes dancing over to the car, and the last thing the Williams kids heard was Sherah going, 'Oh, Aunt Kismet!' And Kismet's boyfriend reaches out and kind of drags Sherah into the Lincoln, and it takes off down the street.

"Well, the kids came running inside, and we didn't know what to do, and a few minutes after that the phone rings. They must have stopped somewhere to make a call. It's Kismet, and she tells me that Sherah is her own flesh and blood, all she has left from her dead sister, and she heard a rumor that somebody else was going to take Sherah and raise her, and she's going to put a stop to that. Sherah belongs with family, and Kismet and her boyfriend are going to raise her as their own, and on and on. She'd been drinking.

"Anyway, she hung up, and we all put our heads together and decided to play it low-key, not get all panicked. We knew Reverend Sims would be back soon, and we thought we'd wait for him and assemble a little group to go get Sherah. You know, attack of the light brigade—"

"What about the police?" Anne asked. "Aren't you going to call the police?"

"Not for something like this," Jordan shook her head. "The boyfriend—his name is James Turner—just got out of Lorton about a month ago. He's probably already broken his parole, and we don't want him getting set off by the sight of a bunch of flashing blue lights and police cars. People like him don't have a real positive response to the arrival of the police force.

"We just want to take it slow, and easy, but still have enough people to make it look like it's a *community* coming for Sherah, not just an individual or two who want to adopt her and have their own agenda."

"Where does Kismet live?" Anne asked.

"We weren't even sure where she stays, but then LaVon came to the rescue on that," Jordan said. "He went with Jackie and Sherah on Christmas Eve to take Kismet a present. I never even knew Jackie did that, but I guess she was trying to reach out to her sister. Kismet wouldn't let them in, they had to leave the present by the door, but LaVon remembers where her place was. It's in Anacostia. Right across the street from the mental hospital. St. Elizabeth's."

"Oh, great," Anne said.

"Yeah, I know," Jordan said. "All the crazies, just across the way. Might as well join right in.

"Which reminds me," she continued, putting her hand on Anne's arm and drawing her aside for a moment. "I'm sorry if I was too hard on you when we talked about Sherah the other day."

"Thank you," Anne said. "We're all on the same side here, right?"

Jordan grinned at her. "Right. No need to shoot our own troops. We'll all try to figure out what's best for Sherah, together; that is, once we get her back from her alcoholic, drug-addicted aunt and her ex-con boyfriend who packs a gun wherever he goes."

"Great," Anne said. "Thanks for easing my mind as we go."

All around her, people were heading off to the bathrooms, getting a drink of water, retying their tennis shoes, tightening their belt buckles. *It's like troops getting ready for battle,* Anne thought. *But we don't have any swords. We don't even have any plowshares.*

And then they went out the door, empty-handed, off to fight for Sherah. Reverend Sims looked over the group, counting. He turned toward Anne. "We're going to take the church van," he said, "but not everyone will fit. Can we take your car, too? If you don't mind, maybe Elder Williams could drive, and you and Molly and Ruth can be with him. That'll work."

"That's fine," Anne said.

They got in the Volvo. Elder Williams adjusted the driver's seat and mirrors to accommodate his bulk. Anne leaned forward from the back-seat where she and Molly sat.

"Do you think it'd be all right if I call Tom Hogan?" she asked. "He's the detective I know. We can trust him to keep this quiet, but it might help to have him with us."

"If he's your friend, it's all right with me," Elder Williams said. "But no squad cars, no uniforms, no badges, no guns."

"Okay," Anne said, squeezing forward between the seats and punching Tom's number on the car phone.

"Hi, Tom, listen," she said when he picked up. It was miraculous that he was actually at his desk and not out poking around some crime scene. She profiled the situation as succinctly as she could.

"Okay," Tom said. "I'll get over there as soon as I can."

"Tom, could you bring somebody with you?" Anne asked, watching the decrepit blue church van in front of them swerve through the streets toward Anacostia.

"Preferably somebody big," she continued. "But there can't be any show of force. Just drive a normal car and take off your ties or badges or whatever you have on and fit in with the neighborhood. You can't look like police."

"Okay, I hear you," Tom said. "We'll come naked. I'll bring my buddy Toby Jackson. He's big."

As they pulled up in front of the crumbling three-story row house where Kismet lived, Anne saw Kismet at the open front door, standing behind the sagging screen as if she was waiting for them. She was wearing a long caftan, her hair in dreadlocks, big silver hoops in her ears. She was swaying a little, one hand gripping the side of the door, the other clutching a bottle.

The blue van stopped at the curb. Elder Williams pulled the Volvo up just behind it. Anne saw her friends move to a clump right in the middle of the street, about thirty feet back from Kismet's front door. Anne and the others joined them.

Suddenly Kismet shouted from behind the dark screen.

"You people just stop and stay right there," she called. "You got no business here. What're you doing, sightseeing?"

"No," Jordan Taylor shouted back. "We just came to see how Sherah's doing."

"You can't take her away from me," Kismet shouted. "That girl's my own flesh and blood, no reason in the world for you people to come for her. She's all I got, now that Jackie's gone."

"Kismet!" Jordan called out. "What are you talking about? You hadn't spoken to Jackie for years! Don't get started with all this family stuff now! It's too late."

"Oh, yeah?" Kismet shouted. "You think so? You come and try to get Sherah then. Come on! I'm ready for you!"

"Oh, Anne," Molly buzzed in Anne's ear, grabbing her arm tight.

"Calm down," Anne said, disengaging her arm. "We'll be all right if Jordan will just shut up."

Leonard Sims was gently moving his way toward the front of the clump of church people and escorting Jordan to the back. "Uh, Jordan, excuse me. No disrespect here, but a hostage negotiator you are not. Let me try something."

He cleared his throat. "Ms. Green!" he called out toward Kismet in his rich, bass voice.

"This is Reverend Sims. How're you feeling today?"

"Oh, Reverend," Kismet's voice sailed back through the screen door. In the shadow behind the screen they could see her throw her head back, the bottle tipped to her lips. There was a chugging sound. "I never been better," she continued. "I'm starting a new family today."

"Tell me about it," Leonard Sims said.

"Well, you know I lost my other babies when I went to prison a couple years ago," she said. "They went into that D.C. social services thing and now I don't even know where they are. My babies!"

There was a choking sound like a sob, then she continued on as if nothing was wrong.

"But now I got my man James here, and little Sherah, and we're starting new."

"Well, how is that little girl?" Leonard sang back to Kismet, melodiously. "Where's Miss Sherah?"

"Oh, Reverend, she's fine. She's so cute and smart! You can tell she takes after our side of the family. She never stops talking, though, does she? We had her wearing a little apron and cooking some lunch for us. She did a great job. Just delicious. She's upstairs now, cleaning out the front bedroom. That's gonna be her room."

"Great," Jordan mumbled from the back row where Michael had her firmly in his grip. "And what kind of stove does Kismet have for Sherah to blow up? Propane?"

"That's nice," Leonard Sims responded to Kismet. "Do you think we could see her?"

"Oh, I don't think so right now," Kismet said, pulling back a little. "She's busy here, and here's where she's gonna stay. You can't fight us for her."

"We're not here to fight, Ms. Green," Leonard responded. "We're just here to talk, peacefully. We don't believe in violence."

"Oh, really?" Kismet said mockingly, tipping the big bottle again. "Look what happened to my sister, right over there in your nice, nonviolent neighborhood."

"I know," Leonard said soothingly. "It's awful. Just because the church is there doesn't mean bad things don't happen. They happen all over the city. You know that. But that doesn't mean we give up. We've got to fight the good fight. But we don't fight it with more violence. We fight it with love. Jackie believed that."

"Oh, yeah," Kismet said again. "I know she did. But she thought she was so much better than other folk ever since she got wound up with you people."

"I don't think so, Ms. Green," Leonard responded gently. "She talked about you all the time. She talked about how much she loved you, how much she missed you, what you were like when you were little girls together, skipping Double Dutch on the sidewalk in front of the stoop all summer long."

There was a pause, another chugging sound, and Kismet's voice came back through the screen, softer now.

"Yeah," she said. "I remember. Those were good days. I remember skipping rope out front, Jackie and me and the girls next door, with Mama sitting on the porch with the neighbors, us just skipping and skipping until it got dark outside. I was always the best. Jackie'd get the rhythm messed up and get all tangled up in the ropes."

"Ms. Green, may can I call you Kismet?" Leonard called respectfully.

"Why?" she asked suspiciously, called back from the past.

"Well," he said, "because now I'm thinking of you when you were a little girl, jumping rope with Jackie and the others, and nobody called you Ms. Green then. So may I call you Kismet?"

There was a gurgling sound.

"Okay, Reverend," she called. "You can call me Kismet. Can I call you Reverend?" Then she giggled, overcome by her own wit.

"Sure," Leonard said amiably. "I was just wondering, Kismet, if you wanted to come out and jump some Double Dutch out here with us. I'm sure we can find some jump ropes around here somewhere. We've got some ladies in our church here who can't jump rope worth beans. And we've even got some white women out here who need some real serious help with anything involving rhythm. Maybe you could give us a hand."

By now a crowd from the neighborhood had gathered. There were women of all ages holding small babies on their hips, some old men drinking quietly from bottles in paper bags, solemnly watching the proceedings like a movie, a few young, restless men who wondered when something more exciting would happen, and a couple of preschool children.

Upstairs windows were opening down the street as well, with suspicious faces softening upon hearing the earnest discussion about jumping rope. The atmosphere was somewhere between a street party and that of a crowd waiting for an old building to be demolished, watching the heavy wrecking ball swing slowly back and forth.

Suddenly Sherah's clear voice broke through the rumble of the crowd.

"Hey, Reverend Sims!" she shouted from the third-story window high above the street.

"I'm up here! What are you doing here? Hi, Miss Jordan, Miss Anne, Elder Williams, Mrs. Williams! Hi, everybody!"

Oh, Anne thought, breaking into a huge grin. *I should have known she'd be okay.*

"Hi, Sherah!" Leonard Sims called. "Are you okay?"

"Oh, I'm fine," Sherah said. "Except I can't get the door to my room here open. I think the doorknob must be stuck."

"Kismet! Leonard Sims shouted. "Where's your friend James?"

"Oh, James," Kismet giggled. "He's just sitting on the living room sofa here. He doesn't seem to be in a very good mood. He's been in a bad mood ever since he got out of Lorton. You'd think a guy'd be happy, coming out of prison. Not James. He's got one of those what you call artistic personalities. He's a little moody. I've been trying to cheer him up. I've been sharing with him a little. That's a Christian virtue, now, isn't it, Reverend? Sharing? Yeah, I gave him his own bottle. Sometimes that helps a person get through the day, you know. We just drink on special occasions. Like when we get new family."

"Oh, great," Molly hissed at Anne. "We got a drunk and a manic-depressive in there, and little Sherah's turned into Cinderella, cooking and cleaning and locked in her room—"

"Be quiet!" Anne hissed back. "If you don't calm down you can just go home."

"Right," said Molly. "I'll just call a cab."

Anne felt a warm hand on her shoulder and turned. Tom had slipped into the crowd while everyone was distracted with Sherah's appearance. With him was one of the largest black men Anne had ever seen.

"Hi, Anne, Molly," Tom said. "This is my colleague, Toby Jackson. He just loves stuff like this."

"Oh, yeah," Toby said, shaking their hands gently with his own huge paw. "Nothing like a little hostage situation to break up the afternoon doldrums."

He paused. "But seriously, your Reverend here is doing a good job. He's doing the right thing, just talking it through, taking it slow, going back to childhood memories. If it was just Kismet in there he'd be done already. But that James guy is a wild card. That's where it could be tough."

"Okay, Kismet," Leonard Sims was calling now. "We've got some people here who are out on a serious search for jump ropes."

There was an indistinct sound from near the front door, and Anne could see Kismet staggering away from the doorway. A moment later, there was a muffled sound, a sort of thud.

Then there was silence.

"Kismet?" Leonard called. "Are you all right?"

Silence.

"Kismet!" he called again. "We care about you. We're your friends. Are you all right?"

Nothing.

Leonard paused a moment, looking back at everyone else in the crowd. Most people shrugged back at him.

"James!" he called loudly. "How are you doing?"

There was no sound or movement from the narrow house.

The tension rose. Anne saw Tom and Toby flex a little, and realized that, yes, of course they had brought their guns.

315

"James!" Leonard called. "Kismet!"

There was no response.

"Oh, no," Tom said. He began to move toward the perimeter of the crowd, and then suddenly, from an alley about four houses down from Kismet's, came the unmistakable sound of Sherah Jones's voice.

"Hey," she called, running out from between the tall houses, arriving in front of the crowd. "Here I am! Everything's okay!"

"What in the world?" Leonard Sims said. "Sherah! Are you all right?"

"I told you," she said, a little out of breath. "I'm fine. I excaped!"

"Well, that's very smart of you," Leonard said slowly. "What did you do?"

"Well," Sherah said, beaming out at all the people, quite pleased with herself.

"After I talked with you that last time, I figured out the doorknob in that dumpy bedroom wasn't stuck, they locked me in! And so I sat there and thought about it.

"You know, Miss Anne," she called in Anne's direction, "I thought about that very first story you ever told us, about that princess in that castle, she's locked in, and then the chewing mice help her, and she gets out.

"So I'm like the princess locked in the castle. I looked around for some chewing mice, but I didn't see any. I only saw some regular dumb mice in that house that couldn't help anybody do anything, and so then, I remembered that Mama told me a long time ago about how when she was a little girl, her mama used to leave the key on the sill above the door in her room.

"So I was thinking that Aunt Kismet is my Mama's sister, right, so maybe she'd do that, since she got this old kind of house that has keyholes in the doorknobs. So I found this box in that old dumpy room, and I put a box on top of the dresser, and a box on top of that, and I climbed up on top of them all and felt up on top of the doorway with my fingers, and sure enough, just like Mama used to say, there's a key.

"And I put it in the doorknob, and it worked, and then I went down the stairs, one at a time, real quiet, and you people were all standing out front, but I tippytoed and peeked into the living room, and there's Aunt Kismet over on the sofa with James. They both had big bottles, and they were sleeping real loud. Real loud.

"I knew they'd be asleep. I just went out the back door from the kitchen into the alley."

"But honey," Leonard Sims said for the rest of the crowd, "How did you know they would go to sleep? Because they were drinking so much?"

"Well, no," Sherah said. "See, when I was making their lunch for them like they wanted me to, they were so loud and fighting and scaring me the way they were yelling, so I thought I'd better do something.

"And then I found some blue pills up in Aunt Kismet's cabinet. They got a big PM on them. Mama used to take two of them sometimes when she couldn't sleep at night. And then it was like Mama was up in heaven helping me think of an idea. So I smashed up a bunch of those blue pills in little bits. I used this hammer I found on the counter. Then I scooped up all that blue powder, sprinkled it in the macaroni and cheese, and stirred it all up real good. I even put in some extra milk to make it more creamy.

"It kind of turned the macaroni a little green, but they didn't even notice. They ate it all up, and they told me I was a very good cook," Sherah said proudly. "And by the time I got out of that room they locked me in, they were asleep!"

The crowd was silent for a moment, digesting Sherah's triumph. "A little child will lead them," Leonard muttered. Tom Hogan stepped forward.

"Uh, Sherah," he said softly. "That's great that you did all that. Uh, how many blue pills did you put in the macaroni?"

Sherah shrugged. "I don't know," she said thoughtfully. "I remember I thought, well, if Mama used to take two, then maybe they needed more than that. I just shook the bottle out. It was about half-full."

"Okay," Tom said, moving back in the crowd again. "Well, we'll just give a call over to D.C. General for an ambulance," he said to Anne, "but I doubt Kismet or James'll have any problem."

"Right," Toby Jackson said. "Their insides are probably made of rotgut. It'd take more than a few little Excedrin PM and a bottle or two of booze to do them in."

Leonard Sims exhaled, and the crowd did so with him.

"What a day," he breathed. "What an ending. Thank God. At a time like this, I think we should all sing a hymn!"

And then he started singing what was evidently the first thing that came to mind, his strong, bass voice flowing over the rutted street and the grim houses, the melody lifting far above the rotting roofs. His wife joined in immediately, and then the others, until the chorus of song rose and echoed over the D.C. streets.

Anne looked around. Here she was, with some of the people she now loved best in the world, right in front of the mental hospital, singing "Amazing Grace" at the top of her lungs.

She looked over at Molly and winked, seeing, as she sometimes did, the two of them in their adolescent fancies so many years ago, and knowing they never could have imagined anything quite so strange as this day they were now living.

She looked at Tom, who was singing away next to his huge friend Toby—who was harmonizing quite beautifully—and her heart swelled toward him. He caught her eye and smiled. She looked toward Jordan and Reverend Sims and the others and grinned as wide as she could, even as she sang along, not caring what anyone else might think.

And as she looked out at the crowd gathered on that bleak Anacostia street, most of the people who lived in the neighborhood were singing along as well, remembering the old hymn from child-hoods buried far too deep for far too long. It was a golden moment that February afternoon, and Anne would remember it the rest of her life.

Sherah was standing in front of her, singing with all her small might. Anne knelt and grabbed her in a fierce hug, and as her arms went around Sherah's warm, compact body, Anne could feel Danuta's pearls resting ever so lightly on the thin skin above her heart.

THIRTY-SEVEN

As the last few lines of the hymn faded, everyone in the crowd stood silently for a moment, suddenly a little self-conscious.

"All right, everyone," said Leonard Sims, raising his arms in a benediction, as if the service was now concluded. "Thank you for coming today. The Lord bless you!"

"Show's over," someone said. The crowd began to break up, people walking away in twos and threes. Some lined up to shake Leonard's hand before they left. "Thank you, Reverend," said one old lady. "Lovely service."

"We should have brought a collection plate," Elder Williams teased.

Toby Jackson went to make the call for the ambulance for James and Kismet. Tom looked at his watch and declared himself done for the day. The church people loaded up into the blue van, and Anne, Tom, Molly, Sherah, and the Williamses all squeezed into the Volvo, this time with Anne at the wheel.

The van pulled out, Anne following behind. She could see everyone in the van bouncing up and down on the seats, clapping in unison. *They must be singing again,* she thought. Then the van stopped at a corner, the window opened, and Leonard's arm motioned the Volvo to draw alongside.

"Hey!" Leonard shouted out the van window toward Anne and the others. "We should celebrate. We were thinking maybe we could stop and get dinner for everyone. We could go through a drive-through and get a bunch of hamburgers or some buckets of fried chicken."

He paused as the people behind him in the van all started shouting their opinions. "Which do you want?" Leonard shouted toward Anne. "Burgers or chicken?"

Anne paused for a moment, hearing an echo in her mind.

Which do you want?

She shook her head to clear the old memory, and then suddenly thought of something new.

"Neither!" she shouted. "I have a different idea. A surprise."

The others all looked at her, eyebrows up. "What is it?" Sherah asked from the backseat. Anne ignored her.

"Hey," she shouted over to Leonard. "How much gas do you have in that thing?" The church van was notorious for running out of gas.

"I just filled it up yesterday," LaVon shouted in a muffled voice from the rear row of the crowded van.

"Great!" Anne said. "I've got an idea. You all are just going to have to trust me on this. Follow us."

Leonard shrugged. "We're game," he said.

Anne pulled out ahead of the van and punched her parents' number into the car phone.

"Hey, Dad, it's Anne," she said when her father picked up. "How are you?"

"Oh, hi, dear," he said, sounding a little out of breath. "I'm fine. I was in Maryland all day; I just came in. What's up?"

"Oh, I thought since Mother is gone, you could use some company for dinner," Anne said.

"Sure, that would be great," Bill Madison said. "There's nothing good to eat here, though. Before she left your mother stocked the refrigerator with a ton of low-fat snacks for me to eat while she's gone. I could not eat non-fat plain yogurt if you paid me."

He paused.

"Would you like for me to call for a pizza like we used to when you were in school?"

"Oh, Dad, that would be so nice," Anne said.

"What would you like?" her father asked.

Anne hesitated, mentally counting the occupants of the van behind her.

"Uh, I think we need five large supremes, thin crust, with extra cheese."

Her father paused for a moment.

"Are you that hungry, Anne?"

"No, Dad," Anne laughed. She looked around the Volvo. Ruth Williams, wedged next to her, and Elder Williams were both grinning. Tom and Molly, in the back with Sherah, were listening earnestly to Sherah's detailed descriptions of Aunt Kismet's interesting collection of liquor bottles.

Anne looked in the rearview mirror at the beat-up blue church van behind her, swaying on the potholed street, its rows of black faces bobbing up and down on the bumps, everyone evidently singing together at the top of their lungs.

"We'll be there in just awhile," Anne said to her father. "I thought I'd bring along a few friends I'd like you to meet."

About the Author

ELLEN VAUGHN, now writing her own provocative fiction, has worked with Charles Colson for more than sixteen years. A skilled storyteller, she has collaborated with Colson on many of his books, including the fiction best-seller *Gideon's Torch* and the modern-day classic *The Body*. A native of Washington, D.C., Vaughn holds a Master of Arts degree in English literature from Georgetown University and a Bachelor of Arts degree from the University of Richmond. She and her husband, Lee, live in Virginia with their three perpetually peripatetic young children: Emily and twins Haley and Walker.